OMEGA

It's the beginning of the end …

LIZZY FORD

DEDICATION

Special thanks to:

BROOKLYNN HUPKE, who suggested the name "Mismatch" for the heroine's gargoyle friend,

and

AOIFE CONNOLLY for naming the heroine's best friend, "Mrs. Nettles!"

ONE
ALESSANDRA

No man or woman born, coward or brave, can shun his destiny.
– HOMER

*F*OR ONCE, TYCHE, COULD YOU GRANT ME A LITTLE
luck?

I slowed before reaching my favorite meadow
in the forest, my heart racing and chest heaving. A grin
stretched my cheeks, and I stopped to listen for the boy I'd
challenged to a race. I heard … voices. Male and at least two
females.

"I guess not," I muttered aloud.

The damn nymphs had him. My giddy excitement faded. I
was the one who managed to lure a teen boy from the nearby
campground into our forest and, as usual, the nymphs stole
him. I couldn't compete with the beautiful women. There were
thirty of them my age, all unusually perfect, feminine and
graceful. Even my guardian said they weren't normal, and we'd

1

coined the term *nymphs* to describe the other girls at the isolated orphanage where I lived under the thumb of strict priests. The other girls were all my age, too, each of them destined for positions befitting their beauty, according to the priests.

It was disgusting. I couldn't stand them.

I was an athlete, uncomfortable in anything but tennis shoes and yoga pants, terrible in school and bearing a scar from childhood across one cheek. No matter how much makeup I plastered over it or how far forward I brushed my dark locks, I wasn't able to hide it. I was always late to class, always the last to understand whatever torture the priests were teaching us, always trying to catch the first light of Aurora in the reflecting pool or scaling a hill to watch the last rays of Hersperides.

The nymphs laughed at me. I hated them for it and me for not being able to fit in no matter what I did. I couldn't change the fact I was shorter, smaller and otherwise imperfect compared to them.

"Lose another one, Lyssa?"

"Yeah." I heard my guardian's approach and looked up into his scarred, ugly face. A mountain of a man with bright red hair, Herakles had never once understood why I was so disappointed to lose every guy I looked at to the nymphs.

"If a man can't outrun you – "

"– I can't bring him home with me. House rules. I know." It was a stupid rule. Surely there had to be one man somewhere who shared my deer-like agility.

My guardian chuckled.

"He was so handsome!" I whined with a sigh, recalling the gorgeous brown eyes and smile of the teenage boy I'd met today. When he had looked at me, my insides turned fluttery and warm. "He almost outran me, too."

"Only because you slowed down."

I rolled my eyes and spun away, headed towards the compound in the middle of a forest where we all lived. "So what? Everyone here has kissed a boy and I can't even look at one without the stupid nymphs taking him away. They just bat their eyes and the boys fall all over them." I made a show of shaking my hips and blinking rapidly in mockery.

"I've never kissed a boy."

"You know what I mean!" Herakles was a jerk sometimes. His rules were designed to prevent me from ever having a boyfriend. My interests generally lay in martial arts and sports. If not for the nymphs conspiring to steal any boys I lured away from the campground and always taunting me about everything, I wouldn't look twice at a boy. But I shared one sole trait with the nymphs: competitiveness. I wanted so badly to best them at something and earn enough respect not to be bullied every day for the rest of my life.

"You could try studying harder," Herakles suggested.

"Right. Like that's going to get me a boyfriend."

"There is more to life than boys and whatever else it is your head is full of," Herakles reminded me. "You don't need a man anyway. You can take care of yourself. I've trained you to survive anything."

"I know I don't *need* one. I want one so the nymphs stop

laughing at me. Just for a day, then I'd let him go like you free the rabbits I catch."

"You noticed."

I arched my eyebrow at him. "I figured it out after I caught the same one every day for a week when I was, like, sixteen. You know the nymphs don't have to hunt rabbits, don't you? They don't have to run every day or build their own campfires and shelters on the weekends. They get to go to town, Herakles, and see movies!" I sighed, tortured by my miserable existence. "Can I be normal? Just for one weekend?"

"Normal people aren't prepared for their world to change or to face the trials awaiting them."

"The zombies apocalypse isn't coming. The priests say the world has never known a time of greater peace and prosperity and the gods are happier than ever."

"An apocalypse is not required to announce itself," he stated.

I bit my tongue. I knew better than to argue with Herakles. He was of a singular mind and convinced the world was going to end any day. Nothing I'd ever said over the past twelve years had dented his obsession with self-reliance and survival. I learned to hunt game bigger than me, forage for berries, survive in extreme weather conditions and other skills the nymphs – and even my teachers – often ridiculed. Sometimes he blindfolded me or hobbled one leg or arm so I had to survive for a weekend alone in the forest with simulated physical impediments. He first dropped me off in part of the forest alone with no compass when I was nine. I bawled for a day until he came to get me. Instead of taking me back, we stayed in the forest, and he taught me to navigate by the stars.

No one understood why he made me do these things, least of all me. I obeyed him because, above all else, I loved my Herakles, as weird as he was. While we were accepted here, we didn't fit in at the school filled with nymphs and priests. We had to stick together, two dented peas in a misshapen pod.

"The man you want will be able to outrun, outhunt and outsmart you. When you meet him, you can marry him. Until then, no man will do," Herakles said.

"I don't want to marry anyone," I said. "I just want to kiss him."

"Then you can kiss the man who catches you."

His conditions for me seeing someone were impossibilities. Herakles alone was the only man who could keep up with me. It was his way of saying I'd never have a boyfriend as long as I lived under his roof.

I glanced up at the green canopy overhead. The blue sky resembled puzzle pieces from this angle, and not a cloud was in sight on this warm spring day. What torture did he have in store for me on such a beautiful Friday? I had to climb a rope or navigate whatever obstacle course he built before I was allowed to go to bed at night. Weekends were worse. I was exiled to the forest for more survival training until Sunday night.

He was conditioning and preparing me for something. I had no idea what, and I suspected he was just a little off. A former Olympian, Herakles was the toughest, most honorable person I had ever known. He swept the annual Olympics for three years in a row before he stumbled upon me, rescued me from the house fire that killed my parents and brought us here. He didn't respect anything but physical prowess. He could barely read, and he had an almost allergic reaction to discussing anything regarding emotions.

But he was my hero in every sense of the word.

To this day, I was unable to recall what exactly happened the night I turned six except it involved Herakles catching me when I fell from the sky. Why or how I was flying, I didn't know. I still occasionally dreamt of falling – but no fire. My life changed that night. Herakles was unwilling to talk about it even after I turned eighteen and was considered an adult by everyone but him.

Herakles tugged the sleeve I'd tucked under my bra strap back down over the strange birthmark on my bicep that looked eerily like a double omega. The omega was the final letter in the Greek alphabet, or, according to Herakles, a sign of Armageddon. "Keep this hidden," he reminded me.

"I know." I pulled both sleeves down so I didn't look stupid with only one up.

Picking my way through the forest back towards the compound where we lived, I considered the topic I'd been meaning to broach to him but hadn't quite figured out the best way yet.

"We haven't talked about graduation," I started. "It's in three weeks."

"The world might end tomorrow. You should not think too far beyond today."

"Omigods, Herakles! I'm eighteen, and I'm graduating in three weeks! I want to go home!" Too late I realized I'd told him what I had hoped to discuss in a calmer manner. I didn't look back at him but focused on the path at my feet.

"You know there is nothing for you there."

"So you've told me every time I asked. But I have to go somewhere," I pointed out. "College. Waitress at a fast food joint. Holy Zeus, I'd become an initiate at a temple."

"No temple would have you."

It wasn't the first time I'd heard that, either. The priests didn't consider me disciplined or selfless or motivated enough to refer me for a position in the elite initiate corps. Half of the nymphs were headed to temples of the Greek gods. The others were being sent to the households of influential politicians and nobles around the world. I could speak English, Greek and French like they did – a requirement to become an initiate – but my grades were sorry and my temperament deemed too unsuitable to be placed in a position where diplomacy and manipulation was required.

"You have more freedom here than the average person living beneath the thumb of the Supreme Magistrate will ever know," he said. "Why do you wish to leave?"

"Because that's what kids who graduate high school do. They get a life. Join the real world."

"Where did you learn this? Television?" He was genuinely confused. He rarely spoke of his childhood, but I'd assessed over the years that his own upbringing had been very different. "I must talk to the priests about censoring the programs they

one of Herakles weekend tests. The priests censored everything that reached us from the outside world, including the news. They removed what they didn't want us to see before letting us watch what was left.

"Hey, is that ..." I asked and walked into her room.

"Yeah." A wistful note was in Leandra's voice.

It took a lot to make the perfect, beautiful nymphs envy someone else. For once, I understood where she was coming from.

"The Silent Queen," I said in awe, gazing at the television. The Queen of Greece, known as the Silent Queen because she hadn't been seen or heard from until this month, was plastered everywhere on the news. A girl my age, she was stunning with white-blonde hair, pale blue eyes and a jawline sharp enough to cut ice. "Wow."

"She's just a symbol of the unity of gods and mankind. No real power." But even Leandra sounded enthralled by the woman on the television. "She can't speak. She gave her first address in sign language."

"Wow," I murmured again. In a sparkling diamond tiara and radiant silk dress, the teen looked more godlike than human. She was flanked by the Supreme Magistrate – the powerful political representative of humanity – and the hooded and masked Supreme Priest – the gods' advocate on Earth. The three most powerful figures in the world were known as the Sacred Triumvirate, and each had his or her own private security force, according to the priests, which was how they balanced their power.

I couldn't look away from the Silent Queen. The priests had drilled the history and importance of the hereditary Bloodline into us since we arrived. The Silent Queen's ancestors were touched by the gods, and it was said only she could appeal directly to them in a way that defied even the priesthood. Throughout history, once Greece fell as a global power, the most powerful nation on the planet was given the sacred duty of protecting the Bloodline and housing the royal leader, which was how she ended up here in the United States. "She's amazing."

"I'm sure she's been Photo-shopped for television," Leandra said somewhat defensively.

I rolled my eyes. The nymphs knew they were special. There was something strange about thirty orphaned women of extreme beauty and charm, all born within three months of me, all under the strict protection of an orphanage run by priests who didn't hold weekly worship ceremonies but taught us instead the Old Ways, as they called them. They were positioning the nymphs in places of eventual power, where they could then share the Old Ways with others.

If our world was strange, we had no idea. As far as we knew, this place and its customs were normal.

"I've been assigned to her court," Leandra said.

"Seriously?"

"Yep."

It made sense. Leandra was a hair prettier than the others and quite a bit smarter, according to the priests. I was suddenly crushed that I might end up taking food orders from hung over college students the rest of my life while the others went off to positions I could only dream of.

"Where are you going?" she asked, green eyes finding me. "To live with the Mountain Man on some isolated peak?"

"He's not a Mountain Man," I said, bristling. "He's the greatest Olympic athlete in history."

"A disgraced one who ditched his wealthy benefactor to live in a forest with us. He's absolutely mad, and he's turned you wild and ruined any chance you had at a decent future."

My anger bubbled. I knew better than to cause a fight. I had stopped that nonsense when I was fifteen, but sometimes I wanted to sock the pretty, perfect women around me.

My biggest issue with Leandra wasn't that she was mean. It was that she was often right, and her words about Herakles stung. Something was wrong with him, and I sometimes thought maybe that meant there was something wrong with me, too. It was why I didn't turn out like Leandra and the others and why I was definitely not going to the Silent Queen's court.

I squinted to see the ticker at the bottom of the news. *Civil unrest grows. Supreme Magistrate places five more states under martial rule over SISA's objections.* That made about forty states under martial rule by my count. The priests refused to tell us about the civil unrest when we asked, but sometimes, like today, tiny pieces of information slipped through their censoring and made it to us. I was dying to know what the world outside our boring forest was like.

"When I get to court, I'll find you a job chopping wood or

something," Leandra said with a wide grin.

I stormed off to my room, followed by the sound of her laughter. I loved Herakles like the father I couldn't remember, but sometimes I was really embarrassed to be me. I hated that feeling. I had trouble making friends, more so because Herakles often had some bizarre requirement for me to hang out with someone. Boys had to be able to outrun me, and girls had to solve a riddle. No one ever succeeded at his challenges, except for the perfect little nymphs who hung out with me only to laugh at me.

Basically, I was always alone, and he seemed determined to keep it that way. I felt even more isolated knowing the nymphs all had plans of where they were going after graduation and I didn't.

I went to my room and closed the door, sitting on my bed. I had barely pushed off my shoes before a tap sounded at the door. "Come in," I said and tossed myself onto my back.

"Lyssa, I have to leave for the weekend."

Startled, I immediately sat back up. "Where? Why?" I demanded of Herakles, who had never left me for half a day let alone a weekend. "Is something wrong?"

"No." His features were scarred beyond recognition, his smile lopsided and frightening. Everyone else winced when he looked their direction, but I loved every knotted scar and burnt piece of flesh on his face. He was my protector, my friend, the only father figure I knew. He had always been beautiful to me. "You are to travel to the eastern boundary and back this weekend. Here's your surprise pack. Open it when you get there." He tossed the satchel onto the bed beside me.

"Ugh." I eyed it warily. He no doubt had planned another weekend of torture. I'd probably have a hat and spoon and nothing more to survive two days in the forest alone. Technically I should have had only three more weeks of this madness remaining, except I had a feeling his plans were always going to trump mine. "You're sure there's nothing wrong? You've never left me before."

"I'm going to scout someplace where we might settle after you graduate," he told me.

I looked up, thrilled. "I won't be trapped here for the rest of my life!"

"No, but you might one day wish you had been." He frowned. Every once in a while, my guardian had a mood I didn't understand. Naturally open, upbeat and focused, his features were now grave and unreadable.

I studied him, wishing I could read his thoughts or make him smile again. "Something is wrong," I assessed.

"Not wrong. It's always complicated to move from one place to another." He shook his head. "Anyway, you have a treasure hunt to complete this weekend. Your tasks are in the bag. You will not wish to wait until morning. I put up several traps and obstacles."

I muttered curses I'd learned from him under my breath. As long as we had been together, I never really knew what to expect on these adventures. "I'll see you Sunday night," I said reluctantly.

"Heed the boundaries and rules."

"I know." I pulled on my shoes obediently and a camouflage windbreaker. When I stood, he smiled at me again.

"Good girl. Don't get lost out there."

It wasn't possible and we both knew it. I'd been over every inch of that forest multiple times. "Have fun in town."

He turned and left.

I grabbed the bag and left my room for the forest once more.

No boys. No future. No town.

There were days when I wanted out of my life so badly I wanted to scream.

TWO

Small opportunities are often the beginning of great enterprises.
— DEMOSTHENES

NOTHING BAD HAD EVER HAPPENED IN FIVE minutes, right?

Just as the sun sank below the horizon, I reached the red cord marking the boundaries of the priests' forest refuge. This end of the woods stopped before a natural lake surrounded by hills. I perched on a tree stump inside the boundaries, gazing at the serene lake with a combination of longing and frustration.

A hundred meters. I ran twenty times that distance five times a week. It would take me under five minutes to run to the lake, strip off my shoes and socks to dip my toes in the water and run back.

I chafed sometimes at the restrictions Herakles put me under. I cared for him too much to want to disappoint him. But tonight, knowing he was gone, and I'd be leaving here soon, too, I just wanted to throw everything aside and be in control of my life for five minutes to see what it was like. With Leandra's laughter still in my thoughts, and my frustration with this place at a pitch, I was tired of being excluded and ridiculed for being different.

No one would see me if I just stepped past the boundaries for a split second. Herakles had left, and the nymphs were in town by now, so they couldn't report me.

I approached the red rope and nudged my toes up against it then looked around. I half expected there to be a siren or electrical shock or something after the constant reminders from Herakles and the priests never to leave the woods.

Nothing happened.

I stepped on the red cord.

Still nothing.

I stepped over the physical boundary of my world, and a thrill went through me. Not only was there no alarm but I didn't feel guilty or bad for doing it, emotions that might derail me from continuing. I stayed where I was, my heels butting up against the cord, and lifted my gaze to the lake.

The possibilities were endless. My whole life started right here and now.

I laughed at my overdramatic thoughts, realizing nothing was about to change except I might upset Herakles. That alone made me hesitate. I loved my crazy mountain-man guardian, and it bothered me to think I was going to make him mad by doing this.

Assuming he finds out. The stubbornly independent side of

17

me he spent hours trying to exhaust with physical activity knew there was only one way he could find out, and I wasn't about to tell him. At least, not for three weeks. Maybe after graduation, when we were on our way to the Burger God I was going to spend my life working at, I'd tell him of the one time in twelve years when I defied him to dip my toes in the lake.

Crouching like it was a race, I breathed in deeply then bolted. I was completely alone, competing only with myself. I laughed as I sprinted, tickled beyond anything to be completely free, if only for mere minutes.

Sprinting to the lake, I vowed to keep to my internal promise of not spending more than a few minutes off the property and threw myself to the ground. Wrenching off my shoes and socks, I scooted to the edge of the lake and dangled my legs over the rock on which I sat.

The moment my feet dipped beneath the cool surface, my world seemed to slow to a stop. I leaned over, marveling at the sensations. It shouldn't have been, but this was somehow different than a pool. This felt … alive.

"Holy Poseidon," I murmured.

The sensation of being united with something living moved through my system, a wave that ran from my toes to the tip of my head, in rhythm with the water, then outward, rippling the grass around the lake. I shivered. Fascinated, I peered into the dark depths of the lake. My feet caused small waves that were pushed back by the natural tides of the lake. Deep within the depths, I caught a glimmer of something odd.

I squinted in the fading light. They weren't fish or rocks or anything. The lake was too deep to see its bottom, but I swore I saw ribbons of soft colors twisting like smoke through the waters. Their movements were too precise to be dictated by the tides. I blinked – and they were gone.

Realizing my five minutes were up, I lifted my feet and dried them on my pants legs then replaced my shoes and socks. I didn't feel nearly as urgent about returning to the forest where I'd spent most of my life and ambled back. It was strange, but I could almost feel the tide of the lake still moving through me, rocking from toes to head and back again before rustling the grass around me. It was gentle, soothing and peaceful. I was an extension of the water, and it felt natural, nice.

I had nothing to compare the experience to and couldn't help wondering if I'd spent my entire life cut off from such small pleasures. It made me despise the nymphs even more, since they probably spent every weekend *feeling* whatever this was out in the real world.

Stepping over the red rope, the internal rocking stopped, and I realized it hadn't only been the lake I felt. The breeze that stirred the surface of the lake stopped at the barrier, too, and its gentle touch on my skin fell away.

I missed them almost as soon as I left them. Facing the lake once more, I smiled. If nothing else, I now knew one of the secrets of the world outside my boundaries, and it was beautiful.

Beyond happy with my secret adventure, I moved five meters from the cord to an area big enough for a fire and built a little campsite. My assigned kit contained a canteen of water and the ingredients for s'mores. Herakles' thoughtfulness only added to my happiness. I went through my tasks of finding shelter, starting a fire and stretching out on the ground to watch the stars with a smile plastered on my face. After my treats, I let the fire die out and retreated to a small shelter I'd created from a poncho and tree branches. I had brought a sleeping bag and crawled into it.

My mind was on the lake, on my future and how incredible it was going to be to leave the compound once and for all and join the rest of the world. I slid into deep, contented sleep.

Something awoke me shortly before dawn. I opened my eyes, senses trained on the world outside my makeshift tent. Animals used their instincts and intuition better than humans, and Herakles had emphasized being more like the locals when camping out. So I listened in silence and stillness.

An animal was rustling quietly, but it wasn't close, and it wasn't in the forest, which meant it was large if I could hear it this far off. The sounds came from the direction of the lake. I crept out of my sleeping bag and covered the distance quickly between me and the boundary. Reaching the stump where I often perched to gaze at the lake, I squatted on top of it and stared.

It was an animal, but nothing like I'd seen before. Monster was probably a better description. The creature had a wingspan of ten meters and was the size of a linebacker with the long, lean musculature and grace of a feline. It stood on two legs and had two arms that looked pretty human. The sound I heard was of its long tail tapping the brush lining the bank of the lake. Its skin was an unnatural shade of stone grey. One of its ears stuck out at an odd angle and its eyes glowed like blue jewels in the night. It had fangs, talons, and a barbed tail, and its eyes were positioned facing forward, all of which were characteristics of a predator of some sort and not something I cared to confront.

It stood where I had sat earlier, peering at the lake, at the surrounding area, at the sky. It crouched beside the lake, tail tapping against the dirt.

It was horrifying – and magnificent. I couldn't have imagined a more incredible combination of man and beast. The raw power it exuded in each tiny, controlled movement exceeded anything a human or traditional predator possessed.

This is a dream. It had to be. No such creature existed, unless it was some sort of undiscovered animal or leftover dinosaur. And if that were the case, I didn't think this would be the first time I'd seen it. I spent too many days and nights in the forest for it to belong here. Where it had originated, and why it chose to stop here, I couldn't begin to guess.

Intelligence was in its thoughtful movement and visual exploration of the environment. The man-beast hybrid wasn't something I was able to explain away. I pinched my arm to ensure I was awake. The light sting wasn't much of a reassurance when faced with a monster from a nightmare.

It stood and unfurled its wings. They were charcoal in color, lined with black fur, beautiful and wide, shaped neither like a bat's nor a bird's but something in between. With ease that left me astonished, one flap of the mighty wings propelled the creature into the sky effortlessly. Within seconds, it had disappeared into the clouds above.

For once, I was grateful for the red cords marking the boundaries of the property. The priests claimed they would protect us from unwanted attention. The creature hadn't glanced once in my direction, which made me think the ropes were working. Or maybe I was blessed by Tyche for once.

I stood on the tree stump, trying to get another glimpse of the beast in the clouds without success.

My gaze returned to the lake. What other surprises awaited me in the outside world? Was this creature the reason why the priests insisted I never cross the boundaries and if so, had I risked being eaten or killed when I left the forest earlier for the lake?

I shuddered, this time out of dread. If the priests knew, the creature would be on the list of animals to avoid that they kept posted in the main schoolhouse as a warning of what wildlife not to engage.

No one, except maybe Herakles, was going to believe me if I told them about the creature. Easing back from the edge of the property, I returned to my shelter but wasn't able to sleep again, not with the knowledge something like *that* was hovering in the clouds above the forest. I silently thanked Herakles for his survival training and insistence I carry a knife with me wherever I went. I clutched it in my hand and remained still until dawn swept across the sky. Only then did I start to relax again and packed up my tent.

Bad things didn't happen during daylight, I told myself. I clung to the childish notion and decided to disobey Herakles for a second time.

I was going back to the school today without completing my assigned treasure hunt. I wasn't spending another night in the forest when some creature big enough to eat me was on the loose. Bears were one thing, but this … this was something even I knew better than to mess with.

It was a four hour trek back to the center of the property. I hiked through the forest, always sensitive to the creatures living here. While I'd catch and eat them if I had to, I also wasn't going to disturb their daily lives by leaving messes or destroying their homes. Herakles was strict about appreciating and respecting the domain of Artemis and Dionysis and all their children.

My mind kept returning to the creature. I wasn't able to flush the image of the terrifying creature standing beside the lake from my thoughts. It didn't seem to be a part of nature, yet it had to be. Everything was, except for the gods and goddesses, who were still part of nature, just a different nature from ours.

Lost in thought, I didn't notice the drone of an airplane until it roared overhead. I looked up, unaccustomed to hearing them quite so low, but not alarmed to see the plane. A municipal airport was nearby. It was how the priests brought in guest speakers and other visitors from outside the area.

Unconcerned, I continued on my hike, unable to prevent the occasional look over my shoulder. I'd hear the creature if it was following me, but similar to my hope that bad things didn't

"Father Cristopolos will tell you." He glanced at me. For the first time since arriving, I sensed he was hiding something. I had always found the monks and their dedication to the Old Ways mysterious, but I never felt like their secrets pertained to me. Whatever he wasn't saying about *me*, however, snagged my attention.

The remaining three priests approached. I bowed my head to each of them as was appropriate. They exchanged looks I wasn't able to decipher but which made me uneasy.

Father Cristopolos addressed me. "Alessandra, why don't you take us to your and Herakles' favorite spot in the forest. I think it's a meadow?"

I nodded. My pulse was starting to race at the calm request. I'd wanted the attention of the priests my whole life and watched them dote over the nymphs instead. Now that the four of them were focused on me, I suddenly wanted them to leave me alone. "This way," I said quietly and spun on my heel, leading them deeper into the forest. "Was Herakles in the house or something?" I asked uneasily, unable to identify why they wanted to go to my favorite place.

No one answered. They simply followed me.

I swallowed hard, edgy and scared that something had happened to Herakles. For all my complaining about the forest adventures and him not letting me near boys, I loved him. He was the only father I really remembered, and I wasn't going to handle it well if something happened to him.

Maybe they know that. Maybe that was why four priests were following me, in case I went crazy and they had to tie me up or something. My sense of dread grew as we approached the meadow where Herakles and I trained. My step slowed out of fear of the bad news they'd give me once we reached it.

Setting foot in the meadow, I faced them with my arms crossed. "Is Herakles okay?" I asked and braced myself for bad news.

"He is well," Father Cristopolos replied.

I sighed. "Omigods. Then why all this?" I demanded and waved at their grave visages.

"We need to talk to you about your future," Father Ellis replied.

"Now? After our home was just destroyed?"

"Our home was destroyed because you left the boundaries," another of the priests, Father Renoir, replied coolly. He was probably my least favorite staff member.

"Renny," Father Ellis said gently. "This is a delicate situation."

"What're you talking about?" I asked. "So I left the boundaries for ten minutes. Am I being expelled for it? The nymphs go to town every weekend!"

"My dear," Father Ellis approached. "This all exists because of you. The school. The orphanage and property."

I waited, not understanding.

"Once every other generation or so, a very special woman comes along," Father Cristopolos started. "Someone with great power that rivals the gods'."

"Yeah. The Oracle of Delphi who becomes the bridge between humans and gods," I recited from class. "They found you," Father Ellis replied. "It prevents your power from awakening. Why else do you think we permitted Herakles to train you as he did? To survive at the hands of humans and gods, you need to be able to adapt to any circumstance if you are to fulfill your destiny."

None of this made sense to me. Something really weird was going on, and only I seemed to realize it. My chest was being squeezed by an invisible hand. I couldn't wrap my head around how any of this was possible – but they truly believed it, no matter how insane it sounded. "I'll play this weird game. My destiny. What is it?"

"To break the bridge and send the gods back where they belong. To return humanity to the Old Ways, to freedom," Father Renoir said quietly. "You only need to outlive the current Oracle. We hoped to hide you until that day when she passed, after which, you could live a normal life once the gods were gone. It is the deal we struck with Lelantos, the reason he wanted you hidden, and the promise we made to Artemis, whose heart has been weighed down with the treatment of each Oracle. When she discovered you were only a child, she offered us her help. We must in turn deliver on our promise."

I wanted to laugh, but something about the severity of their features stopped me. Everyone knew Artemis had a soft spot for little girls in trouble and about the brittle nature of the relationship between the Olympic gods and Titans after the war that saw the Titans exiled to another dimension. The Titans swore vengeance. The idea I was in any way involved in the doings of *gods,* when I'd barely been allowed to participate in a safe place for you now."

"And rescue Herakles," I pressed.

"Herakles is the strongest man in the world. Chances are he will buy us time and won't need our help to be rescued," Father Cristopolos said.

For once, he made sense. I didn't see Herakles staying anywhere involuntarily. "Can I ask where he went at least?"

"Washington DC," Father Ellis answered.

I was born and lived just out side of DC until I turned six. If everyone in the world was looking for me, I doubted I could walk into the nation's capitol and find Herakles unnoticed. Not that I was buying this nonsense ...

Except that I kind of was. I was scared enough to believe what they said without understanding exactly what it meant to be someone of importance. To be hunted.

To be an Oracle, the most cherished and highly regarded human in existence. It made little sense after my humble upbringing here.

"Where do I go?" I asked quietly, unable to dispel the urge to find Herakles, no matter what the priests said.

"We have a backup plan. We're waiting for someone who will take you elsewhere."

"Who?"

Fathers Cristopolos and Ellis looked at one another briefly in silent communication I didn't particularly care for. "You needn't worry," Father Ellis said. "I'll be going with you. In the meantime, I need you to keep this on no matter what." He stepped forward and took my arm, wrapping a piece of red cord

THREE

There is nothing permanent except change.
– HERACLITUS

HOW FAST COULD REALITY, A WORLD, LIFE IN general, transform into something I never knew existed?

I was waiting for Father Ellis to laugh and tell me he was joking about everything. But as the next two hours passed in silence, he didn't change his story. He was quiet and calm, choosing to meditate in the peaceful meadow. I initially paced then sat and stared at the sky, lost.

Everything they'd said began to sink in. When I realized this was real or at least, the priests believed it to be real, I also knew I had to do something. I stood. The monk was seated cross legged in meditation, his eyes closed.

"I'm going to get my emergency pack," I told him. I waited for him to tell me not to bother, because they were messing with me.

He opened his eyes. "Is it far?"

"Half hour."

"I'll wait here."

My insides were shaking when I turned away and started into the forest. Yesterday, I was desperate to leave the forest. Today, I was scared of the same thing. It was stupid of me to be so worked up! I didn't buy the idea of me having power, but I did know we couldn't stay here when the place we all lived was destroyed.

And there's Herakles. He was the strongest man alive and had been for fifteen years. But I worried about him. If something else was going on here, like maybe the priests were lying to me for some reason or hiding something worse, then I wanted him with me. I trusted him. I loved him.

I couldn't leave him trapped in someone's basement or prison or wherever he was. Even refusing to believe that I was the Oracle, I found myself looking closely at the red cord around my wrist and wondering if it really did what the priests said it did – hid me from the world.

I moved through the forest to the place where we kept emergency packs and stopped at the base of the large, old tree in whose trunk we'd stuffed supplies. Pulling on the pack, I tightened the straps and rifled through the other supplies to make sure I wouldn't need them.

The crack of a branch made me tense, and I straightened, listening.

Someone was there. Not the priests, who didn't know how to walk with discipline, but someone who was trying to navigate the forest without being discovered. The occasional brush of cloth on wood, the careful placement of slow footsteps …

Pulling free my knife, I faced the direction of whoever was following me. "I can hear you," I called.

There was a pause, as if the forest was waiting, too. Finally someone spoke.

"I seem to have gotten lost," the man said. He eased out from behind a thick tree trunk.

The stranger was dressed in the type of clothing indicating he wasn't a lost camper but someone who wanted to blend in with his environment. He carried several hunting knives and was built like he knew how to use them. His exposed forearms were scarred and tattooed. A tattoo wound around his neck and disappeared into the clothing covering his chest. He was too handsome to be a priest by far, but it was the gleam in his eyes – the spark of a predatory awareness Herakles had taught me to be wary of – that disturbed me. He had the look of a soldier, aside from his medium length hair.

"Where are you trying to go?" I asked and eased away from the stash of supplies.

"You with the orphanage?"

"Where are you trying to go?" I repeated.

He snorted. "My employers are located somewhere in this forest. A priest named Cristopolos." His gaze went to our surroundings, and one of the tattoos on his neck stood out. The mark of Hermes – a winged foot – was surrounded by other ornate ink work. Herakles had taught me about the different guilds of the underground society of criminals. I filtered through what he'd forced me to learn to identify the marking.

"You're a mercenary," I said, surprised.

"Not a mercenary. A gladiator," the stranger corrected. "But I do merc work on the side during the off season."

I didn't think someone could bear the tattoo of a mercenary and *not* be one. Mixed martial artists belonging to the Gladiator Guild were street fighters paid handsomely for beating the daylights out of another of their kind. The line between the legal and illegal markets of being paid to fight was blurry, and I didn't fully understand it except that this man wore a tattoo that designated him to be something other than what he claimed he was.

"So you fight and kill people for money," I said, recalling what the priests told us about one of the occupations they favored least. They looked upon gladiators with disdain and mercenaries with outright horror.

"Not exactly the godly values they teach you, I know."

"I think it's cool. I can fight, too."

"Sure, kid." He flashed an insincere smile. "Which way is it?"

I bit back my response, irritated he didn't believe me. And to call me *kid* when I was eighteen, an adult by most standards … though today, I felt like I was being treated like a ten year old again. The mercenary was younger than Herakles' age of thirty five, younger than the priests and the age of all my favorite Hollywood actors.

"Whatever," I muttered. "What kind of gladiator gets lost in

nothing like that. The edge of wary arrogance definitely fit the image I'd created.

"You've met your charge, I see," Father Ellis said.

"What? This little girl?" Niko motioned to me. He looked me over critically.

I crossed my arms, irked that even the guy they were paying to take Herakles' place was judging me. Before I could say anything, Father Ellis rested his hand on my forearm.

"Lyssa is humanity's most precious member." Father Ellis had stiffened.

"Coming from a priest who doesn't believe in violence, that doesn't mean much." Niko flashed a quick smile, though his cold eyes were never still. "At least she's tough and can run. I had expected someone more … delicate."

What was worse? Being called a *kid* who couldn't run or fight or being considered unladylike? Niko wasn't winning any points with me. I wasn't a nymph, but I had outraced him.

"Can you really fight?" Niko asked me.

"I can," I proclaimed. "I can climb, camp, hunt, run, fight … I can do everything."

"She had a very motivated guardian," Father Ellis said with some disapproval. "Neglected her studies. But, she can run."

What was wrong with these people? Judging me for being prepared for the situation they knew was coming? "Whatever. Let's go." I shifted my pack.

"Go where?" Niko asked, gaze once more on Father Ellis.

"To wherever you're taking us," I replied.

"My contract was for stationary service in a place with

three squares and a real bed."

I pointed towards the school. "That place was blown up."

"We have a situation," Father Ellis said simultaneously.

Niko planted his hands on his hips.

Seeing the priest squirm under his glare made me very happy after my day. "Are you going to tell him about the ground forces coming?" I prompted innocently.

"Quiet, Lyssa." Father Ellis turned towards the school and began walking. "Come with me. Both of you."

I went, mainly because I had nowhere else to go and a little because I wanted to see Niko and Father Cristopolos in an argument.

"I'm not going anywhere until the contract is defined," Niko stated.

"If you wish to be paid, you will come with me," Father Ellis replied.

I looked over my shoulder as I walked, waiting to see what the mercenary would end up doing. He was watching us unhappily. Finally, he started forward, tense and bristling, eyeing the forest with wariness I didn't share. His long strides closed the distance to Father Ellis and me, and he stepped onto the deer path we walked on.

"Can you really hunt?" he asked me.

"I can."

"Good. At least you'll be useful if your priests try to pull one over on me."

I glanced at him, not liking the sound of that.

"I will take you whether they pay me or not. There's an

underground market for someone like you."

"Niko, do not scare her," Father Ellis said. "You will be paid above and beyond what we promised."

"What do you mean, someone like me?" I asked in confusion. "If I am what they think I am, there's only one of someone like me … of me … of whatever you think I am."

"You're an initiate, aren't you?" Niko asked.

"Do I look like an initiate?" I retorted.

"Lyssa, hush!" Father Ellis shot me a look. "Let us deal with him." He stepped from the forest onto the greens. "Father Cristopolos!" he cried. The head priest and Father Renoir stood with a pile of items that had been salvaged from the building.

I started to follow, but all four turned to yell, "Stay in the forest!"

"Oh, my gods!" I groaned and jerked back to make sure I remained where they told me.

Niko appeared amused then hardened as he stepped past the red rope onto the greens. He paused several steps away and turned to face me.

"Who or what do they think you are?" he asked, leveling dark eyes on me.

I fell speechless, uncertain what to do. It kind of felt like everyone was lying to everyone else. Niko claimed to be a gladiator but was really a mercenary, and the priests told him I was an initiate.

"Hmmm." Niko studied me. He seemed to find answers where I didn't mean to give them. "I'm guessing you're worth much more than they offered. Better hope they're willing to pay to keep me from kidnapping and selling you."

I almost laughed but realized he was serious.

He winked and walked away.

I began to regret not sending him off in some random direction when we met. The fact he was doing this for the money that made me feel a little dirty. Or tainted. Or at least, capable of understanding why the priests looked down upon shady men like him.

Watching them speak, I waited for someone to yell or give some sign it wasn't going well. The distant sound of thunder reached me. The sky was clear, aside from puffs of smoke left over from the school burning.

Weird. Thunder and no clouds. The earth trembled. I waited for it to pass like it might in an earthquake, but it didn't. The tremor remained constant and the thunder loudened.

With the four of them busy talking, I dropped my pack and scaled a tree quickly. I reached the top and poked my head up above the canopy, expecting to see what I normally did: kilometers of woods followed by a break where the road was and more forestry on the other side of the break.

Trees were being knocked to the ground and flattened by machines I wasn't able to see from this vantage point. It had started near the road and was moving towards us, downing whole swaths of trees for a kilometer stretch.

What could do this to a dense forest of mature trees? Was it the work of the ground forces the priests spoke of? I was embarrassed to admit I had no idea whose ground forces they were referring to or even what ground forces really were.. Did the military intend to run over the forest to grab me? Or was it the SISA, the international secret police force tasked with internal security of the human race by the gods?

Was it even legal for someone to mow down an entire forest?

I shimmied down the tree and replaced my pack. The four priests were huddled together a short distance from Niko, whose gaze was on the forest in the direction of the thunder. He alone seemed aware of something being wrong.

Catching my gaze, he lifted his chin back towards the direction we had come and mouthed two words. *Run. Now.*

Fear lit in my blood, followed by concern for the priests. I stood frozen for a moment, debating what Herakles would have me do.

Survive. And if I was what the priests said I was, I was probably putting them in danger by being with them.

I took one step back then another. Not at all certain I was about to do the right thing, I turned and began to make my way quickly through the forest, to the east. The crashing of trees soon became more audible, and I did as Niko said and sprinted.

I ran until I no longer heard the sounds of something crunching and grinding the trees of my forest beneath it and slowed only when the peaceful sounds of nature were present around me. Without stopping, I snacked on a protein bar and continued walking for another hour and a half, covering the distance between the school and the lake in record time.

And then I stopped at the boundary, as I had been trained.

Gazing at it, I couldn't help the guilt that floated through me. I was afraid to leave the forest this time, because I knew what would happen if I did. A part of me remained in denial about all that had happened in so short a time, that it was connected to the simple act of me going one step too far.

I sat on my tree stump, staring at the lake. It was midafternoon, and I hadn't forgotten the creature I saw either. No, I wasn't going to cause more trouble.

My determination lasted until I heard the birds begin to vacate the forest around me. The sound of machines wasn't present, but the animals were fleeing something. I had no idea where to go once I left the forest and remained where I was, on the verge of panicking yet knowing that was the worst thing to do in a crisis.

I miss Herakles. He would know what to do and where to go.

Twenty minutes later, the unmistakable sound of someone running through the forest reached me. I rose and hurried to a hiding spot close by, anxious to see who followed.

"Lyssa!" Niko's quiet cry reached me before he did. "Or ... Alice. Whatever your name is. We need to go. Now."

I peeked at him through the brush. He reached the tree stump, his gaze sweeping expertly around the area. He was sweating – and bloody. One hand was caked in it and there was also blood on his shirt.

"C'mon, you little shit!"

With some hesitation, I stood. "Are you hurt?"

He whirled to face me. "No."

"Is someone else hurt?" I asked.

"You could say that." He strode over the cord towards the lake, oblivious to the importance of the red boundary marking the edge of my world.

I walked until my toes reached the rope, torn about leaving. "Shouldn't we wait for Father Ellis?"

Niko didn't stop. "No."

"He can't move as fast as us."

"What is your name?"

"Alessandra."

He spun to face me, backpedaling as he spoke. "They're gone, Alessandra. They took a different route out of here."

My jaw dropped open. "They left me?"

"These people pursuing you – pursuing *us* – aren't the kind of people I'm used to dealing with. This is SISA. They have the gods' blessings to kill fast and without mercy. Running was the smartest thing for them to do." He wiped his bloodied hand on his pants. "You can come with me now, and we'll make it out of here by the skin of our teeth, or you can stay right there and wait for SISA to get you."

Gone. In all my preparations for the apocalypse, or perhaps this incident, I understood being alone to be a part of the scenario but wasn't quite able to wrap my head around it any more than I could the fact I was allegedly important. How could I go from being constantly surrounded by forty people to … alone?

Why didn't they take me with them? This hurt more than anything.

"Fine. Good luck." He turned away.

"Wait!" I cried and started forward.

Realizing what I had done, I twisted to look at the red cord boundary I had spent most of my life avoiding. I was leaving it, the safety of the forest, my past, my home ... basically everything behind me.

It was scary and exhilarating all at once.

Niko wasn't waiting.

Unable to stop and contemplate the world behind me, I charged ahead and ran to his side. My eyes went to the sky automatically, and I sought whatever creature had tracked me last night. Reminded of the rope around my wrist, I wished I'd thought to ask more questions about its power, about what I supposedly was, about what in the name of Holy Olympus was going on.

And ... how could the priests just leave me with a mercenary they didn't trust? How was I so important – yet not worthy of a farewell?

The idea they were watching over me out of obligation and had never wanted anything to do with me stung hard. I kind of considered them to be my extended family, however dysfunctional that was. I never suspected they didn't feel the same.

"Where are we going?" I asked Niko to take my mind off the pain.

"You tell me. Where did your priests want you to go?"

I was quiet.

Niko glanced at me. "They didn't tell you, either, huh? Great. Well, you're not coming home with me. I don't even think I can go home if you're important enough for teams of SISA special forces to smash through the forest."

"I don't know where to go, Niko."

"Just … pick a place. It won't matter so long as it's away from here."

"Washington DC."

"Worst place to be when the government is after you. Although …" He drifted off, gaze going to the west, as if he could see DC from here. "It might also be the best place to be. SISA won't expect us to go there."

I didn't care what reasoning he found in it. I was going to find Herakles, the only man in the universe who wouldn't abandon me at the first sign of trouble like the priests did. The cracking of tree trunks sounded behind us, followed by the faint tremble of the earth.

"Won't matter if we don't get out of here. I hope you can run as far as you can fast. We need to move." Niko took off running towards another thatch of forest lining the opposite side of the lake.

I followed, unable to shake the sense of guilt, unease and fear churning in my belly. The destruction of our home was all my fault. Maybe that was the real reason why the priests abandoned me – because I destroyed everything they loved.

FOUR
THE GROTESQUE

Not even the gods fight against necessity.
– SIMONIDES

"WHAT HAVE YOUR PRISONERS REVEALED?"

I glanced up at my master and friend as he entered the isolated apartment where I lived on a compound in central DC. The compound housed little else than my quarters; there were too many secrets for me to live among normal humans.

"Nothing." Washing my bloodied fists in the sink at the bar, I dried them and poured him his favorite drink. Unlike most men, the Supreme Priest preferred fruity drinks with umbrellas to shots of hard liquor. "They won't say what's in the forest."

"But you felt something."

"I did." Something ... familiar.

"It bothers you."

My hands paused as I finished his drink.

Lantos sat on a stool at the bar. He removed the mask he wore in public to reveal the face of a man in his thirties with sparkling green eyes and a smile that seemed out of place for someone with such a stately position as the gods' advocate to humanity.

"I know you, Adonis," Lantos chided gently. "Better than you know yourself. What did you sense?"

It was unlike me to hesitate to share any thought with the man who saved my life, yet something about what I'd experienced made me balk at the idea. I closed my eyes and tilted my head, bringing up the memory from the night before, of the calm lake reflecting starlight, the scent of pine and other trees in the air, and the peace that always came with leaving the confines of the city to hunt.

Beyond the pleasures of nature, I'd sensed ... a flicker of awareness, an instinct buried so deeply, it shocked me to feel it. What I'd experienced had nothing to do with the lake or what might've been present. Something inside me was awakening, and I wasn't accustomed to such mysteries or surprises about myself.

"I don't know," I said. "Whatever they hide there, it's familiar to me on a level I should know."

"Your memories have begun to return?"

Opening my eyes, I shook my head. "Not at all. There is nothing before the night you saved my life."

"Your beast instincts?"

"Baffled."

Rustling from below me drew a smile. The tiny creature at my feet – an animated stuffed koala bear – was pawing my leg like she did every time I returned to the apartment. I had no memory of obtaining the toy, no idea how she'd come to life. I only recalled waking twelve years ago to find her and Lantos hovering over me in worry and the life-threatening wound in my side healed by the magic of Lantos' Titan father.

"Hello Mrs. Nettles," I greeted the toy and picked her up. I didn't remember how she came by that name either, but she insisted I call her this.

Pink. She said and shuffled over to the Supreme Priest. At times uncannily wise beyond her years, she was at other times nothing more than a moth drawn to sparkly of bright things. She was currently fascinated by the umbrella in his drink.

"For you, Mrs. Nettles." Lantos handed her the umbrella. "How are you today?"

I shook my head at his look. She was too bedazzled to respond. No one heard her but me.

"Any luck on figuring out if the Silent Queen or Magistrate are involved?" Lantos asked.

"They're keeping things tightly held." I mentally went over the reports and activities of the day. "We destroyed the forest and found these everywhere." I lifted a gym bag onto the counter and withdrew a red cord.

Lantos' eyes lit up. He picked up one and held it over his forearm then lowered it. The rope cord turned to something resembling smoke. His body absorbed it.

"Part of your power," I observed. "What is it?"

Mrs. Nettles on the ground and moved out from behind the counter. It was almost past sunset. I peeled off my weapons and watch in anticipation of the change. "Tonight I'll return to the forest and look for any trace of where she went."

The image flashed once more and this time, brought a stab of pain.

"Your nose is bleeding," Lantos said.

I touched my nostril and gazed briefly at the drop of maroon on my fingertip. The pain subsided and with it, the vision of the girl. "Just sinuses." *Why did I say that?* It wasn't sinuses, and I knew it. The urge to lie to the man to whom I owed my life had been instinctive.

Alessandra, Mrs. Nettles said once more.

Lantos was gazing at me closely, a flicker of something dark in his gaze. Normally, Lantos was the moon and me the night sky. His outgoing, optimistic personality sometimes grated on others whereas my silence was usually taken with caution if not fear. People were able to sense the predator I was without seeing me in my secondary form. It helped that my reputation – well earned – was nonetheless much larger than my deeds.

I cleaned up my nose and felt the trickle of fire that went through me every time I was about to change. "How go your Holy Wars?"

"Exactly as planned. We're keeping the Magistrate's men busy outside the wall and the gods in disarray, fighting one another rather than us. I brokered another truce today."

"Only you could do something like this."

"Stop baiting me. It was your idea. Divide and conquer."

By nature, I tended to toy with the people around me. It wasn't malicious, more instinctual. I made every effort not to do so around Lantos for the simple reason that he was my friend.

"Like a true war leader. How do you come up with such ideas?" he asked, half in jest.

I shrugged. "It made sense for the situation."

"It's tied to your past. Your hunches are too … good for them to be just hunches."

"And I told you I'm not remembering anything yet. If I guess correctly, it's not done consciously."

"Any insight or hunches as to what Artemis is up to?" Lantos asked casually.

Of all the gods stuck on earth, Artemis was the only who hadn't sought him out to help establish a territory or broker deals with the Supreme Magistrate's men. It was common knowledge among the gods and goddesses that Lantos was one of them. Crisis kept them from demanding his exact lineage or asking too many questions that might reveal him as the son of their enemy. "None. The gods are your business, not mine."

"You've proven frighteningly accurate in everything."

"If I knew, I'd tell you," I replied. "I hear nothing through the networks and no indication your fellow Triumvirate members have any insight either."

Lantos nodded.

"I'm about to change," I said and pushed off my boots. "See you in the morning."

"Fly well." Lantos' smile returned. He replaced his mask,

bowed to Mrs. Nettles and left my flat.

I went to my room and stripped out of my clothing before heading to the balcony to change.

Mismatch. Mrs. Nettles never called me by the name I'd adopted after Lantos saved me. Mismatch was the name she claimed was mine before Lantos. She was shuffling after me as fast as her stubby legs would go.

"What is it, Mrs. Nettles?" I asked. "Quickly. It's my time."

Don't hurt her.

"You know what Phase Two is. I must obey Lantos," I replied gently.

You will see.

This was definitely one of her double possession stages when she seemed to have knowledge beyond her or my ability to access.

My attention shifted to the fire growing inside me. The moment the sun dipped beneath the horizon, my body began its nightly transformation. Black wings sprouted and spread from my shoulders outward. The hair on my body disappeared, and my head grew heavy, my features malformed and hideous, my body thickening and growing half a foot taller. Talons sprouted from my hands and toes followed soon after by a barbed, whip-like tail.

Not even Lantos knew how and why this transformation occurred. I resembled the stone grotesques and gargoyles perched on the temples of the gods. Beneath the dark gaze of Nyx, I flew and sat among them, waiting for any of them to come to life and join me for my nightly hunt.

They never did and I was left with a sense of loss to reinforce the knowledge I was alone.

Fly! Mrs. Nettles clapped silently and watched my wings flare out. The vacant look was back in her face. Whatever secondary possession took hold of her, it was gone once more.

Not entirely alone. I had never met another animated toy, either. We were different and unique, thrust together by circumstances I didn't recall.

I bowed my head to her and turned my attention to the sky. My beast senses were strong even in human form and completely unleashed when I was a creature. I swept into the sky, barreling upward until I was above the city, then flinging out my wings to catch an air current and hover. My heart raced from the ascension, and my shoulders warmed from the exercise.

I turned my focus north, towards the forests of Maryland, and began flying. My grumbling stomach would wait for now; I needed to complete Lantos' mission first. The odd instincts were stronger in my beast form, the draw of what was hidden in the forest, the compulsion to find it … her … nearly beyond my ability to curb. I needed to know for certain if the image in my mind was accurate and why I'd done the unthinkable and lied to my only friend about something as unimportant as a nosebleed.

Whatever was going on, it didn't take the primal urges of a beast or warning of a stuffed animal for me to know the world was about to change.

FIVE
ALESSANDRA

Even a god cannot change the past.
– AGATHON

I ALWAYS IMAGINED HOW I'D FEEL THE DAY I LEFT THE forest. The reality, that I was forced out alone with no home to go back to, didn't hit me the way I expected. I was worried about Herakles, sad for the priests, glad to be away from the nymphs.

But I didn't feel like crying. It seemed … weird. How was I so calm watching my life crumble?

"You still with me?"

I blinked out of my thoughts to look at Niko. He was driving a car he had stolen, much to my disapproval. We had fled the area of coastal Maryland, first on foot then by car, and were on a major highway headed south, towards DC. It was almost one in the morning, and I was exhausted. After my adrenaline wore off, I'd begun to wonder why he was helping me if he didn't get paid for the job.

"I'm fine," I said.

"You in shock?"

"Um. I don't think so. My skin isn't clammy and my pupils aren't dilated."

"I meant mental shock, you little shit."

I rolled my eyes.

He was quiet for a moment, eyes on the road, before he spoke. "If we're going to do this, we need some rules."

My brow furrowed and I studied his profile.

"One, you may know how to run, fight and hunt, but your guardian didn't teach you the most important lesson."

I tensed, not about to let him insult Herakles.

"You are out of your gods' damned mind if you think you should be talking to or trusting or otherwise not running at the sight of a stranger, especially one who looks like me. The men hunting you will try every trick under the sun to get you to turn yourself in peacefully or seduce you or outright blow off your legs to keep you from running again. No strangers. Ever. At all. Everyone you meet is the enemy, including any other gladiators or mercs that you think are there to help. You have no friends."

"But you were in the forest because the priests –"

"Wrong. If he looks like me, you walk away." He slapped the steering wheel lightly. "What would you do if you ran into someone like me in the store?"

With a sigh, I stared out the window. "Walk away."

"What about some injured kid or woman in the street?"

"That's different. I know how –"

"Wrong. Walk away."

"But that's not right if I can–"

"Wrong!" he said more loudly. "No strangers. You're not safely tucked away in the forest or at school anymore, Alessandra. You're about to enter the real world, and it's ugly. It will eat you alive if you let it. SISA means business."

I listened. I hated to be schooled like this, and I was pretty certain if I saw an injured child, I'd stop, no matter what the consequences. *Which is why I'm here and not in my bed tonight.*

Ugh. I had real issues and no part of me was able to fathom the idea of people chasing me.

"Rule two, if someone asks you your name, it's Lisa," he continued.

"How can someone ask me my name if I'm not allowed to talk to anyone?"

"Don't get smart. Gods know I hate smart women."

I stared at him. "What do you mean you hate smart women?"

"Different story. No strangers, and you answer to Lisa. Rule three, no temples, police stations or hotspots, or anywhere else where people might be looking for you."

"The police?" I echoed. "I'm not a criminal."

"Who do they think you are?"

An Oracle. I didn't answer, though, because I didn't know who he thought I was.

"That's what I thought. Rule four, don't lie to me, don't

deceive me, don't betray me," he growled. "I have a real issue with that."

"You have a lot of issues," I mumbled.

"Yeah. Keep that in mind. Unpredictable mercenaries make for interesting allies."

"You think they're following us?" I twisted to look out the back window of the car.

"I know they will be if they figure out which direction we're headed. We're going underground. It's my world, not yours, which means, rule five, don't blow this for me. It takes years and money to get to a good place in the criminal underworld. I'm doing you a favor by taking you in. Don't ruin my life."

Criminal underworld? He wasn't really giving me warm fuzzies about our future. "So we can't ever go back to the forest."

"No. What're your rules?"

"No strangers. My name is Lisa. No cops, don't lie to you and no blowing your reputation with your criminal friends."

"Exactly."

The glow of light pollution hovering over DC brightened the horizon. We were getting closer to where I was born, closer to Herakles' location. "If someone was taken prisoner, how do you find them?"

"Depends on who has them. You talking a criminal or someone grabbed by the secret police?"

"I don't really know."

"If you know someone who got grabbed by the secret police, there's no finding them," he said.

"There has to be a way."

Niko chuckled. "Look at you. All wide-eyed and innocent."

"Stop it! I am so tired of people treating me like I'm an idiot!"

"You *are* an idiot if you think SISA will give up anyone without a good reason," he replied. "They're run by a man who doesn't know the meaning of boundaries and who answers only to the gods' representative on Earth. The laws shift around what he does, and no one is going to mess with him or his people so long as they're under the protection of the Supreme Priest who advises the world leaders, among others, as to what the gods and goddesses expect of their elite, sleazy, ass-kissing politician underlings."

I listened. The priests had taught me about the Supreme Priest and his connection to other high level politicians. He was one of the most powerful men in the world, according to the priests, who hadn't liked him one bit because he – and the Supreme Magistrate – stood between the people and free will. The Supreme Magistrate controlled the military and was responsible for securing the borders as well as enforcing international policy and quelling civil unrest. The Supreme Priest had its own domestic security arm – and was more feared than the military.

The security force managing the police state had many names. Secret Police. Divine Police. And other slang names Herakles had told me that offended the priests when I repeated them. Their official title, though, was SISA – the Sacred Independent Security Apparatus of Our Heavenly Fathers and

Mothers, whose members were colloquially known as Sacs, according to Herakles, or Sisans according to the priests.

They were said to be charged by the gods with managing internal affairs of the human race related to matters of law, morality and religion. They answered to no nation state but to the Supreme Priest. I didn't have any idea who ran the SISA. He wasn't of interest to the priests, or I'd have been taught his name.

The world was sounding more dangerous by the minute, and I didn't like it. The priests' claim that the SISA would torture me if they found me was sounding more likely given the grim words of Niko.

But there had to be a way to find Herakles. I couldn't think of him as being completely lost or worse, at the hands of someone Niko said worked outside the laws. The real world outside the forest, however, was completely new to me.

Red signs warning of an enforced curfew and mandatory checkpoint ahead began to appear along the highway. Two miles from the checkpoint, Niko pulled off the highway onto an exit leading into a quiet town near the forest.

"Where are we going?" I asked.

"You have a biotag?"

"I'm not sure what that is."

"Then we aren't going through a checkpoint where we can get thrown in jail for not having one, now are we?"

I rolled my eyes. He was moody at best tonight, probably tired like I was.

He drove through quiet neighborhoods before pulling into a

long driveway leading to a sagging doublewide trailer surrounded by a fence topped by barbed wire. Huge dogs barked at our approach, and a man with a large caliber rifle sauntered out of an outhouse sized guard shack beside the road.

Niko stopped at the rolling gate, and I looked from a scene out of a horror movie back to him.

"Really?" I asked.

"Shut up. These people don't like strangers or fugitives and you're both."

I sank into silence.

He rolled down his window and shook the hand of the man outside. "Hey, Mike. Need some work done."

"You got money this time?" the man named Mike asked and leaned down, peering at me.

"Yep. Quite a bit."

"Who's this?"

"No one. New girl toy."

"They getting' prettier and younger." Mike seemed to find that funny and laughed. He stood. "I'll tell Mama you're here."

"Thanks, Mike." Niko left his window down and waited for the gate to roll open before he began driving again.

"Your mother lives here?" I asked.

"No." He snorted. "Mama is the head of the criminal underground. No one knows her real name. They have to tell her anytime anyone enters her compounds. If she doesn't like you, she'll order you killed on the spot," he answered. "Stay close and keep quiet. We'll get you a biotag and be on our way."

He pulled around back, an area populated by more men

with guns drinking beer kept cold in a kiddie pool filled with ice. I looked at him skeptically.

"Don't judge these people or me," he grumbled. "Your damn priests died before paying me what they owed. If you're worth half what I think you are, you're the one on the most wanted posters so don't tempt me. This is coming out of my pocket, and those rednecks out there might just save your life."

I said nothing. I was too tired for my temper to flare.

"Come on." He climbed out of the car.

I exited more slowly, not at all convinced I wanted to leave the car with the rough men in the backyard. I leaned into the back to grab my knife from my pack and placed it at the small of my back, just in case, then trailed Niko.

He was weaving through the thugs and criminals, greeting those he knew and smiling like he belonged. Which he probably did. I eyed everyone I passed, my nose wrinkling at the stench of beer, marijuana, gun oil and body odor. These were not the kind of people Herakles or the priests would want me around. Most of them were too drunk or wasted to pay attention to us, and others jostled into me or spilled beer on me without apologizing.

I went with Niko into the house – and almost gagged at the cigarette smoke fogging up the air. I sneezed then coughed.

"Knock it off," Niko said and grabbed a fistful of my shirt, hauling me through a living room and down a narrow hallway. He released me outside a door and turned to face me. "Don't talk to anyone. Don't make eye contact. Don't leave this spot. Got it?"

I grimaced, not at all happy at breathing air that felt like it was choking me.

"Hey. You got it?" He pushed one shoulder against the wall.

He wore an expression that warned me we weren't in a place he considered friendly. His muscular frame was tense once more, and an icky feeling slid through me. I knew nothing of this man, and Herakles would say that no one with a shred of honor would go merc.

What if he was here to sell me out?

"Yeah. I got it," I said and tugged free. "Just be quick."

Niko knocked on the door beside us and opened it without waiting for someone to answer. He walked in and grinned widely at whoever was inside.

The door closed behind him. I lingered for all of ten seconds before deciding I really didn't want to be around criminals and had no reason to trust a man who said he was going to sell me if the priests didn't pay him.

Which he claimed they hadn't.

The barrage on my senses here made my skin crawl. I returned the way we had come and stepped out onto the back porch, waving away the last of the smoke. The stench here was muted compared to the inside of the trailer. I gazed around briefly before deciding I'd rather take my chances alone than stay here.

I wove back through the armed drunks and druggies towards the car and paused at the end of the sidewalk before the driveway.

A figure in a hood and cloak stood leaning against the

driver's side of the car. He didn't seem to be armed, and he made no move towards me. Unable to make out facial features or anything about the person, I hesitated to confront someone in this place where everyone was armed. But I did move a little closer and peered at him.

"That's, um, our car," I said awkwardly.

No response. No movement. I felt him watching me.

"Hey! What'd I tell you!" Niko belted from the direction of the house.

"Great." I rolled my eyes and turned. "I couldn't breathe in there!"

"Get your ass back here."

"Are you gonna let this guy steal your car?" I pointed over my shoulder and then turned.

The hooded figure was gone.

"The smoke is getting to you. Hurry up so we can leave." The screen door slammed closed behind Niko.

I walked around the car and searched the night visually for the figure I saw before finally doing what Herakles told me no one ever does. I looked up.

The hooded figure had scaled the tree behind the gravel parking area and was clinging to it.

"Just, uh, don't steal our car," I said and then turned away to obey Niko before he yelled at me again. "I mean, *the* car. It's already been stolen once tonight."

This time I covered my nose and mouth with my t-shirt when I entered the disgusting lair of Niko's criminal friends. He waited for me in the hallway.

"Knock it off, Lisa," he grumbled and yanked my shirt off my nose.

"This place is disgusting," I complained.

Niko got into my space until I took a step back. "You may not like these people, but they're going to help us. So stop acting like a child and pretend to be grateful they aren't asking questions," he snapped quietly enough for only me to hear.

I felt bad after that. He was right. I didn't want to be here, but if they could help me get into DC where I could find Herakles ... "Sorry," I murmured.

"Good. Now go." He pushed me towards the door cracked halfway open.

I entered with some trepidation, not certain what I'd find. It resembled what I imagined a criminal's hangout looked like, only with more guns and beer. The guy working at a makeshift desk topped with bundles of money and small cases of drugs was close to my age. He waved me over. Several more men were in another corner, probably guards by their beefy statures. Two women were sorting pills on another table.

I sat before the kid at the table.

"How do you not have a biotag?" he asked, his direct gaze showing no sign of intoxication despite the beer bottles lining one side of his desk.

"Stop it, Marty," Niko replied.

"It's easier to reprogram an existing tag than insert a new one," Marty said in irritation.

"Yep. I know. New one is twice as expensive, too." Niko nudged me.

I said nothing. Maybe I should've been grateful, but I wasn't feeling it. The hairs on the back of my neck were on end, and my instincts were restless.

Marty snatched my wrist and began waving a wand-like device lined with lights over one forearm then the other. "No tag," he said. "You know where I have to go to get these?" he asked me, clearly blaming me for whatever criminal act he had to perform.

"No," I replied.

"Corpse. I have to dig them out of dead people."

I pulled my hand back, grossed out.

"Niko, keep her still."

Niko gripped my wrist and pinned it to the table with strength I wasn't able to shake. I watched Marty lift a second device resembling a handgun and read something on the small screen on one side of it.

"Your name is now … Holly. Holly Rodriguez, and you're supposed to be Mexican." Marty eyed me critically. "You know Spanish? Because this says it's your only language."

"Who cares," Niko replied. "There are white Mexicans somewhere. Shoot her up. We're in a rush."

Marty positioned the gun in the center, underside of my forearm and pulled the trigger.

"Ow," I muttered at the sharp sting.

"Congrats. You now have a biotag," Marty said and lowered the gun.

I raised my forearm. A drop of blood hovered over a dark, square microchip planted just beneath the surface of my skin.

The idea it had been in some other woman's body, and she was dead, weirded me out.

"You want me to cut off that rope?" Marty asked, tapping the red cord around my wrist.

"Nope. Just the biotag," Niko replied. He pulled a wad of cash out of a cargo pocket and plunked it down on the desk. "As agreed."

Marty counted it then added it to one of the stacks on his desk. "Pleasure, as always. Good luck, Holly."

I stood and moved towards the door, holding my forearm. The pain was gone, but I was still disgusted by the biotag. I turned to wait for Niko and saw him slide money from one of Marty's stacks into his pockets. He had distracted Marty by showing him a knife.

I left, not wanting to be around if the thugs in the corner caught on and shot Niko. Returning to the car, I peered again into the tree branches without seeing the figure I had spotted earlier. I didn't really believe in magical creatures the way the priests and others did. Herakles was very pragmatic, not at all into the supernatural outside of the gods, and I had adopted his realistic view of our world. Sprites and monsters didn't exist, even if the myths claiming otherwise.

Except ... the creature from the lake. I wasn't afraid of whatever it had been by our car, not like I had been of the grotesque. Now *that* was worth worrying about. But a man in a hood hanging out in such a place? No comparison.

"Come on, Holly." Niko strode by me to the car and opened the driver's side door, sliding into it.

Eager to be out of here, I hurried around to the passenger side. "Do they know you stole their money?"

"Quiet, kid." He turned the car around and headed back down the driveway.

The gate rolled open, and Mike-the-guard waved us through.

Ten minutes later, we were driving down the highway toward DC again. Traffic slowed at the checkpoint, and Niko released a sigh as we were waved through rather than stopped by men dressed all in black wearing masks and carrying weapons.

"That's it?" I asked.

"They don't usually wave you through, and my luck has been bad for a while," Niko replied.

"If you're a criminal, wouldn't they be more interested in you than someone without a chip?" I asked.

"I have my ways of avoiding detection."

I had a feeling they were just as illegal as everything else he did. Too tired and interested in DC to speak, I focused on the buildings we were approaching. Signs and banners telling citizens to report terrorists spouting anti-gods and anti-government activity and beliefs to the SISA were everywhere, squeezed between parking meters, fast food restaurant ads and plastered on the sides of buildings.

Graffiti was everywhere, too, and I noticed a theme among the colorful tags as we passed. They all started with *Mama says*
...

... don't trust the gov't.

... destroy the SISA!

... go home gods!

... bring back the Old Ways.

"Mama is popular," I said.

"She's outfoxed SISA for ten years."

"She must be really smart."

"Probably. No one's ever met her. I sometimes think she's a figurehead that doesn't exist. Even us criminals want to know we have someone to take care of us, I suppose."

"Why are you a merc?" I asked. "Doesn't being a gladiator pay enough?"

He laughed. "You know nothing about the real world, kid. I don't know any gladiator who isn't involved in the Merc Guild or some other criminal enterprise."

"I had no idea," I said softly, somewhat disappointed to learn the fighters we watched on Wednesday nights on the Gladiator Guild channel were criminals. "What made you choose that instead of becoming a normal citizen?"

Niko gave me a weird look. "You mean a slave to the gods and their human underlings? Why would I want that? If you don't want to live a life of fear, you end up like me on the streets and make a living where you can."

I frowned.

"*Normal* people are afraid to speak their minds, to live their lives the way they want, to follow their dreams. They are oppressed, Alessandra, by the gods, by SISA, by the Supreme Magistrate. People disappear every day and are never heard from again. No trials, no justification, no real reason. Heresy is the biggest excuse given, and there's no one to tell that the SISA can't do what they're doing. And that mess is ideal compared to what's been going on outside the wall since the Holy Wars erupted five years ago."

"Holy Wars? What wall?"

He eyed me. "Gods damn the priests! It's not my job to school you in the ways of the world. You're lucky I got you a biotag, you little shit! That came out of my salary."

"You stole the money back!" My gods. This guy had issues. Why was he helping me for free when he clearly didn't like me? "We should return to the Old Ways," I said, hoping for a topic that didn't make him yell quite so much.

"Exactly. You're not as stupid as you seem sometimes. You know what the Old Ways are?"

"Of course. I learned in school. A time where humans governed themselves without the influence of the gods. Life, liberty, equality and the pursuit of happiness," I recited from class.

"They don't teach that shit in school. The knowledge has been lost, or would have been, if not for Mama. It's what she wants – to return to the Old Ways." He smiled faintly.

"Strange. Our priests taught us the Old Ways are supposed to return soon."

"I'm liking your priests more and more. They're clearly academics out of touch with the real world, though. It's impossible for the Old Ways to exist alongside the gods."

Unless the gods are gone. Puzzled, I rolled his words and those of the priests around in my head. I was beginning to understand that my world of twelve years wasn't the same as this one. The idea the Old Ways were almost lost when I'd lived every day reciting *life, liberty, equality and the pursuit of happiness* was odd. If the priests were right, if they hadn't been messing with me about being the Oracle, I was beginning to see why they wanted me hidden until the old Oracle died. The Old Ways could emerge only after she was gone. *But why not get rid of me instead of imprisoning me?*

Not a lot made sense to me yet. I had much to learn about the real world and a ton more to think about.

Niko stayed off the bigger streets through DC and angled us to the side of the city closer to Maryland, finally stopping in a rundown section of town that shouldn't have surprised me but did. The buildings were blocky with barred windows, and vehicles that appeared to be abandoned lined one side of the street. The thump of bass came from a house squeezed between block apartment buildings. Masked SISA police patrolled the neighborhoods on foot.

"SISA's everywhere inside the wall and the military everywhere outside it." Niko glared at the police.

"You prefer it otherwise?"

"The military is secular and has a justice system. They answer to the people and don't make people disappear for saying the gods are nuts."

We weren't completely different. Aside from Artemis and Lelantos, I was raised to be able to identify the other gods and Titans but not to worship them.

He parked out front. We got out and went to the door.

There was no mistaking the round chinks in the concrete walls on either side of the door for anything but bullet holes.

Thus far, I wasn't impressed by the outside world or those who inhabited it.

"Are we visiting more of your friends?" I asked.

"No. This is one of my places." He unlocked the door and walked in.

I trailed. He locked the door behind us and went to the stairs on the far side of a lobby with scuffed floors and sagging ceilings. He led me to an apartment on the second floor. It was clean, neat and practically decorated. Grateful not to be stuck in a place like the trailer, I put my backpack on the floor.

"Bathroom through there. There's only one, so lock the damn door if you're in there," he said grouchily and pointed. He walked into his bedroom and flipped on the lights.

The apartment had a small kitchen and dining area along with a balcony overlooking the street behind where we parked. The balcony doors, however, were barred, preventing anyone from using the outside space.

"Hey, Niko?" I dropped the curtain and moved towards the couch, peeking into the cracked bedroom door.

He was on the phone, his back to me. My instincts stirred once more, and I had the same urge I did at his redneck friends' – to leave him sooner rather than later, even if I had nowhere else to go.

SIX

OMORROW I'LL FIGURE IT OUT. I WAS TOO BEAT TO take a shower and slung myself down on the couch. I had spent two nights a week sleeping on the ground; the lumpy couch was good enough for me. As busy as my mind was, I was soon asleep.

Arguing voices pulled me out of a deep slumber. I struggled to rouse my resistant body, lost the battle then forced myself into a sit. I blinked rapidly and sighed. The noises were coming from Niko's room, probably from the television, except …

Instincts. The ones that made me worry about bears during fall and great cats during wildfire season. I rolled off the couch and orientated myself quickly before rising and going to the door to his bedroom cracked open.

"Niko?" I called.

Silence.

I pushed the door open to see him on the floor, bare chested in sweatpants. The hooded figure I had seen earlier stood over him, gun in hand.

"Stay where you are," hissed the person in the hood.

Niko motioned towards my left, and I looked. The top drawer of his dresser yawned open, and I caught the faint gleam of a gun butt. I moved towards it.

"If you try it, I'll shoot him," the hooded form threatened.

"You'd be doing the world a favor," I replied. "He's kind of an asshole." Snatching the gun, I flipped off the safety and walked towards them. "But I need him for now and I do know how to use a gun."

The person was still for a long moment. The tip of the gun lowered, and Niko knocked it away, snagging the hooded person's arm and shoving him into the wall. The hood fell away, and I started to smile.

The figure who bested Niko was a pretty woman with cocoa skin and a tattoo on her forehead.

"You couldn't stay away, could you, Dosy?" Niko growled and searched her roughly.

"I'm not here for you, you arrogant pig!" came the saucy response.

I switched on the lights. The tattoo was the same symbol on the Temple of Artemis: a bow. The woman wore a robe of gray beneath the hood. "Wait, did a priestess just kick your ass?" I asked Niko. I put the gun on the dresser.

"I was sleeping!" he retorted. "No one knows where this place is." He released the woman, angered and tense, and stepped back.

"She probably followed us from Marty's," I guessed.

"I was in the trunk." Dosy turned to face Niko. With a glance at me, her cool gaze fell to him, and her chin went up a notch in what I knew from experience was defiance. "Not the first time I was relegated to a cold, dark place at Niko's hands."

"I had nothing to do with that," he replied.

"Except abandoning me."

"That was ten years ago, Dosy, and you walked away!"

"You can't walk away from someone if he's already gone."

"You must be the smart woman he hates," I said with an uncomfortable laugh, uncertain how else to react to their violent reactions to one another.

The two of them glared at each other. Niko's jaw was ticking, and he appeared ready to pounce. Dosy's unfaltering gaze was cold. The tension between them was so thick, my cheeks grew warm. Whatever their history was, I was guessing it was pretty personal.

"I'm just gonna go back to my couch," I murmured and stepped back.

Dosy started towards me, and Niko grabbed her.

"I'm here to protect you from him! Niko will sell –"

"Holly knows you're full of shit!" He had her arms, and she pushed at him. "I should put a bullet in you and leave you for your goddess to take care of. Oh wait – the gods haven't helped us in five years! They abandoned us the way you did me ten years ago!"

My brow furrowed. Before I could pursue, Niko reached over to grab the priestess's weapon. "Wait!" I cried. "You can't just kill a priestess in your apartment!"

"Oh, I can."

"He can't hurt me," Dosy said calmly. "And since I know that … Holly, I came to give you a message about your birthright."

"Shut up, Dosy." Niko made a show of putting the gun to her head. "You have no idea what I've become."

"Wait, wait, wait!" I scrambled forward and pushed Niko to keep him from hurting her. He pushed me back. "I don't know who I am or what I'm supposed to do! If she does then …" I grunted and shoved him far enough away to squeeze between them. "Then I need to know. *We* need to know."

With me in the way, Niko lowered his gun arm without releasing his grip on Dosy.

"He's already sold you out twice by now," Dosy said, smooshed between me and the wall.

"Stop stirring the pot!" I snapped. "Just think about this for a minute. Both of you. You both want something from me and if you're fighting, I'm walking out that door without either of you."

"I wouldn't let you," Dosy responded.

"Not happening," Niko said at the same time.

"Oh, good. You're agreeing with each other. Niko, go over there. Now!" I ordered him.

He gave me a look that said he wished he'd left me with Marty but reluctantly moved to the other side of the bedroom, near the door. I stepped away from Dosy.

"Glad to see someone here has sense." Dosy straightened out her clothing. "For the record, Holly, he wouldn't have hurt me. He's always talked big, acted small when it came to me."

"In any case!" I shouted over Niko's objection. "Why are you here?" I asked Dosy.

She relaxed some, her focus shifting to me instead of the man she had a history with. "I'd like a glass of water."

"Oh, let's. We must be civilized." Niko strode angrily into the living room, the muscles of his thick frame rippling beneath the colorful tattoos covering his back, shoulders and chest.

I shook my head and followed, as did Dosy. When I reached my couch and sat down, I realized they were both staring at me.

"Um, what?" I asked, unsettled by Niko's fiery look and the odd expression on Dosy's face.

"You aren't what I expected," Dosy replied first.

I sighed and held my face in my hands. Irritated at the latest person who wanted to belittle or insult me, I rose and lifted my pack. "I'm out. You people have issues I can't fix."

Dosy laughed softly. "You took that wrong. I meant it as a compliment. I was expecting a scared, silly teen with no sense. You can use a gun and hold your own with Niko. That's impressive."

I lowered the pack, my ruffled feathers smoothing out.

"Herakles was rumored to be with you. He taught you to have a backbone?"

I glanced at Niko, who was listening intently. Uncertain what to think of Dosy or how she knew Herakles, I hesitated to respond.

Dosy sat on the chair near the kitchen. "Water, Niko," she

snapped. "How did you get through the checkpoint so easily?"

"They waved us through," I said with a shrug.

"That doesn't just happen. I'm betting Niko's made arrangements."

He appeared ready to refute her but whirled and went to the sink. He wasn't kicking her out or trying to kill her anymore, which made me think she was right. As badass as he acted, he wasn't going to hurt the woman he had feelings for at one point.

"Herakles," Dosy prodded. "Why is he not with you?"

"He was captured," I said. "We're here to rescue him."

"We're what?" Niko demanded.

"Rescue?" Dosy's eyes widened. "If he was taken, it was by SISA. There's no way for you to get to him."

"I don't believe that."

Niko brought her a glass of water. This time, the look they exchanged was one of uneasiness.

"Why is a priestess looking for me?" I asked her.

"*High* Priestess," Niko said, using air quotes in mockery. "What do the gods want with some initiate?"

"Not your concern, Niko," she replied.

"But you came to find me, right?" I asked.

"Yes."

"And tell me ... what?"

"I came to find and protect you from people like Niko," Dosy admitted. "People who might figure out who you really are."

Niko was studying me the way he had in the forest when we

first met.

"So do you know what's supposed to happen next?" I asked.

"Pardon?"

"Where I'm supposed to go, what I'm supposed to do. The priests at the orphanage seemed to think I should go somewhere."

"You were raised by priests," Dosy repeated, surprised. "That's not how this was supposed to happen."

"Okay, first, what is *this*?" Niko asked and motioned to me.

"Holly is of –"

"Omigods. My name's not Holly," I muttered. "It's –"

"Lisa," Niko cut me off. "And shut up."

Dosy appeared taken aback for a moment before she met my gaze. "Do you know what you are?" she asked uncertainly.

"Allegedly what I am? I was told yesterday," I replied. "Niko thinks I'm an initiate."

"So Herakles isn't with you, you were raised by priests and you don't know how to be what you really are," Dosy summarized.

"Yes," I said. "And I want to rescue Herakles."

Agitated, she rose and paced. "After hearing all this, I think rescuing him will be the easiest thing you do."

Niko and I exchanged a look. We didn't know enough to share her alarm.

"Okay." Dosy drew a deep breath and approached me. "First off, don't take off the red cord. If it is what I think it might be, it'll keep people from tracking you. Second …" She trailed off, at a loss for words. Blinking rapidly, she shook her head. "I can't even begin to imagine a second. Just stay underground for a while. Niko, if you betray her to you-know-who, I will gut you."

It was a wonder either of them were alive, given how often they threatened each other in the short span we were together.

"Hard to protect what you don't know you have," he pointed out.

"I'm an Oracle," I said. Whether or not I should have, I didn't really care at the moment. I wanted to see what they did when I said it, to gauge how bad things really were.

Dosy gaped. "Don't ever tell anyone that!" she yelled when she'd recovered. "Ever!"

"A what? You mean … you mean *the* Oracle?" Niko was staring at me. "And those damn priests were going to pay me the rate for a typical teen runaway? Now I'm glad I cut them down before the security forces moved in."

I gasped.

"This is what I'm talking about." Dosy pointed at him. "This is why you're better off with me, Holly. Lisa. Whatever your name is."

My ears were ringing from Niko's confession.

"You do not walk into –"

The two of them began shouting at one another again, and all I could think about was the blood I'd seen on Niko's hands. It hadn't belonged to the enemies. It had belonged to the priests he let me think had abandoned me.

"How could you do that?" I shouted above them and pushed at Niko. "How could you *kill* them?" I reached for his weapon, emotion boiling despite my exhaustion.

Dosy stepped back, and Niko grabbed my arms, gaze dropping from her to me. He wrestled with me, finally wrapping both arms around me and shoving me face first into a wall. I struggled in a frenzy until it was clear I wasn't going to best him this way. I panted and went limp, my mind racing.

"Look, kid, it was –"

"Don't call me kid!" I struggled to pull away, but he kept me in place. "You're a murderer!"

"It was an act of mercy."

"Bullshit!"

"No, it was," Dosy seconded. "The secret police would've done unspeakable things to them. Since the SISA chief, Adonis, took over, it's been nonstop carnage and oppression. They're aggressive and harsh. If you've got something to hide, suicide is a better option. It's not something that's easy to explain, except that Niko did them a favor, Holly."

My name's not Holly! I blinked. My eyes were blurred by tears. A tremor of emotion swirled through me. I could imagine no situation under Zeus where the priests committed suicide. Was the world outside my forest that bad? *Why* had they kept so much from me? Did I not need this type of knowledge in order to help them with their plan to bring back the Old Ways?

"You okay?" Dosy's voice had softened.

"No," I replied. "They were my friends."

"Holly, I know this is hard, but trust me. They are better off in Thanatos' hands than SISA's. You learned about Thanatos, the god of death, didn't you? About his realm?"

I calmed some, recalling that good people like the priests weren't really gone. They lived on in a different realm, one ruled by Thanatos. "Yes."

"Then you know death is simply a gateway into a much better place."

It was easier to let myself believe her, trust her, than to sort through emotions I wasn't prepared to feel. The priests had never been close to me like Herakles was. I wanted to believe them better off, the way they taught us in school. But if Herakles followed them into the underworld of Thanatos ...

I would do whatever I had to out of revenge. Herakles was my heart, my life, the only thing keeping me from acknowledging the desolation stemming from understanding that the world I knew was now completely gone. I wasn't ready for that.

"Don't wuss out now, kid," Niko said in a quieter voice. "You're tough. Stay tough. I don't kill unless I have to, but all of us knew what was coming. I did it quick."

"I do agree with him there," Dosy said. "SISA will do anything to find you."

"Let me go." I tugged at Niko's grip.

He did so.

I left the wall and sank onto the couch, trying to rein in the emotions I couldn't quite categorize. Herakles would tell me they were right, that I needed to stay focused not emotional, that the priests were in the part of the underworld saved for the most righteous. Yet the image in my head of Father Ellis falling beneath Niko's knives ... I wasn't happy at the orphanage, but

Dosy said.

"Hmm. So you don't want me to do it. Looks like I'm in, kid."

I snorted, not at all certain if I'd really won or if he was so determined to spite Dosy, he'd get us both killed.

"I'll do what I can," Dosy said, gaze on me. "Niko, make up your mind. You gonna keep her safe, or do I need reinforcements to take her away from you? I don't need to remind you how few men your people have in DC."

I waited.

The two went into stare down mode again. Finally, Niko shifted.

"Fine. I'll take her to find this friend and dump her off at the front gates or wherever," he said finally. "I'm not going to risk my neck for her."

"No surprise," Dosy muttered. "Good enough for me. I'll be back in the morning with any information I can find out about Herakles." She strode to the door.

"Hey. You haven't answered my emails," Niko called as she opened the door. "How's … Junior?"

"He's *not* Junior. He's nothing like you!"

"You guys have a kid?" I asked, astonished. "My gods. That poor little guy." This earned me two glares.

"It's why I'm the only person immune to Niko's knives and guns. We'll talk about it later." Dosy left and slammed the door behind me.

The look Niko gave me made me think I should sleep with one of his guns. But I was just as upset and glared back. He spun on his heel and stormed into his bedroom, slamming the door.

That poor kid.

Although I'd never experienced it first hand, I imagined this was what it was like if my parents were fighting. Except my parents didn't go around mercy-killing priests. I locked the front door and settled down on the couch again, a little out of place and worried about what was going on that no one wanted to tell me.

At least I might soon know where Herakles was. If I were in trouble, he would come for me. It was only fair I did the same.

Father Ellis is dead. I wanted to hate Niko, but ... well, I was horrified to admit I was a little too angry with the priests for lying to me my entire life to feel complete compassion for them.

I was too confused to figure out what I felt. None of this seemed real. I wanted to wake up at home in my bed at the orphanage and trek into the woods with Herakles for another survival lesson.

SEVEN

Hateful to me as the gates of Hades is that man who hides one thing in his heart and speaks another.

– HOMER

T HE NEXT MORNING, I STOOD ACROSS THE STREET FROM the thick metal gates of SISA headquarters located in downtown DC. Maybe it was stupid of me, but I hadn't really considered it might be hard to get to Herakles until I saw those tall, thick gates guarded by half a dozen men on the street side. Herakles had taught me to be self-sufficient in every scenario I could think of to the point I thought myself somewhat invincible. But those gates ...

There's no way I can sneak in.

I had to, though. I'd rather be trapped with Herakles in prison than stuck alone in an insane world I didn't understand. The morning crowd, consisting of tour groups and businesspeople, walked past the wall, seemingly oblivious to the compound. I couldn't look away.

At least, not until one of the masked guards looked my way twice. The masks kind of freaked me out. They covered their entire faces and heads. Each guard was identified by a patch with a number on it rather than names and faces.

I left the sidewalk and went into the café behind me. With the money I'd pilfered from Niko, I bought a Greek coffee and sat near the window. The streets and sidewalks were churning with rush hour activity. Part of me was thrilled to realize I was a part of this world, at least on this surface. Buying coffee, smiling at people whose paths I crossed … no one knew I was different.

I kind of liked that.

The gates across the street opened once to reveal a second set, these much smaller, and guards and tire shredders in between the two. Beyond the second gates sat a white building with marble pillars. I wasn't able to gauge how large it was in the two seconds the two gates were simultaneously open.

Niko had claimed this building was more secure than the White House. Dosy disagreed, claiming this was an offsite and the *real* headquarters was located in Northern Virginia. She said this site was abandoned before a month ago and considered its reactivation a ploy of some sort. I was inclined to take her word over his, out of principal because I had no idea either way.

The two had still been fighting about something that didn't matter to me when I left. They argued about *everything*. I didn't even have to be subtle – just walked out.

Herakles would tell me to evaluate everything I could about the compound. So far, I'd figured out I wasn't going over the gates. I had no clue whether the sewer system was an option. The only thing Dosy had been able to find out was that Herakles was in the east wing, which wasn't visible from the street.

Official visitors entered the gates on foot and by car. Their identifications were scanned, and they, their belongings and vehicles were searched. My eyes followed the walls down the block. I stood, grabbing my coffee to walk the perimeter and see what other gates were present.

Half an hour later, I was forced to admit there was one way in and out of the compound. I returned to the café and sat with another coffee, toying with the red cord around my wrist.

"You little shit."

I looked up to see Niko at my table. He sat down without waiting for an invitation.

"You all clearly had some things to work out," I replied.

"When you meet that special someone who turns out not to be as interested in you as you are them, then you'll understand."

"I doubt it. Herakles told me never to let any boy derail me from my goals, and I won't." It had been easy, if frustrating, to let go of the boys the nymphs stole. I wasn't letting anyone near my heart, because Herakles said that's when bad things happened.

"You think it's a choice to fall in love, to have a kid you aren't expecting," Niko observed.

"Everything in life is a choice."

"No, kid. It's not." He was amused. "But I do hope to see the look on your face when you realize that."

"Whatever. Are we gonna do this?" It was hard to talk to him when I wanted to explode about the priests.

"Do *what?*"

I pointed towards SISA building. Niko looked briefly.

"Let's get something straight. You're insane to want to go to the one place you should never want to be," he replied.

"You know why you're here right now? Because you murdered everyone else who could help me," I shot back.

"Shut up, kid. I was going to tell you, Dosy sent me down here to dissuade you, but I have a different idea."

I waited, surprised to sense he was on my side. And irked he didn't even blink when I mentioned the priests.

"There's only one way into that place," he continued. "We need to be invited."

"What does that entail?"

"A mercenary bounty hunter claiming to have the real Oracle in tow might warrant an invite."

I brightened. "That's brilliant, Niko! Let's do that!"

He eyed me. "Does anything penetrate that thick skull of yours? Like how dangerous this is, how small the chances are you'll be able to walk out the same way you walk in? What they might do to you?"

"Can't be worse than what you might do to me."

"You have no idea how big of a favor I did those priests. They didn't even pay me."

What an asshole. "Herakles will fix everything," I said, missing my friend even more.

"We don't even know where he is."

"Yes we do. The east wing."

"You're not getting it." Niko sighed and studied me. "You might get in but you won't get out."

Maybe he was right. But why did I want to leave if Herakles was trapped and being tortured? My world – except him – was crashing and burning. I was trying not to face that reality and holding out for Herakles to fix things. I didn't care what happened to me if it meant he was gone.

I didn't tell Niko any of this. It was obvious he thought I was insane. To discuss what I felt made it more real. It was easier for me to push away my emotions and put all my faith in the man sitting in a cell somewhere in the east wing of SISA headquarters.

Herakles had spent over a decade taking care of me. For once, it was my turn to do the same for him, and nothing Niko said was going to dissuade me.

"Well, come on," he said and stood.

"Where are we going?" I asked suspiciously.

"Dosy knows some people. You and I are going to walk into SISA and hope she can get us out." He stopped outside the café and pulled out a pair of handcuffs. "I've never seen footage of a potential Oracle walking in voluntarily." He slid one cold cuff around one wrist then the other.

"You're really going to help me?"

Niko met my gaze. "No one else I know would consider me

walking you into SISA *helping*," he replied. "When we're inside, chances are they're going to separate us. Count to a hundred and then pull off your red bracelet. If you really are what Dosy says, it'll cause some sort of chaos and distract them long enough for me to slip away and find Herakles."

"This is a great plan," I said, my hope building.

"It's a terrible plan. We have no exit strategy."

I didn't care. All I could think about was Herakles. "I can take care of myself," I told him when I saw the worried look he cast the walls. "I know self-defense and I can run."

"You have no clue, kid." Without another word, he took my arm and marched me across the street.

My stomach churned as we approached the guard post.

"I found the real Oracle," Niko proclaimed.

"Move along," one of the guards said, unconcerned.

"Look, I'm a merc. I've been tracking her, and I found her," Niko insisted. "If you check with your boss, he's expecting me."

Say what now? I eyed him.

"Whatever, sport. Keep walking," another guard replied.

Niko glanced at me. "Can you do anything Oracle-y to prove it?" he asked.

"Not that I know of."

He muttered something I couldn't hear then reached for the red cord at my wrist. Tugging the knot free, he pulled it away.

A wave – invisible yet strong enough to shatter the glass of car windshields – rippled outward from us. The gate before us shook, and the plastic chairs outside the café flipped onto their sides. Everyone within ten feet of us was flattened. The wave lost power the farther it traveled down the block.

Niko and I exchanged a look. We alone were left standing. The guards were sprawled onto the ground where they'd fallen. Replacing the red cord, Niko faced the nearest guard, who appeared too stunned to react.

"If you don't want her, I can sell her off on the black market for at least –"

The guards erupted into action and shouting. Someone screamed for the gate to be opened while two more charged and grabbed us both.

"It's working," I mouthed to Niko, not fighting the men jostling us towards the gate.

He rolled his eyes.

We were escorted past the first gate where our entourage doubled before we were permitted through the second gate. The compound inside consisted of at least three buildings edging a courtyard and entrance to an underground parking garage.

We stopped there. One of the guards radioed into someone. He was too far away for me to hear, and my gaze fell to the building to the east, where I thought Herakles might be. It was impossible to tell anything about the buildings and what they held by their uniform, blank facades. No numbers or identifying marks were visible. The building on the left was boarded up.

Someone in a suit emerged from the eastern building to wave the guard forward. I was corralled in that direction. Niko remained in the courtyard. I automatically began to count as he had instructed.

The interior of the building was as plain as the exterior. A foyer consisting of an empty space flanked by two doors held two men in business suits and a doctor or nurse in scrubs.

"Just one guard," one of the businessmen waved the others away. He wore spectacles and carried an iPad. "You won't be any trouble, right, princess?" He glanced at me.

What an ass. But I was polite. "No, sir," I replied.

He waited for the door to close behind the other guards before motioning for his assistant to open one of the doors leading into the interior. We walked into the building, and I peered into the offices we passed.

They were empty and appeared to have been for quite some time. The cameras in the hallways all pointed at the floor or the wall behind them rather than in the direction they should. Dosy's claim about this place being a set up for … something began to make more sense.

"Name," the man in the suit said to me crisply.

"Holly."

"A pleasure, Holly. We're going to do some paperwork and then send you in for a medical exam. We've had quite a few frauds lately, so I'm sure you'll understand the precautions we must take. There's a great deal of wealth involved."

"Wealth?" I echoed.

He stepped into an office and motioned me to sit in front of a desk. "Yes. The Oracle of Delphi's fortune has been growing for ten thousand years. It's the number one reason for fraud.

People have been after her money for years."

"So she's rich." I frowned, not understanding the divide between what the priests told me and this. "And the downside …"

"Downside?" He gave me an odd look. "What downside is there to being one of the wealthiest people on the planet, handed power on a platter and having the honor of communicating directly with the gods daily?"

"I guess there is none." Something wasn't right about this. If what he said was true, why did Niko say every potential Oracle who came here did so unwillingly? The priests had only said the Oracle was tortured. They never mentioned wealth or anything else. I knew they favored the Old Ways and found myself wishing once more they'd taken the time to tell me something more than they had. Like, the full truth. Did they fear I'd be swayed to ignore the Old Ways by money?

The guard took off my handcuffs and the assistant scanned my arm. "Holly Rodriquez," he said, reading the screen. "According to this, you're thirty eight and wanted for murder in two states."

All four of them stared at me.

"About that …" I cleared my throat.

Note to self: tell Niko never to use Marty again. Then again, this was probably karma after Niko stole money from his criminal friends.

"It hasn't been reprogrammed," the assistant continued. "Which means …"

"You either killed Holly Rodriquez or bought a biotag on

the black market," Spectacles finished.

"I didn't kill anyone," I said quickly.

"There are no traces of her old biotag being removed. How did you come to have no biotag?" the assistant asked.

"I'm not even sure what a – ow!" I snapped and yanked my arm back. A tiny, sharp prick of pain throbbed on my forearm in the spot where he had removed the chip.

"DNA sample," Spectacles directed the medic. "There's more than one way to uncover your identity."

"I'd like to know that, too," I told him.

They gave me the same look Niko did pretty much every time I spoke.

I was escorted down the corridor, past more empty offices, to a small medical lab, past a hallway with *Prisoners 0-24* listed on the wall, and motioned to a chair in the doctor's office. Realizing I had lost track of my count, I started at fifty and watched the doctor prep a needle. He wrapped rubber around my arm and then tapped the bluish vein inside my elbow.

"You're very calm," he said with a glance at me.

"I've had my blood drawn before," I replied.

"No, I mean with all this." He motioned to the guard at the door and the assistant of Spectacles, who was typing into his iPad.

The insertion of the needle stung, and I watched the plastic vial fill with blood.

"I guess I don't understand what the big deal is," I replied truthfully.

His eyes lingered on my features, as if he didn't believe me.

It was hard for me to be deceptive about something I knew nothing about.

He finished when I got to ninety nine in my countdown, so I kept counting. I didn't want to knock everyone down with a needle in my arm.

"You really don't know, do you?" he asked and slid the needle free.

"I don't even know enough to know what I'm supposed to know about," I quipped.

"Hold the cotton ball for ten seconds." He smiled. "I see a lot here, and everyone is usually trying to get something over on someone else. It's the political nature of DC. Even the frauds are trying to game the system somehow. But you … you're not right."

"I get that a lot, Doc." I lifted the cotton ball to check the prick beneath.

"A place like this will destroy you if you aren't her. The trials might do the same even if you are. The gods are not happy. Be careful."

I looked up, not expecting the compassion, however distant and passing it was. "Thank you. I'm sure I can handle it."

"I'm done." He motioned to the guard.

I joined the guard at the door. A closer look at the mask showed me it was almost sheer. Nothing impeded the breathing or sight of the man beneath it. The color prevented people from seeing his features.

"Where to next?" I asked the guard curiously. This wasn't the ideal area to unleash my strange magic wave. I wanted to be closer to the prison.

"We wait for DNA results to identify you based on the genetic profiles kept in the biotag database," the assistant to Spectacles said. "You can wait in John's office or the courtyard."

"John's office sounds great," I said cheerfully.

Even he looked at me like I was crazy. I didn't understand what everyone was concerned about. I had a feeling I'd be in trouble if I were a fraud. But I wasn't, and I didn't think being the Oracle could be worse than lying to people with no senses of humor who were probably quick to pull the trigger on a fraud.

We returned to the office. John wasn't there, and the guard took up his post outside the room. The assistant started to sit. Wanting as few people around as possible when I took off the bracelet, I spoke up quickly.

"Hey, can I get some water?"

The assistant glanced at me and stood once more without responding, leaving the room.

I had long since passed the count of a hundred and hoped Niko wasn't in trouble. I listened until I heard the sound of the assistant's footsteps fade then crept to the door and untied the cord at my wrist.

In a confined space, the weird shock wave was way worse. It shattered the glass office windows behind me and slammed into walls, reverberating back towards me and knocking me to the ground along with the guard. An alarm went off in response to the building shaking, and the lights in the hallway flickered.

I hastily replaced the cord and made a mental note never to take it off inside again. My ears rang as I scrambled to my feet ahead of the guard.

Before he could stand, I had snatched his handgun.

I bolted towards the direction of the hallway where I'd seen the sign for the prisoners. Darting down it, I heard someone shout for more security forces. The alarm blared. I covered my ears. My heart was slamming into my chest and my adrenaline racing as I reached the intersection at the end of the hall.

This one wasn't labeled. I was a little turned around in the building that had no windows in the corridors. After a split second of debate, I raced to the left, which I hoped would take me toward the wing with the prisoners.

The alarm turned off. "Thank the gods!" I murmured and paused near another intersection. I heard the sounds of mobilized guards from the direction I came from but couldn't determine if or which way was where I wanted to go.

I headed left once more. The boring, whitewashed hallways expanded and emptied out into a courtyard at the center of four buildings. Ducking behind the wall to keep the guards rushing around from spotting me, I saw another sign indicating the prisons across the courtyard from me and waited.

One guard in particular seemed to be directing traffic in the center of the courtyard. Dressed similarly to the others, he wore a red patch on one arm I took to mean he was a commander or someone up the leadership chain. The courtyard was lined by long dead bushes and shriveled trees.

Once the traffic in the courtyard dissipated, he strode away as well, and I inched out from the hall. Herakles had taught me how to hunt without alerting my prey, and I used those principles to move into the courtyard stealthily to the edge of the covered positions behind a post.

I stopped to listen and let my senses read what they could from my surroundings. A good ten meters of open space stretched between me and the building I wanted to be in. Cameras had been placed in the corners of the courtyards, all facing the sky rather than the open area, and no guards. In fact, the courtyard was silent, the calm eye of the compound. I began to think the twenty or thirty guards – some out front and some I had seen in the courtyard – were the only other people present. The large compound was a ghost town.

Despite the fact I saw and heard nothing to alarm me, the hairs on the back of my neck stood up. I didn't move for a long moment, waiting for whatever it was to pass, but the sensation remained. It was more than being watched, more than the surge of adrenaline in my system. If my senses hadn't told me it was clear behind me, I'd almost think someone was there.

Herakles had trained me to trust my intuition over my eyes. I gripped the handgun more tightly and then whirled.

The man with the red patch was behind me, close enough to grab me. He reacted with agility that stunned me, arcing back and knocking my arm away while whipping out his own handgun and pressing the cold metal muzzle to my forehead.

Within the time it took for me to gasp, I had gone from in control to being at his mercy. I went perfectly still. I had never seen anyone move with such speed, even Herakles. His weapon was centered on my forehead. My weapon was trained uselessly beyond his feet.

The mask obscured his face. Unlike the others, the commander didn't wear body armor or carry a rifle, as if it were rare for him to leave the compound or maybe, because he was confident enough not to need such things. He was a good head taller than me, lean and sinewy where Niko and Herakles were thick. He even breathed silently.

"You're fast," I said, unable to help the honest words. "Like really fast."

"So are you."

I tilted my head. His soft, gravelly voice was familiar. I didn't think it possible I had ever heard it before, and I searched my thoughts for why I recognized it.

"Can you use that gun?" he asked.

"It may come as a surprise, but yes," I replied. "Though why it continues to amaze you people that I'm not a defenseless little girl, I don't understand."

"I tend to give my opponents the benefit of the doubt, whether or not they appear to be defenseless little girls." He nudged my head back an inch with the weapon. "You're brave."

"I've been told I'm stupid not brave," I said.

"Entertaining, too."

"Um, thanks." *What in the name of the gods … this guy is messing with me.* "Anyway, I'm just going to leave."

He nudged my head with the gun again as if to remind me of its presence. As if I could ever forget.

"You don't want me dead, or you would've shot me. You

want me scared enough to obey. Which I'm not." I eased back. "I'm leaving. You can shoot me if you want, but either way …" I held out my arms and backed away, not about to lose the gun but sensing this guy wasn't going to be the one who pulled the trigger.

He didn't lower the weapon but stepped with me with grace and silence I envied. Perhaps I should've been more cautious. The man was a predator of a different kind, one without the moodiness of Niko or the friendly warmth of Herakles. Something about the way he spoke to me … the fact I was pretty certain that – however improbable – he had been standing behind me long enough to shoot or subdue me and chose not to … the uncanny sense he wasn't going to call for backup … the suspicion he was as intrigued by me as I was by him …

The masked man was a freaky enigma, one even this brave fool knew was the most dangerous person I'd ever met.

"Are you a gambler to risk your life like this?" He sounded … curious.

"No," I replied. "I'm weird. Everyone says so. But at least I can run fast."

"Faster than me?"

What in Hades? I meant it as somewhat of a nervous joke. I didn't get why he was standing here talking to me, or why I didn't feel the need to run. If anything, something unnatural held me here. It wasn't my will or fear or anything else I controlled. It was … him. Was it a trick? Magic? He moved like no human. Could he be a demigod?

"Maybe." I cleared my throat.

"Down the hallway to your left is a fountain. Make it there and back before I do, and I'll let you walk out of here. Fail and you remain as my master's guest."

"Did you just challenge me to a race?" I asked, startled. *This guy definitely plays with his food before he eats it.* Herakles said this kind of opponent was the worst and to be drawn into their game was the greatest kind of danger in existence.

But … if I really did have a chance to walk out of here by simply outrunning him, I'd be a fool not to play a game I could win.

"Ready."

He put his gun away. At least it was a race. I stood a chance. I kept telling myself this despite the warning from Herakles beating mercilessly against my brain.

"Set."

I put my weapon away, too, tucking it into the waist of my pants at the small of my back.

"Go."

I ran. I beat him to the entrance of the hallway but he soon pulled ahead, making it look easy to outdistance me when I knew how fast I was. Pushing myself harder, I caught up to him before the dry fountain and nudged him aside to take the inside track. I pushed him a little too hard – he caught himself against a wall – and I silently apologized and sprinted ahead.

The man soon caught up to and passed me. I was two steps behind him, my instincts screaming for me to escape before I lost and he devoured me for dinner. The moment we hit the courtyard again, I bolted off towards the wing where I hoped to find Herakles, counting on putting distance between me and the commander before he noticed I wasn't playing his game anymore.

For several steps, I was convinced I'd done it – outsmarted and out distanced him.

And then something smacked into me, driving me to the ground.

I rolled and leapt to my feet, barely putting up my arms in defense of a kick that was aimed at my head. I stumbled back but soon let my instincts take over, the way they did when I sparred with Herakles.

The commander fought with the same agility with which he ran. I struggled to keep up with his pace and when I thought for sure I was about to face plant and end up dead, he eased up.

It hit me then he was testing me. It was a matter of survival to me, but it seemed to be the next level of his game to him. Uncertainty turned to mild panic, and I suddenly had the urge to back down. I wasn't good at games. I didn't like them, and I never, ever won. Something about the mental manipulation component defied my preference for a direct confrontation.

I fought and looked for my out. He could've killed me ten times over by now, but I had one secret weapon. I dropped my defenses completely and snatched the red cord off my wrist. If I couldn't win fairly, I was going to win however I had to.

The cord fell away. The man snatched my wrist and yanked me into his body.

I caught myself against his wide chest and cursed silently.

His arm coiled around me, pinning me in place. He figured out, or maybe just knew, whoever else was in my space wasn't going to be affected by the wave. But it wasn't this that startled me most. It was how I ... *experienced* him. I had hugged Herakles, the priests, the nymphs. But I couldn't recall noticing them – the shape of their muscles, the light scent of their bodies, even their warmth.

Which was silly, because they were no different than this man. Flesh, blood, yadda yadda.

Why did I find it fascinating that I could feel his heartbeat beneath my right hand? Why was I breathing in deeper to try to taste his scent? Why was his smell as familiar as his voice, and I'd never experienced either before?

The shockwave was stronger this time, and I twisted to see behind me at the damage. The earth around us shook while the ground beneath our feet was perfectly still. Alarms erupted once more, along with the sound of glass shattering.

"Dammit!" I murmured breathlessly and pulled at his grip. I was losing my chance to act.

He didn't release me but bent and grabbed the cord to replace around my wrist. The moment it was secure, the world around us ceased trembling. "It's foolish to unleash power you cannot control," he told me. He gripped my neck with one hand and stripped my weapons from my body, tossing them away. He whipped off his mask next and tapped the microphone on his shoulder, speaking one word into it. "Courtyard." His gaze fell to mine.

The man who could outrun, outsmart and outfight me was

a kind of beautiful I didn't know existed. Green-blue eyes surrounded by long, feathery lashes beneath thick eyebrows were so bright, they almost glowed in an olive-toned face. His features were too perfectly chiseled to be natural. A shock of black hair clashed with his bright eyes. He was clean shaven, hard of expression and too strong and nimble to be real.

I knew him. Or at least, like his voice, I *felt* like I did. It was the same weird instinct I had felt when I touched the gem Father Ellis gave me. Like this man belonged to me.

Which was the craziest thing yet in my adventures since setting foot outside the boundaries of the forest.

"Quick, Lyssa." Niko's voice broke the spell. "Get out of here."

I twisted to see him emerge from the depths of one hallway, armed with two weapons trained on the beautiful stranger. "Did you find him?" I asked eagerly.

"Not this time. We need a better plan. Exit that way." He motioned with his weapon to a hall I hadn't been down.

"Ni–"

"Now!"

If I weren't rattled by the man I'd just met, I would've probably argued more. As it was, I wasn't feeling quite right about all that happened. I'd met someone I couldn't physically beat, and I wasn't about to stick around to find out what happened next. I pulled away from the stranger and went in the direction Niko indicated.

But something stopped me before the first intersection. I was so close to Herakles, I didn't want to leave, especially since

I didn't think I'd be able to use the same trick twice to get in here. After running into *him,* I didn't want to risk a second meeting either.

I halted then turned, creeping back down the hallway towards the courtyard at the center of the buildings. Niko had sent me into the north building but I was determined to go to the east.

Niko and the man were talking. Niko's guns were down, and their distance bespoke the comfortable distance between acquaintances rather than enemies. I edged closer and strained my senses to hear what they said.

"... as agreed," the commander was saying.

"Yeah, well, it cost more than I expected to get her here. The finder's fee doesn't cover my expenses."

Finder's fee. Coldness trickled through me, and I thought about what Dosy had insisted to be true about Niko.

"You'll be compensated for expenses," the man replied. "And docked ten percent for not contacting me before bringing her here. We had a plan, Niko, and you bulldozed it as usual."

"Come on," Niko complained.

"I also won't tell your boss you brought her to me instead of him."

"Total dick move."

"Take it or leave it."

Niko started to bristle. Just then, three guards filed out of one of the hallways into the courtyard. Not that the man he faced needed help. Niko didn't know how dangerous he was.

I didn't know how dangerous Niko was. Betrayal hurt more

than leaving my home. It made me more desperate to find the only person I'd ever trusted, the man who could right the world tumbling rapidly out of control.

"I'll take it," Niko said reluctantly, eyes on the newcomers.

You bastard. He had tried to warn me against men like him, and I assumed he was talking about everyone else. I didn't think he'd be the one to turn on me. If not for Dosy's insistence about what he'd done, I'd suspect him of murder rather than mercy-killing the priests.

The commander motioned someone forward. "Take him to John and escort him out," he instructed.

"What happens to her?" Niko asked.

"Not your concern anymore, now is it?" came the cool response. "Oh, and Niko?"

"What, Adonis."

"I know you aren't here as a merc. Whatever your boss is planning, assume I'm going to bill him."

Who was Niko's boss? How were Adonis and Niko connected? The questions were tumbling around my brain, and the only answer I cared about was how I was going to find Herakles and escape.

After several lewd curses, Niko lingered for a fraction of a second then left.

A heavy feeling sank into my stomach. This had been his plan all along. Dosy was right, and I'd been too worried about Herakles to care what Niko's motivations were for helping me. I was a fool of the worst kind, one Herakles would be disappointed in for letting my emotions lead me into danger instead of rationally thinking my suicide operation through.

"Instructions, sir," one of the guards approached the man in the center.

"Secure the exits. I'll take it from here." The commander's gaze went towards me.

I eased back, hoping he hadn't realized I was there. I was alone and no closer to finding Herakles. Slinking back down the hallway, I was careful to tune in at every intersection, both to my senses and to the intuition that might be the only sign the commander had found me. I had never felt anything but confident in myself, yet here, I was a trapped rat in a blind maze. I felt like I did the night I spotted the grotesque; I was waiting for something to swoop out of nowhere and grab me.

The buildings were, for the most part, abandoned. Every once in a while, I thought I sensed something and eased away from the direction I had been headed. I went deeper into the compound, farther from the east wing, and into the center of a building that seemed to consist of old barracks. I peeked into several and identified only about four rooms among the several dozen that appeared to be in use.

It was as I entered the only decorated area in the center of the compound it hit me I'd been herded in this direction discreetly by my opponent. The apartment was the sole part of the compound that appeared to have been used continually. It wasn't possible for me to end up here if I hadn't been manipulated. The airy flat featured high ceilings, its own bubbling fountain, and marble features everywhere. It had to be *his*, because it smelled like him, a faint scent I barely registered when I had met him but which was stronger here. I wasn't able to place it except that it was his.

One wall was jammed with awards, citations, degrees, certifications and other proof of recognition. The largest: the plaque naming him the chief of SISA.

My heart took off again when I realized who I'd been unknowingly messing with. "Only the Big Bad Wolf," I muttered to myself. I mentally kicked my own ass at the thought of teasing the man charged with oppressing opposition and policing everyday people. Adonis Wade wasn't a cop or a security guard but the man charged by the gods with the security of the entire human race.

And he knew who I was because I'd been stupid enough to challenge him. Niko had allegedly mercy-killed four priests to keep this man from torturing them to discover me, and I walked through the front door and challenged him to a duel.

I had never felt real fear until I stood before his wall of accolades and began to understand why Niko and Dosy said rescuing Herakles was tantamount to suicide. I was dying to ask Niko if he'd made a deal to bring me in before he met the priests or if he was looking out for his own interests after I told him what I was.

I'm an idiot. Dosy was right. I never should've said anything about being an Oracle, never should've trusted a situation that appeared too perfect to be true. It wasn't a coincidence Niko helped me break into SISA. It was part of a plan by strangers who knew what and who I was.

"Now that you understand …"

I whirled. Adonis Wade didn't look old enough to be the boogeyman his brag-wall claimed he was. He wasn't much older than twenty five. He was dressed in the dark uniform, hands at his sides and mesmerizing gaze on me.

"Understand what?" I managed.

"Who you're dealing with," he replied.

"As long as you know who you're dealing with." I lifted my wrist to display the red cord. It was self preservation that made me need to put something between us. The intensity of his presence and look was too much for me to handle without help. I slid behind a table with an expensive vase on it.

"Better than you do." His gaze went from me to his wall and back to me. "Stay here for now."

"Um, no. The minute you leave, I'm gone."

"The fate of Herakles is in your hands."

Just like that, my anger and defiance melted.

"I repeat. Stay here for now." He strode towards the door.

"You're not going to tie me up or anything?" I asked. Too late I heard the words. As if he needed me telling him to tie me up.

"I don't need to. If you care about Herakles, you'll do as I say. If you want to know who your parents were, who *you* are, you'll worry about not pissing me off."

His words slammed into me. The one man in the world I shouldn't want anything to do with was dangling everything I wanted in front of me. "My parents." I didn't think of them often, probably because I didn't remember them. I wasn't a complete idiot. I knew they had existed at one point. "You're serious."

"What do you recall of your life before Herakles?"

"Nothing."

"At all?"

"Sometimes I dream of falling." I shrugged. "That's all."

"I'm about to know everything, Alessandra. If you leave, you'll never learn any of it."

He walked out.

I stared at the closed door, not at all certain what just happened. I was trapped in the apartment of the chief of the SISA. *I think I'm in trouble,* I thought, gazing around warily.

But I wasn't about to leave. Not when the answers I needed were right in front of me.

EIGHT

I WAS FALLING AGAIN. IT WAS NIGHTTIME AND THE SKY above overcast. Down, down, down … and Herakles was there to catch me, like always. My hero, my friend, my Herakles.

I missed him even in my sleep. As I awoke, I silently swore it was my turn to rescue him.

"Alessandra."

My eyes snapped open. Three people hovered too close to me. I sat up quickly from my spot sleeping on the couch and stared first at the man with the face that made my heart race unnaturally and then at the doctor and John. It took me a moment to orient to this place and recall I had fallen asleep on the couch of the man who was probably supposed to be a super villain to my super-Oracle self.

Herakles would not approve.

"We have your DNA results," the doctor said and held up a file folder. "The reports are going to the Triumvirate. They'll decide whether or not to release them to you. I imagine the press will figure out your identity before we can alert the gods."

"What made you voluntarily – and quite publicly – walk into this place?" John – Spectacles – asked. "Controlling the media's response has become a nightmare."

Everyone was searching for me, but no one actually wanted to find me? I couldn't catch a break. It was too early for nonsense and questions. I needed coffee and a toothbrush.

Swinging my legs over the side of the couch, I was at a loss as to how to respond. For having found the Oracle they sought, none of them appeared remotely pleased.

"I have no idea what's going on," I said finally and stood. "I know you're god around here, Adonis, but do you have a spare toothbrush?"

Silence.

"I can use yours. People act like I have rabies, so I figured you wouldn't want that."

"Second drawer in the bathroom," he replied at last.

"Thank you." I walked towards the bathroom, unusually aware that he was watching me. It was weird how my instincts picked up on him and only him like that.

After I had freshened up, I returned to the living area to find all of them gone. Truth be told, I was kind of relieved. Adonis made me nervous. I wanted to think it was because he was a badass in his own right but ...

I recalled that tiny moment of something in his arms yesterday. My fingers remembered what it was like to touch his chest, and his scent drifted in the air around me. It was more than a memory, though. I *felt* him. As if we were connected somehow and I was being drawn towards him when every part of me knew that was completely wrong. It was stronger today. Twisting around, I sought some sign of him being present and spotted him on a balcony overlooking a courtyard that hadn't been tended in years.

What made him *live* on an abandoned compound?

I wanted to know what was going on, if Herakles was safe, yet feared dealing I with *him,* the man four people I knew had committed suicide to avoid.

There's something here. Something unnatural I didn't yet understand. I wasn't afraid. I had a list of reasons I should have been, but I wasn't. Neither was I comfortable around him.

The fact he could outrun and outfox me left me unsettled. Herakles had taught me to take care of myself but never bothered to mention what happened when someone bested me and I was subjected to being trapped by mind games. We never talked much about emotion or mental strife, and he scoffed at the priests' attempt to teach me diplomacy. I rarely found fault in my guardian, but I was starting to suspect I'd missed a few things.

Like how to deal with a man resembling Adonis Wade. He was too young to be in such a powerful position and not to be a super genius, ambitious, and strong enough for anything I could throw at him. I had to figure this situation out – *him* out – get my answers and help Herakles escape.

As if feeling my gaze, he spoke. "You haven't asked about him," the head of SISA said without turning. One hand rested against his temple as if he had a headache.

It bothered me that he could sense me better than I did him. I was really hoping he wasn't able to read minds, too. "How is he?"

"In one piece for now."

I shifted feet, not liking the response at all. "Can I see him?"

"No."

"Why should I just take your word?"

"What choice do you have?"

"Yesterday, I might have been compelled to agree," I replied. "Then Niko sold me out and you decided to threaten Herakles with bodily harm if I didn't cooperate ... you can see why I'm not really interested in trusting anyone right now."

"Nonetheless you have no choice but to behave in the hopes I don't do to Herakles what I'm known to do to people like him."

It was probably the scariest thing I'd ever heard. The priests always told us straight out what the consequences were for acting out or disobeying, and rarely was their discipline discouraging to me.

I knew only tiny hints about what this man was capable of and that four priests had committed suicide via Niko so they didn't have to fall into his hands. Add to that a High Priestess that feared SISA and even Niko – a mercenary who stood to make money off me – who was at first unwilling to deal with this man, and my imagination knew no bounds as to what someone had to be capable of to scare so many people.

"You were testing me yesterday," I said quietly. "Why?"

"Curiosity."

"Hmmm. That's it?"

"What else is there?" He faced me, his intent gaze rattling me.

My cheeks grew warm for reasons I wasn't able to figure out, and I crossed my arms, feeling exposed. "I don't know. It seems beneath you." At his silence, I continued. "You have a billion awards and citations and run this mega huge security force that terrorizes the entire world. How does one person rate your curiosity?"

"How does the Oracle not know who she is?" he countered.

"I know exactly who I am. It's everyone else who seems surprised I'm not someone else," I said, perplexed. "I can defend myself, survive under any conditions for any length of time, and am generally what I consider to be a good person. Who cares if my Greek is basic, I hate chic flicks and have never kissed a guy?" Too late I heard the part about kissing and flushed. Not that I cared what he thought, but … was this all going in some sort of official record? Was I going to go down in history as the Oracle who never kissed a boy? Because I couldn't think of anything more embarrassing.

"You don't know everything, or you wouldn't have stayed here voluntarily."

"You call me being here voluntary?"

"You want to know what you really are," Adonis stated. "You want to know where you came from. You want to know why. You may think you know what you're capable of, but you don't have any idea and that's why you stayed."

I drew a deep breath. He was like Leandra – the wrong person delivering the right message. And I hated that. "Okay, yes. I want to know those things. But I stayed for Herakles. I will always stay for him."

"At the risk of everything you are and could be?"

"I really don't care what *you* think I am or could be, and I definitely don't have a problem with who I think I am. I care about him."

Adonis was hard to read. He didn't seem to know exactly how to take my honesty. Or perhaps he was offended by it. I wasn't able to tell except I had the impression he was constantly evaluating me. I had no answers for him. He already knew more about me than I did.

"Can you tell me who my parents are?" I asked.

"Not unless the Triumvirate approves the disclosure of such information."

"How can their names be of any importance whatsoever?"

His silence was stifling. This line of discussion appeared to be closed, to the dissatisfaction of both of us, if I read his tight features correctly. "Why do I get the impression no one wanted to find me?" I asked.

"Politics."

"I don't understand."

"I know." He clearly wasn't willing to enlighten me. "The Supreme Priest will see you soon and the Supreme Magistrate when he's done. I would recommend you be on your best behavior."

Like I'm not now? "And if I'm not?" I asked, a little irked by anyone telling me how to act.

"You probably won't like the consequences." His words were too casual.

His vague threats were a million times worse than anything Herakles or the priests had ever threatened me with.

For the first time in my life, I had the feeling I was so far out of my league, there was no bridging this gap. "You are really good at this game," I whispered.

"Game?"

"Passive intimidation."

"I've never heard it called that." The smile was cool and fleeting. He left the balcony and approached me.

My senses, and a few random emotions, were thrown into a frenzy that caught me completely off guard. I was finding it hard to focus on the fact I never wanted this man within striking distance. Instead, I was lost in a state of confusion until he was almost toe-to-toe with me and then, not about to back away because …

Well, I never backed away from a challenge. And that's what this was. A predator sizing up how hard his prey was going to fight back. I'd fight to the death, and I wasn't afraid for him to know it. I met his dazzling gaze.

"People are cautious when dealing with me," he said. "They hide their true intentions, lie when they feel threatened and stick to the peripheral because they sense the danger inherent in drawing my complete attention. You tend to walk in blindly swinging a bat. You know no fear, and you're honest beyond a fault."

Heat spread up my neck and face. I sounded like an idiot. I didn't want to care what he thought, but some part of me was acutely aware of the fact I was always too different.

"Intimidation is an art form with one key component: uncertainty. How will you react when you don't know what I'm capable of?" he continued quietly. "My *game* is people, and you're not playing it like others do, hence my –"

"– curiosity." The word was almost choked out.

"Yes."

I couldn't handle his intensity or my growing unease. I shifted away, wanting to put something between us, even if it had no chance of standing up to him if he chose to attack. "Just putting this out there." I was starting to babble, too, unable to control it. "You are scaring me. Kudos to you for that. I'm probably going to have to try to escape so whatever punishment you're planning ... *this* is already pretty freaky. I'd probably rather choose physical torture then this mind twisting stuff. If you take suggestions."

"Not usually." Was he amused?

I had no idea. I'd never met someone I had less of a read on, and more of a sense about, than him. In fact, that's what was bothering me foremost: the draw. The uncanny familiarity of a man I had never met, the need to know more about him despite suspecting he was constantly on the verge of killing me. "Who are you? Do you have some sort of magical power?" I asked. "Or have we met before?"

"It's a game. Nothing more."

Of all he had told me, this was the only thing that sounded false. It was intuition again, whispering secrets I couldn't quite make out. "That's not true," I said aloud. "This ... *I* am not just a game to you. You do know me. I mean something to you."

"A promotion."

"No."

"Stop there."

The low threat was almost a growl, and he was tensing. My breath caught. I didn't dare look away from him, not about to be caught with my guard down if he came at me.

"There are limits you are not ready to push," he added.

He knows me. Not the Oracle or someone he had a dossier on. *Me.* But how? My mind raced with possibilities, none of which were remotely feasible. I kept coming back to the suspicion he had some sort of divine power that gave him insight or maybe even foresight. With the senses and reactions of an animal, he had to be more than human. According to the priests, the discreet offspring of gods and human women existed in several high up positions in the governments. Viewed as competition by gods, and distrusted by humans, demigods were said never to announce what they were.

Or ... did he feel what I did? The draw?

So engaged was I in figuring him out, I barely noticed he had left until I heard the door close.

Adonis Wade freaked me out. I wasn't about to stay here.

I counted to twenty then went to the door. To my surprise, it wasn't locked and no guard was posted outside the door.

Closing the door, I gazed at it for a long moment. This was

a dare. That much I figured out. I had no clue what this guy's end game was – but I doubted I wanted to be involved.

How did I find and rescue Herakles?

I debated for a moment before an idea dawned on me. Spinning around, I went to the bedroom of Adonis and searched it for a guard uniform.

NINE

TWO HOURS LATER, I MANAGED TO SCOUT AN EXIT route and made it to the prison in the east wing. It went quickly, since no one was present to challenge me in two of the four buildings on the compound.

Similar to Adonis' apartment, the prison area showed signs of regular and continued use. Having never been in a prison before, I still thought the cells were too small. Maybe six by six, which meant my poor Herakles couldn't stretch out on his bed. It took some self control not to plant in the middle of the corridor and yell for him. I had to pretend like I belonged, which mainly meant not drawing too much attention to myself. Adonis had an iPad in his apartment, and I pretended to walk and check it, like I was doing something.

Entering the prison cells, though, required me to cajole the reluctant guard and convince him I'd lost my pass card. He let me in – probably because no one in their right mind would want to break *into* a prison – and I pretended to check my iPad screen and peer into the one-foot square window of each cell.

They were all empty but well maintained. Unable to understand the purpose behind the compound, it was beginning to weird me out.

When I found him, I nearly squealed. Herakles was alive, lying on his side on his bed and staring at the wall. One arm was in a cast and he had a black eye. I didn't see any other wound or bruises, though he appeared paler than usual. Resisting the urge to tap on the window, I used the loaner pass card the guard had given me and swiped the door open.

Herakles twisted towards me.

I strode in. I didn't dare take off the mask, not with the camera in the corner. It appeared to be the only live one on the compound. "Hey," I said. "Pretend like it's not me."

He sat up. "What are you doing here, Lyssa?" he hissed, his face draining of all blood then flaring red. "You cannot be here! Everyone –"

"Yeah, yeah, I know. I'm the Oracle."

Speechless, he stared at me.

"Aaaaahhh. You didn't think anyone would tell me, did you?" I said, unable to prevent the note of pure glee that entered my voice. "Well they did. The SISA razed the forest and the priests committed pre-emptive suicide. I came here with a mercenary, ran into a High Priestess then got captured by a guy named Adonis who turned out to be the head of this horrible place. Now I'm here to rescue you."

He listened, unable to help the upturn of his lips at my

story. "If you were any other person, this might surprise me." He rose. "What's your plan?"

I glanced at the camera. "We need to get rid of that first."

Stretching upwards, he knocked it to the side. "Done."

I didn't hesitate. I tossed the iPad on his bed and shimmied out of the outer layer of clothing. I had overlapped two pairs of the guard clothing and gave him one and the oversized boots I'd stolen from Adonis.

"To leave, go out the way you came in and follow the signs to the D Street exit," I instructed him.

"You can show me."

"Um, no." I straightened and turned my back to him while he changed. "I gave it some thought. I think you should leave without me."

"Absolutely not."

"Okay … he's tracking me, Herakles. Don't ask me how, but he's keeping an eye on me. I need you to leave, so he can't threaten me anymore."

"Who?"

"The head of SISA."

"Terrible plan, Lyssa."

"Or is it secretly brilliant and you don't want to admit it?"

"Not at all."

I sighed. "Look, Herakles. They're onto me and for whatever reason, this Adonis guy is serious about messing with me. But he also knows things I need to know. About my parents. My life before we met. About *me*," I explained.

Herakles gazed at me.

"I want to stay long enough to find out some things. That's it. If you leave, you can find help and break me out."

"You make it sound simple," he said with a concerned frown. "Do you know what he is?"

"Sort of," I said. Truthfully, I didn't. I knew he was more than I could see, that he was connected to me.

"Did he hurt you?"

"No. He's trying to play mind games with me."

"You suck at games."

"Yeah, I know. But he wants me alive and has information I want, too." I wasn't about to tell him I was afraid of Adonis.

"I won't leave you here, Lyssa."

"Herakles ..." I sought some kind of argument(argument does not make sense here, possibly agreement?). "Please. I'm not a little girl anymore. You prepared me for this my whole life. Give me two days here then knock the front gate down and rescue me."

He was considering me. I didn't know why my overprotective guardian hadn't already dragged me out of here, unless ... would he betray me, too? He knew I was the Oracle. Were the priests and he working together on whatever was going on? I crushed the thoughts. My Herakles would never disappoint me.

If he was listening, it was because I had to be making sense or he thought me old enough to make my own decisions.

Or ... something else was going on here. I was skating on the semi-frozen surface of a lake waiting for it to crack and me to plunge into the dark, cold waters below. No matter why my stomach was churning, no matter what reason he might have for leaving me here, I had to know he was safe before I'd feel comfortable skating onward.

"Really. There's no way for both of us to leave here. He can sense me somehow. I'll endanger you. Our best shot is for you to escape and bring back an army of … someone. Just avoid the mercs, cuz they'll stab you in the back. Adonis has said he won't hurt me, at least not before I meet the Supreme Magistrate in a few days." *Yeah, I totally just lied to my only friend.*

A brief silence fell, and then Herakles chuckled. "My Lyssa. All grown up after two days on her own." The terse note in his voice was one I hadn't heard before.

"It's been a learning experience," I said, quoting him. "Will you go? Please? I don't think I'm in any danger right now. If anything, I think Adonis wants to see what makes me tick."

"I can see that about him. But the members of the Triumvirate will destroy you. I imagine they will wait for the full moon, when the barrier between our worlds and that of the gods is thinnest. That gives me a week, but I wouldn't take that long. They won't harm you before submitting you to the trials, either."

Trials. More evidence he knew so much more than he had ever shared. It wasn't the right time to ask him to share. I wasn't remotely scared about some stupid trial. I just couldn't live with myself if Herakles was hurt or worse because of me.

"Exactly. It's a plan. Leave, go get help and rescue me. Then things will go back to the way they were, and we'll be happy in the forest again."

"Lyssa," he said gravely and turned me to face him. "Things will never be the way they were."

"Yes, they will. They have to be. You can make them be," I said, a tremor of emotion in my voice. I didn't want to admit this was my life. Gazing into his dark eyes, I was forced to face some of the emotion I'd been avoiding. "I love you," I said, my throat tight. "I want us to be happy again."

He hugged me to him hard. "Then I will do as you ask, Lyssa."

"Thank you." My eyes were brimming with tears. We both knew my hope wasn't founded in reality, but I wasn't yet able to admit how far gone my comfortable world was. I needed him to buy into my dream, however crazy it was. "Now go, before someone figures out what happened." I pulled away.

"I will make it out of here," he assured me. "And I know who to ask for help. I just have to find them."

"Sounds good." I gave him the pass card and boots then sat on the prison bed. With a long, final look at one another, Herakles pulled on his mask and left. I closed the prison door behind him and sat down on the bed, suspecting Adonis was going to figure out what I had done soon enough.

As I waited, I struggled not to doubt my guardian. He had given me no real reason to. *Except lying to me my whole life.* It was too quiet in the tiny cell, too small for me to exercise or work off some of my apprehension and worry.

The guards came to the door and opened it an hour later.

Ugh. I was hoping not to deal with Adonis directly. He stepped into the room. I lifted my head from the wall behind me and waited to hear what he had to say. A man this striking should speak in rainbows and puppies, not be in charge of the organization that suppressed humanity and tortured people.

"You had the chance to leave," he noted and studied me. "Why didn't you take it?"

"You have information I want, Adonis." The subtle draw was back like an itch I couldn't reach. It left me warm and agitated. "You can leave me here, by the way. I'm happy in a cell."

"Far be it from me to make you unhappy, but since I'm the only one you can't outsmart or outrun, you'll stay with me," he replied with cool sarcasm.

The reminder of how unnatural his skills were didn't help my irritation. He motioned me out of the cell. I went, mostly because I was afraid to push him when I was trapped in a room that small. The nearness of Adonis made my instincts so sensitive, everything agitated me. A guard escorted us out of the prison building.

I couldn't take the thick silence between us or the fear I was in the kind of trouble I didn't know how to get out of. I kept telling myself that Herakles was free and would come for me. I just had to survive on my own here a day or two, and I could do that.

But *this* … I stared at the back of his head, not understanding how I was dutifully following him down the corridor like a puppy when I knew I should at least *try* to run.

Because he knows me. I wanted to learn more about being an Oracle and my past, and this man claimed to have that knowledge, if I could survive him long enough to learn.

"On a scale of one to ten, one being stuck on the couch again tonight and ten being flayed alive, where am I in terms of trouble?" I asked finally.

"Three."

I invented the scale and had no idea what that meant. What alarmed me: his response wasn't *one*. "So you are upset about Herakles leaving?"

"Not at all. He served his purpose. I didn't impede his escape."

Holy Zeus. Adonis knew all along. He was toying with me, once more the predator.

"Then why a three?" I demanded.

"You moved slower than I expected. I'm a little disappointed."

I almost choked to keep from speaking. *Stop falling for it, Lyssa! He's playing games with you!* It was unnerving. I had to stop folding to my discomfort and just shut up, as Niko had ordered me.

So I did. I said nothing all the way back to his apartment.

He left me there. Alone. No guard. No handcuffs.

This was the part of his game where I cringed – and admitted he was right. I was blindly volunteering to stay in the hopes he at least enlightened me about who I was before he did whatever they did to Oracles.

I had the distinct feeling I'd one day look back on this moment and wish with all my heart that I'd run.

But for now, I was staying put.

going on. This was a Triumvirate turf war – over me.

Adonis was the first to act. He launched at Niko and smashed him into the men with him before he kicked Dosy back. Settling into a fighting stance, he waited.

"I'm not picking a fight with you, Adonis," Dosy said.

"You entered a SISA property without permission. I call that picking a fight," Adonis replied.

"Agreed. Whereas I was invited," Niko said.

"You were not invited," Adonis replied in the same tone. "I've already alerted the Supreme Priest who will ensure the Silent Queen and Magistrate are aware."

"This was authorized," Niko replied. His preference for the military over SISA began to make sense. Niko was one of them.

"Same," Dosy said and stretched for the knives at her back. "By all rights, protocol, custom and tradition, she was supposed to come to us first. I was authorized to use lethal force. How about you boys?"

Niko glared at her.

"Thought so. May Ares bless your weapons like Artemis has mine." Dosy drew her weapons and lowered into a fighting stance. "The usual rules. No firearms. Let's get this over with."

Mesmerized by the three of them, I could deduce several pieces of information. The first: they all knew each other well enough to tell me this type of *politics* happened often. Second: if they were messing with each other, their leaders weren't all on the same page like the news claimed they were. Third … Dosy could fight.

And that made me extremely happy after being told by the

nymphs and priests at school fighting wasn't a proper womanly pursuit.

The three all drew weapons and began circling one another. Their companions stood back. I assessed my situation. The fastest – and safest – exit strategy was probably going to be the balcony and the ropes Niko's men had used to drop onto the balcony. I couldn't see whether the rest of Adonis' forces were outside the closed entrance door of the apartment. Three of Niko's men were between me and the balcony. With their attention on their fighting leaders, I just had to time this right.

Sparks flew off the weapons smashing into each other. Dosy had started – and Niko joined in. The three began a deadly dance as skillful as it was scary. Adonis was unmatched as far as speed, but Niko and Dosy managed to team up on him between taking swipes at each other. The two of them were amazing, and the dynamic of all three of them locked into a battle to the death held me in place.

Until I realized the others were equally entranced, and no one seemed to think I was capable of anything like I planned. For once, I wasn't upset about being underestimated. I inched closer to the men in my direct path, eyes on the three warriors holding nothing back. I was secretly rooting for Dosy, hoping Adonis didn't get killed and not at all concerned about Niko.

Their fight moved away from the balcony, pulling one of the military members with him. With two between me and escape, I didn't wait.

Snagging a knife from the nearest, I smashed him over the back of the head with both hands then sprang forward to knock the other off balance as he turned to see what the noise was. Herakles had taught me to disable rather than use lethal force, though I knew how to kill as well.

But I didn't. I smashed an elbow into the second man's nose then punched him in the throat. He bent over, gagging. I slid the hilt of the knife between my teeth and darted to the nearest rope. The courtyard below held five of Adonis' men.

"Up it is," I murmured. With a quick tug, I confirmed it'd hold and began to half pull, half walk my way up the side of the wall. I was close to the roof when I heard someone shout to alert the three fighting.

The sound of them pounding into one another ceased. I focused hard on moving as quickly as possible, not caring about my burning arms and thighs as I neared my destination.

"Kid!" Niko shouted and grabbed the rope I was on, wrenching it back from the wall. Dosy was scaling her way up a second rope. Adonis had disappeared.

I'm not a kid! Clamping down on the knife so hard it hurt my jaw, I hauled myself the rest of the way up with upper body strength and reached the top. I dragged myself over the top and dropped, panting from the effort. Not about to give someone like Adonis the time to take the stairs to the roof, I decoupled five of the ropes rapidly before starting to cut Dosy's free.

"Go back, Dosy!" I called, sawing through it.

"Not on your life!"

She was as stubborn as Niko. I didn't bother to check and see if she was okay after the rope snapped free but stood back and looked around wildly. Niko's men had gotten up here somehow; I could escape the same way.

My gaze settled on the grappling equipment on the far side of the roof. I dashed towards it and caught myself on the wall, leaning over to see the rope dangling into another of the plentiful courtyards. This one butted up against the wall of the compound. With any luck, I could scale that wall too or find my way back to the exit I'd found earlier for Herakles.

People were shouting from somewhere in the buildings. I wasn't sticking around to find out which of the security forces was going to win and grab me. I slung one leg over the edge of the roof and gripped the rope.

A throwing knife grazed my calf, and I glanced down. It pinned my pant's leg to the wall behind me. There was only one man I'd bet money on to make that shot, and I wasn't about to let him near me. I bent over to pull at the knife only to find it was too sleek to grip. Dropping the cable rope, I strained to wriggle the knife free frantically.

"Stop now, Alessandra!" Adonis warned.

"Gods dammit!" I straightened and wrenched back.

The knife didn't give on the first try, so I yanked again.

This time, it did, and I toppled backward, clutching at the rope. A rush of adrenaline flooded me as I began to fall. A sense of déjà vu swept over me, and I was once more in my dream, falling … falling … waiting for Herakles to catch me.

Adonis snatched my wrist, and I looked up, startled. I shook off the weird sense.

"I won't let you fall," he said.

I laughed. "It's okay. It's not far and I'd rather have a broke leg than …" I yanked at his grip. The rope was right beside me anyway; I wasn't going to fall more than a couple of feet.

"You're a fool!" he breathed.

"Yeah. Now let go!" I tried to pry his hand off my wrist with my other hand. When that failed to work, I reached for the red cord around my wrist.

"Stop!" Adonis snatched my other wrist. I heard the sounds of more than one person running towards us. From the look he cast over his shoulder, they weren't his men.

He kept his grip on the wrist with the red cord and released my second hand. I expected him to draw a weapon but he snatched the rope. Seconds later, he leapt over the edge of the roof.

The man had a serious set of feline reflexes. I could barely register what was happening, while he was reacting. He grabbed me around the waist and slid us both down the rope until my feet hit the ground. It happened too fast for me to react, and the moment we were safe, the arm around my waist was around my neck.

"If you kill her, Adonis …" Niko yelled from the roof.

I was able to see the shadows of him and Dosy on the ground, along with several other forms of their guards.

"Game over. Leave, both of you!" Adonis returned.

"Don't give up now!" I called.

"The Triumvirate wants you alive. They don't care if you're missing limbs. Do *not* tempt me." These words were for me, spoken close enough to my ear for his warm breath to brush my skin. I shivered. His grip was tight but not yet severing my air supply. Herakles would say he was going for control rather than the kill. I was hauled against his hard body, once again aware of his scent and the strange sense of familiarity I hadn't yet shaken.

This wasn't the calm Adonis that challenged me to a race. This was the Adonis who was about to use one of the weapons he carried, and I didn't think even he knew who he was going to use it on.

I stretched for my knife, not about to ruin the only good escape opportunity I had.

Dosy was descending the wall rapidly. Niko was gone, and I assumed he was taking the stairs.

Adonis hauled me to face Dosy, one of his weapons out. I waited until she was close enough to engage him then smashed my heel into one of his feet, stabbed him in the arm with my knife, and wrenched away.

Adonis released me. I stumbled away, caught myself, and bolted. He showed no sign of pain but deflected Dosy's strikes and then pushed her aside.

"If you run, you'll never know who you are!" he called after me.

I stopped at the mouth of a passageway. The words were kryptonite. I wanted away, yes, but I wanted to know who I was, too, why I was important.

"Run!" Dosy cried. "You don't know what they'll do to you."

"I can return your memories to you," Adonis added.

I turned to face him. "No one can do that."

"It's one of the benefits of working for a demigod

representing the gods on Earth. A direct line to Mnemosyne."

I glanced at Dosy, who hadn't yet lied to me that I knew. "Is that true?"

"Probably, but it's irrelevant. Assuming you survive the trials, the Supreme Priest and Supreme Magistrate will enslave you with your magic."

It sounded a lot like what the priests had told me.

"I'll spare the girls and priests we found in the town nearest your compound," Adonis added and took two steps towards me.

My breath caught. The other priests had died because of me. I couldn't let that happen to those remaining or to the nymphs, however many hadn't escaped. They were in SISA control because of me.

"Okay." I dropped my knife and raised my hands.

"Alessandra," Dosy objected.

"I'm with SISA. For now," I replied.

Adonis strode towards me, none too pleased, and kicked the knife away. He pulled my arms down and cuffed me.

"Leave, Theodocia," he said to the High Priestess. "Take Niko with you, or I'll toss him in prison."

"You can have him." Dosy was frowning. "What're you planning on doing with her?"

I looked at Adonis at the question.

"Submit her to the first trial," he replied.

"Before the other members of the Triumvirate interview her?"

"I have my orders."

"And you always follow your orders." The look they shared

told me they knew a lot more about each other than I did about anyone I'd met. "I don't have to tell you or the Supreme Priest this is highly unusual. She deserves some prep time or something."

Adonis dropped my hands. "If she's the Oracle, she'll survive. If not, she won't."

My interest increased. "Why? Is it dangerous?" I asked, excited at the chance to put the skills I spent a lifetime learning to use. "Like really dangerous?"

Dosy appeared ready to chastise me the way she did Niko. Adonis' expression was that of scrutiny, as if he was trying to figure out if I was messing with him.

"Shut up, kid," Niko growled, emerging from a nearby hallway. "Even you aren't stupid enough to want to go through the trials without preparing for them." He sheathed his weapons. "My employer called me off with a promise he's got some words for your boss about how she's being handled, Adonis. You win this round." Niko stalked towards the front of the compound, trailed by his entourage.

"Next time," Dosy promised the quiet head of SISA. "Find your way to the Silent Queen and me, Alessandra. We won't imprison you."

"Sounds good," I replied. I watched her leave as well before Adonis stepped away. "Do you really have my friends?"

"I do."

"Niko killed three of them."

"They're better off."

I didn't like that at all. "But you'll spare the others now?"

"Will you go through the trials without me forcing you into them?"

"Yeah, sure. Can't be that bad."

He shook his head. "You're something else. If you're not the Oracle, you're the bravest fool I've ever met."

From him, I was certain it was a compliment of sorts.

"Submit to the first trial, and they'll be freed," he added. "Try to escape again, and I'll kill them off in front of you, one by one."

"No need for threats." I raised my hands and took a step towards the center of the compound. "I'm cool with this. What are these trials?"

He gave me an indecipherable stare.

"Assume I know absolutely nothing about what's going on," I said impatiently. "I'm not fighting you. I'm just asking a legitimate question."

He studied me. "Usually, three gods sponsor the incoming Oracle and design trials to challenge her, test her magic, mental toughness and willingness to obey them," he explained. "The gods were too preoccupied to nominate sponsors for you, so each member of the Triumvirate is giving you a trial instead. You'll receive three tasks you must complete."

"Hmmm. What happens if I don't?"

"You'll never have full access to your power."

I can do more than create earthquakes? "It can't be that bad."

Adonis lifted his chin towards the hallway behind me in a silent command.

I retreated to the passageway leading into the compound then stopped.

No voices came from the area, but my intuition was doing it again. Tingling.

I returned to the corner looking into the courtyard. Adonis was alone. He was on his knees, holding his head, face scrunched up in pain. I watched him, not expecting the man with the strength and agility of a great cat to be vulnerable or hurt. He didn't look as if anyone had touched him from the fight with Dosy and Niko. I'd nicked his arm, but he didn't seem affected by the wound. His hands lowered to his sides, and he shook his head and rose.

I eased back and hurried away on tiptoes through the compound to the apartment without crossing any of his men. It would be so easy to flee ...

But I wasn't going to risk the lives of anyone else I'd grown up with.

I returned to his apartment and nudged the door closed behind me with my hip. Something was rustling again. I inched forward, towards the source of the sound in his bedroom, and pushed the door open.

I was expecting to see someone left behind from Niko or Dosy's camp, but no one was present. The sound was gone, too, and I scoured the room.

Spotting the last thing I ever expected to see in the room of a man like Adonis, I laughed. "I forgot about you!" I crossed to his bed and sat down, grabbing the stuffed animal resting against one pillow with my bound hands. "No way he has a toy like this." The stuffed koala bear was ancient, its original tan fur visible in the crease of one ear. The rest of it was darker, dirtier brown. It smelled clean despite its grungy appearance. "You wouldn't happen to have any handcuff keys would you?" I asked it playfully.

Dresser.

I looked around. It was almost like a whisper but not quite audible. Like it was in my head. Taking the toy with me, I went to the dresser I had ransacked earlier for a weapon and this time searched out a handcuff key.

"Awesome," I said and set the toy down. I unlocked my cuffs then tossed them on the dresser. "Come on, little guy." I picked up the bear and went into the living area.

TEN

M
Y LATEST ESCAPE PLAN FOILED, I DID WHAT ANY
teenager would do. I flipped on the television.
Accompanied by Adonis' toy, I sank onto the
couch, my attention at once snagged by the news.

Real news. None of the censored stuff the priests fed us at
the orphanage.

Except, as soon as I began watching, I began to feel … ill.
The world outside my forest was ugly and the people
untrustworthy, but it seemed far better than what was going on
outside of the region entirely.

"The death toll this year outside the wall has reached ten
million, ten percent lower than last year. Experts claim the
trend has been decreasing every year since the Holy Wars
began five years ago, which they take as a sign the wars
between the gods are losing steam due to the political posturing
of SISA and the military," claimed one anchorman.

"Fantastic news, James," said the woman beside him. "With

153

forty three states under official martial law, many are crediting the military and Supreme Magistrate with keeping the peace."

I watched in interest as they showed stock images from the wall and a map of the territories claimed by the gods and goddesses as well as those currently conflicted. The map of North America was riddled by colors indicating pockets of different deities' territorial claims. Images from those areas were … horrifying. Smashed towns, long breadlines, massive temples in perfect condition where the gods and goddesses lived surrounded by destruction and images of the extreme poverty and disease afflicting humanity.

The television flipped off.

I blinked, stunned, and faced the door. Adonis had a second remote and tossed it on the couch.

"Is this real?" I asked.

"Is what real?"

"The wars. The wall."

He eyed me. "How do you not know anything?"

"We were sheltered. But you're telling me the continent has been torn apart by gods infighting?"

"Not the continent. The world, except for about a thousand square miles of the eastern seaboard and Mount Olympus in Greece, their adopted home here."

My jaw dropped. This wasn't what the priests had taught us!

"The deities grant favors for a price and manipulate humans as required to amass their power and money. It's the way it's always been," Adonis said.

"But the Sacred Triumvirate is supposed to balance their power with humanity."

"They did at one point. Power is all that matters now, Alessandra. Power, influence, control. The gods have been at war with one another on Earth for five years. Which is why it's important we found you. We weren't planning on you appearing quite so soon, before my master had a chance to complete his preparations."

Five years. There it is again. But I was too incensed to follow that line of thought.

"Isn't the Supreme Priest the liaison between gods and people? Can't he make the gods stop hurting everyone?"

"Politics at this level are about one thing: power. No cause, no morality, no concerns other than power and survival matter once you reach the Triumvirate." He gave me a look saying he didn't quite believe I was so naïve.

I stared at the blank television screen. I was beginning to understand better why the Old Ways were needed, but I didn't know why the priests hadn't just come out and told us all about what was going on in the world. What else were they hiding?

"Your first trial awaits," Adonis said. "My master has given me your tasking."

A trial didn't sound that bad. If anything, it sounded easy. I knew myself well enough to believe I could withstand anything.

"After the trials, I get my powers and I can stop the Wars, right?"

"If the Triumvirate wishes it."

"Like I care if they do! Ten million people have died this

year. The Oracle helps people."

"The Oracle obeys her masters."

"No." I shook my head. "I don't care what they want. I'm going to do what's right. Send the gods home and free the people."

"You think you have a choice."

I hated it when he said something like that. The only way to uncover exactly what was going on was to face these trials and come out on the other side an official Oracle. Whatever this test consisted of, it couldn't be that bad. I was trained for everything and I had the additional motivation of knowing I could save the world.

I picked up the teddy bear. "You stay here," I said sternly. "Hey, why do you have this?"

Adonis' cold glare was his only response.

"Whatever. Where is the first trial?" Propping up the stuffed animal where it could see the television, I stood and went as close to Adonis as I dared.

He tilted his head towards the entrance to the apartment. "Courtyard."

"It's ... here?"

"Yes. But first ..." His eyes went to the bear and lingered. "... first you have been blessed by Mnemosyne."

Mnemosyne. The goddess of memory. Excitement rushed through me. "What does that mean? I meet her? She returns my memories?"

"You're the brave fool. Go find out."

Intrigued yet certain he was setting me up for something

quite awful, I went to the door.

"You'll need this," he called after me.

Turning, I caught the sheathed hunting knife he tossed me. "Thanks. How long does it take for her to return my memories?"

"Do I look like a god?"

"Yeah, but …" Hearing my response, I groaned. "Never mind. I'll go see the goddess then to the courtyard."

He stood stoic and still, hands crossed in front of him. I was getting no information out of him, but at least he hadn't reacted to my comment about him looking like a god.

A trickle of red seeped from one of his nostrils. "Nosebleed," I said.

He touched it gingerly then rested his knuckle on his temple temporarily.

"You have a headache?" I asked, sensing the strange weakness in him I'd witnessed in the courtyard. A man this strong didn't seem susceptible to the headaches I got with my fall sinus infections.

"Not your concern."

"Peppermint helps. Or, you could …" My eyes swept over the couch again. "I thought I put it up on the cushion." His teddy bear was lying on its head on the floor. Crossing to it, I plucked it up and replaced it, this time in a corner. "Stay! Your daddy has a headache and can't pick you up."

"You are the most bizarre person I've ever met," Adonis said. "Is there any sense in there at all?"

I shook my head at him and returned to the door. "See you

in a few," I said. This time, I didn't hesitate but opened the door and stepped into the hallway.

Or … more accurately, into a forest. I stopped in place, startled, and stretched out one hand towards the side of the hallway I should've been able to feel, if this were a mirage.

Nothing. A warm breeze swept the scents of flowers and earth by me, and pine needles rustled far overhead. I started to turn to see if I could still see Adonis.

The forest surrounded me on all sides. The door had vanished. As far as I could tell, I'd stepped into a different world.

Could be stranger, I told myself. "If my trial were surviving the woods, I'd be set!" But … supposedly, I wasn't here for my trial. I was here to find a goddess who held my memories.

I started into the forest. And then I glimpsed it through the foliage. A wall stretching from the earth towards the heavens, made of what appeared to be concrete. *Different world or somewhere else in my world?*

Eager to see if what the news said was true, I headed in that direction.

ELEVEN

Know thyself
– THALES

T HE WALL WAS SHEER WITH NO STAIRS, DOORS OR ladders with which to scale it. After trotting back and forth along a kilometer stretch, I rested my hands on it. It was cool to the touch, and my palms came away chalky.

Not concrete. Not stone.

I had no idea what the material of the wall before me really was, though I was grateful it appeared to be porous and more prone to chipping than say, marble. I retreated to the forest. I had a knife and the forest to supply me with materials to help me scale it.

Because I was meant to. The woods extended in all other directions with no end, and yet, I was drawn only to the wall. I gathered some moss, flexible branches from saplings and

159

misplace any hand or foot and end up plunging to my death before I'd seen what was on the other side of the wall.

Just as I was beginning to wonder how long it would remain midday in this odd place, the sun plunged towards the horizon and disappeared. Within seconds.

Startled, I twisted as far as I dared to see the sky. I was half a kilometer above the tops of the forest. A bright moon worthy of the goddess Selene herself was nestled into the bosom of Nyx. Stars glimmered around it.

"Herakles will never believe me when I tell him about this place," I murmured. The moon kept my climb from being impossible, but it was far more difficult to place the branch tips well without squinting to see. I took one and began chipping away at a new spot, using the now dulled tip to create a small hole in the wall.

Tap, tap, tap. I squinted to see if it was deep enough only to realize the sound continued.

Tap, tap, tap. Three more times it went. I froze and then shook my head, sensing I was close to exhaustion.

I tapped twice more with the dulled point and stretched back, ready to plunge the branch into the concrete with what strength remained.

Tap, tap.

I lowered my arm. More than my exhaustion was at work here.

I tapped the wall again, and more tapping answered. Forcing my tired mind to focus, I swiveled my head to my right, the direction the sound came from, and gasped.

A hippolectryon was pecking the wall with its beak. With the body of a horse and the legs, head and tale of a chicken, it had wings and was uglier than I expected. I stared at it, wanting to dismiss the possibility it existed, before recalling that I was in a magic place where the sun stayed overhead for over twelve hours and then dived across the sky to set in the time it took me to sneeze.

"You're smaller than I expected," I said to the creature not two meters away from me. It was the size of my foot. "Too little to eat. Too little to carry me on your back."

The creature looked at me, as if waiting for me to tap again. I did more out of curiosity than anything else. It pecked in response.

And then it hit me. The creature wasn't flying. It was *walking* up the wall on spindly chicken feet.

"How in Hades is that possible?" I muttered. I tapped the wall beside me. The creature tapped back, moving closer as it did. When it was within reach, I picked it up to study its feet.

It squirmed with a clucking sound, but in the moonlight I could see its feet weren't magical or suction cups or anything else. I dropped it away from the wall, unconcerned about it falling since it had wings. Rather than drop downward, the hippolectryon landed on the wall again.

With some caution, I drew one leg up from the branch it was on and rested my knee against the wall. My balance shifted to it, as if gravity itself were changing around me, and I felt the heavy sense of lying on my stomach.

I lifted my second foot into place next, not about to lose my death grip on the two branches preventing me from falling. With incredulity making my heart sprint, I cautiously sat up. I was kneeling, bent over my handholds.

The hippolectryon began pecking again and walked on, as if bored now that I wasn't playing with it anymore.

Disorientated, I released one hand then the other and risked a look in the direction that had been down seconds before.

The forest was where it had been, and my stomach lurched at the idea I was about to fall.

But I didn't. I breathed deeply and released my final grip on the branches. The hippolectryon was two meters away again, pecking and pacing.

With some apprehension, I stood. I didn't topple into the forest, and the wall beneath me didn't give out. "Ha!" I couldn't help the baffled laugh. "I'll take it. I'm sick of climbing. Thanks for rotating the world for me, Atlas." Wrenching my remaining foot and handholds out of the wall, I tucked all but one into my cargo pockets and clenched the fourth, in case the world's gravitation changed on me again.

I began walking then trotting up the wall, towards the top, followed closely by a hippolectryon that sometimes ran, sometimes flew to keep up.

"You have an interest in what's over the wall?" I asked, slowing. It landed beside me without answering. The distance to the top of the wall was much greater than I expected, a full kilometer and a half past the point where I began walking. Finally, after fifteen minutes, I saw the edge of the top come into view and silently admitted I'd never had made it if I had to climb all that way.

Readying my stake in case I was about to plunge down the other side, I knelt and leaned over the edge. The top of the wall was about a meter wide. I tapped on the surface, waiting for the hippolectryon to test it out.

The creature went. He didn't fall. Just … stood there.

"Okay. Please do it again, Atlas," I begged the Titan quietly. Blowing out a breath, I lay down on my stomach and crept over the top. My stomach dropped, and the same lurching sensation returned as gravity changed around me once again. "I'd think this was a dream if I didn't know I was awake."

I rolled onto the top and lay on my back, staring at the sky briefly. The hippolectryon pecked at one of my hands, and I moved it out of reach. Tired, I nonetheless was exited to move on and shifted to my knees to peer at what lay at the bottom of the wall on the other side.

A single, solitary house stood half a kilometer from the foot of the wall. Otherwise, only darkness existed. Not the kind of darkness that occurred when the sun set. This was unnatural. Nothingness. I wasn't certain what I expected of a blessing from Mnemosyne but it wasn't this. I readied myself for the odd sensation of gravity changing and leaned carefully over the side of the wall, waiting for the unsettling sensation to leave my belly.

"All right. We're set," I said cheerfully and stood. "You ready?" I looked back.

The hippolectryon was gone.

"I guess not." I started forward, down the side of the wall, not looking at the house for fear of becoming disoriented once more. When I reached the bottom, I knelt and placed my hands on the grass ahead of me.

"Atlas, just one more –" I toppled onto my face. "Gods dammit!" I muttered and sat up. "Thanks anyway." With a sigh, I looked around. Nothing else had appeared. Just the house. I dropped the stakes and rope at the wall and strode down a sidewalk towards the house. Nothingness ran on either side. I peered over the edge of the sidewalk once then not again, not about to wade into the void on either side.

Pausing in front of the two-story house, I studied it. Was I supposed to know it? Because it wasn't remotely familiar. A small porch and several windows faced me. It seemed so very normal, the kind of cookie cutter suburbia I imagined everyone lived in, before learning the world was in a state of chaos brought on by warring gods.

"Mnemosyne?" I called. I wasn't expecting her to magically appear and wasn't disappointed. I'd never been blessed by a god or goddess. I knew less of the protocol handling one of them than I did about the people who lived outside my forest.

Uncertain if I was supposed to waltz in or knock first, I decided to be polite and knocked. The door creaked open under the force of my knock. I pushed it the rest of the way open. Lights I couldn't see from the outside glowed from the second floor of the house. Stairs were ahead of me, a formal dining room on one side of the foyer and a formal living room on the other side. The hallway to the left of the stairwell led to a kitchen. Nightlights positioned in outlets along the walls lit up the bottom floor.

It was quiet, calm and … familiar. Not like Adonis, who I felt I'd never met before, but familiar as if I had been here before. As if I should know this place.

"Hello?" I called.

No one answered. I started up the stairs, to the part of the house beckoning me to it with bright, cheerful light. Three bedrooms, a study and bathroom. Thus far, everything about this place screamed ordinary. The door to one bedroom was wide open, and I went to it.

Stuffed animals and dolls were scattered on the floor. A television with a pink remote control was at one side, a twin bed with a purple canopy on the other. The dressers and furniture were bright white, the curtains overlooking the space behind the house pink and green. Purple, heart-shaped rugs were on the floor.

I smiled, liking the bright, happy colors of the room. Beside the TV remote, in front of a blanket that appeared to have been wrapped around a small form before being pushed off, were a shoebox and a scrapbook. I knelt beside the scrapbook, curious to see the child who lived here.

Flipping open the cover, I was surprised at the title page.

The Oracle of Delphi

I turned the page. The scrapbook was filled with articles cut out of newspapers and printed from computers about the current Oracle of Delphi. Pictures, news reports, tabloid covers. Nothing about the book was personal to its owner at all.

"Someone's obsessed with the Oracle," I said and closed it. The shoebox beside it was empty, and I stood, puzzled as to what I was supposed to do next.

I started towards the door, wondering if I'd find more in the next room over, when I tripped over something hidden in the blanket at my feet.

"Hey. I know you." I bent and retrieved the stuffed koala bear I'd first seen with Adonis. It appeared almost new, and it was ... rumbling. My fingertips vibrated with the strange sensation. "Some kind of talking toy?"

Mrs. Nettles.

The voice from Adonis' bedroom.

"Uh. You're not talking to me are you?" I asked, holding it away from my body.

Mrs. Nettles.

I dropped it then gasped. "Oh, gods, I'm so sorry." I picked it up and gazed at it. "Are you hurt?" My face turned hot at the idea of talking to a toy.

The stuffed animal blinked. It *blinked.*

This time when I dropped it, I leapt back. "The flying horse-chicken was a little weird. But this ..."

The koala climbed to its feet. I had the sudden flashback to a horror movie I once watched where a doll came to life and slaughtered people.

Mnemosyne sent Mrs. Nettles to guide you.

"What does that mean?" I demanded of the quiet world around me. "What is a Mrs. Nettles?"

The koala pointed to itself then began to stroke one of its

ears.

"You're ... you're Mrs. Nettles."

It nodded.

"Oh." If this world weren't surreal, I might short out. I decided to accept a walking, talking teddy bear as I did the wall. "Okay, Mrs. Nettles. I'm trying to figure out what Mnemosyne wants me to do here."

Mrs. Nettles extended her arm in my general direction.

"I'm not sure what that means."

It did it again.

Not getting whatever she wanted me to know, I knelt and cautiously drew nearer to her. "Do you know Adonis?"

Mrs. Nettles nodded and waddled towards me. She paused at my knees and then shifted forward to try to grasp the red cord around my wrist between her two chubby paws.

"You, uh, want me to take it off?"

It nodded.

"You know what happens if I do?"

Another nod.

I'm in some weird world where toys can talk. Why not? I tugged the red cord off and braced myself to hear the shattering of glass.

Immediately, the world around me erupted into activity and color. Thin, shifting ribbons twisted and twirled around every single object in the room. I'd seen them before, and I racked my brain to figure out where.

The lake. In the water, I had witnessed smoky, faded ribbons like these twisting in the depths.

"What are they?" I asked, stunned by the life in the room filled with inanimate objects. The toys on the bed had two ribbons each, one blue and one yellow, though the exact hue and widths were unique around each toy. Mrs. Nettles, however, had three – blue, yellow, and faded green.

Mrs. Nettles had no answer.

Mesmerized by the colors and movement, I let my gaze roam over everything in the room. Even the television had two ribbons. I looked up towards the ceiling to see if I had any floating above my head. If I did, they were invisible.

Rustling came from the direction of the window. I blinked out of my amazed stupor to find Mrs. Nettles had moved. She was beneath the window, staring up at it, unable to reach the pane or see out of it.

"Don't tell me you fly," I said with a half laugh and rose. I crossed to the window and froze.

The nothingness had retreated. The house had a backyard, complete with a picket fence, tree house and a sandbox. Toys were scattered across the yard, and if I leaned out the window, I'd see a small herb garden beneath the kitchen window, next to a ...

How do I know that? I didn't recall ever seeing Mrs. Nettles or the house or the backyard before. Why was I certain of the herb garden?

I was starting to remember.

"Mrs. Nettles! Can you find him?"

I whirled. A little girl around the age of six bolted into the room, faded and transparent, a ghost in every aspect. She was trailed by the ghostly version of Mrs. Nettles. They searched for someone or something before she crossed to the dresser and opened the bottom drawer. She pulled out a brilliant blue-green gem that glowed unnaturally before she hurried out the door.

My heart was starting to pound harder, and my instincts tingled. I touched the teal gem beneath my t-shirt and tugged it out. It was identical to the little girl's.

My Mrs. Nettles was waddling towards the door.

I followed her and reached the door in time to see the spectral girl race down the stairs. Sweeping Mrs. Nettles up, I hurried down the stairs, following her. She darted out the back door and towards the tree in the corner of the backyard. I watched her climb the ladder on the trunk to reach the tree house then disappear inside.

The sounds of men shouting from behind us made me reach for my knife. I slunk through the house to the front door just as it burst open, and I was overrun by men in black uniforms.

I cried out, startled, and stumbled back, slashing at the figures.

But these were ghosts, like the girl. After the brief heart attack, I realized they couldn't see or hear me at all and grew braver. I walked out front to see the world had grown once more. The house was one of many identical ones lining a street in the suburbs. The men originated from one of five black vans. Several were huddled around one van. I was about to go inside to see what happened to the little girl when I caught a flash of red in the moonlight.

I'd recognize Herakles' hair and size anywhere. I started towards him, wondering if he could see me. My step slowed as I waded through the spectral figures around him. This Herakles I'd only seen in old pictures.

Gorgeous, handsome, bearing none of the scars he did now, Herakles was twenty three, at the peak of his physical shape, dressed in black fatigues like the other men and issuing orders from the iPad in his hands.

"No parents!" someone cried from the door of the house.

"They're already dead," Herakles said without looking up. "Saw to it yesterday, after they revealed her location."

My breath caught. *This isn't my Herakles.* I'd never heard that tone or seen that expression on his face. I didn't like either. My Herakles was a gentle athlete, not ... this.

"We've got her! She's trapped in her tree house," a soldier said, hurrying towards them. "This way."

"Thank the gods. I'll be glad to get this over with," Herakles said.

"Quite a change from being the People's Champion," another man said beside him.

"Yeah. Master's orders."

Master? I didn't want to see what happened next. My Herakles didn't deserve to have his honor and goodness besmirched by this bizarre place. As far as I knew, he never had a master, unless he was talking about the benefactor who sponsored him at the Olympics.

"What in Olympus is that?" someone gasped.

They all looked up, and I did as well. A creature I never knew existed before last week soared overhead, its grey body blending in with the partially cloudy sky. Eyes glowed teal, and he passed with the threat, silence and intensity of a thunderhead.

Grotesque. My heart quickened once more. The creature was headed towards the backyard. I watched it, unable to explain how my whole body seemed to come alive when I saw him. My heartbeat turned erratic and blood roared in my ears almost too loudly for me to hear. I was fevered, thrilled yet scared, curious and dreading all at once.

I raced through the house to the backyard, wishing I could warn the little girl it was coming, and stopped cold.

The grotesque was tearing into Herakles' men. His tail, fangs and claws shredded anyone that came near. I watched, somewhat disgusted, and uncertain whose side anyone was on. His agility, his feline speed and strength, were somehow … familiar.

The four men were soon in pieces, torn limb from limb. The grotesque straightened and looked around, tail tapping the tree, before he lifted into the air effortlessly. He went to the opening of the tree house, and my breath caught.

I hurried forward instinctively. "Don't hurt her!" I cried at the ghost that couldn't see me.

To my surprise, the girl emerged cautiously from the house and smiled at the grotesque. It wrapped her in one arm and picked up Mrs. Nettles as well. She laughed as the creature lifted her into the air over her house. The monster wobbled in midair, as if unaccustomed to carrying others.

Herakles and two others raced around the side of the house. The men with him fired their weapons at the grotesque, which hovered closer to the rooftop. If he were hit by a bullet, he didn't show it.

"We need something bigger!" one of the attackers called.

The grotesque began to rise straight up into the sky.

"I got this." Without any sign of strain at all, Herakles wrenched a picket free from the fence, positioned himself as if throwing a javelin, and launched it straight up.

Even I doubted he'd get anywhere close to the grotesque flying twenty meters over the house.

But he did. The picket pierced one wing and pinned it to the side of the monster, running all the way through him to stick out of his other side.

A roar shook the windows of the house, and suddenly, the creature – and girl – were falling.

"No," I whispered, horrified.

The girl came free from the monster's arms as they tumbled out of the sky, screaming as she did.

One of the men cursed, but Herakles trotted a short distance, spread his legs wide and held out his arms.

Falling ... and Herakles caught me. I shook my head, suddenly dizzy, suddenly able to feel the air rushing through my hair as I fell once more ...

Down, from the night sky ...

Down, from the arms of the creature trying to rescue me ...

Down, into Herakles' arms.

I dropped to my knees, struggling to right myself. Mrs. Nettles tugged free and waddled away. Blinking, I forced my mind to focus here and now and not on the dream.

Herakles had the girl. The grotesque smashed through the roof then crashed through the first and second floors, sounding as if he landed on and crushed the kitchen table.

"It's okay." Herakles' voice was gruff.

The other men were panicking, one calling for an ambulance while another barked for someone to bring a first aid kit.

I climbed to my feet and approached, fearfully watching Herakles and the girl. She was shaking and scared, staring not at Herakles but into the air above his head.

"Is your name Alessandra?" he asked.

My heart dropped to my feet.

The girl nodded.

"My name is Herakles."

"Bad people," she whispered.

"Not bad. You're special, and we've been trying to find you."

"You're … hurt." She was staring at the air above him. "Broken."

Herakles breath caught audibly. "What did you say?"

"The ribbons. They're broken."

I blinked. I'd done my best to cancel out the ribbons around everything to concentrate on what I was watching. I saw what she meant. Herakles had four ribbons, but the colors were tie-died rather than solid, the edges jagged instead of smooth. They appeared to have been stitched together from other ribbons.

Frankenstein. He referred to himself as such on occasion. I thought it was because of his size. I saw the truth now, the confused Franken-ribbons unique to him.

"I can fix them." Baby Alessandra raised her hands and began to manipulate them, using her fingers to smooth and shift them.

Herakles staggered and dropped to his knees, releasing her. She rolled free of him with a grunt and then sat up, appearing irritated to have been disturbed before she finished. She continued to manipulate the ribbons until the edges smoothed out and the colors were uniform.

Herakles contorted on the ground as she worked. When she was finished, he fell still, panting and sweating.

"Now we have to save Mismatch," the girl said and stood.

"Mis … what?" Herakles struggled to lift his head.

"My gargoyle." She started towards the house.

"Stop!" he called. "You can't … it's dangerous." With some effort, Herakles pushed himself to his feet and staggered forward before regaining some part of his composure. "What did you do to me?"

"The ribbons." She pointed.

Herakles passed a hand over his head as if to see what was there then brought his hand before his face. He stared at it before he looked down at his body. "This isn't me. This isn't who I am."

"Mismatch!" Alessandra cried.

I circled Herakles. The coldness was gone from his features, and he appeared … aware where he was mechanical before. He had been broken or at least, not quite right, as little-me said. I didn't understand the source of his Franken-ribbons. Something terrible had happened to him, perhaps in the youth he refused to reveal to me.

"Herakles! The Supreme Magistrate is on the way. We need to get her to the House," someone called.

His face skewed in response, and he glanced towards the girl making her way up the stairs. Herakles snatched her.

"But – " she started to object.

"Quiet. The bad people are coming. We need to leave."

He took her out the back gate and disappeared into the night.

The scene faded. I was standing behind the house. The yard was gone, along with the men.

Realizing how tightly my chest was clenched, I bent over and took several deep, steadying breaths.

I was slow sometimes, but even I understood what I'd seen.

Me. Herakles. The forgotten events of the night that changed my life. But was it real?

Yes. I felt it just like I felt the gem at my chest belonged to me, like my grotesque had belonged to me.

Herakles killed my parents. He was going to turn me over to the people he hated most in the world. My protector, like everyone else in my life, wasn't who I thought he was. I *ached* inside. The man I never thought could disappoint me had turned out not to exist.

"Don't freak out, Lyssa," I whispered, sucking in air.

Aurora was lining the horizon. With no concept of how time worked here, I forced myself to straighten. Mrs. Nettles was standing in the doorway.

"So, were you … mine?" I asked as I approached, straining to control the emotions.

She nodded. *Mrs. Nettles.* Turning, she pointed towards the kitchen.

Not at all certain I was ready to see what happened next, I went.

The grotesque lay in the center, a pool of dark blood beneath him. The ghost Mrs. Nettles was tugging the picket out of his side. I felt bad for her, wanting to tell her no one could survive such a wound except …

I had seen him. I knew he did. Somehow.

Five ribbons floated around him, one of which was green.

The sun came up, albeit not as fast as it went down, and something even more incredible began to happen.

The monster became human. Its change was silent. Wings melted away, and the athletic, feline body turned from gray to olive-skinned. Dark hair grew on his head, and the talons withdrew into him.

"No!" I breathed. "It can't be!"

By daylight, the grotesque was Adonis.

"No, no, no!"

But, similar to Herakles, he wasn't the Adonis I knew. He was younger for one, in his teens. When he awoke, his expressions were open and aware instead of cold and withdrawn, his gorgeous eyes warm. He sobbed out of pain, and spoke gently to Mrs. Nettles.

"Is no one who they seem to be?" I whispered, stricken by the sight of anyone in pain. "He tried to rescue me."

He's yours. Mrs. Nettles' tiny voice said into my head.

"Mine." I didn't understand fully what that meant or how this man was the same who slaughtered people right and left, who kidnapped Herakles, destroyed my forest and was universally feared and hated by everyone. What changed? Why had he wanted to rescue me when I was a child and turn me over to the Sacred Triumvirate now?

Confusion was trumped only by helplessness at seeing him hurt. Whatever our past and present, I ached for him strongly enough that tears pricked my eyes and I resisted the urge to weep. We were connected on a level I had no clue existed but which made his pain real to me.

I wiped my eyes. "Dream. Memories. Not real."

Mrs. Nettles pointed towards a door I guessed would lead to the garage if this were reality. In this version of things, my name was written on it, and I instinctively knew I wasn't going to find two cars behind it.

I didn't want to leave, but she waddled in the direction. I trailed, this time apprehensive about what lay behind the door.

She stopped before it and looked up at me.

"You want me to … open it?" I asked.

A nod.

A sense I wanted to ignore was creeping up on me. It was more than familiarity this time. It was the idea that Adonis was right. I basically knew nothing about anything and had to acknowledge there was a piece of me that had been hidden from everyone for too long.

I didn't know me, either, and this scared me. Terrified to learn more about how Herakles wasn't the man I thought he was, I was likewise starting to tremble to think I was about to find out who I was. What if I were as bad as Herakles had been? What if my secrets were the worst?

Who – or what – am I?

TWELVE
THE HIGH PRIESTESS

If all men were just, there would be no need for valor.
– AGESILAUS THE SECOND

"FAILED MISERABLY," I REPORTED AND TOSSED my weapons onto the table beside one of the Silent Queen's gardeners.

Sometimes success takes a different shape than one expects. This was supposed to be a sphinx and ended up a griffin. It's still beautiful, she replied through the telepathic link we shared. Mute since the age of six, she spoke to no one but me.

I glanced over at my mistress and the keeper of the Bloodline, the stunning Queen of Greece. She perched on a bench beneath a shade tree, her crystal clear blue eyes on the gardener shaping one of the many fantastical bushes in the gardens.

"Ran into Niko. We're not the only ones pressing Adonis. He has absolutely no concern for the Oracle discovery protocol."

You need to make a decision about Niko, she reminded me. With cool beauty, mild manners and the large eyes of a doll, the Silent Queen was often mistaken for being simple, naïve, weak.

Such a person didn't request a High Priestess to assassinate an ex-lover, among others. The cunning teen was brilliant and ruthless in the way of a royal fighting for her title. I had lost track of the people we'd seen to an early grave to protect our secrets from the other members of the Triumvirate.

"I know," I said. "He's been a pain lately. We have a son together. Makes things complicated. If he were anyone else …"

He'd be gone. I know. The Silent Queen patted the seat beside her. *How are preparations going?*

"Perfect. Ready to take the next step when commanded."

And the Oracle? Do we strike or wait? What is your impression?

I dwelled on the question for a moment, trying to sort things out in my own head before responding. "She's tough. Smart. Adonis was in a hurry to start her on his master's trial."

Adonis has never been an easy man to understand.

"Not at all. But he was even harder than usual. He went out of his way not to hurt her when she tried to escape. The Adonis we know and loathe would've shot her in both legs to make it easier."

Perhaps he has orders from the Supreme Priest.

"Maybe." I wasn't convinced. "Anyway, I think if we can

get her alone and present our side, we'll be able to sway her. She'd be an asset to our plans, and your trial for her would only hasten our ability to act."

As long as the cost isn't too high. We also risk discovery once we reveal our trial to her.

"She seems ... honest. I think an honest person would side with us when she hears the alternative."

True. Where do you go next?

I glanced at my watch. "Downstairs," I replied, referring to the secret city beneath DC. "The military intercepted a train of supplies coming from outside the wall. I'm going to see the damage and check in with our friend."

Ask him about the Oracle.

"That's a bit difficult without telling him the truth."

I trust your judgment.

Beautiful and powerful, the Queen was also the best boss in the world. "I'll be back for your dinner."

She bowed her head, and I stood. I was the only one who could hear her, which meant I was required to attend every official dinner, gala, and ceremony she did. I didn't bother changing clothes but whirled a hooded cloak around my shoulders and collected my weapons.

I entered her airy villa and trotted down to the wine cellar, past the thousands of bottles of wine, and to a secret passageway behind a wall.

Moments later, I was descending in a small elevator into the secret city below DC. Always dark and drab, it teemed with activity and movement. Two story buildings and city blocks had been established in the central hub of the city located beneath her villa.

Leaping out of the elevator, I strode through several roads named after former Greek kings and queens. The scent of food and gun oil were in the musty air, and those I passed bowed their heads or greeted me with a smile. The armies living here consisted of mostly men wearing run down clothing. Part of the duties for those present was to spy in DC, and vagrants made for the least noticeable spies. Each of them wore a patch with an *M* on it when visiting underground.

"Docia!" someone called as I entered the warehouse district where the supplies were kept. "You heard?" Gus, the man in charge of this district, was red-faced and fidgeting. He had a tick in one eye that was twitching faster than usual as a result of his agitation.

"Yeah," I said and approached him. My gaze was caught by a shock of red hair and the towering frame of Herakles. He'd found a small gang of Mama's men doing reconnaissance and beat them all until one finally agreed to take him to the leader of the underground world. The Queen and I alone knew his importance and instantly welcomed him. He was walking with someone else among the weapons. Not touching, just looking. "What's he doing here?"

"He knows his guns. He's helping with this week's inventory," said Gus.

"Hmmm." Someone so close to Alessandra didn't need to be in the middle of my weapons depot even if he didn't know yet what our plan with her was.

"The men love him. He's been sparring with them. Tough."

"Herakles!"

I watched my son race out of the neighboring building towards the red-haired giant with the scarred features. Herakles whirled and pretended to fight with him before feigning injury and dropping to the ground. Tomas laughed.

"Tommy loves him too," Gus added. "Here's a list of what was seized."

My gaze lingered on Tommy, who lived below ground with the armies of Mama. I pursed my lips and took the iPad, skimming through the missing supplies. "Figures it was the shipment with the missiles we need to penetrate the wall."

"Those cost a fortune to pilfer from the military."

I studied the numbers. "They're in their supply depo or seized assets warehouses?"

"Seized assets."

"Damn. We haven't cracked entering that area yet." I handed back the report, gaze falling to Tommy again. Gripping my phone tightly, I debated not going down the road I was about to before I punched the number for Niko.

"Whatever it is, no," he said bluntly when he answered.

"All right. Then I won't bring Tommy by," I snapped.

Silence and then, "You always demand something in return for me seeing *my* son. What is it?" he demanded tersely.

"Ten minutes alone with your computer."

I knew he was cursing the day he met me. I was, too. We'd had something once, long ago, when I was too naïve to see Niko for the selfish person he was. I rarely thought of those days anymore, but I did wish he was a better person for my son's sake.

"Okay. After hours."

I checked the time. It'd be a squeeze to attend the dinner with the queen.

"And I get him for the weekend," Niko added.

"One day."

Niko grumbled. "Fine. Friday." He hung up.

I lowered the phone, feeling dirty for being willing to use my son to manipulate someone else. But only one place in North America manufactured the wall-buster missiles, and it had recently been smashed to pieces by angry gods. Even without this complication, the Silent Queen was running close to broke. She had spent the fortune her family built up over millennia to create the underground world and the armies it contained. The weapons were irreplaceable – and a vital part of our plan.

"I'll get them back," I said to Gus. "Keep an extraction team ready."

"Will do."

I moved away from him to Tommy. Herakles was back on his feet, talking Tommy through the parts of a machine gun he held.

"Hey, kid," I said and ruffled Tommy's hair. "Give your mama a minute with the greatest Olympian alive."

Tommy smiled and raced away.

"Good kid," Herakles said. His scarred face held me in quiet curiosity for a moment before I realized I was staring. It wasn't like me to be distracted by a man.

"You have time to talk?" I asked.

He nodded. "Any word on Alessandra?"

"I saw her today. She's doing great."

We began walking, leaving the warehouse area for the streets of the underground city.

"All this … you control the criminal underworld, too?" Herakles asked.

"Most of it. There are parts we haven't been able to wrangle into order or we've purposely not touched. The arena is one. Too popular. It's sudden disappearance or change would draw the attention of too many high level politicians who like to gamble."

"Would be a good place for money laundering."

"That's what we use it for."

"Lyssa would like you. Smart and strong."

I felt his gaze on me and wasn't certain what to say in response. "About Lyssa," I started. "What do you think she'll think when she sees what we've built? What we plan?"

"I'm not really sure what you plan, except a rebellion against the gods."

"Good place to start."

Herakles was quiet briefly. "She was raised to fight and to believe in the Old Ways. Assuming the Old Ways are part of what you're doing here, I imagine she'd be eager to join you once she discovers what her fate will be otherwise."

There were moments when I recalled the scarred man was more than he seemed. He'd been chosen by someone to take care of the next Oracle. All I knew about him was that he vanished twelve years ago after winning three annual Olympic games. To participate, he had to have had an incredibly wealthy benefactor, possibly a politician or god whose honor and pride depended upon Herakles winning.

How much he knew, his connections with the elite and who he might be working for, were not mysteries I could guess. They also weren't questions one simply asked. I didn't want him offended or driven off or otherwise outside our reach and control. Adonis had the right idea to trap him as a way of assuring the Oracle cooperated. I wasn't going to cage the man, but I was going to give him as many reasons as possible to stay under our influence.

"You designed all this?" He swept a hand out towards the city.

"A good chunk."

"It's impressive."

From him, the compliment was unexpected. "It's a privilege to know you think so."

The silence between us was charged. We continued walking, each in thought, and at least me overly aware of the two inches between our forearms. He was close to my age with the body of someone who hadn't lost any part of the edge he held in the Olympics. The only thing I didn't understand about him: the scarring covering his face and neck. A combination of fire and knife, if I had to guess, and he'd never bothered to obtain surgery to fix it.

"Docia, I want to see Lyssa, " he said quietly.

"I understand." And I did. For all intents and purposes, she was his daughter. "Adonis has started the trial the Supreme Priest dictated."

"Which is ..."

"Gods know," I replied. "None of the Triumvirate members are willing to share."

Herakles stopped and faced me. "She's not prepared."

"She's very well prepared," I countered. "I've seen her fight and spoken to her. She can take care of herself."

His jaw ticked, his dark eyes on mine. "I would've liked to have spoken to her first. To warn her not to trust anyone."

"I think she's figured that out."

Herakles expression didn't change. Whatever was on his mind, his gaze was troubled.

"I'm sure she'll do well," I said.

"Yes. She will," he agreed. "I fear more for the things she will learn that she might not be prepared for."

"Such as ..."

"The truth."

Concern fluttered through me. Was it the kind of truth that would drive her away from our cause? Sensing he wasn't about to discuss it, and not knowing him well enough, I didn't ask. I had two people digging into his past for more information about him. Whatever they turned up would give me more insight. Until then, I wanted to keep him content here in the underground city.

"Are you comfortable here? Have everything you need?" I asked.

"Very. Thank you. I only worry for her. Her fate is out of my hands, and I can't yet fully accept that."

I didn't want to imagine what I'd feel if Tommy were at the mercy of the Triumvirate. But Alessandra was tough. She didn't strike me as someone to wallow if she was knocked on her ass. "Let me know if you need anything," I said and started away.

"I would ask one favor," Herakles said.

"Sure."

"I'd like to be involved on some level with the operation you're planning."

I considered him. "It's a very delicate political situation, Herakles. I don't have to tell you this."

"You fear giving me too much knowledge or power."

"We've built this underground city in the shadows. Should Alessandra not choose to support our cause, I risk much by granting you access now only to have you side with someone else later."

"Fair enough. Training? You have a lot of green troops. I can help. It'll do me well to stay busy, too."

"I think that'll work," I said with a nod. "Report to Commander Zeuson. He'll know where to put you."

"And could I trouble you for information on Alessandra, whenever you have it."

"I'd be happy to share."

He smiled. "Thanks, Docia."

Sadness was in his eyes despite his calm manner and acceptance of his adopted daughter's absence. I started away, thoughts on how we were going to steal the missiles once I used Niko's computer to unlock the facility, and then paused.

Herakles' suffering bothered me. Perhaps it was because I, too, had a child I'd never want to see go through Alessandra's fate.

"Artemis has kept watch over her this long," I told him, turning. "I don't think she'll forsake Alessandra anytime soon, but I'll say an extra prayer for her this evening at the temple."

Herakles' crooked smile was warm. "Thank you."

Without responding, I strode off once more. I had enough to think about without allowing the sorrow of one man to weigh me down. Yet something about Herakles, and his love for Alessandra, made me want to pray harder than usual this all worked out the way we planned.

THIRTEEN
ALESSANDRA

Be still my heart; thou hast known worse than this.
– HOMER

MY HAND SHOOK AS I GRIPPED THE DOORKNOB TO the pseudo-garage. With one last look at the man in agony behind me, I stepped through the door.

I was ready for the worst, for an abrupt, if not violent, re-acquaintance to whom I was.

Instead, I was in little Alessandra's bedroom once more. It was light outside, and a warm summer breeze swept through the bedroom and past the little girl seated in the center of her floor. The spectral figure was playing with Mrs. Nettles and several other dolls and toys she'd brought to life. Those that were alive had three ribbons while those that were inanimate had two. Alessandra had a thick rainbow of greens, from the most brilliant yellow-green to teal to the darkest green moss. The room swirled with ribbons whose purpose and power I didn't understand.

"Do you want to play?" she asked and looked up at me.

I shook my head. I wanted to leave.

"Well, you should!"

I've always been saucy. A smile slid free. Sensing no danger, I sat down near her. "What's going on?" I asked. "Why am I here?"

"You're remembering."

"I was afraid of that. Is everything true?" I looked around the room. It was feeling more like mine this time around to the point I knew she kept the scrapbook about the oracle in the bottom drawer of her dresser.

"Yes."

"Even the part about Herakles and ... my ... parents?"

"Yes." Her eyes were sad. "He loves you still." The wisdom in her eyes was out of place for a six year old, and I gradually began to suspect she was ... an image. Like the rest of this place. A surreal delivery system to provide me with the truth I needed.

"I love him." The words were a tight whisper. I swallowed the knot in my throat. Thinking of him made me ache. "And Adonis ... how can he hate me now?"

"He doesn't remember who he is, but I've begun to remind him."

"You ... you're Mnemosyne?"

She nodded. "Too weak to appear to you in person. The Holy Wars tax us all. I was forced to use your mind, and your magic, to create all this." She waved around her before returning to the toys. She picked up Mrs. Nettles then deftly grasped the green ribbon. "This is yours. Only you have it. Not even the gods can use it."

I accepted it. It had no weight whatsoever and yet stuck in my hand. "What does it … oh." Mrs. Nettles went still, became inanimate once more, as I leaned back. When I leaned forward, she returned to life. "So that's what I do? Bring toys to life?"

"You can do many things. Each has a purpose." She motioned to the other two ribbons. "You can change them." She manipulated the ribbons floating around Mrs. Nettles. The stuffed animal faded until she was a ghost then returned to normal and then ended up with her feet where her hands should be and her eyes on her butt.

I can manipulate matter. I had never heard of anything so incredible. "This is what gods do, isn't it?"

Mnemosyne nodded and returned Mrs. Nettles to normal before bringing her back to life. "We control nature, time, space, and so do you. Initially, gods and goddesses learn to create and destroy. You have to train yourself to do other things."

"Like what?"

"Premonitions. Teleportation. Telekinesis. There is no limitation to what you can do. You simply have to learn." She handed me Mrs. Nettles. "When you bring something to life, it's yours. You are bound to it. You must protect it. You can never harm one of your creations." These words were so solemn, I almost smiled at her cute, serious expression.

"I brought Adonis … the grotesque … to life," I mused. "He's not the same man I saw in the kitchen."

"You must help me remind him. I am too weak to do it myself."

I wasn't certain it mattered if I told the SISA chief who he was to me. He had changed too much. He didn't seem capable of compassion or empathy or even reason, and he worked for the Supreme Priest. Basically, he was everything I didn't need in my life right now, even if he could turn into a grotesque and fly at night.

"What else should I remember?" I asked, hushed. "More horrible stuff?"

"No."

"And the trials? Is that what this is?"

"No. You will need to know who you are before you start them. Mismatch remembers you; he doesn't know it yet. I asked him to bring you to me, and he did. If he didn't feel the connection between you, he would've denied me."

Ugh. I was already feeling … unsettled, to say the least. I yearned to talk to Herakles, to ask him to tell me his version of events the night I fell from the sky. To understand how he could kill my parents then raise me as his own.

This kind of betrayal was too deep for me to feel anything but profound confusion. I didn't remember my parents, but that didn't mean I was able to brush off their deaths. He had hidden away his entire past from me, and I never bothered to ask him too much about it out of respect for the man I loved. Was this wrong? Should I have insisted instead of blindly trusted him?

"These trials … what is the purpose of it?" I asked, puzzled.

"The gods created the trials to challenge you so you understood how to serve them. I fear men will choose trials to further their goals as well."

"I need to get this over with," I said. "I need to talk to Herakles."

"If you are ready." Mnemosyne pointed to another door I suspected didn't lead where I thought it should.

I had no idea what I should have been ready for. Mnemosyne went back to playing with her toys, and I stood. "Thank you." I went to the door and stared at it, stilling my emotions to handle whatever came next.

"I do know you can't kill him," she called after me.

"Kill who?"

"The opponent the Supreme Priest chose to face you."

So next is a battle. I faced the door. I could deal with a battle better than I could learning I knew even less about the world and those in it than I thought. "I'm not afraid. I can handle a battle."

Mnemosyne said nothing. With a deep breath, I opened the door …

… and stepped into the courtyard on the SISA compound. It was empty – aside from the ribbons that flowed around everything – quiet and late afternoon with lights from the recessed corners of buildings illuminating the shaded area around me.

"Shit." Until I turned, I could assume I wasn't being

matched up against the one man who could not only beat me, but who could do so very, very quickly, before I had a chance to convince him not to kill the person who brought him to life.

Grotesques lining the rooftop of a temple. I was on a class tour of the temple when teen boys began to torment one of the stone monsters. I stopped them, tried to fix the creature and in doing so, brought it to life. The memories were trickling in. With a start, I realized I wasn't wearing the red cord. The world didn't quake, and I focused for a long moment on the ribbons. I could manipulate them, allegedly, yet had no idea what each color meant or how to maneuver them without making the entire world crash down around me. Mnemosyne's warning about being able to create or destroy out of the gate concerned me. How on earth had I as a six year old managed to learn to use this power safely?

I felt him near me. This time, the uncanny sensation was stronger. I hadn't yet recovered from the revelations or the trek through my mind to release my memories.

"The Supreme Priest has ordered your trial to be as such: you will face me in a battle here and now. If you fail to defeat me, you will swear a blood and life oath to serve him and obey him without question."

"Can we, uh, talk about this first?" I asked. Coldness pierced me. I drew a breath and faced Adonis. He was dressed in his black uniform, cool gaze on me, panther body tensed and ready for a fight. He carried two knives and appeared serious about using them.

Except, I wasn't seeing him as he was now but as he had

been – the weeping man bleeding out on the floor of my kitchen. He nearly died to save me, and he had murdered several government men to protect me.

What happened between the moment he fell from the sky and when he rediscovered me? Did any part of the man he had been remain?

You can't kill him.

Mnemosyne wasn't telling me I'd fail. She was warning me I physically could not destroy something I had brought to life.

"What if I win?" I asked as the silence drew out.

"Then you owe him nothing."

It was simple and smart. The Supreme Priest managed to cut out the other members of the Triumvirate up front. I imagined he intended to use my powers for the reason Adonis claimed earlier: to expand his influence and control over the world. If I were truly what Mnemosyne claimed, I could grant him this, and help him rule the gods as well.

"Quick question," I said, my heart starting to race. "Do you remember me?" It was lame.

"Choose your weapon." He pointed with the tip of one knife towards the windows of the second floor overlooking the courtyard. I watched his ribbons shift around him with each movement, fascinated by them. "The Supreme Priest is watching on behalf of the gods."

"Of course." I blew out a sigh. "Adonis, I don't –"

"Weapon of choice."

I studied him. Some part of him had known me, but it was buried under years of him being a different man. I went reluctantly to the display of weapons on a table. My hands were shaking as I picked up one knife and tested its weight.

"You are not so eager for your trial," he observed.

"No, I'm not."

"You had some sense knocked into you since we last spoke this morning."

"Not sense. Knowledge." I set the knife down and picked up another. No part of me was involved in choosing a weapon. I was wishing instead that I'd never gone in to open my memories. Not that I wanted to kill Adonis or anyone, but knowing I couldn't, with his pain and effort to save me still fresh, with the confirmation that we truly were connected, I was worried. Terrified even. Because all that emotion meant I wasn't going to be able to pull the trigger if I had the chance. Not in self defense. Not out of anger for what he'd done to Herakles, the forest, my adopted family. Herakles had trained me to contain my emotions when it came to survival and I wasn't able to do that now that I knew the history between Adonis and me.

Seeing him for the first time in the backyard, when he came to visit the night after I'd woken him ... the fleecy softness of his wings ... his scent ... how he'd gently wrapped me in his wings ...

Oh, gods. That was where I first smelled him. It was why he was familiar to me even in the human form I never saw as a child.

How could I defeat him when I didn't think I'd have the heart to try?

There's another way to win. Help me remind him who he is. The voice was almost too soft to hear.

"You're stalling," he said.

Blinking, I shifted towards the next set of weapons, short swords. Images from the night he tried to save me, when he picked me up gently from the tree house and hovered off the ground, flew through my mind.

I love you, Mismatch.

Mismatch. It was the name I gave him when I was a child.

Shivering, my hand dropped from the table. "I remember how soft they were," I said.

Silence. For a moment, I didn't think he had heard.

"Softer than velvet. Blacker than night, and wider than the courtyard."

"What're you talking about?" A tight, hushed note was in his voice. I heard him pad closer and tensed, uncertain if he believed in fair fights or just winning, and what he'd do since he knew the stakes.

"Your wings."

His breath caught. He was so tense, I eased a hand toward a knife.

"You're a grotesque by night, human by day, brought to life around twelve years–" I continued.

His fist smashed into the table, and I leapt back, without one of the precious knives.

Adonis was unhinged for the first time since I'd met him. "Who told you?" he demanded, eyes blazing and face flushed. He stepped towards me, and I had the impression of a lion about to attack.

I really had no other way to defend myself except with words. I raised my hands and kept my voice low, steady and calm as I responded. "No one told me. I remember. Mnemosyne showed me what I forgot."

"Which was what exactly?"

"Mismatch."

"That's not possible." He snatched the material of my shirt and shoved me into a column, keeping me in place with his strong frame and the forearm across my throat. I was silent and too aware that I was out of knowledge about him. I hadn't known much about him at all when I was younger. "No one knows that name." His low voice was a threat, his eyes pinned to mine.

Uncomfortable yet not about to try to move, I struggled to pin down emotions that were starting to race within me. My first instinct was to either run or fight, and it was the wrong time for either reaction. I hadn't learned everything about handling the world I thought I had when leaving the forest. Determining the best way not to get killed was unexpectedly difficult.

We stared at each other in a thick silence. I had never been this close to a man – other than Herakles, who didn't count – never had my body pressed to another's. I was torn between believing the grotesque who risked his life for me when I was young would never hurt me and knowing the muscular body I was once more experiencing could destroy me before I had a chance to speak again.

And then there was the other emotion, the one tied to my fevered insides and the fluttering of my stomach that seemed ridiculously out of place at a time like this. Adonis was ... attractive. More so now that I knew he could turn into a mythical monster, which was beyond intriguing. Even more so after seeing him rescue me when I was a child. From the eyes that resembled the gem at my chest to the quiet intensity and self-assurance, he could outrun, outsmart and out maneuver me, all of which were Herakles' conditions for any boy to get near me.

He was kind of incredible.

Assuming he didn't kill me. I studied his perfect features. He was ... struggling. Though against what, I couldn't tell. I sure as Hades wasn't resisting. It had to be the goddess trying to make him remember.

"Your nose is bleeding again," I ventured.

He touched it with his free hand and gazed briefly at the blood. Glassiness crossed his eyes. With no warning, he stepped back and shook his head, stumbled another step and weaved on his feet.

I stared at him, not expecting the weird weakness to return. He had displayed none of it upon our first meeting.

"How did you know of my ... condition?" he asked and rested the heel of one palm against his temple.

"Condition?" I repeated. "Sounds like you're sick, but you're not. You're a grotesque."

He shot me a warning look and this time, I saw the pain.

The image of him on the kitchen floor distracted me long

enough to cost me the chance to reach for a knife on the table. Able to read his opponent, he shifted between me and the table without raising his guard.

I did the only thing I could. "We met twelve years ago," I started, at a loss as to what else to do except to talk. My new memories were crisp and clear. "You were a statue on the Temple of Artemis. I woke you up one day, and you came to visit me later that night. I awoke ... your stuffed animal, too. Her name is Mrs. Nettles. I didn't understand why you had her at first but now I get it. She's kind of alive and has been since you met her."

He lifted his head, the tension creeping back into his frame. *He does not like to talk about this.* "You tried to rescue me when I was little but got uh ... hurt." I barely stopped from mentioning who hurt him. How he let Herakles go when he'd nearly killed him ...

"Hurt," he repeated. His intent gaze shifted to me.

Unless he can't remember either. His scrutiny supported Mnemosyne's claim.

"You know. Fell out of the sky. Both of us did."

"I don't just fall out of the sky. Something happened."

"You, uh, have a scar here?" I asked and touched one side then the other. "And here?"

His head lowered, and his predatory glare gave me chills.

"You were rescuing me and got stabbed," I continued.

"By whom?" He stepped towards me.

I very wisely began to step back at the same speed. "Not by me!" I exclaimed. "I was six."

"But you know who did it."

"It was kind of a long time ago."

A knife appeared in one of his hands.

"What's important is that you don't want to hurt me. You shouldn't hurt me, I mean," I said. "We aren't enemies."

"Enough. Draw your weapons."

"I don't have any."

He winced and ceased stalking me, one hand hovering at his head again. I didn't know enough about the ribbons to understand what they were supposed to tell me.

"This isn't a normal headache, is it? "I asked. "Mnemosyne is trying to show you what you've forgotten."

"Not your concern." He wobbled on his feet. Seconds later, he dropped to his knee, holding his head.

I studied him. "You can't remember me but when we're around each other, something happens to you," I guessed. "You feel the connection, don't you?"

He said nothing. He was regulating his breathing as if to calm himself.

"I named you Mismatch," I added. "After I awoke you. Do you remember that?"

No response.

Squatting to see his face better, I kept my distance, not about to end up shredded because he snapped.

"How do I help you remember?" I studied the ribbons around him. All were agitated, though one in particular had ragged edges along one side. I had seen the little-me of twelve years ago smooth out Herakles ragged, discolored Franken-ribbons.

I stretched out a hand the way I saw myself do it twelve years ago and began tracing the edge of the ribbon with my finger, trying to smooth it out. Just when I was about to give up and flush with embarrassment about swiping at random things no one else could see, the edges folded. One by one, the ridges disappeared.

Adonis shuddered. His eyes were closed.

"Did that do anything?" I asked awkwardly. "If you didn't feel anything then never mind. If you remember falling ..."

"I dropped you." The hoarse whisper carried a note of pain. "We were both falling."

My heart leapt. "Yes! You went through the roof and Herakles caught me."

His head flew up. "Herakles threw the javelin." By the flare of fire in his eyes, he wasn't going to be content to imprison Herakles next time they met.

"Yeah. We need to get past that part," I suggested. *Although, if it's true Herakles killed my parents ...* It wasn't the right time. Not until I was certain Adonis wasn't about to try to kill me. "You remember me. You know why you can't kill me?"

A guarded smile tugged up the side of his lips. "You love me."

I flushed. "No. Baby Alessandra did. I think ... I think we might one day get along, so long as you don't decide to kill me."

He held my gaze, amused yet still tense.

"And, for the record, she loved the gargoyle version of you. She never met this you," I added self-consciously, hating my blush and flustered disclaimer.

"Grotesque. Gargoyles have water spouts." He stood as he spoke. I did as well and resisted the urge to put more space between us.

"Adonis ... Mismatch ... whatever you want to be called. Are you going to force me to fight you or not?" I asked. "Because I ... I can't live with something happening to you." These were dangerous words born of emotion, but I couldn't get the image of him falling, bleeding, out of my mind.

He was holding his head again. "You're older." He faced me. "I forgot how quickly humans age."

"I have no idea what to say to that. You didn't age much at all."

"I'm only human half a day."

"Right. Anyway ... about this." I gestured towards the table. "The trial."

He cocked his head to the side, as if listening. I tried to hear what he did with no success.

"What is it?" I asked.

"Either I fight you or we're both in trouble."

Even as I said it, I inched towards the table. "Trouble doesn't sound so bad."

His gaze settled on me. I had a feeling he was trying to reconcile a bunch of new information, freed memories, before he revealed his intention. I wanted to empathize after the experience I still couldn't wrap my head around, but my greatest concern was surviving.

"It's the kind of trouble we may not escape." He strode to

the table and picked up two more knives. "The Supreme Priest is furious."

"We," I repeated, my heart accelerating. "So ... we're a *we*."

He glanced at me before tossing over two knives.

Catching them, I almost shouted with relief. *Thank the gods.* I wasn't going to be forced into a battle with him this day, and I'd managed to defer it without shedding a drop of blood.

Adonis approached once more, this time holding out a third knife. Gazing up at him, I accepted it.

"We're, like, BFFs now?" I asked skeptically.

"I do not understand everything yet," he replied. "But I remember you. I remember you giving me life." He was quiet for a moment. I sensed turmoil though he displayed none of it. "I remember swearing to protect you."

"I can take care of myself," I objected softly.

"Not against me."

The truth scared me.

"If I refuse to face you, I cede the trial. You will triumph by default."

"I'm okay with that," I said.

He bowed his head once, and a thrill rippled through me. I'd passed my first trial, even if by accident.

I had the sense of gravity shifting, of the world around me changing rapidly enough to make my stomach turn. Rather than move, I gazed up at Adonis, once more mesmerized by his gaze and the sense of connectedness between us. And ... more than a little worried he meant to betray or otherwise feed me to his boss at some point.

The sensations ceased and were replaced by a different sound: the roaring of a crowd. Blood and sweat were in the air. The ground beneath our feet turned from concrete to dirt.

"What's happening?" We were at the center of a crude arena, surrounded by an audience on bleachers that stretched twenty meters upward. The shape, scents and ceiling overhead gave away our location as being one of the seedy, criminal underground fighting rings, the type Niko probably frequented.

"My master is displeased."

"Did you do this?" I breathed.

"No. This is where he sends me to punish me."

I stared at him. "You work for a man who sends you to a death match when you mess up?"

"You're weak on your left," Adonis said and shifted to that side of me.

"You're going to … defend me on that side or kill me?" I asked.

"Swords." His gaze was on a weapons display at the side of the arena. Without answering me, he trotted towards it and withdrew two short swords, twirling them to test them.

I watched. It made sense to know how to use a knife in this day and age, but a sword? He was deftly checking their balance, maneuvering them with his normal fleeting agility and running quickly through a few weapons forms. Satisfied, he returned, pausing to gaze at me. I saw the flicker of confusion, the only indication he was about as clear about us as I was.

"I can't remember why I saved you all those years ago," he

said finally. "Did you deserve it?"

"Dude, I was six." I shifted under his intent look. "Truce for now?"

"I don't do things without a reason and I can't decipher why I should spare you."

"It's a feeling."

"Instinct."

I rolled my eyes. "Whatever. You just know you can't hurt me because we're bound somehow."

"Yes."

The gates at one end of the arena rolled open, and the crowd hushed in anticipation. I stared into the depths of the doorway. I wasn't feeling as enthusiastic as usual about the prospect of fighting someone. Whatever was there had four ribbons. Not that I had a clue what that meant. Adonis had five.

"C'mon, Adonis. Just tell me we have a truce so I'm not paranoid about you stabbing me in the back."

"None is needed." He stepped forward and tested his swords again.

"Stop with the mind games!" I snapped. "I just need a yes or no. That's it!"

"The Supreme Priest had one chance to win you with his trial. I ceded it to you. Do you think I'm going to kill you now?"

"No offense, Adonis, but I don't have a clue how your mind works." I withdrew two knives and faced the direction he was. "What in Hades is that?" I stared as some … thing began to emerge from the darkness of the doorway. It wasn't human, and it was huge. Just when I thought my world couldn't become any more foreign to me ...

ℱOURTEEN

In all things of nature there is something of the marvelous.
– ARISTOTLE

"ℐS THAT A *MANTICORE?*" MY MOUTH WAS OPEN.

"Yeah," Adonis answered. "Big one, too. Their breeding program is getting better."

"Breeding …" I couldn't think let alone ask. The male version of a sphinx had a shaggy human head, the body of a lion and bat-like wings. He was also the size of a Clydesdale with fangs and talons that were twice the length of my index fingers.

"The beast games are the Triumvirate's covert way of keeping local citizens focused on this side of the wall. Largest gambling events in the world. Technically illegal and secretly supported by the Triumvirate."

"That's impossible," I managed finally, watching the creature emerge from the depths of the arena.

"I'm beginning to think you grew up in a hole in the

ground, not in a forest."

It was the worst time possible to tease me. I was about to pass out.

"Snap out of it." He nudged me. "It's just a fight. You're good at fights." Adonis was focused yet not worried.

I was. I'd seen a tiny monster in a dreamland that didn't exist. I had no idea monsters were real. "Okay. I can do this," I murmured and drew a breath.

"Can you use a sword?"

"Normal people don't use swords, Adonis."

"Not sure where I learned. I can't remember that far back yet." A smile pulled up one side of his mouth. "You're far from normal. Try it." He handed me one of his.

It was well balanced but somewhat awkward and a bit heavy. But considering the distance I'd need to be to wound the beast with a knife …

"You're enjoying this," I said, studying him.

"I need the outlet."

We both did. From strangers and enemies to a shared history where we were besties, I doubted even sharp Adonis knew what to think. My shock began to wear off as I evaluated the creature for weaknesses.

"It doesn't bother you that your boss sends you to fight monsters when he's mad?"

"No."

This guy is something else.

The monster roared and the packed auditorium cheered.

I handed the sword back, eyed the beast standing outside its gate, and jogged to the weapons. Tucking knives in a cargo pocket and one at my waist, I hefted two swords and returned to the center of the ring beside Adonis.

"Any tips?" I asked. *Aside from begging Ares to bless us.*

He moved a meter away then two. "Beware the tail. Keep its attention divided. You have the speed and ability. If we can coordinate our attacks, keep it off guard, one of us will have a kill shot."

I didn't have time to thank him before the beast was upon us.

It charged towards me first and swiped with a paw the size of my torso. I arched back and watched razor talons soar inches over my head. Instincts kicked in, and I smashed one arm into it to keep its momentum from shifting back. It rounded on Adonis.

The whip like tail smashed into my calves and knocked me onto the ground. I rolled, the world a combination of dirt and monster, and leapt to my feet, ducked a second swipe and slashed a scratch in its side.

"Tail!" Adonis called.

I jumped up. The tail swept beneath my legs, and I was starting to feel somewhat smarter than the beast when the manticore donkey kicked me with one leg. I sprawled onto my back, the air knocked from my lungs.

Its tail sailed over my body as Adonis kept it occupied.

"You alive?" he called.

It took a moment for air to reach my lungs once more. "Yeah." I climbed to my feet.

He was moving and fighting with the agility I envied. The crowd roared when the manticore knocked him off his feet. Adonis rolled away.

"Hey!" I shouted to the ugly creature. With some timing and a whole lot of luck, I plunged a sword into its writhing tail. It snapped the tail another direction, taking one sword with it.

The manticore rounded on me, and I glimpsed its fanged mouth up close. With a roar, it began swiping and snapping.

Pure adrenaline drove my reflexes. It was all I could do not to get smashed by the creature, and I focused on movement rather than striking.

"On your left." Adonis' words were quiet, half a second before I smacked into him.

He steadied me with one arm, lashing out with the other, and nudged me back to my feet. He bore a red streak down one arm.

"New plan. Move with me!" he ordered.

We maneuvered and faced the beast. It withdrew to study us, paced and then launched again. I stayed with Adonis, finding it easier than I thought to fight at his side. I didn't have to look at him or worry about whether I was about to crash into him again. His enhanced instincts kept us in tandem, and my sense of connectedness gave me a sixth sense about where he was.

I finally began to see where I had a shot to attack rather than deflect and duck and made my first effort to slash at the beast. I cut it across the cheek. Rather than retreat like I had hoped, it roared and flung itself at me instead. This time, its speed was more like Adonis' than mine, and all I could do was watch it leap in slow motion, immobilized.

The beast was fast; Adonis was faster. He smashed into me milliseconds before the enraged beast. One of its talons tore down my back, and fire spread throughout me.

We hit the ground and rolled, landing side by side, Adonis on his belly and me on my blazing back. I cursed, unaccustomed to this level of pain.

"You overextended," he said and hopped to his feet. He hauled me up.

The beast was pacing once more, blood seeping from several wounds into the dirt. The crowd was at a roar, and both of us were now hurt.

Adonis spun me to check my back. "Superficial. Will bleed a lot," he said after a quick assessment. He stepped in closer, until his body met mine, and gripped my wrist. "Quick lesson in sword fighting. The blade is an extension of you." He moved my arm through several motions. "You're not used to having a six foot reach but you need to use it. Here" he stabbed "not here." He did it again, this time pulling me off balance. "You need to feel the space between you and the tip of the blade. Got it?"

I nodded.

His warmth left my back but not my body entirely, and I faced him and the beast, not understanding the draw or why his touch stirred up something inside me. Grimacing, I stretched back. The wound was hurting bad, and blood trickled down my pants.

"You remember how Bellepheron defeated the cerebus?" he asked.

"Yes! He flew away on Pegasus. Are you going to turn into Mismatch soon?" I asked, excited.

"No. I was thinking you could be the one who flies." The gleam in his eye was new, and I didn't know him well enough to know if it was humor or … opportunity that caused it. Or maybe he was having *fun* fighting a monster because his boss was mad.

"Explain."

"I'll launch you onto his back. You ram a sword through the back of his skull."

The beast was starting towards us again. "That's your plan."

"You got a better one?"

Sadly, I didn't. Reading my expression, he whipped off his belt and looped it around my hand and the sword hilt.

"Not that I don't trust you to hang onto it," he said. "Ready?"

"Sure." My heart was flying, my back burning, and I had the urge to push reset on everything that had happened the past few days.

We both looked towards the creature barreling towards us. Adonis bent, and I placed one foot firmly in his clasped hands. He twisted us to where my back was to the creature.

"We're a good pair," I said, needing some affirmation when my heart was ready to leap out of my chest. I wanted to trust that he wasn't going to feed me to the charging beast I couldn't see.

I could hear it, though, even above the roar of the crowd. It sounded like it was on us.

Adonis gave me an odd look, neither agreeing nor disagreeing. Heat warmed my cheeks. We really weren't on the same page, despite being trapped here fighting monsters and our shared experiences in the past.

"Or whatever. Just throw me."

"Land on your feet." It was the only warning he gave. One moment I was holding my breath, afraid of having my head snapped off and the next, I was soaring through the air. He hefted me high enough that I did a flip and watched as he slashed at the beast and ducked below it as it leapt.

I didn't land on my feet. I pancaked onto its back and grabbed the mane with both hands, grateful Adonis had thought to tie the sword to my wrist. I straddled the beast just as it reared and clung to it with thighs and hands. It bucked the moment its front legs hit the ground, and I was flung forward.

The jarring ride left me thinking I'd never have the ability to steady myself.

"Ready in three …"

Startled, I sat up the best I could at his countdown and managed to grab the flopping sword.

"Two!"

Holy Hades! There's no way I –

"One!"

I gripped the hilt with two hands, pushed my torso as far back as I could, and planted the sword at the base of its skull. It reared, impaling itself, and suddenly went limp.

217

Tumbling off the back, I hit the ground hard and heard it hit the ground beside me harder. The crowd was going nuts, screaming and air horns blaring. I stared at the pipes running across the ceiling.

Adonis crouched near me. "We'll make a good team after you learn a few things."

I twisted my head. "What in the name of Olympus does that mean?" I groaned and pushed myself up.

He didn't answer. The man lived to be enigmatic. Standing, he held out his hand. I glanced up at him and took it. He pulled me up easily, and we both turned to gaze at the dead beast.

"So do we win? Is your boss no longer angry?" I asked hopefully.

"Too easy to appease him." His gaze went around the crowd and settled on the gate on the opposite side of the arena from the one the manticore entered. "Yeah. Too easy."

"Just tell whoever runs this place who you are."

"This was ordered by the Supreme Priest. Who I was to him stopped mattering when I refused to fight you."

Of everything he'd said, this hit the hardest. "You potentially walked away from your job and him for me?"

"Come on. We need what rest the crowd will give us." He started towards the gate yawning open. "You need a few lessons in sword fighting, too."

I watched him, unable to shake my astonishment. I thought him undecided about assisting me when the opposite was true. He was all in.

Maybe some part of the man I knew twelve years ago

remains. I hurried after him, grimacing at the pain in my back.

We stepped out of the bright arena into the low lit area behind the scenes where a line of fifteen guards with guns stood waiting for us. These were mercenaries if I'd ever seen them. Dressed differently than one another, some unkempt, in different levels of quality of dress.

"This way." One motioned for us to head down a hallway wide enough for a car.

I walked with Adonis, and we trailed the man who spoke down a long hall. It emptied out into an area of crude cells, some with handcuffed men and others with men lying on cots or eating.

We got our own cell, this one with four concrete walls, as if his boss had a clue what Adonis became at night. The man we followed opened the door, and we stepped into it.

"You fight again first thing in the morning," he said as he closed the door behind us.

A small first aid kit and two trays of mushy cafeteria food and rolls sat on one cot. A five gallon container of water was at the foot of the second, and the corner contained a metal toilet and sink. At least, a curtain shielded the bathroom area from the rest of the cell.

"Home, sweet, home," I murmured and looked around.

Adonis went to the first aid kit and picked it up, opening it to check its contents. "Shirt off. We'll get bandaged up and work on some moves."

I hesitated. I'd never taken off my clothes in front of anyone. He glanced at me.

Turning my back to him, I peeled my shirt over my head without removing it completely. I used the material to cover my breasts. "Ow!"

He said nothing. The moment his fingers touched my bare back, I jumped. Embarrassed, I cursed myself silently and was still when he tried again. He cleaned the wound quickly.

"You take a beating well," he stated.

"Thanks."

"It's more important than people realize."

I sighed. His version of small talk sucked. "Do you have a plan?"

"Survive until my boss forgives me or makes enough money on the odds that he's appeased."

"Or they leave you out at night."

"He knows what I am. That won't happen."

Will he let you die? I didn't want to know the answer to the question and kept it to myself. The silence was awkward, and I sought a new topic. "So you kept Mrs. Nettles all this time without remembering why."

"I assumed she came from my childhood."

"Why couldn't you remember anything?"

"Why couldn't you?"

I had no idea. Was this a secret Herakles would know? "You know it's not normal for a toy to walk and talk, right?"

"It's not normal for a man to turn into a grotesque every night. I knew she was special. Just not why."

"Did you feel a connection to her?" I asked, mind on the gem at my chest.

His hand paused. "Of sorts."

I tugged the gem free and turned. "This is yours. Do you remember it?"

He wiped his hand on his pants and lifted the gem, studying it. "It's familiar. But I can't remember."

"You gave it to me after I awoke you."

"From the Temple." He met my gaze. "I see glimpses of the past. I was someone else before I was stone."

Feeling a little claustrophobic with him so close, I pulled the gem free and turned once more. "I didn't know you then." I focused on the ribbons in the room around me as he finished. "I need to learn to use them."

"Swords?"

"No." I waved at the cell. "I can ... see strands of ... life. Around everything. I smoothed out one of yours and you remembered me. I used them to bring Mrs. Nettles to life when I was little and to ..." I paused, not sure I was ever going to be ready to figure out what I had done to Herakles.

"To what?"

"I'm not sure. I changed Herakles. Somehow."

"Herakles." His voice was a pitch lower. "You remembered something that makes you doubt you should've saved him?"

"No, never. I'll always save him."

"Something changed."

"Nothing."

"You were a terrible liar before you fixed me. It's easier for me to tell now. You're curling your toes."

"How in Hades do you know that?" I looked down, not

realizing I was doing as he said until I focused on my toes.

"I can feel what you do."

"What?" Pulling my shirt back over my head, I faced him and stepped back. "That's kind of creepy."

"Your ribs on the left side are stiff, probably bruised, and your wrist is burned from the belt."

I rubbed my wrist. "I take it back. That's freakish."

"When you felt the connection, it was normal. When I do, it's freakish?" He tossed the rag he'd been using on my back.

"This," I swept my hands down my body, "is mine to know what's going on. Don't mess with me! None of your damn mind tricks, Adonis!"

He gave one of his almost smiles. "I wasn't this time."

"Oh, but you do admit to doing it before?"

"It's in my nature. Predators sometimes toy with others."

"I think I want my own cell," I complained. My body was starting to cool down and stiffen. "Can you read my mind?"

"No."

"Would you tell me if you could?"

"No."

I glared at him.

"It's a matter of self-preservation," he said. "Don't sit down. You need to learn to handle a sword."

I was almost looking forward to it, to compare the training methods of the Chief of SISA and Herakles, and to get out of the awkward discussions I had with him.

"Basic drills …"

For the next hour or so, Adonis showed me a few basic

moves that would've been useful in the arena. He was surprisingly patient, more so than Herakles. When the basics were done, we spared lightly in the confines of the room for another fifteen minutes before he called it quits.

He ate like the beast I knew him to be, and I watched, amused that someone who came across as polished held the very definition of a feral side. "You ever hear of a fork?"

"Ever kissed a boy?"

I gasped. "That is not cool!" I flung my roll at him.

He caught it and bit into it without responding verbally, but my appetite was mostly gone. I *hated* to be embarrassed, to know he was probably judging me like the nymphs and priests and everyone else did.

He lifted his head and tilted it. His gaze went to the door a full twenty seconds before I heard a key in the lock. A man armed to the teeth and flanked by four more guards entered. His guards stayed outside, but he didn't close the door.

"Niko," I growled.

"Hey, kid. You put on quite a show." He gave a sly smile. "Welcome to the underworld. This is a good place to supplement your income, assuming you survive or know how to gamble."

"Ever the mercenary. Can you get us out?" I demanded and set the tray aside, standing.

"I don't plan on it." His gaze went to Adonis. "You in trouble, Adonis?" His smile was wide, his expression almost gleeful. "What's it like to view the world when you can't look down on it anymore?" He stepped forward.

A surge of protectiveness, or maybe possessiveness, shot through me. I recalled too clearly seeing Adonis hurt twelve years ago and moved to block Niko's progress into our cell.

"What do you want?" I demanded, glaring up at him. "Like you haven't already messed up my life enough!"

"Shut up, kid. You're damned lucky I came along when I did, or you'd be sitting on that stump afraid to leave your forest."

I flushed.

"Someone like you need a guard dog?" Niko directed this to Adonis.

If I had any idea how to twist or tug the ribbons over him to turn him into some sort of animal, I would have.

"You came to gloat." Adonis stood at my back, close enough for me to feel his heat once more.

"Damn right I did," Niko said. "The Supreme Priest told my boss what happened with the trial. No way even he would forgive something like this. I might apply for your position at SISA."

"They don't take your kind."

"No matter." Niko's jaw ticked, but he forced a smile. "Hey, kid. Your new friend tell you about his prisons and the heretics he collects? People like the priests you knew get thrown into melting chambers where they're dissolved alive. The worst end up at the House. I can't even imagine what kind of torture Adonis commits there."

I didn't back down, though I had to admit, I was wondering about the extent of Adonis' actions, whether the fear of the priests and others was justified. To know he was connected to me, that I had brought him to life, and he massacred people …

"Leave us alone," I said quietly. "Watch from the stands like everyone else."

"Trust me, kid, I'll be there next time you fight. No love lost between Adonis and me, though I don't wish you a slow death like I do him."

"I can feel the love," I said sarcastically. "Dosy know you're here? Probably why she won't let you see your son."

Niko reached out to grab me. Adonis snatched his wrist with his lightning speed. I blinked but didn't otherwise move.

"Watch it, kid. The Supreme Magistrate still wants you. When Adonis is gone, I'll be there to pick you up, the only thing standing between you and your fate." Niko growled. He wrenched free, turned and left.

The door slammed behind him.

"What possesses you to challenge men who can beat you?" Adonis asked.

I shifted away from him and went back to my cot to sit. "I'm not afraid of men. Monsters, yeah."

"You should feel the opposite."

"How so?"

"Men can think. They can act maliciously. Monsters are instinctual by nature. Some are more aggressive than others and some trained to fight but they're not malicious."

"You're both?"

"The worst of all. An intelligent predator."

"Are you upset the Supreme Priest might let you die here?"

I asked.

"I'm not the regretting type." He set his empty tray of food on the ground. The question was on the tip of my tongue, and need to know what kind of horrific acts he'd committed sending guilt through me. Herakles had killed my parents, but what had Adonis done? How many people had died because I let something like him loose into the world?

"The muscles between your shoulder blades. They get tense when you're … upset," he said.

"Stop!" He was right. Not that I'd ever noticed that, either. My wound was painful and blazing despite the medicine he smeared on it. "How do you know how to use a sword anyway? Are you from the same place as Niko?"

"The Gladiator Guild? No." Adonis sat on his cot. "I'm not sure. It's from the life before I was a grotesque. It has something to do with my mark." He traced his thumb over an omega shaped birthmark on his wrist.

"I've got one, too." I pulled up my sleeve to display the double omega.

He studied it. "That explains a few things."

"Meaning …"

"Part of an old legend that spooks the gods," he said. "There's a prophecy about a final Oracle as strong as the original who opened the gate for them to come here. The legend foretells that this second Oracle will be strong enough to cut them off from their power and banish them permanently from Earth."

"I've heard that before. It's what I'm supposed to do. And

bring back the Old Ways."

"Do you know what it would take for them to return?"

"Please don't say Armageddon."

"Then you do know."

Such destruction was beyond my ability to imagine. But I could see Adonis setting fire to the world without a second chance. "Why ... how can you be this way with me and scare everyone else to the point they'll commit suicide rather than deal with you?"

"You want to know if I'm as bad as they say."

My mouth was dry. I nodded.

"Yeah. I am." His features were calm, his gaze steady. "Does that change things for you?"

I no longer wanted to discuss this with him. I looked away, seeking yet another subject that wouldn't end with my body so tense, I felt ready to pop. "Do you think the same person wiped both of our memories?"

"It's possible. It happened around the same time, and we knew each other."

I nibbled on the last of my food then sat back.

Adonis and I stared at one another. In addition to his bright eyes, his perfect features were worthy of visual exploration. Wide shoulders and chest, a lean frame and long legs with thick thighs completed the man I could not for the life of me figure out. I wasn't even certain I wanted to. While I respected his physical prowess in the arena, I was uncomfortable in the downtime when his attention was on me. I always had been. Always wanted to put more space than I had between us. His

body, and I flushed when they fell to his groin.

"Thank the gods. Monsters come with …" I motioned to him and silently screamed at myself for being stupid. "… loin clothes."

I can remove it if you find it offensive, the soft whisper came from inside my mind.

"No! Oh, my gods!" I'd never been more humiliated.

He was amused. His fanged smile was scarier than Herakles'.

"Okay," I said and swallowed hard. "We survived your first change." Although I felt like hyperventilating at the thought he could morph into a creature. He resembled a gargoyle with his heavy, uneven features built to scare.

You clench your right fist when you're scared.

"Wait a minute!" I yelled and shook out the tension of my right arm. "A teddy bear talking in my head is one thing. You don't get to do that!"

I cannot communicate with you otherwise.

"I'm good with not communicating. Be a good monster and don't talk to me."

He tilted his head and pointed behind me. My eyes stuck to the long talon extending from his grey hand. He had torn four men limb from limb to protect me. I had the sudden desire to sleep with a sword this night.

He pointed again.

I turned and leapt back. The cot and cup were both alive. The cot was bumping silently against the wall. The cup rolled back and forth, unable to right itself with the handle in its way.

"Holy Hades," I breathed. "I really did it."

The cot changed directions and started towards me. I backpedaled, amazed yet … sort of freaked out by the weird display. I smacked into Adonis, who steadied me. Shoving his hands away, I tripped over the walking cot and went down with it, both of us tangled and thrashing. Something ripped, and I shoved the cot off me and scrambled to my feet.

"Shit. Okay." I caught my breath. The cot had gotten stuck on the other one and torn down the center. The cup began to roll towards me. "Nope. We're done with this." I plucked the green ribbon from it and the cot and lowered my hand, not sure what to do with them. Light as air yet mine to control, I finally patted them against my thigh. They disappeared.

Well handled.

I risked a look at the creature, who was watching with his arms crossed, exposing roped forearms. The muscles of his athletic frame were perfectly defined under tight gray skin. I caught myself staring too long and shook my head. "You seriously look like this every night?" I managed finally.

He bowed his head.

"I see why I called you Mismatch. Your ears and face are …"

He growled.

"… lopsided but beautiful. Like, you are incredible, Adonis." I cleared my throat. "Never mind. I think I destroyed the cots. Hope you don't mind sleeping on the floor."

He extended a wing.

I eyed it.

I sleep on them.

I hesitated then touched the inside of one wing carefully. The downy fleece lining it was softer than anything I'd ever felt. "Wow." I ran both hands through the strange fur, smiling despite being weirded out by everything that had happened recently. "I can see why. These are incredible." I also innately understood little-me's fascination with the creature. Stunning did not begin to describe him, and the wings made me want to melt into them and sleep forever.

Because I was finally beginning to feel the drain of the insanity I'd been through.

You are tired. I can feel it.

"Bad monster!"

Mismatch moved the dead cots to the back of the cell and wrapped himself in one wing then lay down, spreading out the other on the ground. Oddly enough, I was less nervous around the monster. He was scary, yes, but something about Adonis left me self-conscious and rattled.

"You don't bite do you?" I asked.

Only when warranted.

I rolled my eyes. The monster that so gently picked up Mrs. Nettles and me was less scary than the man I couldn't read.

"I won't hurt them will I?" I asked, pulling off my shoes and socks. I sat down with a grimace, my back hurting.

No.

I rested my hands on the wing then let them sink into its plushness, soon grinning from the softness. "This is amazing!" I stretched out carefully onto my belly and rested a cheek against it. His scent was everywhere, and I sighed.

The wing rolled around me, and I went with it, surrounded by warmth and softness unlike anything I'd ever experienced. The rolling stopped and loosened, easing out from around me without releasing.

"I'm a human burrito!" I said cheerfully. "Do you eat humans?"

No.

I closed my eyes, intending to relax for a few minutes, but ended up toppling into deep slumber.

FIFTEEN

Gentleness is the antidote for cruelty.
– PHAEDRUS

BANGING ON THE DOOR JARRED ME AWAKE. I BLINKED, not recalling where I was until I saw the dreary concrete walls. I was warm despite the damp chill of morning underground in a place with no central heat or air conditioning and lifted my head. My body was sore, my back aching and feeling like the wound would tear if I dared move. The sound of metal trays sliding on concrete floors came a second before the door clanged shut.

Falling asleep with a monster wasn't as strange as waking up with Adonis. One of his arms was draped over me, and we were spooning. He was wearing pants, thank the gods, or I would've totally lost it. I did sneak a peek at the smooth, rounded muscles of his chest and biceps. There wasn't much about him that didn't amaze me.

"How's the back?" he asked without opening his eyes.

I really despised how he did that. "Awesome. Ready for another go!"

"Good."

I wasn't fooling either of us, but I didn't care. I pushed to my knees and moved away from him, sweeping one last look down his body. Ugh. He was perfect. Aside from the homicidal tendencies, the mental games and the fact he had access to too-much-information when it came to me.

I got to my feet, and groaned aloud. "Oh, gods that hurts!"

Adonis said nothing. He stood, displaying none of the aches and pains I did. I straightened all the way. I didn't feel remotely ready for another day in the ring.

Someone had brought us a mushy breakfast. I bit back another groan as I picked up both trays from the door and brought them to the center of the room. Adonis was dressing, and I sat heavily.

"You know you snore?" he asked.

Awkward did not begin to explain the close quarters. I ate without responding and willed my body to stop aching quite so much.

"You ready for today?"

I continued to ignore him, not in the mood for shape shifting grotesques or their annoying SISA chief personas.

"Not talking." Was he amused? I didn't dare acknowledge him with a look.

We ate, and he pulled out the first aid kit. I watched for a split second as he rolled up a sleeve and prepared to bandage the nasty looking wound on his arm.

"I can do that," I said.

He said nothing about me breaking my silence but held out the bandage. I shifted forward and took it. I wrapped his forearm carefully, how Herakles taught me. When finished, I sat back and admired the work briefly.

"Your guardian taught you well," Adonis said.

"Yep." I looked at him for the first time this morning. It was true. I had already begun to reap the rewards of his training. And yet …

My parents. Today, after some good rest, I was starting to think differently about the issue I brushed off yesterday. I was good at denying things I didn't want to deal with. Or … emotional issues, because I'd been taught by example to ignore feelings in favor of action. Was that because Herakles himself didn't know how to deal with what he'd done?

Lost in dark thought, I was gazing into Adonis' eyes. Heat warmed my cheeks. He was too enigmatic for me to begin to guess if he knew what I was thinking.

"You razed my forest." I needed the reminder that the man before me was no better than the man Herakles had been. I was kind of afraid of learning to trust someone to find their secrets unbearable, and Adonis struck me as someone who had a lot to hide.

"I did. No better way to drive out a herd of deer than to take their home away."

"I saw you at the lake. I gave away the location, didn't I?"

He nodded. "I can sense more than how you feel. I can

sense where you are, when the red cord is off."

"That's creepy." Adonis wasn't the kind of man to offer condolences or sympathy, but at least he wasn't messing with me. In fact, he'd been brutally honest when we spoke last night.

I didn't know what to think about the people around me or what I was supposed to be doing. I wasn't about to trust him. If my own guardian, who I spent twelve years treating as a father, had a past that horrified me, what had this ... creature done?

"I will protect you," he said quietly. "I make few promises in life, but this is one."

I'm not sure I believe him. I sensed he felt my turmoil. My body probably gave me away, and I rolled my shoulders to loosen the tension between them.

"I'm ready." I stood and stretched back. "You think the monster will be bigger today?"

"Much. And we'll know how mad the Supreme Priest still is."

Fifteen minutes later, we found out.

"What in Hades is that?" I whispered, staring through the gate into the arena at the monster facing off with no less than eight men armed with lances, swords, knives and axes.

"A sign the Supreme Priest isn't going to forgive me this time."

I searched his face. He was tense, but this was different than the man ready for battle. This was the tension of a man who was worried.

"I'm sorry," I murmured.

"For what?" He appeared genuinely curious.

"For you being punished because of me."

"Why would you apologize for someone else making a decision about his life?"

"Because I'm a nice person, you asshole!" I sighed. "Why are you so difficult?"

He studied me, the half-smile back. It never quite reached his beautiful eyes. "Obviously I enjoy baiting you."

I hadn't really found the side of him capable of being truly human yet. I rolled my eyes and tested the swords. My back was quaking, my strength half what it was yesterday. I went through several slow exercises.

"Thank you," he said softly.

"For what?" I grumbled.

"For caring about my fate. No one I can remember ever has."

My anger crumbled. Then he said something like this. Or rescued me. Or defied his boss, a member of the Triumvirate, and ended up in a death match with a monster. I began to suspect he simply didn't know how to be human, because he was good at it when he tried.

"That was a very good, human response," I told him. "People are supposed to care for one another. They aren't supposed to send their friends to face monsters."

"This is foreign to me."

I glanced at him to ensure he wasn't baiting me again. To my surprise, the self-admitted butcher of who knew how many people was serious. "You've never loved anyone? Been loved?"

"Only you."

I flushed.

"As a child, when you loved Mismatch," he added with a glimmer of amusement in his eyes. "That is all I know of love. Friends."

How did he do this? How could I want as far away from him as possible one moment and to hug him the next and assure a mass murderer that he, too, deserved to be loved?

"You never had a chance to be a real human, did you?" I managed.

"Why does that make you want to cry?"

"Stop with the body reading!" I sighed and swallowed the tightness in my throat. "Because … you might make a good human if you were given the chance to learn. You can be very kind, very thoughtful."

"And yet my kindness makes you tense."

"Yeah. Your bluntness, too."

"Thank you."

"You're welcome," I said. "Now we just need to teach you some eating manners, and you'll be set."

"And get you laid so you stop tensing up whenever I touch you."

I pushed him.

This time, his smile was real. It was dazzling, more beautiful than his eyes, and revealed dimples in his cheeks.

"Can you manipulate its ribbons?" he asked.

I blinked out of my surprise, grateful to focus on something outside of the two of us, even if it was the largest monster I'd ever seen.

The crowd was already twice as loud as yesterday when we'd won. People were on their feet, cheering on the creature shredding men two at a time in the arena before us.

The Typhon possessed four ribbons. I stepped forward and lifted a hand. Where I was able to grip the ribbons of anyone or anything, I couldn't quite grasp these. Whenever I tried, they shifted just out of reach. "This is weird. It's got some sort of defense mechanism."

"It's a Typhon. It's supposed to be buried beneath a mountain. It wouldn't surprise me to discover he's under the protection of some god or other."

"Looks like he got out," I said, distracted.

"Zeus alone was able to subdue him."

My hand dropped, and I faced him. "You can't be serious."

Adonis said nothing, and my eyes returned to the arena. I believed him. The massive monster had the upper body of a man and the lower body of an octopus, except each tentacle was a snake with fangs that exceeded the size of my hand.

The crowd burst into a frenzy.

The beast was tearing through the men as if they were standing still and not hacking at the snakeheads darting towards them. What the snakes didn't snatch and bite in two, the double-headed axe the creature held did the same.

I had never seen men die. In my dream or memory was one thing, but here … watching their blood spray into the air and coat the ground, hearing the crowd roar louder the more blood was shed …

I felt a little ill. It had never occurred to me to imagine what the inside of a human body looked like, and I was disgusted to see it didn't look much different than beef.

"I think I want to be a vegetarian," I whispered, not entirely certain how to handle the sight.

"You've never seen a man die?"

"No. Definitely never seen one torn in two."

"It's a quick death. There are many worse ways to die."

"You would know, wouldn't you?" I meant the words to be said too quiet for him to hear, but they came out normal. "And it's my fault you do know."

"Your fault?" I felt his eyes on me.

"I brought you to life. I unleashed whatever you did. Whatever you are."

"You make it sound as if I'm like this thing." He lifted his chin towards the arena.

"I don't know what you are. I've heard a few things about what SISA does to people," I replied. "Everyone is terrified of you in particular. Niko –"

"Niko can't be trusted with his dick."

I laughed, startled by the warm anger. "You guys don't get along. But even Dosy said you were dangerous."

"Dangerous, yes. A monster, no."

"You said you were as bad as everyone says, and I'm not about to trust you of all people after Herakles."

"Ah. There is something."

I didn't mean to say it aloud. He was far too curious about the relationship between Herakles and me. I didn't understand exactly why and prayed it wasn't because he knew something else about Herakles that would hurt me worse.

"What is it?" Adonis asked, nudging me in the side with his elbow.

"So you can't read minds. Thank the gods!"

"Is there more you don't want to share?"

"There's a shit ton that's not your business!" I snapped, glaring at him. "Why do you think *anything* about me is?" I was almost relieved that the gate chose that moment to open.

Amusement at my outburst glowed deep in his eyes. "You've been needling me since we met. I'm returning the favor."

"I haven't needled you," I retorted. "And I know that's not true. You may be able to feel what I do, but some of that carries over to me. I knew you were lying when you said this wasn't personal, and I know you're lying now. You want something from me, Adonis."

"Maybe." He drew both swords. "Or maybe there aren't many people I'm interested in, Alessandra. You're strong, beautiful and unique. You're destined for things you can't begin to imagine. You intrigue me."

"No more honesty! I preferred it when you barely said two words to me!"

"The Typhon awaits." He started into the arena. I was about to demand to know his plan when it hit me what he'd said.

Beautiful. The most incredible – yet freaky – man I'd ever met thought I was pretty. The knowledge made my insides warm and fluttery, and more adrenaline fed into my bloodstream. Adonis was definitely on a different scale than the silly boys I used to lure from the campground into the forest. The two were on opposite ends of the man spectrum. If we weren't about to die horribly at the hands of a monster ...

Focus, Alessandra. It didn't feel like a lie from him, but I sensed he wasn't telling me the full truth either. I followed into the arena.

Adonis waited for me to near before speaking again. "He's vulnerable from the waist up like any human. We're going to try to behead the snakes one by one. And ... if we're lucky, you'll figure out how to crush him with magic before he pulverizes us."

"This is a terrible plan," I muttered and joined him. My eyes went to an arm and head that had landed on this side of the ring before finding the pyramid of bloodied heads on one side.

The creature had killed dozens here today. For a long moment, I couldn't look away, and my stomach churned.

"Hey."

I blinked at Adonis' quiet voice and looked up at him.

"Herakles trained you well. You need some polishing, and it starts with focus. Eyes there." He pointed his sword at the creature headed towards us. "Never take them off your opponent."

"Okay." Not that staring down the monster was better than seeing the pile of heads. I stretched out a hand and tried again to grasp his ribbons. They remained evasive.

"He's going to swing the axe. We'll duck. And strike at the

same time at the head closest to us. Then bolt. Use that speed of yours to get clear of the head beside it."

"How do you know he's going to swing?" I studied the monster. It was almost upon us, and I was fighting the urge to run.

"Instinct." Adonis stepped a meter away, eyes trained on the target. "Wait until I say to move."

I trust you. For now. It wasn't possible to fight for our survival at his side and not trust him, even if my faith in him didn't extend outside the arena.

"Ready to duck on three …"

The hissing snakeheads were my size with long tongues and fangs that were far too close for my comfort. But I didn't move. If I knew one thing about Adonis, it was that he had a sixth sense when it came to predicting his opponent.

"Two."

A tongue nearly reached me. The giant swung his axe back.

"One."

The massive axe swung over our heads. At the same time, the snake nearest us darted forward. I stumbled to the side, not expecting its speed. It shrieked suddenly, and I saw Adonis raising his swords for a second strike. I hurried forward and joined him. The writhing snake body knocked me off my feet, and I vaulted back up, all too aware of the neighboring snakehead that was now trained on me.

"Drop and roll!" Adonis shouted.

I obeyed. I wasn't about to doubt him when my life was in his hands. The neighboring snake snapped into the air above my head then followed me, digging its fangs into the ground by my thigh as I rolled.

The monster bellowed in pain and anger, and I saw the axe start to drop again. With no more momentum to roll, I launched to my feet and ducked a swinging snakehead before diving out of the range of the axe. Back on my feet, I saw Adonis had been driven off as well, one of his swords still stuck in the half-severed head of a snake.

He used hand signals Herakles taught me, and I nodded to show I understood.

But I definitely didn't agree. His plan was to scale the wounded head in order to get to the vulnerable body of the monster.

He drew the third short sword he had at his back.

The monster charged at me. Instincts warned me against getting stuck in the corner behind me, and I darted to the side. Slashing, weaving, hacking ... the dangerous dance was too fast for me to track my movements or the monster's. I didn't have a chance to think about survival – I just reacted.

"Left!" Adonis' voice reached me through the haze of movement. I obeyed and ended up knocked to the ground by a snakehead rather than eaten. I rolled, feeling one tooth graze my arm and whipped my swords up blindly.

I stabbed one head through the mouth. Adonis was suddenly there, and he smashed both his weapons down on the creature's neck.

This time, the head fell lifeless next to me. I didn't have a chance to catch my breath. He stepped between me and the next attacking head to give me time to bound to my feet.

"Axe!" I cried.

We both dove to the ground and hopped up again quickly. Adonis snatched me around the waist and whirled twice before his movement stopped, putting enough space between us and the beast for us to breathe.

"Thanks," I gasped.

We stood for a brief moment, leaning against one another to recover. His scent was as soothing as talking to him was not.

"They grow back," he said.

I followed his gaze. The first head had completely healed despite the sword in its neck. "That's ... impossible!" The second had healed over but not yet grown back.

The axe fell towards us once more. We dived away from one another and were quickly back on our feet.

"Stay fast!" Adonis called and then bolted.

I wanted to watch. His speed was incredible. But a snakehead darted my way, and I began the deadly dance again. I smashed my sword into the fangs, and it withdrew. The chink in the monster's defenses gave me more breathing room for sure, and I played it to my advantage. I moved with the monster, keeping the not yet regrown head to my weak left while battling the nearest snake and glancing upwards towards Adonis.

He wasn't getting very far. The snakeheads could move up as well as out and away, and he was struggling to climb past the monster's belt. As if fed up with him, the creature snatched him and held him up and away with a huge hand.

He began to squeeze. I saw the grimace of pain cross Adonis' face. For the first time, I began to think we might not make it out of here. All of Adonis' speed and strength, all my training, wasn't going to defeat something like this. The sight of him in pain. Trapped, helpless ...

Well, not helpless. He plunged one sword through the hand of the monster. But I knew he was hurting, and I involuntarily ached for him.

Herakles killed my parents before adopting me. Adonis tried to rescue me before turning in to a mass murderer. No matter what I felt for either, one truth melted out of my confused emotions.

I'd never let either of them die. Deflecting the lunge of the snakehead nearest me, I dropped one sword and reached for the ribbons around the creature. They evaded me, but I had a plan. I dropped the second sword and ducked a swipe with the axe.

This time, when I reached for the ribbons, my other hand hovered close enough to catch them when they darted.

Adonis gave a roar of pain. The monster shook him hard. Two snakeheads were headed my direction, and I had no weapons within reach.

Not understanding how to disarm my opponent, I closed my fist around the ribbons, crushed them with my hand and yanked them all towards me.

The Typhon vanished. Adonis fell ten meters out of the air and landed in a still heap, his ribbons agitated and at least two jagged.

The crowd fell silent.

I looked down at the jumbled ribbons in my hand. Afraid to release them to the world in case a new Typhon formed, I did what I had done with my green ribbon and pressed them against my thigh. They disappeared. I uncurled my hand hesitantly. The ribbons were gone.

Mnemosyne had said I was born with the power to create and destroy. I'd just proved her right, and it felt … icky. Like watching the Typhon pulverize the men it fought before us.

People were beginning to whisper, then talk then boo. Furious they were angry we survived, I looked up, and my anger faded. It wasn't us they were booing. Soldiers in urban camouflage had begun to pour into the grandstands of the arena. Boos turned to cries for people to flee before the military captured them.

I stood, breathless, and made my way to Adonis, dropping to my knees beside him.

He wasn't moving. Distracted by the invasion, I nonetheless did as he had instructed and focused on the challenge at hand. I smoothed out his ribbons with some effort, still not certain how or why this worked, and then untangled the one that was knotted. The gate nearest us rolled open, but I ignored it, continuing to work until I was satisfied the ribbons were as they should have been.

"Just hope you're not dented like the cup," I whispered. I didn't need to see the soldiers pouring in to know they were there. "Adonis! You gotta wake up!"

He did so slowly and shook his head. Pushing himself up,

his gaze settled past me on the soldiers.

"Damn. Here I was hoping Adonis would die." Niko's voice made me want to scream. "Good job, kid."

I twisted to see him and then pushed to my feet, exhausted. Adonis caught my arm, and instead of turning to give Niko an earful, I looked into his gorgeous eyes.

"Your old boss wants to see you, Adonis," Niko said. "Might be willing to forgive you after the money he won on this round."

My eyes widened. "No," I whispered fiercely to Adonis. "You can't go back to what you were!"

"Remember what I said," Adonis said, gazing down at me.

"That I'm beautiful?" As soon as I heard the words, I knew they were so very wrong.

"I'll protect you." Adonis was amused. "No matter what you perceive to be going on."

"Adonis, this isn't –"

Ignoring me, he released me and walked past me towards Niko. "Been a pleasure, Niko," he said. "Looks like you won't be killing me today."

I turned, fuming and confused, to see the two men staring one another down.

"Not today," Niko agreed. "Leave. Before I forget my boss's orders to make sure you make it back alive."

Adonis slid away, without bothering to look at me again, and disappeared into the depths of the gate.

I watched him go, stung, and nowhere near trusting him enough to place any amount of money on a bet he was serious about helping me. It made no sense that his betrayal hurt me as deeply as Herakles' but it did.

"Good show, kid," Niko said to me. "Time to meet the Supreme Magistrate."

I glared at him. I was in no mood to meet anyone. I had no forest to return to, no Herakles to comfort me, no choices of my own to make. The military had cleared out most of the grandstands, and the other exit was blocked by a line of them.

"Go on." Niko nodded his head towards the nearby gate.

Disliking him more every time we met, I also had nowhere else to go and moved forward reluctantly.

This isn't how it's supposed to go. Adonis was supposed to stay with me, and we were going to leave this place.

Thus far, no part of the real world lived up to my expectations. I was starting to understand why Herakles was so insistent I not leave the forest before I was ready. What he failed to understand was that nothing could prepare someone for a life like this.

Niko caught my arm as I passed. A sharp sting pierced my forearm. "Ouch!"

Immediately, the ribbons around everyone vanished.

"Not taking any chances," he said and released me. In his other hand was a small gun like the one Marty had used to give me a biotag.

I looked down at the red dot of blood above an equally red … something he put under my skin.

"Created a solution out of one of your cords. Easier than a bracelet. Not something you can readily remove, either."

"I hate you, Niko."

"But I love you, Alessandra," he said, amused. "You know what kind of bonus you earned me?"

I marched away angrily, dreading where they'd take me. A prison. A torture chamber. To feed me to another monster. My mind was whirling with horrible thoughts but it was the vision of Adonis walking away from me that was the worst.

SIXTEEN

An alliance with a powerful person is never safe.
– PHAEDRUS

*M*AYBE I DIED AND WENT TO THANATOS' WAITING *room.* I stood in the middle of the open foyer of a Greek style villa of endless white marble. Airy, open, spacious, serene. Even Adonis' apartment wasn't as beautiful as this place. A waterfall laughed from somewhere deeper in the house, and the scent of roses and other flowers floated through open windows from a garden courtyard. A crystal chandelier was overhead, and the décor was simple, sleek and expensive, if I had to guess. Two servants stood in traditional white robes, a male and female, with their eyes straight ahead of them and their poses still enough to resemble the statues that dotted the interior.

Dressed in a dusty, bloody, sweaty black SISA uniform and nowhere near fitting into the place, I shifted back onto the plush rug so as not to mar the pristine white marble flooring with the blood of my reopened back wound.

Niko's escorts remained at the door of the villa.

"It pleases you?"

I turned at the unfamiliar voice.

The distinguished man in his forties was well dressed in a suit, clean shaven, and radiating a similar level of confidence bordering on arrogance that Adonis did. With dark eyes and hair, he looked familiar, though I was too tired and wary to place him.

I shrugged in response.

He smiled politely, the kind of smile that was reflexive rather than sincere. No other part of his façade changed with the token gesture, and his eyes remained cold.

"This is yours," he stated. He held nothing in his hands, and he didn't point at anything either.

"What is mine?" I asked cautiously.

"The villa. It belongs to the Oracle."

"I don't understand."

"This is your new home," he said again without blinking. "It took some negotiating with a furious Supreme Priest, but Niko finally managed to bring you where you belong."

"You're saying ..." I looked at my surroundings anew. Adonis' men had claimed the Oracle was wealthy. It wasn't really clicking this meant *I* was wealthy.

"Yes."

"Who are you?" I asked.

"Among others, I'm known as the Right Honorable

Supreme Magistrate. Among my equals, of which you are one, I'm simply called Cleon."

Magistrate. Niko's boss. I'd seen this man on the television, though he looked a little different in real life. Maybe because the feed we received in the forest was always somewhat fuzzy.

It took me a moment to move past my surprise that the man at the top of the food chain was addressing me. What did one do when meeting such a person?

"Oh." I kicked myself for the stupid response. "Sorry. I didn't recognize you."

"I understand from Niko your upbringing was sheltered."

"I feel like I was raised on another planet."

This time, his smile was genuine, or trying to be. He quickly suppressed the warm amusement in his gaze. "I'll save the tour for later. I've called for a physician to attend you. The wound on your back appears deep."

"Doesn't hurt," I murmured. "What tour?"

"I will leave you to explore your home on your own. If you need anything, ask your servants. But the tour I speak of is of the grounds."

I started to smile. I was the one who used to get stuck with kitchen duty and maintenance of the school because I was too wild. I was the school's sole servant. I had never dreamed of having my own servants!

"You may want to be more appropriately attired."

I smelled and knew it. I wasn't sure I cared. For a man with immense power and influence, he was being … nice.

Which wasn't good. People weren't nice. If I was learning

anything about life, it was this. Yet something was subtly pleasant about this man. I innately knew his suggestions were gently disguised orders – and I didn't really mind. It was a first for me not to mind being told what to do. "You're a good politician, aren't you?"

"I am adept at my position, yes."

I didn't roll my eyes but wanted to. "You're sure this ... place is mine?" I asked, puzzled by the notion. I left the forest with nothing but my knife, the clothes on my back and the gem Mismatch gave me as a child. I had never really had possessions, never been concerned about obtaining them.

"The Oracle's trust falls to her successor upon discovery."

"Where is the other Oracle?"

"She works with the gods. Once you assume the mantle of your position, you no longer need such luxuries from humans when you have the gods to provide for you."

He made sense ... to a point. I still felt like everyone around me had a huge secret and no one was willing to share it.

"I'll wait for you," he offered. "After the tour, a soiree is planned to begin introducing you to prominent members of the social strata in which you now belong."

Soiree. Strata. His use of pretty words made me feel more backwards than I already was. I wanted a tour, particularly of this villa that I allegedly owned, but I also wanted some space. Some time to clear my head of the monsters and almost dying. Of Adonis abandoning me and Niko dragging me here.

I was back where I was when I met Adonis. Struggling to understand a stranger's game and feeling ill prepared to handle something that didn't involve direct confrontation, survival or weapons. "Thanks." It wasn't really the right thing to say, but I was feeling too self conscious to know what was.

Turning away, I started into the villa.

"Right wing," he said quietly as I started to go left.

I turned mid-step and walked down a hall. The padding of bare feet behind me made me slow, and I twisted to see the female servant following me.

This is weird. From an arena filled with monsters to this. I could see Leandra or the other nymphs squealing in delight to be handed a villa, but I was uncomfortable, overwhelmed. Four chambers lined this hallway and a fifth was at the very end. The servant motioned to that one.

I opened the double doors and gasped. Forty foot ceilings, a bed larger than any I'd seen, and a ceiling depicting the gods in gold and gems. Pale neutrals created a seamless line from floor to wall to ceiling, and the scent of jasmine was in the air.

The servant padded to a door on one side, and I trailed, flabbergasted by the luxurious room. The bathroom consisted of a large shower, dressing and powder room, an antique style heated bath the size of small pool, waterfall and multiple sinks. White marble was everywhere, dotted with white vases and flowers.

"Wow," I breathed.

I began to see why I needed a servant when I crossed to the shower. It was controlled by a touchscreen in the wall.

The servant punched few buttons. Instantly, overhead rain showerheads and jets lining both walls sprang to life. I knew before I set foot in it that it was going to be the most incredible experience yet.

I stripped out of my clothing slowly, my back aching and tight despite my reassurance to Cleon I was fine. I dropped the dirty clothing on a chair and stepped into heaven.

"Oh. My. Gods!" I exclaimed, melting into the hot water. I rested my hand against the wall and sighed deeply. Blood and dirt colored the water swirling at my feet, and I watched it, content to stay put for the rest of my life.

Except ... Cleon was waiting.

He seemed young to be in charge of the world. I almost laughed at the thought then closed my eyes and let the water stream down over my gritty face.

With some reluctance and a silent promise to return later, I showered and left the most awesome place on the planet. A towel and slippers were left out for me. I dried off quickly and left the bathroom, looking around the bedroom for a dresser or something.

"I'm Doctor Khan," said a pretty woman dressed in white scrubs. She had set up the chaise at the windows overlooking the gardens as a triage station. "If you would take a seat."

I did so. She was quick, taking my vitals then moving to stitch the wound at my back. I felt only the prick of the local anesthesia and within five minutes, she began packing her bag.

"Thanks," I murmured. My numbed back was almost a relief. I was sore enough from fighting.

"My pleasure." Doctor Khan smiled and left.

I stood and stretched. The servant stood beside another

open door, this one with the light on.

"Clothes?" I asked.

She nodded.

I went to the walk-in closet and stopped so quickly in the doorway, she ran into me.

It was a two story closet with a wall of shoes and purses, a dressing area complete with couch, and every item of clothing color coded. The rainbow of clothes stretched around the closet.

"This is ridiculous!" I said and then laughed so hard my back hurt. "These can't all be mine! No one needs this much clothing!"

"They were tailored especially for you," the servant said. "Niko called in your measurements. It's taken ten seamstresses three days to make these."

I shook my head. "I appreciate their efforts, but it's not like I can wear all of this. Where in Hades do I even start?"

"The Oracle wears traditional garb for her official duties. What's your favorite color?"

"Blue, I guess."

Still grinning, I watched her cross to the spiral stairwell in the center of the closet.

"Tacia, you've been reassigned," came a soft voice. "Kitchens."

The servant paused, and then left the closet, replaced by none other than perfect, beautiful Leandra.

"Leandra!" I exclaimed and hugged her. "But I thought you were placed in the Queen's court!"

"Hush, Lyssa. You always were a tad slow." She shot me a look. With a quick glance out into the bedroom, she closed the closet door. "I'm here undercover."

"You're a spy?" I started to laugh again. "This keeps getting crazier!"

"Shut up." Leandra moved gracefully towards the clothing. "I'm picking your clothes. I've seen how you dress."

"Whatever." I sat down on the couch. She went up to the second level and began pushing clothing aside. "Why does the Queen need a spy?"

"Because apparently, none of them at the top trust one another."

"Ah. Yeah. I've seen that. It's nothing like what I expected it to be."

"What isn't?"

"The real world."

"It's different than I expected, too. But … I think we were prepared for this better than you."

"What do you mean?"

"The priests trained the rest of us in methods of subversion on the weekends while you were hiding in the forest."

"I thought you went to town to watch movies."

"Nope. See how good we are? You never figured it out!" she said with a smirk.

"So you were trained to spy and I was learning how to survive in the forest," I mused. "Kinda jacked up, isn't it?"

"Very. But the priests knew what you were. We didn't find out until the place blew up and SISA bulldozed the entire forest."

My smile faded. I hated recalling the circumstances of leaving the forest. I wanted to pretend it'd still be there when this crazy dream was over.

"They groomed us to protect you and further our cause. Your own personal spy network in the most prominent families in the world."

"Seriously?"

"I'm running it, so don't get any ideas." She shot me a look. "The others are moving into place."

"Why didn't you warn me about anything up 'til now?" I complained.

"Because we had no access to you." She carried a blue-green dress when she descended the stairs and set it down on the table in the dressing area.

"A dress?" I grumbled.

"You're on the same level as the Queen. She only wears dresses. So do you."

It was weird to see even Leandra accepting all this. The nymphs made fun of me my whole life. If anyone was going to be more surprised than I was, I expected it to be her. But she appeared fine with circumstances I was having trouble swallowing.

"Towel off," she told me. "This will be like wrestling a pig into an oven."

"Gee, thanks." I tugged the towel off and let her wrestle the dress into place. It was light and airy, layers of silks so sheer, they were transparent. The bodice was wrapped in a gold rope that hugged my body and moved and stretched when I breathed. "This isn't bad. I can still fight in it."

"No fighting! This dress is worth a fortune," Leandra chided.

"You never know when you'll run into a monster that shouldn't exist."

"I saw you on television. You and the SISA chief in the arena." Her hands paused from tugging the layers straight. "You did really good, Lyssa. Herakles trained you well."

"I didn't die," I agreed. I played with the ruched portion over my breasts. The square neckline was low but not indecent, and the gem Mismatch had given me glowed just above the seam. The thought of Adonis made my sad confusion return. "Have you heard from him?"

"Not directly. One of the girls heard he went underground. He might be waiting it out until SISA isn't looking for him anymore."

Was he serious about helping me if I got stuck with SISA? Before my memories, I never would've entertained such a thought. "Do you know what's going on? For real?" I asked quietly.

"You're meant to return us to the Old Ways, according to the priests."

"Is that really possible?" I met her gaze.

"Yes. You're the Oracle, Lyssa." She believed what she was saying. "No one else can stand up to the gods."

"But am I *supposed* to?"

Her hands dropped.

"I mean, they're the gods."

"They're destroying the human world for material gain," she answered.

"Not all of them. The priests said some were good."

"The gods created this world. They did their part. Now they need to leave us alone," she reasoned. "Artemis and the Titan Lelantos agree and have protected us for this reason."

"Hmm. Really? Or is this the latest alliance in territorial gods?" I challenged.

"It's possible, I suppose."

We gazed at one another. I didn't have answers. I never really did. Leandra knew what we were taught, and I suspected both of us were going to learn more about the truth of the world before we understood how we were going to convert it to the Old Ways.

"Sit down. I need to do your hair," she said.

Neither of us was satisfied with the discussion, but I obeyed. She primped, curled, dried, gelled and gods knew what else to my hair until it shone and the plump curls stayed in place. I admired her work in the mirror. I had always wanted to spend time on my hair like the nymphs did, but Herakles usually had other plans.

"Now for shoes." She was cheerful again. She went to the wall of shoes and selected delicate high heels.

"No way I'm wearing those," I said instantly. "I can't fight monsters in heels."

"You're going on a tour, not to fight monsters."

"No heels!"

She sighed noisily. "Fine. Your fat feet would look funny in them anyway."

"My feet aren't fat." I glanced down.

"How about these?" She held up strappy sandals with an inch heel.

"Okay."

She dropped them near me. I slid them on. They were comfortable.

"I'll carry a shawl and satchel for you."

"You're going with me?"

"Yep."

I was relieved. I didn't realize how nice it was to be around a familiar face until I thought about leaving her here to tour with strangers. "Am I presentable?" I whirled, grinning at the layers of silk that swirled around my legs.

"Until you speak."

Ignoring her, I left the closet.

"You can't let anyone know we know one another," she warned me as I started towards the door.

"I won't."

She trailed me out of the bedroom. I marveled at skylights of the hallway. Natural light poured into the house from every angle. I wasn't certain I'd ever get used to living here, but I could admit secretly that I loved the idea of trying.

Cleon waited in a sitting room near the foyer. He rose as I approached. He didn't acknowledge Leandra at all as she took up her station nearby.

"Hard to believe you faced down a monster or two," he

said, gaze going over me.

Not fully at ease in the fancy dress, despite its comfort, I crossed my arms self-consciously. His gaze returned to my features, and he held out an arm towards the entrance.

I began walking, and he joined me. Servants opened the doors for us to leave, and I paused outside the front door, beneath a marble canopy shielding the sidewalks of the compound from sun. A small entourage awaited us. It consisted of a man with a bottle of wine and two glasses, a woman bearing delicate hor d'oerves on a platter, Leandra, and four guards.

It was almost sundown, and I was disappointed to realize that meant Adonis wouldn't be at the soiree. Not that I wanted to see him, but ... ugh.

The Supreme Magistrate and I were handed a glass of wine, and we began walking.

"The Supreme compound houses the White House, where I work on a daily basis, the residences of the Supreme Magistrate and Priest and the Silent Queen's secondary court." As we walked towards the Congress building, Cleon began to point out residences, temples and official offices, describe the benefactors behind the various gardens and courtyards, whisper about the underground bunkers, and generally orient me towards the most exclusive and well-guarded compound in the world. At its center was a massive white temple to Zeus surrounded by a dozen smaller temples dedicated to other gods.

The wealth and beauty of such a place, designed after an ancient Greek city, left me speechless. Cleon's general knowledge was underscored by the pleasant charm of a servant fascinated with his world rather than the boastfulness of a Supreme Magistrate.

He, like Adonis, was nothing like what I expected, especially after meeting the acid-mouthed Niko. My fascination with this new world and the man beside me grew as wine lifted some of the dread that had been following me around for days now.

We watched the sunset from the private, uppermost balcony in Zeus' temple. The sky glowed with different hues of orange, pink and red. I was even more mesmerized by the reflection of those colors on the marble temples in the compound. Several people were out in the quiet sidewalks and walking across the greens. The scent of earth and flowers filled the air, combined with incense from the priests on the temple floor. It was quiet, calming.

Closing my eyes, I leaned against the railing, unable to recall when I last felt this relaxed. It had been since I was in the forest. Perhaps it was the wine and my exhaustion, or the subtle personality of the charming man beside me, but I was enjoying the peace of a compound I knew to be a breeding ground for political dissension among the Triumvirate. I suspected Cleon was the latest who wanted to manipulate me into doing something.

But it was still … nice to take a breather.

"You are enjoying it," Cleon observed, a warm note in his voice for the first time. He stood beside me on the balcony.

"Yeah," I murmured. "I know it's not real. I wish it was."

"It's real enough to touch."

My eyes cracked open, and I shifted my hip against the railing to gaze up at him. He was handsome in a way as subtle as his charm. Unlike Adonis, who had to have been chiseled by the gods themselves, Cleon had a quiet beauty. Symmetrical features, wide forehead and jaw, eyes that were well spaced, and an aquiline nose. Nothing stood out as especially good looking about his features but nothing to take away from them either. His clothing was tailored and fit well, adding to the air of stateliness.

Like the compound, he was outwardly flawless.

"It's what's beneath the surface that bothers me," I said.

"You are troubled by what you have learned since leaving the forest?"

"You could say that."

"Niko is a brash man but he is my best, and I trust him. He obeys without thought. I sent him there to protect you once word leaked of what SISA planned."

"You? I thought the priests hired him."

"The priests were naïve to believe no one knew they were there. I knew. I didn't know what they were hiding, but I had a source providing me information. It wasn't hard to manipulate the situation so Niko was hired rather than another mercenary."

There it is. The conniving was starting to emerge. More secrets I was afraid to learn. More claims I'd never be able to verify. The moment one of these people opened up to me, or my memories shared new insight, I was tense. I clutched the railing, gazing up at Cleon, waiting for the other shoe to drop.

"I've worried you." Cleon rested a hand on my arm.

"No. I've been waiting for that. And worse."

"Your position is one of political maneuvering. There is much of that on this compound."

"It's not my thing. Like, it's the farthest thing in the universe from my thing."

"How can I make you comfortable talking to me?"

"Give me a knife."

Without dropping my gaze, he motioned one of the guards over and held out his hand. The guard removed a knife and sheathe from around his thigh and gave it to him.

Cleon handed it to me.

Surprised by the gesture, I accepted it. "Thanks."

"I want you to know you can trust me on some level."

I gripped the knife, and it helped ease some of my tension. My response to him wasn't going to be favorable, but I owed him some level of politeness after he handed me a knife.

"I have to ask. I know you have a trial for me. What is it?" I asked and braced myself for the response.

"I am to task you last," he replied. "I made a deal with the Queen for the privilege. But, honestly, I want only what is best for both men and gods."

"That sounds fair."

Adonis was right about the unknown messing with someone's mind. What could a man this powerful task me to do? The Supreme Priest had wanted to use my powers for his own personal gain. Was it safe to assume everyone in power would do the same?

I kept quiet and turned to face the sky once more.

It was as I saw the last of the sun dip below the horizon that it hit me why this was so awkward. Cleon was the first person I'd ever met who treated me like an equal. He didn't talk down to me. Didn't assume I was an idiot. Didn't try to control, cage or coerce me yet.

It made me want to be less hotheaded and watch my tongue for once, to remain in a position where he thought of me the way he seemed to at the moment. I wanted him to think me his equal, because no one ever had. It was gratifying to be considered such by someone at his level and wanted to try to live up to the expectations of a stranger.

He really is a good politician.

"Your guests await us," he said.

Blinking out of my thoughts, I walked with him down the stairs, out of the temple and through a maze of sidewalks. Before we reached the outdoor party, the sound of a harp and low beat of drums reached us. Laughter and the scent of food soon followed.

The soiree was teeming with close to a hundred people with a small orchestra in one corner, servants with trays of food and wine circulating among guests, and an area of tables. At the center was a fountain, and torches lit the perimeter. No one looked twice at us when we entered, for which I was grateful. I was feeling more self-conscious in the clothing, more afraid of making a mistake.

I don't belong here. Women were drenched in glittering

jewels and designer gowns.

A servant with a tray approached and held it out. Cleon took the masks and handed one to me.

"I thought you might be more comfortable with a semi-anonymous event," he said.

Busy ogling the biggest diamond I'd ever seen, I hadn't noticed everyone down to the servants were wearing masks over the top halves of their faces. At Cleon's words, I started to relax. He was really, really good at keeping me chill.

Leandra plucked it out of my hand and carefully pinned it in place with hairpins. She wore one already.

"This is awesome," I said, gazing around at the masked strangers. "No one will notice if I eat all the snacks."

Cleon chuckled. "You are welcome to. It's your party."

That seemed too weird to be true, but I was thrilled by the idea of interacting with the highest levels of society – and no one knowing it was me.

"Who are all these people?" I asked.

"The most affluent men and women in the world. Favored by the gods. The elite. Those whose fortunes and fates rest with those of the gods."

"They are probably excited to see me."

"They are. You are the promise of continued good fortune and wealth for them."

I didn't really like the idea of an elite when the rest of the world was in chaos because of the Holy Wars. I started into the crowd, absolutely entranced by the amount of bling the women wore. Did they dress like this every night and go to soirees?

I bet none of them have ever skinned a rabbit for dinner. I swallowed a giggle at the ridiculous thought, torn between admiring the people around me and critical of the idea they couldn't survive in the arena or forest if the world ended tomorrow.

Checking out the fountain, I stopped to perch for a moment and watch the world. I couldn't tell Cleon from the other men or Leandra from the other women. For some reason, being anonymous helped me relax more. I was somewhat free, if only temporarily, from being the person they thought I was.

"Beautiful smile, beautiful lady." The man's voice was the opposite of Cleon's carefully controlled one.

I turned and eyed the masked stranger with two hotter than hot women hanging off him. He was grinning, and his hair dark. I saw a gleam of green eyes through the mask, and a star was printed in the middle of his forehead. "Right," I said and rolled my eyes. I started away.

He laughed.

I stopped. I'd heard that laugh somewhere. Not recently. Not in the memories I'd always had. It was ... trapped somewhere in the new memories that hadn't yet completely emerged.

"Go on, ladies. Let me talk to our friend," he said and shooed the girls away. I stared after them. Leandra would give them a run for their money but I never would. The man pushed up his mask to reveal striking green eyes. His jaw was heavy and square, his brow low, and his face wide. He had a widow's peak and long hair held in place at the nape of his neck.

"Lantos." He held out a hand.

I shook it. "Have we met before?" I asked, the same strange sense I got around Adonis present once again.

"Possibly." He winked. "I've spoken to many women before this night."

No surprise there. He was Hollywood handsome with sparkling eyes and a quick smile. He held my hand after our shake.

"You are?" he waited.

I pulled my hand away. I knew Adonis because I had brought him to life, and we'd met when I was a child. I knew this man because ... the memory was completely blank. If I hadn't been through the strangest week of my life, I'd be blushing that someone who looked like this had sent away two models to talk to me.

Instead, I was suspicious.

"Lyssa," I said finally.

"Ah. The reason we're all here." He said and spread an arm out towards the crowd. "It's my honor and pleasure." He rested a hand over his heart and bowed his head in yet another show. "I saw you take out the Typhon. You won me a small fortune."

"I had help," I replied.

"Yes. I saw." A flicker of something – irritation? – crossed his eyes before vanishing. "Care to walk with me?"

"Not really," I said.

He laughed and moved closer. "If I sweeten the deal, will you give me a couple of minutes of your time?"

Sweeten? "What're you talking about?"

Some of the flashiness faded, and I saw a genuine smile on his features. "Sweet girl. I'll take the device out of your arm placed by the Magistrate that's caging your powers if you'll speak with me in private."

I felt the soft skin of my forearm, studying him. "I'm armed."

He laughed again and stepped away, lowering his mask. "I'll keep my hands to myself. Promise. Come!"

I stared after him, dazzled by this charisma yet aware he hadn't accidentally stumbled upon me like he tried to play off. I trailed him through the crowd.

He led me past the orchestra and down a cobblestone path leading into the garden. Other couples posed in embraces, some talking, the others quiet, throughout the fragrant garden. When we reached a small fountain out of earshot from the others, Lantos turned.

"First. I always keep my promises. Your arm." He held out a wide, strong hand.

I placed my arm in it. Rather than pull out a tool of some sort, he rested his other warm palm on top of the area where Niko had shot the solution into me. While far from intimate, heat rose to my cheeks. His touch stirred my blood. I was grateful for the lack of lighting in this part of the gardens.

"What're you doing?" I asked after a long quiet.

"Removing it."

I gazed up at him and waited for more. Seconds later, he lifted his hand. A stream of red liquid ran from his palm to my forearm. He wrapped it around two fingers. It solidified into a cord resembling those I'd grown up around.

The last of the string left my arm, and the world erupted into ribbons.

I gasped, a little overwhelmed by the sudden reemergence of color. Lantos' hand went to my hip as he steadied me.

"How did you do that?" I demanded and swatted at ribbons floating between us.

"Easy. This is mine to command." He held up the cord then tossed it into the air. It disappeared. "Who do you think gave it to the priests to protect you?"

Tearing off my mask, I stared at him.

He removed his mask as well, eyes sparkling with humor I didn't share.

"You're not ... not a Titan," I stammered.

"Alas, no. My father is. I'm the son of a Titan and a human. I'm stranded here with my mother's kind. My father, Lelantos, is your benefactor. I am his humble servant."

If he hadn't done what he just did, I'd walk away.

He touched his forefinger to his lips. "But that's a secret." His eyes glowed with amusement. "You can keep a secret, I believe?"

I nodded, speechless.

"Then I'd like to show you one more thing." He drew too close once again, entering my personal space. He was wide and athletic, and his body heat made a chill run through me. I craned my head back to see his face. "But I need you to promise you won't reveal what I show you."

Even when attempting to be serious, light and laughter

glowed in his gaze. I didn't think I could turn down such a request if I wanted to, not with his light cologne and presence so near me. It was easy to believe he was the son of a Titan. Like Adonis, he had five ribbons and an air of something not quite normal.

I nodded.

"Come!" He slid his arm through mine. "We move through shadows."

I had no idea what that meant. We walked through the garden to a small building sandwiched between the Congress and another official government building. At first, I thought we were headed to a toolshed and started to worry. Until I saw the guards. Herakles had taught me that guards didn't stand in front of a place or person of no importance.

I slowed as we approached, but Lantos urged me on, upbeat and unconcerned that we were about to run into two heavily armed men.

But we didn't. We walked right past them. Neither so much as flinched as we strolled into the building, past another one, through a metal detector and down a hallway. He led me to an elevator, and we stepped in.

"Simple," Lantos said. "Right?"

Puzzled, I met his gaze again. He was smiling. "How is that possible?"

"My father is the Titan of the Unseen. I inherited some of his skills, like the ability to move as a shadow, to hide what's in plain sight from being seen."

"That's amazing."

"Not as amazing as your skill."

"I can't figure out how to use it."

He smiled and motioned me out of the elevator.

The first thing I noticed in the dark room: the scent. I breathed it in – and felt like I was melting again like I had in the shower. Amber incense, tinged with exotic smells I couldn't quite name, ignited a fever inside me and made me nearly giddy. I stepped deeper into the room, wanting to experience more of the scent.

"The fumes are like catnip for an Oracle," Lantos said, amused.

"What is it?"

"You know the origins of your kind? How the Oracle of Delphi used to sit over a cavern, one whose fumes helped put her in a trance?"

"Yes. They said she ..." I breathed in and felt like floating away. "... could use it to help her communicate with gods." I had never felt so good.

"Exactly. They moved those caverns here. What they learned after some time was that the bridge that let her speak to the gods could be enlarged into a portal that let *them* walk across it into our world. But the portal must remain open or the gods cannot access the magic whose source is on their world."

I didn't care. I wanted to lose myself in the smell. It was warm and comfortable, as if I was being hugged all over. "Oh, my gods! I want to live here!" I all but sang and began to twirl. Ribbons encircled and swirled around me, and I laughed.

"Be careful what you wish for," Lantos warned with a low

chuckle. He caught me and wrapped an arm around me to steady my body.

Pressed to him, I grinned, enjoying the sensation of his strong form and the giddiness of the aroma. "Can you feel it?" I asked.

"Not like you do." He grinned down at me. "Do you like it?"

"I love it."

"Good. Now I must show you something you will definitely not love." Lantos scooped me up in his arms and walked with me across the room to a railing overlooking an empty space. He set me down. I gripped the railing to keep from dancing off into oblivion and waited eagerly, praying it was something as amazing as the Oracle catnip.

Lights flipped on into the empty space, and I froze.

"Let the catnip calm you," he said quietly. This time, his humor was missing. He leaned into me, keeping me in place against the railing, his hands on either side of mine. "I'd like to introduce you to the current Oracle, Cecilia."

I couldn't breathe for a moment. "No. This can't be real!"

SEVENTEEN

There will be killing till the score is paid.
– HOMER

THE BODY – IF IT COULD BE CALLED THAT – BEFORE ME was straight out of a horror movie. A naked woman was suspended in what looked like an oversized petri dish with wires and tubes running out of her. Each limb had been severed and connected by a tube to the rest of her body, and her head the same. She was in pieces – yet alive, glowing with the green ribbons I had witnessed over little-me's head. She was awake, her eyes the only sign she was still alive as she occasionally blinked.

"To keep her alive, they use computers and drugs. She must be kept on the verge of horrific pain, for that is when the mind is sharpest. Her body is torn apart over the course of thirty years, and she remains in the level of pain one experiences when having limbs torn off. Drugs keep her immobilized and her body functioning. Meanwhile, her magic is used by gods and men to do whatever they wish. The gods simply need the portal behind her open at all times. Men ... it's never that easy with men."

Behind her were the glowing edges of a portal.

I blinked, wanting to believe I'd been thrust into a dream, that this tortured woman wasn't the fate everyone wanted me to accept. The Oracle's eyes were on me, and I tried to back away, to run, to return to the surface where I wasn't struggling to control the affects of the drugged air.

"Stay, Oracle." Lantos took my wrists and pinned each to my chest, his strong arms defying resistance. "You need to see this. You need to understand."

"Understand what?" I gasped, unable to look away from the woman before me.

That you cannot follow in my steps, came a soft, strained female voice.

"Cecelia is different. Stronger. She was never displaced from her own mind, so to speak. She wrested a piece of her mind and power from the machines the day they did this to her, gathered her strength over the course of thirty years despite the anguish of her existence and five years ago began to act. She started to level the playing field between men and gods. The portal to the gods is open, but they cannot move through it. It's made them desperate. It's the source of their fighting. In case they're trapped here permanently, each wants his or her own kingdom to rule over. Ostensibly, my job is to help them, at least until it's my turn to act."

That I could end up here, torn apart slowly, in agony … I was almost panting and on the verge of panicking.

"Talk to her. She is you, Alessandra. She is your destiny, if you trust Cleon."

Lantos released my hands but maintained one arm around my body as if he could feel my insides quaking and my knees about to give. I placed a hand on the cool glass separating the Oracle from me.

"Who … who did this to her?" I asked hoarsely. Tears pricked my eyes.

It is the way it has been for millennia, came the airy voice once more. *There is not one person to blame but a tradition accepted as necessary.*

"I don't want to…" My throat was too tight to finish.

The Old Ways. The time before the gods became the puppet masters of mankind.

I listened.

I have been dying for two years. I am nearly too weak to hold the portals open, no matter what they do to me. You must leave this place until I am dead. Avoid capture. Trust carefully. Act faithfully. Our power comes from this world. Once the gods are cut off, you can execute them. One by one.

A trace of fury was in her thin voice. Her eyes closed, and I sensed more than saw that she was weakened by the speech.

I trembled in place. How could anyone do this to someone else? How could anyone think of doing this to *me*? I no longer questioned why Herakles drilled me so relentlessly. He wanted me to have a chance to avoid this. He wanted me to survive.

He knows this is my fate. The second secret he kept from me was as damning as the first, and I began to crumble. My emotions were spinning out of control once again, egged on by the amber scent wresting control of myself from me.

"Oh, gods," I whispered. Monsters, my forest, betrayal … nothing compared to this moment, when I was finally able to see my fate, when the secret no one wanted to tell me revealed itself at last. "We have to save her. We have to get her out of there!" I was vaguely aware of the hysteria in my voice, vaguely aware of struggling against Lantos and him trying to speak to me. "Let me go!"

But he didn't, and I began to cry, overwhelmed. I collapsed against the stranger who dared show me my fate. His arms went around me, and he hugged me to him tightly. Aside from Adonis, I'd never been touched like this by a man – but I liked it. I liked his strong frame, his masculine scent and the sense he could support me.

It was hard for me to cry for long with the catnip pushing me higher. I began to lose some sense of reality, to slide into a state of heightened dream, and calmed, clutching Lantos' suit jacket.

For all I knew, he was going to be the one to strap me down and flip on the computers that would tear me apart. A man with magic like his had to be powerful. I was no closer to knowing who to trust, or what to do, than I was when I left the forest with Niko.

"We must go before you are missed," Lantos said quietly. "Do you understand that this is what Cleon wants? What all the people attending your little party really want for you?"

I couldn't answer. I eased away from him without looking up, embarrassed to cry in front of someone else.

"Do you?" he repeated, gaze intent.

"Y…yes." And I did. Cleon had admitted this much already, only I hadn't known exactly what it meant to follow the path he wanted. "What do you want?"

"Later." He winked. Stabilizing me, he kept one arm around me and as we walked to the elevator.

Moments later, we emerged into the cool night. The Oracle catnip wore off quickly, leaving me with nothing to dull the horror of what I'd seen. We started back through the garden to the soiree. I paused when we reached the fountain and tugged free of him.

"I can't go back there," I said, eyes on the happy people at the soiree.

"You need to play your part, pretty girl." He tipped my chin up.

"Do all of them know about … her?" I asked.

"Every one of them. They are counting on you assuming your place so things can return back to the way they were before Cecilia began to fight back."

"And you?"

"I'm the son of a Titan. There's no love between the Olympic gods and Titans. I want to see Cecilia succeed in disrupting the order of things forever. I want the gods dead or at least, expelled from here and to restore my place with my father and the rest of the Titans."

"It can't be that simple," I retorted. "Everyone I know has another side to who they are."

"You're learning how deep and murky the political waters are." He rested a hand on my arm. "Come on, I'll walk you back."

I shook him off. "Why in the name of everything holy do you think I'm going back there?" I demanded.

"Because if you let them know you know, they'll strike with force and speed even I can't counter. They'll have you pinned to that wall the way Cecilia is before you can blink." He moved closer, voice lowered for my ears only. "Right now, the elite are celebrating having found you. They will let you enjoy what they believe to be the last few days of your life in peace, if you play along."

My heart was racing. What he said made too much sense.

"Come with me," he said and offered the mask. "Play the game."

"I hate games." I gazed into his sparkling eyes. After a moment, I snatched the mask and slid it into place to cover eyes red from crying.

Lantos took my hand with a wink and began walking back towards the soiree with me. He replaced his mask as we walked.

Every step was like being on a death march. I wanted to cry again, to break out my knife and ram it through the hearts of every person present who wanted me tortured and held for the rest of my life in misery so they could retain their fortunes. On the verge of hyperventilating, I allowed him to pull me towards the party and struggled to regain some sort of balance between my reason and emotions.

"Lantos?" I recognized Cleon's voice. "My apologies, Alessandra. He's known to be improper with women despite the title."

"Title?" I managed to speak without screaming.

"Supreme Priest."

Wrenching my hand free from Lantos, I glared up at him. I was tired of surprises, of the two-faced bastards weaving in and out of my life. Lantos was grinning again, and I couldn't even begin to fathom how he was the son of a Titan – a sworn enemy of the gods – in the highest-level priestly position in the government.

But ... it fit him. He laughed at all the world and the fools who appointed him the representative of the gods. He was perfect for the role, the ultimate double agent. He hadn't shown me the Oracle out of a sense of compassion but to make me distrust Cleon.

"You're the one who sent us to the arena!" I exclaimed.

"I have a bit of a temper," he admitted. "I placed my one chance to task you in the hands of the man I trust more than myself, and he failed me." He shrugged. "But you survived." He offered another smile. "No hard feelings."

"No hard ..." I started to repeat in astonishment before stopping myself. Cleon was watching us closely. "I need to rest."

"Your time at the arena must have been draining," Lantos said.

"Yes."

"I would be happy to escort you home," Cleon said.

"Thank you." The words sounded forced even to my ears.

My mind was too busy for me to attempt small talk. I wanted to scream, and it was hard to prevent myself from racing ahead. Trailed by the entourage, Cleon was quiet, and he stopped at the doorstep of my villa.

"I took the liberty of booking an appointment for you tomorrow afternoon."

I was about to tell him to go to Hades and take all his rich friends – and Niko – with him, when he continued.

"The Silent Queen is eager to meet you."

Since seeing her on the television during her first appearance, I'd been intrigued by her. I was afraid to learn what she wanted with me but I was also interested in seeing her in the flesh.

"Thank you," I said once again. I stepped into the villa and closed the door behind Leandra.

Ripping off the mask, I flung it and the sandals and sprinted to my room, no longer able to bear being calm and still when I wanted nothing more than explode. I closed my door behind me and wiped my tears, crossing to the open doors of the balcony. Moonlight spilled into my own private garden and lined the flowers with silver.

All this was mine – until the day they decided to tear me limb from limb. I shook with emotion and exhaustion.

Lantos sends his apologies for upsetting you.

"Don't!" I spun to face the silent predator landing lightly on my balcony. "Don't make excuses for that piece of shit! He knew exactly what he was doing!"

It was impossible for me to see Mismatch for the first time and not be awed and just a little terrified. He folded his wings and tilted his head, his muscular frame poised.

"Tell your master you aren't welcome here," I breathed at last.

I help you fight monsters, and you turn your back on me. You were such a sweet child.

"You ditched me and left me with Niko!"

I fought with you and left you with someone I knew wouldn't hurt you. I couldn't take you with me without my men.

"Your boss ..." My chin trembled. I clamped my jaw closed and wiped more tears away. "I hate this place. I hate them!"

Deception is not your game.

"It's not. I'm so sick of people and their secret agendas!"

The duality of Mismatch – the creature I worshipped as a child and the man I couldn't trust – always confused me. He stretched out a wing and nudged me with it. I pushed it back but followed it with my gaze, once more entranced by the softness of its lining. I was about to tell him to stop messing with me when I realized his nature was to provoke me.

Lantos showed you the Oracle.

I hesitated then nodded. Tears of fury and fear were in my eyes again. Mismatch nudged me once more. This time, instead of pushing his wing away, I buried my hands into the soft lining. He stepped closer.

"Why couldn't you tell me that up front?" I demanded, looking up at his glowing eyes.

It wasn't my place.

"It damn well was your place! You're my creation, aren't you? Isn't there some sense of loyalty there?"

My master bid me to let him reveal it to you.

His wing wrapped around me and rolled me into him the way it had last night. Surrounded by the heavenly softness and his scent, I didn't resist for once. I was too tired, too angry, and too cognizant of how much I loved and trusted Mismatch as a child. Those emotions were unusually strong, as if part of me was capable of separating what I felt for him during daylight from what I did at night.

At least you know I'm a monster.

His touch and presence, soothed me. I didn't want it to. I wanted to stay angry. I rested my head back against his chest, thoroughly exhausted. His arms circled me, and I pulled up one hand by the thumb. "My gods, Mismatch. You gotta trim those nails."

Can't kill with them short.

"You shouldn't be killing at all!"

I hunt my food at night.

"That's really weird." I relaxed into him and gazed at the gardens. "What does a gargoyle eat?"

Grotesque. Usually something the size of a full grown sheep or deer.

"The whole thing?"

Flying requires a lot of energy.

His wing unwound and fell away, tucked at his side again, leaving me pressed against his body. I felt a tingle when Lantos flirted with me; when Mismatch or Adonis touched me, my insides ignited. At least when he was a monster, I could pretend there was nothing between us.

"I don't know what to do," I said before I could stop myself.

Sleep. Your fate isn't yet set. You must complete two more trials before you are of use to any member of the Triumvirate.

"I can't sleep knowing I might be dragged out of here and chopped into pieces!"

I'll stand watch.

"You have to go kill a cow."

I already ate.

His tail was tapping the glass of the French doors. I sighed and stood with him at my back. I shouldn't have trusted him more than I did anyone else. But I did. At least, at night I did. During the day, Adonis couldn't be far enough away.

"I want to go back to my forest. The one you chopped down."

He said nothing.

Recalling how he'd destroyed my home, I moved away. "I'm going to bed." I closed the doors behind me, leaving him on the balcony.

A nightgown was laying out for me in the dressing room part of the bathroom. I changed and tidied up for bed, fatigue driving me to skip brushing my hair in favor of arriving to my bed a minute earlier.

Sinking into the massive bed, I stared out the window.

Mismatch was perched on the balcony railing, wings tucked and muscular thighs drawing my gaze. His teal eyes were on the world outside of us.

As much as I hated to admit it, I liked the creature side of Adonis. A lot. Enough to want to curl up in his soft wings again and fall asleep. And I knew if he were here, no one could drag me away to torture me. I was safe with my monster watching over me.

I fell asleep facing the balcony.

EIGHTEEN

I SLEPT IN LATE AND ATE A HUGE BREAKFAST BEFORE getting ready for the afternoon event. No one wore masks the next afternoon when I arrived at the garden party at the Silent Queen's court. The crowd was smaller, and the servants and guards in purple. Leandra had picked my lavender gown and done my hair and makeup again. She trailed me closely, and I could feel her excitement at being in a place more suited to her than me.

The bushes of the gardens were shaped into fantastical animals from Greek myths. Smartly dressed men and women holding champagne glasses spoke quietly in small groups around several of the bushes. Serving staff armed with trays of food and drink wove among the partygoers.

I couldn't look at anyone without thinking they wanted me torn to pieces and strung up. I ended up focusing on the rainbows of ribbons everywhere. The ribbons calmed me, fascinated me.

"Is that all these people do?" I complained to Leandra. "Go to parties and drink?"

"Yeah," she sighed wistfully. "And wear amazing clothes."

I was in another traditional dress and wearing shoes that – according to Leandra – didn't remotely match. But after my night, I wasn't going near anything with a heel. I also had the knife Cleon procured for me strapped to my thigh.

"Ugh. We don't want anything to do with those two," Leandra said and nudged me the opposite direction in which she looked.

"Who?" I leaned around her to see.

My heart leapt. Adonis was in a fitted charcoal business suit and the Supreme Priest in a suit and mask. "Why does he wear a mask?" I asked.

"One of the priests thought it was out of respect for the position. He appears as neither human nor god so as to bridge the two."

Or he's hiding the fact he's a Titan. "Those two are shady."

"All the more reason to avoid them." This time, Leandra pushed me.

I went, thoughts on Adonis.

"Alessandra."

I turned at Theodocia's voice. She wore the robes of a priestess this day. If I had to guess, she was probably also packing some sort of weapons. She smiled at me.

"You have time for a chat?" she asked.

"Sure," I replied.

"Come with me. You've got a private audience with the

Silent Queen." Leandra's gasp was audible, and Theodocia glanced at her. "You come, too, in case your mistress requires you."

The giddy excitement inside me seemed out of place, and I blamed Leandra for infecting me with curiosity.

Theodocia led us into the villa and into a parlor where the Silent Queen waited. She was smaller than she looked on television and far more stunning in person with large blue eyes, chiseled features rivaled only by Adonis, and white blond hair pulled back from a round face and sharp jaw. She wore a tiara dotted by the same color aquamarine gems as her gown.

Ask her if she would like a glass of champagne. The voice was strong and feminine.

Theodocia nodded and turned to me.

"No, thanks," I said before she could speak.

The Silent Queen's eyes fell to me. *You can hear me?*

"Um, yeah." I glanced at Theodocia, who appeared surprised as well. "Is that okay?"

The two exchanged a look. The Silent Queen lifted her chin in silent command.

"Leandra, would you come with me?" Theodocia spoke.

Leandra nearly tripped over her feet as she left, her gaze on the Silent Queen.

I shifted feet when they'd gone, not at all certain how I was supposed to act around someone like this. When the Silent Queen continued to study me, I finally stepped forward with my hand extended.

"I'm Alessandra," I said awkwardly. "Which you probably

know because everyone does."

Phoibe. She shook my hand. *Please. Sit with me.* She perched on a couch with more grace and dignity than I'd ever done anything. I tried to follow her lead, saw my ugly shoes and then quickly tucked my feet back into the layers of my gown.

Phoibe raised an elegant eyebrow.

"My shoes don't match." My cheeks were warm. "So, I'm learning people aren't who they claim or appear to be. You have any sort of ambitions of chopping off my limbs or throwing me into an arena to face monsters? It'd be nice to have a heads up for once."

I learned long ago to trust no one.

I started to smile. She was impossible to read – her expression pleasant but without emotion, her rigid composure unflappable. Around my age, her eyes were soulful, as if she'd already suffered through what I was just learning. I sensed more about her, though, a sort of hyper awareness I got when I was around Adonis. They both saw more than anyone should.

Oddly enough, the sense put me at ease.

"I am," I said and began to babble the way I did around Adonis when he was watching me. "I guess I thought the world would be, too. Do they make you wear dresses every day or do you choose to?"

I like them.

"I guess no one tells a queen what to do."

You'd be surprised. When you are defined by your position rather than your personality, you are subjected to the expectations of others.

"I can see that." I started to relax more, liking her. "I hope they don't want to torture you."

We all bear a curse of some kind. She glanced towards the door. *But I do not wish you to succumb to the fate for which you're destined. I would see you freed to live your life.*

"You are at odds with the others."

No two of us in the Triumvirate are playing for the same reward.

"Games," I snorted. "The Supreme Magistrate wants me to become the Oracle. I don't know what the Supreme Priest wants." I did, but I wasn't about to reveal aloud he wanted to kill off all the gods to gain favor with the Titans.

Power.

Adonis had claimed the same about everyone involved in this game. "And you? What do you want from me?" I asked in an even voice. "What trial would you have me perform?"

There are two things I wish of you. The first, to disrupt the gods and politicians. To put an end to the world as we know it to create anew.

"Is that it?" I laughed uncomfortably. "Just hit the reset button?"

You disagree.

"No. I want … I was raised to believe in the Old Ways and to think I'm the one who's supposed to change all this." I motioned to the empty room.

They trained you well. For the first time since meeting her, a flicker of emotion – satisfaction – went through the Silent Queen's eyes.

"You know who trained me?"

I suspected after Docia met you for the first time. One of my fellow Triumvirate members found you and hid you away?

"Sort of. I mean, I don't know for sure." Cleon had known where I was, and Lantos had created the cords that allowed the priests to hide me. "I think everyone knew pieces of information but not the full picture or I would've been hauled out of my forest long ago."

I was too young to have had a hand in hiding you. My deception began when I saw the gods begin to tear apart the human world five years ago. She rose as she spoke and crossed to a delicate china box on the mantle over a quiet fireplace. *Docia and I looked around at what our options were and made a choice.* She pulled a piece of cloth out of the box and returned, handing it to me.

I unfolded it. "Mama's mark. I saw it driving into DC with Niko when …" I looked up at her. "You …" The idea would make even her laugh if I was wrong. "… created Mama?"

Insurgency. My security detail is small. I needed an army to start to wear down the other two.

"A mercenary army can't really be trusted though, can it?"

Some are mercenary. Most are people from around the world who have lost loved ones to the Holy Wars that began five years ago. They want revenge. The criminal underworld offers us a place to fund and hide such an army as well as create dissension.

It sounded absolutely dangerous to trust an army of people either paid to be there or present for revenge. The more I learned about the political maneuvering of the Triumvirate, the more amazed I became that they'd lasted as long as they had. "Wow. So … the other two can't know."

They suspect. Just as I suspect the Priest has other plans for you. Cleon wishes only to keep the elite happy, but I've learned he's devised an alternate method of doing so involving you. What exactly that is, I do not yet know.

The reminder they were all after me sent a streak of cold fear through me. "It doesn't seem real. So you want to overthrow the system with a mercenary army and bring back the Old Ways."

I want to sever the gods from their world and force them to suffer as the Bloodline has. Anger was in her voice.

"Suffer?"

Another time, we will discuss the second favor I ask of you. What you need to know is you have a part in my revolution, and your trial involves my plan.

"Destroying the gods?"

No. I want them to live stranded here with their curses, placed in gilded cages and paraded around for the people to see. The current Oracle prevents them from moving between worlds and your presence will discourage them from acting against us directly. Your trial is to kill the current Oracle. After you succeed, then you and I will lead the rebellion against the human elite for the sake of the rest of our kind who live in oppression.

If these people were remotely serious, I had a lot to do. Kill the gods, the Oracle, rebel against the humans and end up crucified.

"How does anyone think I can do anything of the sort?" I asked in frustration. "I can't use my magic yet."

Then learn. I cannot keep you too long, or the other two will become suspicious. Send messages through Leandra.

Theodocia entered, and the Silent Queen rose.

Tucking the cloth into the drawstring purse Leandra chose for me today, I stood as well.

It was an honor to meet you, the Silent Queen dipped her head with characteristic elegance.

"Thanks." I didn't know what to do so smiled and stepped away.

Theodocia led me to Leandra, who waited at the doorway leading into the gardens. Leandra appeared excited still, but I was finding it hard to sort through the politics of being an Oracle.

Of everything I'd learned, though, the thought of putting an end to Cecilia hit me hard. It had never occurred to me that I might be able to rid her of the pain once and for all. Yet … killing her was so personal. The last woman to bear the title of Oracle. She deserved so much more and I knew she'd never get it in this life. Her body was destroyed, and soon, her mind would be as well.

The only thing anyone could give her was peace. I'd killed monsters. Could I do the same for her? Would I want someone to end my life if I were in her position?

"Walk or do something. You're drawing looks!" Leandra hissed.

I blinked and registered what I was doing. I was standing in front of a topiary piece of art, staring dumbly into space. I sighed.

"You okay?"

"Not really. I miss Herakles."

"I put the word out last night for anyone who finds him to contact me."

I met her gaze, surprised. "Really?"

"Duh. It's my job."

"You're such a turd, Leandra."

"You're a bigger one."

I bit back my response as someone walked past us. "Thank you," I murmured when they'd gone.

"I don't think the priests prepared you enough for this," she observed.

"Try not at all!"

"You did kill monsters."

"With help from Adonis."

"Yeah. He's got the body and face of a god." Leandra sighed as she gazed in the direction of the Supreme Priest and SISA chief.

A stirring of jealousy went through me before I reminded myself the man scared me more than the beast. "I wish ..." *I hadn't awoken him.* But that wasn't right, because the tiny voice in my head was fiercely in his court. It had to be the instinct of an Oracle who brought a creature to life, the connection created by sharing my ribbons with another.

"What? He didn't destroy our home? Didn't torture

innocent people for information?"

"Yeah," I said, troubled. "I don't know what to think about that. I feel like the whole world is on my shoulders. Everyone expects incredible things from me, and I can't even match my shoes and dress let alone understand who I should trust."

Leandra's sympathetic smile was comforting. "How do we make you better prepared?"

Her considerate question caused a stir of confusion after our dealings with one another at school. However, I also innately knew my whole world was different now, and so was everyone in it. "I need to get a handle on my magic."

"Do it."

"I'm not sure how."

"You made a Typhon disappear. Maybe you're overthinking it. Maybe that's why Herakles taught you to fight rather than think." She winked.

I flushed. Not everything had changed. Too irked to respond, I looked around and focused on the ribbons. She had a point. I hadn't thought twice about how to tackle the Typhon once I realized Adonis was in danger, and I'd brought the cup and cot in our cell to life without thinking either.

"Here. Drink some alcohol. It might help." She handed me two glasses of champagne. "Quickly!"

I chugged one and ended up coughing at the burn. Leandra took the empty flute glass and handed me another. She handed me three more, and I chugged all five before I started to feel untethered from the world.

"Ugh. No more." I pushed the sixth away.

"How do you feel?"

"A little fuzzy."

"Good. Go sit in the shade and use your magic."

"It's not that easy." The alcohol was working quickly, and my first step wasn't as certain as the second. "It doesn't just come to me."

"Yes, it will. Shut up and sit down." She nudged me towards the empty bench under an orange tree that smelled of sweet citrus flowers.

I sat. She took up a position behind me while I observed the ribbons. They were brighter with the alcohol, or perhaps, I was just blocking out the rest of the stimuli. When I'd awoken the stuff in our cell, I'd been startled. When I defeated the Typhon, I'd been scared. The barrier between my world and my emotions was lowering with the alcohol. I had a sense of euphoria once more like I experienced in the Oracle's horrible building.

I plucked two ribbons from the many and focused on them. *Wake up,* I said without knowing what exactly they were connected to. Doubting it'd work, I shifted to another set of ribbons and ordered them awake.

Something tickled the back of my calf, and I stretched down, digging through the layers of silk to reach a grasshopper clinging to me. I flicked it away.

"It's not working," I said, disappointed.

"Um, depends on what you did exactly." At Leandra's note of uncertainty, I straightened.

One of the topiary creatures had begun to stir. It lifted one leg then the other and stepped from the dirt onto the path. Murmurs of alarm went up. The twelve foot tall Pegasus swished a tail made of roses and shook out a mane of tulips.

I watched it. It had three ribbons, one of which was green. I stood, thrilled, and wobbled.

"It's beautiful," Leandra breathed. "You did that?"

"Yeah."

People began glancing my way, at first in worry. Then a round of applause went up, and they crowded around to watch the bush creature walking slowly through the gardens. The second creature I'd awakened soon began to move as well. It was a griffin, and it roared a handful of leaves when it dropped its jaw to speak.

The attendees were snapping pictures and marveling over the mobile topiary.

"The Oracle entertains us!" someone said with a laugh. "Magnificent!"

The Pegasus began grazing on a plain hedge, much to the delight of those watching.

"Her Majesty may not approve of you moving her bushes," Lantos' upbeat words were quiet. "Awaken more and give her a scare!"

He, trailed by Adonis, was one of the only people not mesmerized by the sight and lingering back with me. I glanced from him to Adonis then away quickly, not confident about dealing with Adonis during daylight.

"Do it," Leandra whispered her support.

I was buzzing, but I focused on a small topiary of a winged

sheep near us. *Wake up!* Without knowing what exactly I did to cause it to stir, I saw the green ribbon that floated through the space between us. It settled onto the ribbons already hanging over the creature, and it began to stir. I woke up two more and watched with a grin as they joined the others roaming through the gardens.

"Fantastic," Lantos said from beneath his mask. "Here I thought you could only use your magic when someone you cared about was in trouble."

My jaw went slack at the words. Adonis was close enough to hear them. Before I could muster a retort from among my cheerfully buzzing thoughts, he moved away to join the others.

Adonis remained beside me. I risked another look at him. Meaning to glance quickly, I found myself stuck staring at his perfect features.

"You will need more than an army of bushes," he said.

"For ..."

"Whatever the Silent Queen said to you that made you so tense."

He felt it. Like he always knew where I was. I dropped my gaze and waved Leandra back. "I want to hate you, Adonis," I said, frustrated. "Everyone I've ever met considers you a butcher."

"Most people fear the beast more than the man. But you are different. As usual."

"I love the beast," I said before I could stop myself. Cleaning my throat, I rushed on. "Do you recall everything you say and do as a beast when you're transformed in the morning?" I asked, somewhat hopeful he didn't remember holding me last night. My insides ignited and soared at the memory.

"I recall more, because my senses are heightened at night."

"Are you really as bad as they say?" I faced him.

He turned to look down at me. "Do you need me to say it again?"

"Yes." It was getting harder for me to recall what he was when we were together, and I needed the reinforcement.

"Then I am twice what people have told you." His gaze didn't waver and I felt no tingle to indicate he was lying.

My heart fell and with it my mood. I didn't know how to respond. I had held out hope that there was some goodness in him, that the rumors were false and the fear of the masses misplaced.

But he was every bit the monster people believed him to be.

We gazed at one another in silence, and a familiar pain stung me. I didn't want to lose Mismatch, but I couldn't associate with a man like this. One who tortured, slaughtered and mowed down whole forests with no concern for who might be hurt in the process. One whose sizzling look managed to drive every sensible thought out of my head and make me too aware of the hardness of his body, the incredible reflexes.

"Stay away from me, Adonis," I whispered at last. "Night and day." Turning away, I retreated to the bench in the shade where Leandra sat. I felt his gaze on me and sat with my back to the crowd.

"You have a lover's quarrel with the SISA chief?" Leandra

said with a small laugh.

"We don't get along."

She rolled her eyes. "When a man looks at you like that, you're beyond the getting along stage."

"Whatever." A warm flutter ran through me. I suppressed it quickly, determined not to be associated with the man. "He's a murderer, Leandra. Even if you were remotely right, I couldn't be associated with him."

"He saved your life in the arena."

"He's a bad person."

"Maybe he had a reason."

I glanced at her. "What reason is there to slaughter hundreds or thousands of people?"

"I don't know," she admitted. "He's bad news. I get it. But he looks at you like there's more to his story."

Sometimes I hated how smart Leandra was.

"You guys have a thing?" she pressed.

"No of course not! I'm doomed to be alone. You all used to steal boys from me but I'm starting to think it was a good thing. If I've learned anything since leaving the forest, it's that I can't trust anyone. Ever."

"You have us."

"You're a spy!" I exclaimed softly.

"For you!" she retorted. "Herakles. You are his world."

I clamped my mouth shut. Leandra's attention was on the guests.

"The Supreme Priest is kinda creepy with that mask."

"Yeah." I twisted to follow her gaze.

Lantos and the SISA chief were talking privately apart from the crowd. Whenever I thought of Lantos, I recalled the Oracle. Studying him, a new idea formed, and I rose.

Leandra scrambled after me as I approached the two. Their talking ceased, and they looked at me as I neared.

"May I have a word?" I asked Lantos.

"Of course." He stepped away from Adonis to join me. Leandra lingered behind.

We walked for a short distance into the gardens, away from anyone else, before I was comfortable enough to speak. "Will you take me to see the Oracle again?"

Lantos was quiet, his eyes the only part of him visible from beneath the mask.

"Please," I added. "I don't know how else to go see her if you don't help with the shadows thing."

"My instincts tell me I'm not going to like this answer, but for what purpose?" he asked. His cheerful voice and sparkling eyes made him so much easier to talk to than Adonis.

"Not your concern."

"You learned those words from my chief." He chuckled. "I have the choice to take you or not, based on your response. Perhaps you should try again."

"Fine. I want her to tell me how to use my magic."

"And that's a lie."

I growled in frustration. "It's partially true. I want to kill her."

His eyes widened.

"To put her at peace," I continued.

"You speak to the Silent Queen and come away wanting to murder the Oracle. Can I assume the two are linked?"

"I saw her, Lantos!" I exclaimed. "I saw what they did to her. What they'll do to me. How can I leave her that way? If I were her, I'd beg for someone to kill me."

He began walking again. I went with him, agitated. "There is a flaw with this plan," he started. "Aside from accelerating your fate at the hands of the Magistrate, you'd also risk exposing me while simultaneously chopping off my ability to draw off my power. I'm connected to the same place the gods are."

"You said you want them to suffer. You had to know that would mean losing your power, too."

"At the right time, Alessandra. At a time of my choosing."

A chill went through me. "What if that time is after the Oracle dies of natural causes? Are you willing to let me meet that fate?"

"It would be temporary and of short endurance if so. Only until I can ensure the passage of … we'll just say something important from the other side of the portal."

I stopped walking.

"It's not what I want. Adonis has taken to you, and I want to respect my friend enough to spare you," he admitted.

"If you throw your friends into the arena, they're probably better off without you," I said, a surge of protectiveness flying through me.

"You're not helping your case," he chided. "My hope is to be in position well before her natural death. But I'm not willing to expedite it."

"You won't help me."

"Not unless the timing is right." The skin around his eyes crinkled in a sign he was smiling beneath the mask. "Trust me, Alessandra. I showed you your fate when no one else would. I've protected you since you were a child, and you know my motivation to seeing the gods cared for properly. I ask only that you give things time to fall into place. It'll work out. I promise."

If I do this ... if the Oracle dies soon ... he'll see me crucified. I said nothing, understanding too well what he meant.

"Don't look so dour! There's plenty of champagne and beautiful bush creatures to amuse us," he said and slid his arm through mine and walked me back towards the party.

The more I thought about it, the better idea it was to help the existing Oracle find peace. Even so, he had presented a problem I didn't think through: I didn't have anywhere to go if she died and I was next in line. Except maybe ...

My eyes went towards the villa in whose gardens we were. The Silent Queen had a network of some kind, a plan for rebellion. I wanted to think she'd be willing to protect me if the Oracle died.

But I was learning more and more that I couldn't trust anyone. Even those who seemed to be willing to help. In the end, they were out for their own purposes, and I was a means to an end. I wanted to believe the Silent Queen, but I was afraid to.

I had to break away from these people. I had the magic

needed to fend off entire armies, the survival skills to live anywhere, and the ragged red cord needed to hide from even Mismatch.

A different kind of plan began to form, one that fit my own purposes rather than those of everyone around me.

Escape. After giving the existing Oracle peace.

"I'm ready to go home," I told Leandra as we rejoined the party area.

"Should you turn off the monsters first?"

Glancing around, I saw guests gathered around the creatures. "Nah. They seem happy." *And I hope they eat some of these people.*

Leandra trailed me as I left the gardens and walked around the villa to the covered sidewalks.

"I want to run away," I told her.

"I don't blame you."

"No. I'm serious."

Leandra drew abreast of me and met my gaze. "To where?"

"That's what we need to figure out. Somewhere they won't look."

"Outside the walls, then."

"Yeah."

"That's risky. If they found you in the forest, they'll find you wherever you go."

"But I have my magic. I'll keep learning to use it. Even if they do, I can make them disappear like I did the Typhon."

"True." She was frowning. "Didn't you talk to the Silent Queen about her plan?"

"Yeah. But, Leandra, every one of these people wants me for their purpose. To play a role in their plan. No one is looking out for *me*." The image of the Oracle was in my head once more. "Just like no one is looking out for her. They only want what she can do for them."

"Who?"

"The Oracle."

Leandra was quiet for a long moment before speaking again. "I understand, Lyssa. I don't disagree. But you need to consider the idea the Silent Queen might be a better option. One that helps us bring back the Old Ways."

The wisdom in her words held me in silence as I reconsidered. She was right. But so was I, to want my freedom. On the surface, the Silent Queen appeared to be the best option I had.

"And … you need to complete your trials before you can access all your magic. Think about it. Do you want to be caught outside the walls by a desperate god?" Leandra advised as we entered my villa.

"No," I answered.

"You've had a rough go of it lately. Try to see your situation with less emotion."

"You always make sense," I said moodily. The buzz of alcohol had faded, and I was starting to feel heavy. "I'm gonna take a nap."

Leandra left me at the doorway of my bedroom. I changed quickly and dropped into bed, troubled and needing some alone time to think.

NINETEEN

Love is composed of a single soul inhabiting two bodies.
– ARISTOTLE

L ATER ON, I WAS ON A JOURNEY TO EXPLORE THE VILLA – to find some shred of insight into Cecelia's life – when Leandra found me.

"You have a guest," she said.

"Ugh. Who?" I leaned back from searching beneath the bed in one of the guest bedrooms.

"And you're in jeans. Great." She eyed the designer jeans I'd uncovered in the massive closet. I was barefoot and wearing the most dressed down blouse I could find. "Probably someone you don't want to see."

"There's a million people on that list!"

"Adonis."

And he's number one. "Can you tell him I'm … I don't

know. Dead."

"He's the SISA chief, Lyssa. Whatever is going on between you two, you need to keep in mind he's in a powerful position. We might be able to use that."

Over my dead body. But I rose. "Fine."

I trailed her out of the bedroom. I steeled myself to tell Adonis to leave and walk away.

Entering the foyer area, my tongue stilled when I saw him in his black uniform once more, the one that clung to his muscular thighs, displayed his flat abs and outlined the shapes of his shoulders and biceps. In the end, I stopped and stared at him speechless long enough for him to beat me to it. Not that it mattered. Nothing he could say would sway me from my intention.

"Care to spar?"

Except that. I crossed my arms. "You have an entire organization of people to spar with."

"None of them are as fast as you."

A trickle of pride slid through me. "Okay. Meet me in the garden." I spun on my heels and returned to my room to seek out clothing for the event.

And then I sprinted from my room to the door leading to the garden. Not because I wanted to see him, but because …

Well, I did. It was impossible to deny it. No matter what I knew about him, I didn't want him completely gone yet. Slowing, I exited into the garden and finished tying my hair into a ponytail. He stood ready in the stone courtyard at the center of the garden.

Adonis said nothing but lowered into a fighting stance. With a deep breath, I did the same.

We began to warm up with slow movements, lazy strikes and soft blocks. I half expected him to speak, but he didn't, except to offer advice as we sparred.

Warm ups transitioned into bouts of heated combat that galvanized me. I was angry with him, at my world, at everything. I fought him harder than I had in the SISA building.

I was soon sweating in the late afternoon sun, focused on obliterating his guard or at least, beating myself against it until I could no longer think or feel. His technique was flawless, his reflexes otherworldly. It was easy to let go, to unleash every last ounce of conflicted emotion, and channel everything into physical struggle once again.

In the end, he'd win. I knew this. But I didn't care. We went on for an intense hour or two. My breathing grew ragged, my movements lethargic and tired. At long last, he put me out of my misery and pinned me. An arm bar around my neck, his thighs locked around mine, I was immobilized on top of him, facing the sky with him between me and the ground.

I went limp and tapped out.

Adonis released me, and I rolled off him onto my belly. He remained on his back, breathing hard. Sweat dripped down my neck and soaked the roots of my hair.

"It won't work ... next time," I said between breaths.

He didn't ask what I was talking about. He already and always knew.

"Why are you here, Adonis?" I asked and pushed myself to my knees. "Really."

"To spar."

"No. I felt a ping. That's not true. To spy on me for Lantos?"

"He told me what you wanted him to help you do." He rose and held out his hand.

I accepted and let him pull me up. "And he told me if I end up crucified so he can get whatever it is he wants from the other side of the portal, he'll have me torn limb from body."

"He has his reasons."

New anger tore through me at the calm claim. "His reasons," I repeated. "Because that's all that matters."

"There's a lot at stake."

I started away, furious I'd been drawn in again. After the arena, I wanted to believe there was a part of him capable of being good.

"Alessandra." He caught my arm.

"I'm not going to let anyone do that to me!" I snapped and pulled free.

"Neither will I."

"You'd disobey your boss?"

"Lantos wouldn't take it that far."

"You doubt the man who threw you into the arena out of a hissy fit?" Adonis was too smart for this! "Your loyalty blinds you, Adonis! He claimed he would. Whatever game you're playing, stop!"

"No game. He sent me to tell you his intentions to protect you."

"Ah. Another deception from Adonis. You didn't come to spar of your own free will."

"If I recall correctly, you told me to stay away."

"And yet you're here."

"I was left … dissatisfied with your command."

No ping this time. The tension between us was of a nature I didn't understand. Thick and energized, ripe with promise, despite our sparring. The urge to put something between us was back.

"I meant it," I managed.

"I don't think you do."

"I don't care what you think!" Adonis twisted me into knots. The words were difficult to say. "Don't come back, Adonis."

"Alessandra."

I waited, arms crossed, forcing myself to recall all the bad news I'd heard of him to keep from remembering the human parts that left me raw, vulnerable to him.

"I don't want this," he said finally.

"Then stop being you." The moment the words left my mouth, I heard how cruel they were. "I'm sorry. I mean … I know who you were once. The creature who saved a child because you knew she was in danger. I don't know who you are now, Adonis, and that terrifies me. I can't … I can't let you in my life." My voice quivered. "Do you understand why?"

"Because you're afraid of me."

I nodded.

"Yes. I understand. You have been hurt by too many people

and you think I will hurt you, too."

Gods when he wanted to be, he was so ... sweet. Lethal yet sweet. The combination was perfectly him – and so complicated and confusing, I was starting to panic. I waited for him – *willed* him – to say more. But he didn't.

This time when I walked away, he didn't try to stop me. My victory was bitter. Even I had to acknowledge I didn't really want him gone. Part of me hoped Mismatch didn't listen even if Adonis did.

But he did.

That night, after I pulled on a t-shirt for bed, I turned off the lights and waited for him to appear.

Mismatch didn't come. I stayed up as late as I could and fell asleep feeling sad – and angry with myself for it. No grotesque perched on my balcony.

I was alone, and it hurt more than sending him away.

TWENTY
THE GROTESQUE PRINCE

A man's character is his fate.
– HERACLITUS

HE SECOND THE LAST GOLDEN RAY OF HERSPERIDES left the sky, I began to hear them. Thousands of voices. They filled my head. Subtle whispers, and sometimes louder calls, turned into a form of soothing music. As I flew into the air to hunt my dinner, they were joined by memories. The voices felt like they belonged, old friends returned, even if I didn't understand who or what they were yet.

But the memories were strangers to me, from a different time and world, of a man who had been buried deep inside me for too long. A man I didn't know anymore.

The voices drowned out the memories as I flew over the central Temple of Artemis. I was drawn to her temples without understanding why and this night, many of the voices seemed to originate from there. Hovering over it, I decided to stop and walk among the grotesques and gargoyles, as I often did.

I dropped to the ground and folded my wings, tilting my head to listen.

Welcome back, brother!

Where have you been?

Did you not hear us asking you to visit?

The stone statues were speaking. Each had a voice. I walked from one to another to yet another, listening to his or her distinct voice before stepping back into the center.

Spotty before this, the memories began to flow more rapidly, of the day Alessandra visited this very temple as a child and awoke me from the stone. Twisting, I spotted the platform where I used to stand and crossed to it. No other creature had taken its place.

"I'm from here." The words were a growl when I was in my monster form but I needed to hear a sound from outside my head to help me focus. The stone creatures around me were excited and drowning out my ability to think. "How is this possible?"

The voices fell silent, and I closed my eyes, sensing the answers in my own head.

This time the memories hit me with such force, I was driven to my knees. Gasping, I rested my clawed hands on the roof of the temple. These weren't recent memories but those of a life long passed.

"Don't fight them. They're a part of you. Let them flow."

The soft female voice came from behind me.

Too overwhelmed, I hadn't noticed the priestess approach. She wore the glassy-eyed look of a woman in a trance. Her body was stiff, and she didn't even seem to breathe. Only her mouth moved.

I had seen this before. Gods and Goddesses spoke through their respective priests and priestesses, possessing the bodies of the willing to send messages.

"Ar … artemis?" I growled.

"Yes. It is time for you to recall who you are. What you are."

With some apprehension, I did as she said and allowed the memories to flow.

Mycenaean Greece. Four thousand years ago. I rode my warhorse along a beach whose white sands were soaked with red from my latest battle. Victorious, I'd once more defended my kingdom from the sea raiders from the south. The last rays of sunlight reflected off the armor of the army at the other end of the beach.

I rode away from the army for the sole purpose of relishing my victory. Rejoicing in the bloodshed of the enemy and the crushed hulls of their ships listing in the bay.

"Another great victory that will be spoken about for years to come," said the priest beside me.

"Had you any doubt?" I replied.

"Never, your grace. The Oracle of Delphi foretold your victory."

I smiled. My kingdom was enjoying a golden era of wealth, military conquest and glory.

"You have doubled the size of your kingdom. You will conquer all peoples by the time you are twenty five."

"I will leave the world to my heirs."

"The first of which I bring you news. The child is a boy," the priest added. "Healthy and strong like his father."

"The gods bless us." I smiled. An empire, a son, an army unlike any that had ever been created. I would be the one to realize the dreams of my forefathers.

"They do. He is likely the first of many of the servants and slaves you've taken to your bed."

"You wanted heirs," I said with a wink.

"One will suffice." His grave features were even more serious than before. "The Oracle believes he will be as mighty as his father."

"Good."

"Which leaves us to the final message I wish to impart to you."

I glanced at him. Final? He was elderly but not yet near the age when men died naturally in their sleep. At seventeen, I was a feared warrior not about to die in my sleep either.

"Artemis has seen your battle and requested your service."

"Artemis?" I echoed. "The goddess of women? Not a mighty warrior like Ares?" After each battle, I was summoned by a god and usually given the location for the next battle and advice for defeating my enemies. We worked together, the Gods and the Bloodline, for the glory and power of my kingdom.

Artemis was not known to favor battles, though, unlike some of the other gods who were constant benefactors. I was curious what peoples the goddess of women and hunting would have my army conquer next.

"She offers you this." He handed me a small pouch. I accepted it and dumped the glowing teal gem into my palm. Holding it up to the dying sun, I admired the sparkle and facets.

"Flawless. Fit for a king," I said in approval. "Tell her I will go where she wishes."

The priest bowed his head. "We thank you, your grace." He left me in peace to ponder my next great battle. I listened to the ocean in case Poseidon sent word through the waves of enemies trapped in the bay in need of slaying.

The sun sank beneath the horizon, and an immediate chill seized me, tickling my toes and traveling upward through my body. I felt ... stiff despite the battle lust still in my system and glanced down at the toes that suddenly didn't move.

They were gray, and the strange color and stiffness was climbing up my body.

"Priest!" I bellowed.

My thighs, hips, lower back and torso were soon too stiff to move. My fingers went next and it raced up my arms and shoulders, finally swallowing my neck and head.

I fell from the horse, helpless. I couldn't even blink.

"The curse of the Bloodline," came the priest's sad voice. "The price for the blessing of the gods."

My eyes opened. The memories flooded my mind. Scenes of previous victories, of battle, war, blood-edged politics and strategy that explained my ability to see what others didn't in the manipulative maneuvering of the Triumvirate.

And then there were the four thousands years frozen in stone where my mind and senses were alert in my role as a temple guardian even though my body never moved for four millennia.

I looked anew at the others around me, understanding why I resembled them, why I was comfortable visiting them. Why we were connected. Horror spread through me and I crossed to the nearest grotesque. It told me the answer without me asking.

Two thousand years.

The one next to it had been frozen for only a few hundred.

I was surrounded by my family, Bloodline, forefathers and heirs. My heart twisted inside me to recall what it was like to be among them and then the ecstasy of the first breath I took after Alessandra awoke me.

Phoibe. I froze in place. I had been seventeen when I sired a child. The Silent Queen, a descendent of mine, was eighteen, but the image in my head was of her as a child close to Alessandra's age when she woke me.

"Do you remember why the queen is silent?" Artemis asked through the priestess.

"Because I told her never to speak so the priests couldn't trick her into the curse. She was supposed to remain mute until I returned for her." I was struggling not to feel, not to let the emotions inside me take over. "I never returned. That was twelve years ago."

"She's never spoken since."

I said nothing, overwhelmed by the idea I'd let a little girl suffer for twelve years. I'd dealt with Phoibe as the queen, neither of us knowing who the other was. As a child, she knew only my Mismatch form and I had been forced to forget everything about her.

The protective instinct surging inside me was the same I felt for Alessandra. It had first emerged in the responsibility of a ruler charged with the welfare of his people and later tempered by my duty as a stone guardian of a temple. Ingrained into me, I didn't understand its source and strength until this moment.

"You were hurt. Lantos saved you. Your memories were likely deemed … dangerous," Artemis said, pulling me from my thoughts.

Lantos wiped my memories. I saw these images, too, of him wiping my mind as I lay helpless and dying beneath him.

"You swore once to serve me."

"An oath that turned me to stone." I faced her.

"The oath to me did not do this. Your word was given to fight a battle on my behalf."

I was struggling to contain the beast side of me that wanted to fly, to lose itself in physical sensation.

"Lantos is your friend. Your master. But he's not your ally when it comes to a particular issue."

"What exactly would you have me do to fulfill my oath? Kill

him?"

"No. I'd have you protect Alessandra."

"Alessandra." Another thought occurred simultaneously. "She can save them!" I motioned to the members of my Bloodline trapped forever in stone.

"Not yet."

I paced. "Then our purposes are aligned. Protect her so she saves my kind."

"Protect her so she saves all peoples."

Anger was crowding out my surprise. The gods and their priests had cursed me and every ruler of Greece for ten thousand years. What did I care for her cause? If I protected Alessandra, it was because she had truly acted out of a desire to help me and in doing so, had lifted the curse on one monster otherwise doomed to an eternity in stone. If she did it once, she could do it again and stop this nasty curse that imprisoned feeling, thinking, sensing men and women in stone.

"I don't care about other peoples," I said at last. "I owe them nothing."

"And Lantos?"

Lantos wasn't bad. He was driven and desperate enough to use Alessandra in a way neither of us wanted simply to reach his end goal. Without my ability to strategize, he looked for the quickest method to succeed, no matter what the risk and cost ultimately was. Erasing my memory … sending me after Alessandra when he knew what she was to me … they were the means to his end. I didn't fault him for doing what he felt necessary, but I did fault him for his insistence earlier this day that Phase Two was the only option we had.

"He's a misguided friend," I replied. "One whose purpose no longer serves mine."

"I hear the voice of the ruthless prince of Greece you once were."

I touched my forehead. The familiar headache was back. "That man is dead, his brashness tempered by four thousand years trapped in stone. I have no desire to become him again."

"But you may need to if you are to take your place in this prophetic end of times."

I lifted my head, liking our discussion less and less. "Alessandra is the Oracle. I'm nothing to the Triumvirate, and Phoibe is the current heir to the Bloodline and crown. What place does a rogue monster, awoken by the good humor of Tyche, hold in prophecy?"

"The place beside *her*. I don't need to tell you this. You've felt it since you became reacquainted."

What I'd felt had been too unclear for me to understand, except that I knew I couldn't let anything happen to her. How deep that dedication ran, whether or not it was more than gratitude and fidelity for her rescuing me, I didn't know. But I suspected it was more than I was ready to handle at the moment. "You're wrong," I said.

"Then let me prove it to you." Artemis sat on the back of one of the stone creatures. "Do you remember your real name?"

"Of course. It's …" I stared at her. I recalled every moment of my life before being stone, every military campaign, every slave I slept with, even the names of politicians I'd ordered assassinated and my forefathers for a hundred years before me. Adonis was a name given to me when two police officers found me in an alley shortly after Alessandra awoke me.

But it wasn't *my* name. Not originally at least.

"Your name is written on a plaque buried beneath the beach where you turned to stone, a memorial of sorts to the great warrior prince," Artemis said. "Go there. Find it. Tell me what else is written. When you see it, you will understand."

Usually it was me who toyed with others, but the goddess was having her day – or perhaps, more accurately, her latest day the past four millennia – to play with me. I didn't like it one bit.

And I didn't have a choice either. If I wanted to know what secret she hid, I'd have to do as she said. "What of Alessandra?" I asked uneasily. "She's not safe here."

"No, she is not, and I fear her fate will become much worse soon. Like you, she needs to learn. Those lessons will be painful."

"Then I'll stay."

"You can never truly help her if you don't find the plaque."

I clenched my jaw. A goddess was offering to help me for reasons I didn't understand. This same goddess was the only one rumored to be trapped on Earth who hadn't spoken to Lantos. And she wanted me to help Alessandra, the person who could awaken the other members of the Bloodline and perhaps prevent Phoibe from being turned into a temple guardian.

My personal feelings held no place in this discussion. I

detested being manipulated or lied to. I hated being sent away from the action knowing full well I left Alessandra in danger.

"I have guided you the best I can the past few years," she added. "Like Mnemosyne, I have spoken to you as well."

"Through Mrs. Nettles?" I asked. The double possession. The sense that Mrs. Nettles was two people living inside her, one of which only responded to flashy items. The other was wiser. Different. "I wish you all would leave her alone." I had no way of knowing if my long time companion experienced pain when overtaken by a goddess, and I loathed the knowledge I'd been spied on.

"The faster you go, the faster you return," she baited.

"I will do it for them," I motioned to the statues, "and for her. Not because I gave you an oath."

"Very well."

My head snapped in the direction of Alessandra's villa, and my body went rigid. It wasn't yet comfortable to feel what she did, despite teasing her about it. Fear slid through me – her fear – followed by her pain.

Without saying another word to the goddess, I leapt into the air.

TWENTY ONE
ALESSANDRA

I am not afraid of an army of lions led by a sheep; I am afraid of an army of sheep led by a lion.
– ALEXANDER THE GREAT

IT HAPPENED TOO FAST FOR ME TO REACT.

Hands yanked me out of slumber, bound and gagged me and tied a hood over my head. Hushed voices were too soft for me to understand, and I was slung roughly over the shoulder of someone I didn't need to see to know how big he was. His jarring gait smashed into my ribs with each step, waking me further. Immobilized, I did what Herakles had taught me and trained my senses on anything I could identify: sounds, smells, touch.

And I tried not to panic. It was one thing to be tossed into an arena with a monster and provided weapons. It was something else to be blinded and helpless. I *hated* the feeling of being out of control of my own body.

I identified four people by the different pitches of their voices. I was slung into the backseat of a car that peeled out fast enough for me to be pinned to the backseat. Struggling to make sense of what was happening, I heard two men in the front seat. They had bound me with duct tape, and I almost smiled.

Noob move. Herakles had trained me for this, too, for getting out of bindings of almost any sort. Sometimes, I wondered if he knew what I'd face one day or if his paranoia was simply paying off.

Face planted against the seat and seatbelt fasteners jabbing me in the ribs and thigh, I stretched backwards until I could reach the tape around my ankles. With some embarrassment, I realized they'd snagged me in nothing more than underwear and a t-shirt. I wasn't even wearing a bra.

It made me hate them more, whoever they were.

I prodded the tape with my fingers, searching first for any tears I could exploit and second for any single layers that would be easier to rip. I found one, and ripped it. Duct tape was the easiest of all bindings to get free of for the simple reason that it was more vulnerable to tears. A good tug, and it'd rip down the center to free my legs.

The hands would be harder since I'd need leverage. Behind my back, it was almost impossible. I shifted with some effort until I was on my back and began sawing at the tape with the seatbelt fastener. I didn't need a clean cut – just a hole in the integrity of the tape.

The car turned several times, and the men were silent. The

journey was longer than I expected; they had a specific destination, which could either be good or bad. In my head, I began to drill myself on the different scenarios that might occur, all the while praying for this to be some kind of huge misunderstanding or joke or similar.

The long drive ended about twenty minutes later. The driver parked, killed the engine, and seconds later, the large man who carried me was hauling me out of the back. Stairs came next. Lots of them. The cool night air brushed my exposed legs, and I sought some explanation as to why there were so many stairs outside.

The footsteps of several other men sounded on the solid, cement or stone steps behind us. We reached the top finally. Thank gods, the giant didn't run again. My ribs were burning from the jolting trip out of the villa. I was slung into a chair somewhere outside.

I listened. It was impossible to count the number of people moving around me, but it had to be more than five or six. Heart throbbing, I began to think my chances of escaping weren't going to be good. I tested the bonds as discreetly as possible, unwilling to act until I could see what I was up against.

The hood was ripped off. A man with crossed arms stood before me, flanked by four more. A quick look around revealed three more lingering in the shadows.

But it was our location that left me the most surprised.

The wall. We were on top of it with the lights of DC lighting up the left side and the darkness of what lay outside on the right. The wall's width was easily ten meters, too wide for me to see what was at the bottom of it.

"This is her." His voice brought my attention back. "She's young. Little."

"She beat a Typhon."

He nodded, considering yet skeptical. I watched their ribbons for a moment, debating how far I'd be willing to go if I had to fight my way out of this. I hadn't yet killed a person, and I wanted to keep it that way.

The men were dressed in mixed combinations of fatigues, jeans, workout gear, and other non uniform clothing, although, every one of them wore the patch of Mama on their left bicep.

Shit. Had the Silent Queen been dissatisfied with our discussion? Was this the latest demonstration of duplicity that plagued my world? Of everyone I met, she was my favorite, even if I suspected her beauty hid cunningness characteristic of the other members of the Triumvirate.

"This is it," the leader of the small gang said with pride. "The day we prevent the gods from destroying the rest of our world. The day we rise up against them and their elite!"

The men around him roared and clapped in encouragement.

In that moment, I didn't blame them for wanting me dead. But I wasn't about to die without a fight, either.

"Remember. It has to look like an accident," he added and motioned to the two men on either side of me. They lifted the chair and tilted it back to keep me in place.

Fear tore through me. I had no plan – and no time to make one. They were all armed; I had to risk being shot or beaten or shocked to get to one of them.

Eyeing the edge of the wall they intended to throw me off of, I shifted and ripped the tape around my ankles first and twisted, lashing out at the man to my left with a hearty kick to the throat. He dropped his side of the chair, gagging, and I rolled onto the ground. Springing to my feet, I struggled with the tape around my wrists and instead of fighting, resorted to dodging the attempts of the second man to grab me.

Two more men came forward. I tore through the tape finally but didn't have time to remove the gag. I dived for the man on the ground holding his throat and ripped what weapons I could off his body then danced away.

A baton and a knife. Neither were going to stand up to a gun.

"So she has some fight in her left." Their leader's hand rested on his weapon. "Look, girl, this isn't about you. This is about righting a wrong."

I yanked off the gag. "I … know that. But there's another way."

"No. There's not. Without you, the political elite lose power and the gods can't crush us."

Some part of me knew this. I had never – not once – in my life questioned my existence. Never contemplated suicide or whether the world was better off without me. And I wasn't about to start now. I was a fighter to the bone.

"You're wrong!" I insisted. "There are other ways of –" I stopped as one man lunged at me and smashed the baton across the hand holding his gun.

"Instead of a trip to the wall gone wrong, it'll have to be a mugging," the leader said. "Or you can make this easy for me and painless for you and simply jump."

I shook my head.

"Being beat to death is not a quick way to go."

"I'll take my chances," I retorted.

"No guns," he ordered his men. More of them appeared, and I suspected I was about to enter a battle I didn't have much of a chance of winning.

But I'd always try.

The men began attacking. I did my best to use my environment to line them up, so I only faced one man at a time. The wall didn't offer much in terms of obstacles, with the exception of a couple of ventilation boxes and maintenance closets. I maneuvered close to them.

Pure instinct took over. This time, when I let go, it wasn't because someone like Adonis was capable of handling it. It was desperation and fear that drove me. I was alone again to determine my fate, to decide if I'd lie down and die peacefully or if I'd make them take me down by force.

Though well armed, none of them knew much about fighting. At least, not like Adonis, and no one moved like him. They had numbers, but I had speed and skill, and I used both.

Ducking, striking, whirling … my lethal dance saw the first three sprawling on the ground. The next fell beneath a kick that smashed him into someone else and knocked him out cold, and the next got in one good slash of a knife before he, too, was knocked silly by the club in my hand.

"Enough!" their leader roared at last. He withdrew a gun that didn't quite look normal.

I started to dive for cover when he shot.

It wasn't a bullet but a shock wave of some sort, one that slammed me backwards into one of the obstacles I'd been using to manipulate his men's attack. My head hit hard, and I slumped then caught myself. The world was spinning, my ears ringing.

Too disoriented to move, I braced myself when he raised the gun to do it again. This time, I slashed my thigh as I sailed past the ventilation box. I sprawled onto my back, stunned, the weapons having fallen from my hands.

I stared into the night sky above me, dazed. With a start, I realized it wasn't a carrion bird silhouetted against the clouds above.

Mismatch. At first, my hope surged and heart gleefully flipped at the thought that he really hadn't abandoned me. But he was so far away in the night sky, too far to help me. *Is he here to watch me die?*

I wanted to cry at the thought. The connection between us left me rattled and emotionally raw, unable to know which way was up when it came to him. I could protect myself from anyone but him.

The leader appeared in my view, the gun pointed at my head.

"Wait!" I cried and held up my hands. My ribs and back hurt, and the slashes in my abdomen and thigh burned. "Just …wait."

He did.

"I'll jump," I said quietly.

"Good girl," he said and stepped back without lowering the gun.

A commotion started towards the rear of his gathered men. I glanced towards it but away quickly, more concerned with the man before me. With some effort, I climbed to my feet and tossed my long hair over my shoulder.

"There is another –"

"I'll count to ten. If you're not dropping to the ground, I'll bash your head in and toss you."

I had no idea what kind of gun he held, but it had knocked my body into a state of sluggishness I wasn't able to shake. Blood streamed down my leg and soaked my t-shirt. I raised my hands and glanced up at his ribbons again. I didn't know how to use them. I either brought something to life or robbed it of life and didn't know how else to use my power.

If I survive this, I'm going to ask the Oracle how it all works.

"Four," he said.

"What happened to one through three?" I retorted.

"Six." He motioned towards the edge.

"I'm going!" I clasped my hands behind my head and walked to the edge of the wall. Small lights were visible in the distance. Otherwise, it was dark, almost as dark as the wall in my dream. I couldn't even tell how tall it was and I doubted I'd be able to defy gravity as I had when recovering my memories.

"Eight."

"Zeus, man!" I muttered, unsettled at the prospect. "You won't recon–"

"Nine."

I closed my eyes, more aware of the ruckus from the direction of his men but not about to spend my last second alive giving them the time of day. Instead, I closed my eyes and drew a deep breath.

"Ten."

My instincts screaming, I stepped off the ledge and began to fall.

But I didn't fall for long. At about three meters down, I hit something hard as a rock. Soft wings grazed my body, and we spun in midair. His strong arms were around me, my legs locked between his, and the rest of me pressed against his muscular form.

My eyes flew open. Mismatch had caught me flying on his back and twirled us several times, until I started to get dizzy and nauseated.

Hang on, he instructed me. Disoriented, I wrapped my arms around his neck and buried my face into the nape, breathing his scent. The wings flared out on either side of us, catching us and putting an end to the spin.

My Mismatch. What part of me truly believed if I sent him away he'd stay away? Why did I bother, when being held in his arms felt so natural? We were connected and had been since I awoke him. No matter what emotions left me in a constant state of confusion, he was always – and would remain – my Mismatch.

"Lyssa!"

I jerked at the familiar voice coming from above on top of the walls.

I'll take you home then deal with these idiots, Mismatch said.

"Wait," I murmured. "That's Herakles."

"Lyssa! These fools didn't get the message you're hands off."

I listened, thrilled to hear his voice yet sorrowful as well.

"Tell that thing to bring you back here."

I debated what to do for a moment. Mismatch hovered. "Take me back, please."

They hurt you. I won't let anyone else do that.

His words touched me on a level I hadn't expected. I lifted my head from his shoulder and gazed at him briefly. His tension was clear in his hard body, and his eyes glowed with a feral flare. He cared – no matter what he was during the daylight. No matter how scared of him I was.

"I'm sorry for sending you away. I won't do it again," I whispered. "Please take me back."

Mismatch hovered for a moment longer before relenting. He landed a safe distance from the men, and I slid to the ground. Before I had a chance to turn, he had a palm pressed to my ribs.

"Ow," I muttered.

He lifted my shirt to peer at the spot and the slash. The sensation of his warm hand on my bare skin made me shiver. *Bruised, not broken. The gash on your thigh needs looked at.* I pushed my shirt down self-consciously. I'd been aware of my relative state of undress with the others, but with him …

My face burned as hot as my blood.

Meeting his glowing gaze, I studied him briefly. "You came for me. That's pretty cool."

I will always come for you. His tail flicked the wall, and his wings were held out in a show of what I took to be readiness combined with intimidation.

It was working. The others wouldn't get near us.

"I've seen this thing before," Herakles was the nearest, his treelike form tense.

"He's not a thing," I said and turned. "He's a grotesque."

I met his gaze. The happy glow in his faded. His arms were outstretched for a hug.

I didn't move. All I could think about was what he did to my parents.

"What lies have they told you?" he asked in a low voice.

Mismatch drew me into his body once more, prepared to fly, but I pushed his hand away and stepped forward.

"No lies. I learned the truth about a few things," I replied. "You're with these people?"

"I am. I already tossed their leader over the side of the wall for disobeying Mama's orders. No one else will hurt you, Lyssa."

Gods help me, I trusted him. I stepped forward and grimaced at the pain then limped towards him, throwing myself into the arms of my guardian. I had done this a million times in the forest, but never had his strong embrace been so welcome.

"I've missed you," he whispered fiercely into my hair.

"I missed you, too," I said. He felt like home, as usual, despite the revelation of what he had done before me.

"Is your pet dangerous?"

"Mismatch isn't a pet."

"He's one of your creations isn't he?"

I twisted in his grip to see the grotesque. Mismatch's wings were folded at his back, and his hard gaze was on the men behind Herakles. "Sort of. He kind of grew a life of his own, though."

"My Lyssa. Always changing the world around her," he said with gruff affection. "Send him away so we can talk."

"No," I replied softly. "He stays with me."

Herakles gazed down at me, and I saw his disappointment. "You have changed much already. I wanted to protect you from the ugliness of the world."

"From you?"

"Yeah, sweet Lyssa. From me and all the people like me."

My eyes filled with tears at the admittance. I wasn't ready to lose my hero, my adopted father. I wasn't ready to feel so alone facing my fate as I watched the layers between me and reality peel away. I wiped my eyes.

Your leg, Mismatch said.

"I know," I said and left Herakles' grip. "I need a doctor."

"We have one here."

I glanced doubtfully at the ruffians behind him. "Really?"

Herakles laughed. "Welcome to my world, Lyssa. We live beneath the city. Come. I'll show you." He started away.

"Are we really safe?" I didn't follow. "Both of us?"

"I give you my word."

Mismatch drew abreast of me. I didn't have to ask to know his opinion on accompanying my guardian anywhere. The two looked at each other with anger, if not death, in their eyes. Rather than try to convince him, I slid my hand into the monster's.

He glanced down at me but didn't object when I began to follow Herakles.

"Out of curiosity, what did you learn?" Herakles tone was terse. "About me."

"It's not important," I said, recalling how curious Adonis had been about my relationship with Herakles.

Your toes are curling, Mismatch said a second before Herakles spoke.

"I can always tell when you're lying."

"Oh, my gods! Can't a crippled girl get some compassion instead of an interrogation?" I complained.

Herakles stopped and scooped me up in his arms. Mismatch growled, but Herakles ignored him. "Now. What did you learn?"

I sighed. "About my parents."

Herakles stopped walking and stood rigidly in place, eyes on some point in the distance.

He killed them? The flying creature sounded surprised for the first time since we met.

I didn't answer.

"Then why are you here with me now?" Herakles' question

was barely audible.

"Because I love you," I whispered. "Because you're my Herakles."

I am sorry, Alessandra.

I stretched to see the creature trailing us and offered him a small smile. He was learning how to be a better human.

"Let's get you to the doctor," Herakles started forward once more. His face had blanched, and his eyes were blank.

TWENTY TWO

True wisdom comes to each of us when we realize how little we understand about life, ourselves, and the world around us.

—SOCRATES

NEITHER SPOKE THE REST OF THE WAY TO THE medical facility. We entered the walls and walked along roughly hewn tunnels slanting downwards gradually, until they met stairs that took us beneath the ground level. Mama's men had managed to expand the sewer systems and underground bunker and tunnel network beneath Washington DC to the walls and beneath the city.

The result was a shadowy honeycomb of uneven tunnels and paths that smelled sometimes of rot, sometimes of must, and led to cavernous rooms, some as large as a city block. It was amazing yet scary, as I wasn't entirely certain the men around Herakles would listen to him.

The medical facility was its own private chamber the size of my villa and partitioned into sections by curtains. Herakles set me down on a bed next to a man in a white lab coat.

I wasn't about to admit weakness in front of Herakles or Mismatch, but I was a little lightheaded. The two waited outside the exam room. Gritting my teeth, I bore through a shot to numb the area around my thigh so the doctor could clean and stitch it then tugged up my shirt for him to check the slash along my ribcage.

"Lyssa, clothes!" Herakles called and stuck his arm into the room. The doctor grabbed them and set them on a stool near the table. After a shot of antibiotics, he washed his hands.

"You're done," he said. "Local anesthesia will wear off in an hour. Painkillers on the table."

I stood. He left me alone to change, and I did my best to clean up the blood remaining before pulling on black cargo pants and a sweatshirt that smelled of Herakles and fell to my knees. Weary and achy, I tested my body before joining Herakles outside the exam room.

"Good as new," I said. "Where's …"

He pointed up. Mismatch was perched on a cement beam high above us, appearing ever so much like the grotesque he was.

"That thing tried to kidnap you when you were six," Herakles said quietly.

"He was trying to rescue me," I replied and met his gaze, once more thrown into deep confusion. "How much do you know about me? About what I am and what they want to do to me?"

Herakles was silent for a moment before he spoke hoarsely. "You really have grown up." His emotions were too jumbled for me to read.

I wasn't certain I wanted to know what he felt. I needed distance between me and the world, or thought I did. The moment I saw pain and sorrow on his features, my desire to remain impartial to my caretaker melted.

Crossing to him, I hugged him. "Don't be sad," I murmured. "Just be honest with me. I don't need you to protect me anymore."

"You need it now more than ever, Lyssa."

"I need to know what I'm facing. What I am. How I can possibly survive this."

"I've been as cut off as you from the world since we entered the forest." He eased away. "Let's find a place to sit and talk." He led me out of the medical area and into what appeared to be a community space filled with old furniture and televisions and a few old video games.

I knew without looking Mismatch was tracking our movements from his perch above. Mama's men stopped speaking and whatever they were doing as I passed. I understood their resentment after the incident earlier, and I began to wonder how I was supposed to fulfill the Silent Queen's purpose and lead people who wanted nothing to do with me unless it was to throw me off the wall.

Herakles led me to a quiet area and started to sit when he caught sight of someone behind me and rose.

"Didn't expect to see you here," he said. A flicker of warmth was in his gaze.

Turning, I saw Dosy as she lowered the hood of her cloak. "I was on my way here when the Magistrate raised the alarm about the kidnapping," she said. "Sorry, Alessandra. We are working out the kinks in the alliance. You'll need to magically reappear in your villa soon." Though speaking to me, her eyes were on Herakles, and I sensed … more between them. It was different than the level of intensity between her and Niko. Far less homicidal.

"You two know each other?" I asked curiously.

"Only met recently," Dosy replied. "Am I interrupting?"

"Sort of," I said.

"No," Herakles replied at the same time.

I rolled my eyes and sat down. "Fine. He was about to explain how messed up things are. You might as well join us."

Theodocia is Mama. Interesting. When Mismatch sounded this intrigued, I didn't think it was good. His loyalty was to me and Lantos. I didn't know which one won out, though, when it came down to Triumvirate business.

Resting my head back on the couch, I gazed up at him. "No. The Silent Queen is," I replied aloud.

"Who …" Dosy followed my gaze and gasped. She uttered several foul curses. "You brought him here?"

"You know each other?" Herakles asked.

"Yeah. Unfortunately. If you tell your boss, Adonis, I'll hunt you down!"

I laughed.

"Adonis." Herakles was frowning. "That thing is Adonis."

"At night," I supplied.

"I met him when I was younger. He appeared out of nowhere and a couple of cops brought him in off the street. Disappeared that night but not before he shredded the police station." Dosy was glaring up at the creature. "That was before his boss twisted him into a monster worse than that."

My amusement faded. Mismatch was watching me, unconcerned with Dosy.

"So that's what happened," I murmured.

No. Lantos saved my life after Herakles almost killed me, but I was the person I am long before Lantos. I've begun to remember what I was.

"It'd be nice to know."

"Not to butt in, but do you want to talk?" Herakles eyed the grotesque. He sat on a loveseat opposite me.

"Yeah," I said and shifted to see them both.

"I'd advise you to make it quick. You need to be back where the Magistrate can find you before the Queen's efforts to calm him wear off," Dosy said.

"You'd turn her back over to the man who wants to steal her life and turn her into a monster like he did me?" Herakles bristled.

"My orders are to avoid confrontation with him and his people at all costs. All this," Dosy swept her arms out around her, "is at risk. We aren't in the position to act yet."

Herakles' jaw was ticking.

"It's okay. I get it," I spoke before he could argue. "I'm under the impression I'm relatively safe for now."

"You're never safe," Dosy countered.

She's right, Mismatch agreed.

"I'll give you ten minutes. Then I suggest you have him take you back." Dosy pointed at Mismatch. She rose and moved away, leaving Herakles and me alone.

Now that I had the chance, I didn't know what to say. I'd already seen the look on his face when I mentioned my parents.

"You want to talk about that night," he assessed.

My guardian always knew how to read me. I nodded with some reluctance.

"After I knocked that thing out of the sky and caught you, you changed me. It was your magic. You took what I'd become and reversed it until I knew who I was again."

"I don't understand," I said.

He studied me. I saw he didn't want to reveal everything. "When I was ten, I was twice the size of the other kids in my class. Twice as strong, twice as fast. I caught the attention of a wealthy man who specialized in grooming Olympians. My parents were thrilled. We were poor, and he offered them a stipend if I'd live with him and train. He became my benefactor. But ... part of his program didn't involve training until after I'd been transformed genetically and physically into the person that could survive his training. I spent ten years on my back alternating between surgery and recovery. He replaced every part of me he deemed weak. Add to that genetic manipulation, and facial reconstruction surgeries so I resembled his illustrious grandfather when he was younger, and the real me became lost. Buried beneath scars, body parts that weren't mine, and new genes. I couldn't remember what my real face and body looked like or my parent's names."

My mouth was agape. I couldn't imagine rebuilding someone's body the way he described or the amount of time, money … *pain* he went through to become the most athletic, successful Olympian of all time.

"I became what he said I was," Herakles continued. "I couldn't even think for myself. I obeyed. You saw that when you looked at me. Even at the age of six, you knew how to … help people." He waved over his head at the ribbons I alone saw. "You undid what he did, and I began to remember. To understand. To feel like a real person again. And the buried part of me that had a conscience knew you were going to be crucified if I let them take you away."

"You grabbed me and ran," I whispered.

He nodded. "We were on the run for a week. It was impossible to keep you hidden. I took a razor then a flame torch to myself. I was so sick of what I'd become, and too accustomed to pain to care." He rubbed his scars. "I wanted to burn and cut away the man he made me into. With the stamina and strength he'd built into me, I was able to keep ahead of SISA, the military and the Royal Guard, but even I needed help and rest at some point. I didn't think we'd survive much longer, until Father Cristopolos found me and began talking to me about the Old Ways and how you were part of a prophecy to bring them back. That's when I went to my benefactor once last time and begged him for a favor. He granted us the forest, and Lantos wiped your memory."

I listened, unable to recall the story he told from my own mind. "Why didn't I recognize Lantos when we met again recently? Why can't I remember the time between when I fell and when I arrived to the orphanage?"

"Lantos explained there were levels involved in compartmentalizing memories. His magic sealed away some, but it was his father's magic that tucked away most of them."

"And his father is a Titan."

"As opposed to a half-breed demigod."

It wasn't the history I expected. Perhaps because I was waiting for something horrific to cross his lips. "I changed you," I said, fascinated by the concept.

"You fixed me."

Studying my guardian's face, I began to pity him. Turned into some sort of Frankenstein and then shown what he was, he had tried to destroy himself. My sweet Herakles didn't deserve such a fate, even if I didn't yet know how to tackle the idea of him killing my parents.

"And the priests created a spy ring out of the nymphs," I mused. "You knew about that, too?"

"I did. I don't know if it survived, since the priests didn't."

"It did. Leandra took it over."

"Always the sharpest of them."

A little jealous, even now, about how perfect Leandra was, I changed the subject. "Who was your benefactor?" I asked.

"The man known now as the Supreme Magistrate. He was a low level politician with his daddy's money when we met. My Olympic wins propelled him upwards into the strata he's in now."

"You're afraid he'll do to me what he did to you."

"I know he'll destroy you. It's what he does."

My hands were clenched together. I shook them loose self-consciously and glanced up at Mismatch. He was close enough to have overheard everything. Was that a good thing or not? I hated not knowing where he stood.

"You're here," I said. "Do you trust Dosy and the Queen?"

"I think they are the least evil of the three."

I bit back a smile.

"That said, I feel like I didn't raise you anywhere near right. You are too good and sweet and honest to deal with manipulative bastards. All of them want something from you, and each is willing to bulldoze the world twice over to get it."

"Yeah. I've kind of figured that out. Just not sure how I do anything without ending up torn to pieces or dead."

"I wish I knew."

Ouch. If Herakles didn't know either …

"Time's up," Dosy said and approached once more. "Hey! Come down!" She motioned to Mismatch.

I stood, my body stiffening up already from the night of being beat down. Mismatch floated down from the rafters and landed near us.

"If you breathe one word of any this to Lantos …" Dosy said, glaring at Mismatch.

What I tell him is not your concern, Mismatch replied.

I cleared my throat.

"What'd he say?" Dosy asked.

"Probably what you'd say in the same situation," I replied.

"Look, Adonis, as far as I know, the Queen is the only person not out to have Alessandra killed or ripped apart. I don't know what Lantos is planning, but I don't trust it."

I will always protect you, Alessandra. But I owe my loyalty to no one else and if I act, it's out of concern for your safety. I don't care who I ally with.

I almost asked what had happened that he wasn't claiming loyalty to Lantos any longer but stopped myself. "We're good," I said to Dosy, uncertain if it was entirely true.

"Good. We'll take you to the top of the walls. He can fly you home?"

Mismatch bowed his head.

"You're probably kind of wanted by the Supreme Magistrate, too, huh?" I asked Herakles, not wanting to leave him behind.

"You could say that." He stood.

We followed Dosy through the underground world to the wall that ran on one side. She motioned to a wide stairwell. "Take it straight up," she said, eyeing Mismatch once more.

I waited for them to come with us then realized they were staying. I crossed to Herakles and gave him another quick hug before joining Mismatch in the stairwell. We began to climb, me with some difficulty given the state of my right thigh.

He kills your parents and you forgive him so easily.

"I don't know what to think," I mumbled. "He raised me, Mismatch."

You are much quicker to judge me.

349

I said nothing. My confusion was growing by the day. I felt deep inside my time to decide what to do with my life – which side to choose – was rapidly becoming closer.

I wanted away from everyone. I wanted to return to the forest and start over. This time, I'd know better than to step outside the boundaries.

How did Dosy expect me to lead people who thought, quite accurately, that the best way to win was to kill me? How did I trust Lantos when he claimed he'd only torture me if necessary, and only for a short term if so? Cleon hadn't tasked me yet, but he clearly wanted me in the Oracle's place.

"This would be so much easier if I had a fourth option," I said quietly as we continued to climb.

Unless it was worse than the other three.

"Is that even possible at this point?"

Perhaps.

"And you. What's your angle in all this?"

I have none.

"That's not true. You work for Lantos. You should want what he wants."

He has not the mind for strategic thinking. I do his thinking, and he manipulates. I've always known I could be where he is but never cared for the position. I had no purpose but to serve the man who saved my life until the courtyard when I began to remember.

"What became your purpose then?"

You.

My heart fluttered.

Protecting you. Ensuring Lantos doesn't go to Phase Two. Trying to understand what you're struggling with – who to trust. Who can offer you safety. Who won't turn on you. How you can survive this.

"What's Phase Two?"

You don't want to know suffice to say it's not ideal.

"Okay. So you're the strategic thinker. What do you see when you look out on all of this mess?"

What do you see? He challenged.

"My mind doesn't work that way. I can't get over what my next move should be."

I held my breath, waiting for him to answer. *I see why you bear the double omega.*

It was another of his vague almost-riddles, another sign he was likely toying with me, at least a little, unless he was truly uncomfortable saying the words. Herakles wasn't preparing me for Armageddon. He was preparing me to *be* Armageddon.

We reached the top of the wall. The air was fresher, the night sky sparkling with stars. I was hurting from the climb and pretty sure the warmth sliding down my leg was from a soaked bandage.

You need to see the doctor first thing.

I rolled my eyes. "Like Cleon's not going to wonder how I ended up stabbed?"

I forgot you couldn't lie to save your life.

"You say it like it's a bad thing."

His wings flared out on either side of his grotesque body, and I hesitated. He was absolutely incredible in a really freaky way.

Mismatch held out his hand. I took it, and he drew me to him then released me. I didn't move, not wanting to breach whatever sort of protocol involved in flying with him. And just a little unnerved by the excitement and heat in my blood.

It's a rough ride with someone else, he warned.

"I'm good with heights. Generally okay with flying."

Generally?

"You probably don't want to do any quick ascensions or loops again," I replied.

You'd rather walk?

I sighed. "Don't be cranky. Just get me home. I'll warn you if I'm going to throw up."

Much obliged. He slid an arm around me and pulled me into his hard body.

My breath caught in my throat. Staring at his chest, I ordered my face not to turn pink.

Not used to men touching you. He was amused.

"Stop it. Fly me home, you stupid oversized bat."

His other arm went around me, and I lifted my arms to circle his neck. Mismatch lifted me first then sprung into the air. I squeezed my eyes closed, half expecting him to mess with me and twirl or dive or something, and breathed in his calming scent.

He didn't. He didn't fly too high and kept us steady, my legs between his and his arms firmly around me. I ventured a look over my shoulder once and not again, equally amazed and horrified to be *flying.*

His grip around me loosened, and I clutched at him tighter.

We're there.

I risked a peek over my shoulder and saw the balcony overlooking my gardens. He flew as close to it as possible then released my legs and lowered me to the marble flooring. The horizon was lightening, and I began to hope no one had plans for me so I could sleep for a day.

My dangling feet met the balcony, and I slid down his arms until I was standing on two feet. "Are you leaving?" I asked without thinking.

Unless I'm invited to stay.

"No!" I replied too quickly and moved back. "Stupid question. Thanks for the ride." Even so, I wasn't able to look away. I also had the distinct sense of disappointment that he was leaving. As if the bond between us was becoming stronger or at least, more insistent than it had been.

Mismatch said nothing more. One gravity defying stroke of his wings sent him into the sky. Rather than retreat for what little sleep I could get, I stood at the balcony and watched him. He soared overhead, wings dipping and form circling, floating on invisible currents briefly before he twirled and tucked his wings for a steep dive towards the side of the city where his compound was. He disappeared from sight, and I returned to my bed. Seconds after my head hit the pillow, I was out.

TWENTY THREE

... any moment might be our last. Everything is more beautiful
because we're doomed.
You will never be lovelier than you are now.
We will never be here again.

– HOMER

"**Y**OU WERE HERE ALL NIGHT."

I was a terrible liar, and the Magistrate wasn't buying anything I said. "I told you already, yes." Tired and bruised, I was trying not to move too much because it hurt to breathe.

"And this?" He indicated the cut in my thigh the doctor was stitching up after it tore when I fell out of bed. I'd forgotten it and made too quick an attempt to stand.

"I fell. Into my nightstand," I replied.

He pursed his lips, managing to judge me without losing his pleasant expression. Herakles' story played through my thoughts as I studied the regal politician. I didn't know how anyone could torture another to the extent Herakles had been tortured. Nothing – not all the fame, honor and money ten Olympics brought – would tempt me.

I was also all too aware the people around me didn't have the same moral boundaries. Not Niko, not Adonis, not Lantos or the Silent Queen, who gave off vibes of being able to do so much more than I cared to imagine. I didn't know where Dosy stood.

Herakles …

"We have a luncheon planned for you at one," the Magistrate said.

"Sounds good," I replied with no enthusiasm.

"My apologies for doubting you."

I searched his face. He had relaxed. Either he believed me or was willing to move past it, a reaction I wasn't certain how to take. "It's okay. I was up partying too late last night. I should've answered your calls."

"No hard feelings. There are ambassadors here to see you at lunch. The world is quite abuzz with you." He appeared pleased.

"Yeah." I didn't trust myself to say more.

The doctor placed a bandage on my thigh. I watched him clean up the area, dreading standing up for fear of pain. He handed me a small bottle of painkillers, and I rose, testing my leg. My thigh was completely numb, though nothing was helping my bruised ribs. I joined Cleon at the door of the small medical clinic on the compound.

He led me away. Leandra and two security guards trailed. Dressed in workout clothing, I suspected I'd probably spend the rest of the day in a dress again.

We crossed the compound to my villa, and the Magistrate paused at the entrance. "Niko is beefing up security in anticipation of the ambassadors and politicians who will be in attendance. I'll leave my personal guard here for you."

I tensed. He made it sound like he was doing me a favor, but I had a feeling he no longer trusted me. "Thanks," I said and walked in the front door. "I'll be ready before one."

Which was in about forty minutes. I groaned internally.

"What the hell happened last night?" Leandra demanded the moment she closed the door.

"I don't want to talk about it."

"You completely disappeared and show up torn up!"

I sighed. With Cleon gone, I wasn't afraid to limp or hold my bandaged ribs. "I got no sleep. Please, *please* can I lay down? I promise to tell you but I gotta do it horizontally."

"Fine." Leandra stalked angrily back to my bedroom.

I stretched out across the bed and sighed deeply. "You have a gown picked out?"

"Don't try to change the subject!"

I rolled my eyes and stared at the ceiling. I told her in as few words as possible about my adventure. The bed beside me sank beneath her weight. She perched and listened intently, frowning.

When I finished, I waited for her reaction, not completely sure I understood everything that happened.

"Glad to hear Herakles is okay. We knew where he was but not how he was," she said, pensive. "What is this between you and … Adonis? He's a *monster* at night?"

"Yeah. Long story. He's a nice monster who helps me."

"And an asshole human butcher during daylight who was supposed to kill or crucify you, if I recall."

"It's complicated."

"I wish …"

I twisted my head to gaze at her. "What?"

"I wish we'd had more time to establish our network. I get nothing about the intentions of the Triumvirate in my reports."

"I still can't believe you nymphs are spies."

"Good ones. We should know something."

"Look, Leandra." I grimaced as I sat up. "I don't think it's possible to know what members of the Triumvirate are planning. Did you have any idea there was a secret city beneath this one?"

"None."

"Exactly. They hide their secrets too well even from the other members."

"Still. We owe it to you and the priests to know more."

"You'll figure it out." I pushed myself off the bed. A platter of bakery items was on the breakfast nook table. Brightening, I went to them. I always ate too much when I didn't get enough sleep. "Omigods these are amazing!"

"If you eat too many you won't fit into your dress."

I ignored her and stuffed the rest of the croissant into my mouth before double fisting a fresh raspberry scone in one hand and Danish in the other. Trailing her into the massive closet, I chewed and looked around tiredly.

"The Magistrate insisted you wear something the traditional colors today," Leandra said. "I don't like it." She held up a cream colored dress with a high waist tied by a sunny yellow silk sash.

"It's pretty," I said through mouthfuls of pastry.

"Not the dress, idiot," she said with a noisy sigh. "I don't like that he wants you dolled up more than usual."

"Ambassadors."

"Ambassadors attended the soiree. He wants this occasion to be special."

I was too fatigued to really care. "He won't do anything to me yet," I said. "Right?"

"I've heard absolutely nothing indicating he will."

"So ... maybe it's just super formal."

"Maybe." She frowned. "Put that down and change!" She snatched the remains of the scone out of my hand and tossed it into a garbage can.

I did as she told me then sat at the vanity where she did my hair and makeup. She grumbled about the amount of effort it took to hide the dark circles beneath my eyes and the bruise on one cheek from my altercation atop the wall. When she finished, I gazed at myself in the mirror.

"Wow. You can't even tell I got punched," I said. "I look good."

"You'll pass."

"I'll never be as pretty as you. I know."

She smiled at me in the mirror, a wicked gleam in her eyes. "You're wearing heels."

"Oh, my gods, Leandra! I can barely walk today!"

"Shut up. I picked them out for you already."

I didn't think the Silent Queen had servants talking to her like this. I sighed and rose, sliding my feet into modestly high platform heels. "Hey, these aren't bad."

"You'll kill yourself in stilettos, but these are sturdy. Like you."

"You're such a bitch, Leandra!"

She laughed.

I smiled, unable to stay angry with one of the only people I could trust.

"Excuse me." A second servant came to the door and offered a shallow curtsey. "You have a visitor."

At least this one knocked instead of dragging me out of bed. I walked a few steps cautiously then found the shoes steady enough. Limping to my bedroom door, I exited into the hallway and didn't make an attempt to stop the hobbling movement until I was about to enter the foyer.

I paused, already sensing who was present without seeing him. Facing the balcony overlooking the gardens, I saw Adonis at the railing in his normal black SISA uniform, sans mask. His clothing clung to his tall, lean frame, and my eyes drifted down him.

Leandra was frowning again. She trailed me to the double doors but remained there while I approached Adonis. His gaze was on the garden.

The awkwardness of my trip home last night was forefront in my thoughts, despite my attempt to pretend Adonis and Mismatch were two different people. I crossed my arms and stood in the middle of the balcony.

"Mine's not dead," I said in the tense silence. "The garden." *Gods, I'm such an idiot.* What was it about the man I should want nothing to do with that left me … fevered? Stupid beyond normal?

"I don't have minders, either," was his response. "Send her away."

I hated when he told me what to do. But I turned and waved Leandra back. I drew nearer as well, sensing … something about him that wasn't normal. I leaned against the railing as well and gazed at the flowers below.

"I'm leaving for a while," he said at last.

"To where?"

He glanced at me.

"Not that it's my business. In fact, it's not. Why are you even telling me?" I babbled. "It's not like …" *I care.*

Amusement lifted the strange darkness in his gaze. He seemed more aware, more present today.

More like Herakles the day I fixed him.

"Something happened to you," I said.

"Yeah. It did."

"I didn't do it this time."

"No. My memories returned. Those from before I met you. From a time too long ago for records to exist and those of the four thousand years I spent as a stone beast before you reanimated me."

"Four thousand. My gods."

"Yes, the gods. Only they could devise such a brutal fate." The bitterness in his tone was unmistakable.

"Who were you before?"

He turned over his right wrist, where the faded birthmark of an omega letter was present. "Prince of Greece who fell under a terrible curse."

"The grotesque prince. Your history is amazing."

"It's something." He turned to face me. "But I have to leave to find something I left behind."

"From four thousand years ago?" I arched my eyebrow skeptically. "It won't be sitting where you left it. That's for sure."

"Which is why this might take me a while. I'll be back as soon as I can."

Why are you telling me this? I didn't voice the words this time, afraid of the potentially damning response. Our connection was strong enough I could assume it was why. "Okay," I said finally, aware he was waiting for me to speak.

"You remember how to contact me if you need help?"

"In case you can't feel my body or something?" I asked then laughed awkwardly.

He gave an almost-smile before closing the distance between us. He reached out to lift the teal gem from its place at the center of my chest. I barely remembered to breathe watching his long, strong fingers caress it.

"Hold it in your fist and think of me," he said.

I met his gaze, fluttery and fevered as usual when he was close enough for me to smell him, and nodded. It was so much more intense dealing with him during daylight than the monster at night.

Leandra would tell me I was slow, but it dawned on me in that moment what was between us. I'd mistaken the tension between a man and woman attracted to one another for the natural connection I shared with Adonis. Part of what I felt was the natural bond, but this was deeper, more intense, less fleeting, than anything I'd ever experienced for the boys at the campground.

I didn't want Adonis to leave because I did care – too much.

"I know you're in danger," he continued, oblivious to my thoughts. "But I have to do this. I have to understand who I am … or was."

"You're on a journey like I've been on," I replied. "I do understand. Were you like … you now?"

"A butcher?"

I nodded half-heartedly.

"The world was very different then. But yes, I was every bit what I am now. Enslaving or slaughtering entire races of people I defeated in battle. My edge comes from who I am, not what Lantos made me forget."

Gods how his words bothered me! I had never been as confused by one person as I was him, either. An admitted butcher with no remorse – yet the capacity for gentleness and kindness.

"Your fists are clenched," he observed quietly. "It's not

anger, is it?"

"No. I don't know what it is." I forced my hands open. "I have no idea what this is."

He studied me, mercifully quiet, even though I suspected we both knew what *this* was.

"I never expected you to rescue me or help me. I'm finding out I can't expect that of anyone," I said and shifted back onto solid ground.

"No, you can't."

I hated that he agreed with me. He dropped the gem without moving out of my space and cupped my cheek with his warm palm. Sparks of electricity tickled me from the inside out. I had no real urge to move and began to sink once more into the spell I always did around him. Half amazement, half fear. I'd found the one man who met Herakles' conditions. Not only did Herakles hate him but he was downright scary. I resisted the urge to nuzzle his wide palm, uncertain how to react.

"You have to survive until I return," he warned me. "Do what you must, however bad you feel about it. Lie, kill, steal. Your focus must be on surviving."

What does he know about what's coming? "This isn't how humans give pep talks."

"Survive, Alessandra."

I swallowed hard, overwhelmed by his intensity, and nodded. "I will."

His hand fell away from my face. "I brought you something." He averted his gaze as he said it.

I started to smile curiously. He bent to retrieve a satchel I hadn't noticed leaning against the railing. Wordlessly, Adonis handed it to me and moved back. I opened it and then laughed.

"Mrs. Nettles!" I exclaimed and reached in to pull the squirming animal out of the dark satchel. I hugged her, now fully aware of her connection to me. "I can't believe you kept her all these years!"

Adonis cleared his throat in discomfort. He was as adept with emotion as Herakles was. "Yeah. She can't go with me."

"So are you lending her to me or can I keep her?"

His jaw clenched. I was struggling not to laugh, always tickled when I thought of tough Adonis-Mismatch and his stuffed toy.

"She's yours," he replied curtly.

"Aww. You'll miss her."

He muttered a curse and turned away, striding towards the front door.

"Wait, Adonis!" I called after him.

He stopped without turning. I had no reason to ask him to wait, and I wracked my brain for something that wouldn't leave me yet again humiliated in front of him.

"Thanks," I managed finally. "And safe travels."

"Read the card."

I almost laughed. A card and stuffed animal from the butcher? Mrs. Nettles handed it to me. I opened it, read the names present, and gasped.

"It was all I could take before they locked up the file," he said.

"These are ... my parents."

"Yes."

Emotion jammed my ability to speak. I stared at him in surprise for a long moment then at the names on the card.

"You're coming back, aren't you?" I asked at last.

"Your name is seared into my soul. I will always return to you."

My breath caught. "That's ..." ... *the most incredible thing I've ever heard.* "... uh ... good." I became the stupidest person on the planet when he looked at me like that. Warmth bloomed within me beneath his intensity, leaving me fevered and speechless and oh-so-aware of the significance of this meeting. I no longer had to doubt his intentions, his loyalty. Him.

He tilted his head, his lips turning up in a half smile. He was feeling what I did, the fire in my blood, the furnace at my lower belly. *Humiliated* did not begin to describe what it was like knowing he was so intimately connected to me.

"Survive," he said softly one last time. He walked out, and the front door closed behind him.

Mismatch, Mrs. Nettles said, watching him retreat.

I bit back tears. Why did it feel like he was never coming back? "It's ... okay. He'll be back." *Or ... something.* I didn't know why I wanted it to be true. "Let's show you your new home." With a deep breath, I tucked the card inside my bra for safekeeping, repeating their names over and over as I walked with her towards the bedroom.

Leandra was waiting inside and stopped in her pacing to stare. "What ..."

I smiled and introduced them, explaining how I'd brought Mrs. Nettles to life when I was little. Leandra picked her up and studied her before placing her on the bed. "Did that asshole make you cry?" she asked, returning to me.

"No."

She waited for more.

I didn't know what to say about Adonis, but it wasn't anything bad. His thoughtfulness was beyond that of anyone I'd ever known.

"You're almost late." Leanne snatched a handbag from the table near the door.

I did my best to stop thinking of Adonis and focus on what happened today. "Ugh." I waved at Mrs. Nettles, who waved back.

"Your escort is waiting. The Magistrate said only you are to come because of the level of those attending." Leandra handed me my knife and said again, "I don't like it."

I strapped it on my good thigh as we walked towards the foyer. "I'm sure it'll be fine. Too many people are watching me for him to act. Right?"

"You are way too trusting."

"I just mean I don't think the Triumvirate members are on the same page, and like you said, I don't have my full powers yet."

"I'll take care of Mrs. Nettles if you wind up dead."

"Oh, my gods, Leandra! Doom and gloom everywhere." I smiled at her despite the outburst, warmth blooming inside me from Adonis' gifts and touch. "You do love me!" I wrapped her in a tight hug.

"Stop it!" she hissed and pushed me away. "You'll ruin your dress!"

Grinning, I left her in the foyer and went outside, where the two guards had doubled. My instincts tickled the back of my neck. My happiness faded at the idea I'd be going to an event without Leandra or Adonis.

One of the guards led me down the opposite way I'd gone every other time I left the villa. The compound was large enough for the change in direction not to be suspicious, so I went, limping after him. I didn't start to worry until I recognized the closet-sized entrance to the underground cave where the Oracle lived.

Leandra's warning made me slow. When I saw the first guard enter, I stopped completely.

"Ma'am," said one of them behind me.

I stretched for the knife.

"It's okay, guys. Back up a bit." I turned at Lantos' voice. He wore his mask and was dressed in a tuxedo. My hand hovered over the weapon as he approached. "I reconsidered the request you made of me," he said for my ears only. "We have ten minutes before the luncheon. If you can promise to keep this quick, we'll go down and see her. You can ask her how to use your powers. But – you cannot kill her. That's the deal."

I gazed up at him. "What made you change your mind?"

"A common friend."

Touched by Adonis bringing Mrs. Nettle by, I felt my guard lower knowing he'd set this up. Gods help me, I trusted him.

"You'll need this." Lantos handed me a familiar red cord bracelet. "My magic protected you from the fumes last time. This will help you stay focused this time."

"The Magistrate is letting us visit her?"

"I paid off some of his guards." He winked. "Shift change is at one, though, so we need to go quickly."

I gazed at him for another long moment before nodding and stepping forward. I slid the bracelet in place. Immediately, the ribbons around me disappeared. We walked into the facility without any challenge from the guard. Lantos and I went to the elevator, and I sneaked a look at him.

Something felt off. He was open and friendly as always, but …

"Adonis is going on vacation for a few days," he said. "Lucky bastard."

I smiled. "He's a different kind of guy."

"You figure out what makes him tick?"

I shook my head.

"Me neither. Makes me think I don't really want to know."

We agree there. I wiped sweaty palms on my dress. My stomach was turning over at the thought of the tormented woman mere steps away.

"You okay with seeing her again?" he asked as the elevator ceased moving.

"Yeah. A little nervous."

The doors opened, and the heady scent of amber, sulfur and other exotic spices filled my senses. The band at my wrist wasn't really helping it. I was cartwheeling mentally from the

Oracle catnip before we left the elevator.

I exited and closed my eyes, breathing the intoxicating scent deeply. It calmed me, and a faint tingling at the base of my skull reminded me of how I felt around Adonis. With my senses dulled, I didn't feel the strange coolness at my neck until a sharp sting penetrated my addled brain.

My eyes flew open, and I slapped at it. It wasn't a bug bite. Niko stood beside me, a medical gun in hand. Struggling to focus, I brought my hand away from my neck to see a dab of blood.

"What did you do?" I demanded.

"Injected the red magic into you. A safety measure," Lantos responded.

I faced him, suddenly aware of the people present on the far side of the room, opposite the direction of the Oracle where I faced. "What is this?"

Two guards – one SISA and one military – slid between me and the elevator door.

"This is your one o'clock." Cleon emerged from an office area near the other well-dressed men and women I didn't recognize.

I looked from Lantos to him and back again. "You set me up."

"For which I'm not too proud." Lantos lifted his mask. "But … my end goals depend upon your cooperation. I need that portal open, and Cecilia refuses me every time I ask. Cleon and I agree for once the gate has to be opened, which leaves … you."

Coldness slid through me. I stretched for the knife, focusing hard on him to keep the catnip from stealing my attention once more. Niko snatched my wrist and wrenched it behind me.

"I figured you'd be armed," he said.

I shook my head, too affected by the scents to fight him when he lifted my dress to tear off the knife. It was all I could do not to float away.

Niko steered me towards the others. The moment I saw the surgery table, I dug in my heels.

"Tough luck, you little shit," he said and shoved me forward.

I caught myself on the cold stainless steel and backed away. Niko pushed me forward again. This time, I stayed. My injured thigh was hurting, the pain battling the effects of the catnip.

"For your third trial, you will fulfill your fate, Alessandra." Cleon said. "It's traditional for this to be the third trial of the Oracle, to submit to her place here, above the caverns."

Never, since learning of the trials, did I suspect this was one of them. It was perfectly evil. In order to access my powers, I had to complete the trials. No god or man was going to risk me developing full powers and challenging them, but they needed them for the portal. The solution: to make the third trial enslave my power for them to use.

"Oh, gods," I whispered, no longer wondering why Cleon waited to tell me his trial.

"But you do have a choice." He motioned a team of surgeons forward. They wore masks over half their faces and surgical gowns.

I reached for the gem at my neck. Adonis couldn't sense me with the shit Niko put in me, but I could still reach him.

"Niko," Lantos moved forward quickly. "The necklace."

Niko caught my wrist. He planted an elbow in my bruised ribs, and I gasped. Before I could gather myself, he had yanked the necklace over my head and handed it to Lantos.

"As I was saying, you have one choice," Cleon continued. "You can go the way of the Oracle" he pointed to the opposite wall.

I was afraid to look.

"Or you can try this new method I had developed that allows me access to your magic without you ending up in pieces."

This didn't feel real. I knew it was. But the smells were confusing me, making me feel like I was trapped in a dream.

"Neither," I said.

"We thought you might say this," Cleon glanced at Lantos.

"I don't want to take this step, but I will," Lantos said almost gently. "I know how to use this." He held up the gem. "I can call him back here. I won't harm him, but Niko and Cleon don't share my respect for the friendship I have with him."

Coldness streaked through me at the veiled threat. "You would have your own friend killed?"

"I threw him in with a Typhon. What do you think?" Lantos returned. "It's for the greater cause. Adonis would understand."

I searched his gaze, stated to drift away, then shook my head and concentrate on his sparkling eyes. Images of

Mismatch or Adonis being murdered by Niko played through my thoughts. I didn't want to care. I shouldn't have cared. I didn't owe Adonis anything.

But the idea made me sick to my stomach. My Mismatch being hurt made my chest ache. He was a murderer, a man of untold depth and emotion, one I hardly knew.

He's mine. It was as the little-me of my dream had warned me. I couldn't hurt my own creation. I couldn't stand by and let him die either, not when my emotions were entangled with his.

"What is the alternate method?" I asked hoarsely.

"It's simple and fairly painless compared to our traditional methods." Cleon held up a microchip the size of his thumbnail. "We insert this into your brain. It has been blessed by Dolos and enabled by his magic to undermine your ability to control your magic. The chip sends signals to me that a chip in my brain interprets and helps control." He tapped the back of his skull. "This is a perfect marrying of technology and magic requiring sums of money that would leave you staggering."

"We'd be connected," I said.

"Yes. I'd be in control of your magic. Capable of opening the portal."

"In theory," Lantos added.

Cleon ignored him. "Your trial is to submit to your fate. Either the microchip or by taking Cecilia's place."

My eyes went to the table. I already knew I wasn't going to choose Cecelia's path. I didn't exactly love the idea of brain surgery or having a man like Cleon in my head with access to my magic.

"He'll have the power of a god," I said to Lantos. "You're okay with that?"

"It's a means to an end." Lantos winked.

At least I don't have full access to it yet. I had yet to kill the Oracle, the trial tasked to me by the Silent Queen. I doubted Cleon knew of it, and I wasn't going to volunteer the information.

"I'll do it. The microchip," I said.

This time, I didn't resist when Niko and his goons grabbed me and strapped me face down on the table. I began praying to Artemis and squeezed my eyes closed. Doctors with gloved hands moved my hair and shot me up with some medicine.

This was the only choice. The Oracle's soft, sad voice was in my head as I began to fade into unconsciousness. *At least you have a chance to survive. To murder him. To see yourself free of our cursed fate. I will hold out as long as I can to keep your full powers from emerging.*

TWENTY FOUR
THE HIGH PRIESTESS

I WAS MID-PRAYER KNEELING BEFORE THE ALTAR OF Artemis when the cell vibrated in the pocket of my robes. I ignored it initially, but today was Niko's day with the kid. Which meant ... I was expecting a message about someone burning down the apartment building or worse – Niko forgetting Tommy at the park again. Tommy carried a cell phone for that very reason. It had happened twice this year alone. Niko was good with his dogs, but kids were different. They couldn't be left alone.

Excusing myself from the goddess, I rose, extinguished the candles before me and bowed my head before breathing my last lungful of incense. I exited the temple on the compound where the Silent Queen's villa was located.

I checked the phone.

He's making his move against your boss, Niko had messaged.

I stopped in place, coldness streaking through me. My eyes went from the villa, where the Silent Queen's elite guard was in clear sight, to the entrance to the underground caverns where the Oracle was kept across the compound. SISA and military guards were gathered there, and a full platoon of the combined forces was marching in my direction. It didn't take me more than a split second to understand his warning.

I activated the silent alarm. The politics and alliances among the Triumvirate were constantly shifting. The Supreme Priest had been reluctant to side with the Magistrate fully about the Oracle's fate. The Silent Queen's stance, of course, was not to allow the traditional fate to befall her.

From the text and approach of the cooperating security forces, Lantos had finally made his decision.

What's the plan? I hurried towards the Silent Queen's home as I typed.

Niko responded fast. *Not sure. But we're putting the Oracle where she belongs. Only way to stop these wars.*

"There's so much more at stake, you asshole." Fury filled me. Niko's arrogance – and his blind allegiance to the Magistrate – had always angered me. It was worse this time, because he knew what it meant if Alessandra took her place, if she fell into the hands of the Magistrate.

Rather, he knew what it meant to me. Niko had never cared about the bigger picture I tried on more than one occasion to share with him. He was more interested in the money paid him to enforce the Magistrate's will. I wanted so badly to pretend I didn't care, to expect the worse from Niko. But with Tommy between us, with the moments of kindness Niko showed his own son, I was weak. Always ready to believe there was a shred of decency in the mercenary's heart, always willing to pray for Niko to become a good man so our son had a worthy role model.

But Niko didn't have one ounce of goodness. He didn't care about leaving the world a better place for our son or anyone else.

What about Tommy? I texted as I passed the guards. A servant opened the door for me. I dashed into the villa.

"Phoibe!" I rarely broke protocol by calling her by her name rather than her title, but my instincts were screaming. I raced through the villa and shoved the door to her private bedchamber open.

She was meditating next to a mini-altar near the window. At my entrance, she rose, concern on her features.

What is it? She asked.

"We need to go. Now. Remember the worst case scenario?"

The teen girl nodded and strode to her closet. I heard her change as I gathered the packs we'd prepared from under the bed. Whipping off my robes to reveal the uniform of a Royal Guard with an M patch on one bicep, I strapped and tucked weapons into every place I could.

Gunfire broke out from the front of the villa as the security arms clashed. "Now!" I called.

The Silent Queen emerged from her closet, dressed practically as I'd taught her, and accepted the pack I handed her.

I bolted out of the room. She followed.

The front door was being smashed to pieces. We raced through the villa to the wine cellar, down the stairs, and into the darkness of the basement.

"Rendezvous point at the wall," I snapped at the Royal Guard members present. "I'm blowing the cellar. You've got ninety seconds to vacate the villa. Got it?"

They nodded and ran. We'd all practiced for a quick exit many times, but my hands still shook knowing this was it. This was the day the protection of Artemis we'd always enjoyed was going to be tested by the merciless intensity of Ares.

The Silent Queen was halfway through the cellar, headed towards the secret elevator in the far corner. I paused as I went and triggered the bombs hiding in several of the kegs along the cellar. We had enough plastic explosives to level the entire villa, and an engineer had placed the explosives in such a way that would completely destroy the secret entrance to the underground world.

Niko's text drew my gaze as I trotted to the elevator. *I'll take care of him. He's better off with me since you're in hiding anyway.*

I missed a step.

Sometimes, in my anger and emotion, I forgot how shrewd Niko really was. He had survived the underworld, the monster arena, and the Supreme Magistrate with nothing more than physical strength and street smarts. Bullheaded, selfish Niko had been planning this. I didn't think it possible it was a coincidence he asked for Tommy on this weekend when he was close enough to the Magistrate to know his innermost plans.

My ex was smarter than he let on, and that infuriated me more than anything.

Theodocia! The Silent Queen signaled me.

Shoving my emotions and phone away, I hopped into the elevator. "You remember the plan?" I asked her. "To the wall and out of here to our Virginia safe house."

She nodded. The unflappable royal was pale. She was cutthroat at politics, but this was my area of expertise: keeping us alive and her from falling into the clutches of gods or men.

The trip to the underground city had never felt so long. No sooner did we touch down and exit than fire flashed and a distant boom sounded overhead as her home was destroyed.

The city was a flurry of activity. As practiced, Royal Guards in civilian clothes greeted us. They surrounded the queen and started herding her towards the emergency exit. I raced through the crowds to Gus, my chief of operations during a crisis.

"Gods, Gus, please tell me you got those wall busters out this morning!" I exclaimed as I burst into the active arsenal area. He stood overseeing his staff checking out men and weapons as fast as possible.

"Two," he said grimly. "We stopped when you triggered the alarm. They're on their way out of the city."

"Two is better than none. Activate the training units, and send out orders to liquidate all holdings and bring the cash here."

He nodded, typing in the orders.

"Docia."

I turned. Herakles stood frowning, watching the movement around us. My heart dropped to my feet at the thought of revealing that his adopted daughter was at the mercy of a man who wanted only to return things to the way they were. How would he react if I told him the truth?

"What's going on? Is this a drill?" Herakles' sharp eyes took in everything.

"No, it's not."

"Then what do you need me to do?"

I considered. His size, training and strength were beneficial, and he had the added bonus of raising a spirited teen girl with magic powers. "I need you to make sure the Silent Queen gets out of the city," I said finally. "To a safe house."

"What has happened?"

"The other two made their move," I said vaguely. "She's in danger, and our plans just got moved up."

"What're you not telling me?" He was studying me closely. "Is Alessandra safe?"

Gazing up at him, I couldn't find the heart to lie to him. "No, she's not. But they won't kill her like they will Phoibe. I'm staying here because –"

He started to protest, and I raised my hand.

"– because I know the city, Herakles," I said firmly. "I know the players, the danger and the best way to help her. If you want to assist us, go with the Silent Queen. She is Alessandra's best hope of surviving this."

"Docia –"

"Please." I rested a hand on his chest. The warmth of his skin reached me through his t-shirt, and I found myself pausing at the intimate sensation, once more experiencing attraction I shouldn't. Shaking off the thoughts, I continued. "Artemis has plans for Alessandra. I will stay to ensure those plans come to fruition. But this is about to become a war zone. I need you out of here. I need the Silent Queen alive for us to succeed. Please."

I saw the torment in his eyes, the same in my heart when I realized how true Niko's words were. My son was safer with him, under the protection of the Magistrate and military, than he'd ever be with me down here, now that the next stage of our struggle had begun.

"I will see her to safety. And then I will return," Herakles said at last. "War or no, I will not leave my Lyssa in the hands of these monsters."

"Fair enough." I didn't have time to argue or negotiate. "Gus, call if you need anything!" He nodded. "Herakles, come with me." I jogged through the armies mobilizing for battle beneath the city towards the exit where the Silent Queen would await me. She and her small force of elite guards stood at the foot of the wall, and her eyes were on her phone.

I approached her and saw the tightness around her eyes, the sorrow in their depths, a rare sign of emotion from the queen of stoicism. "What is it?" I asked immediately.

Lantos sends his love and his apology for betraying me. How am I to take this?

I squeezed her arm, aware of the affair between them no one else knew about. "You are to survive. Always survive."

He says the Magistrate will turn Alessandra against us. He suspects what we've been doing.

"And Lantos? Is he going to tell what he knows?"

He says not.

"Like I trust that rat bastard." I waved Herakles over. "I'm sending Herakles with you. Extra security."

The Silent Queen squared her shoulders and lifted her chin, all emotion gone. Even so, I knew the depth of her emotion for the Supreme Priest. Years ago, he had brought me to her to become her mentor and seen to it I had the training and skill to protect her. He had loved her far longer than she loved him, but it didn't make the intensity of her feelings any less.

Neither of us really ever thought he'd go this far as to lash out at her. But it fit. No member of the Triumvirate was any less ruthless than the next, when it came down to it. If Lantos were in the Queen's way, she'd order me to take care of him, no matter how much it hurt her.

We were alike in this. The greater good, our higher calling, meant more than the life of any one person.

"It's an honor," Herakles said softly. "I swear on my life I will see you to safety."

She nodded her head in a simple bow.

"Go. Don't look back. Ditch your phones and any other electronics," I instructed her. "Herakles, you kept Alessandra safe and hidden for twelve years. I need you to do the same for the queen."

"Of course."

The Silent Queen gave me a long look then threw her arms

around me, squeezing me to her tightly. *You must survive, too. You are all I have, Dosy,* she told me. Moments like these reminded me of how young she truly was. I'd helped raise her since she was six, and I didn't want to be apart any more than she did.

"I will. I swear it." I released her. "Now go. Don't stop until you're safe."

She pulled up the hood of her coat and nodded with a glance at Herakles.

I stood back and watched them enter the wall. Our revolution was not yet ready to launch, but we no longer had the luxury of waiting.

Turning away from them, my mind went to Tommy. Every maternal instinct in my body was screaming for me to make his rescue my first priority. But Niko wasn't going to let anything happen to him. He probably planned on using our son against me, but he'd never hurt him or let anyone else near him.

These kind of reassurances had to do for now. I had to prepare for the first stage of our rebellion, which left no room for distraction.

Take care of our son, I texted to Niko. I didn't wait for his response. With a heavy heart and dread twisting my gut, I dropped the cell phone and smashed it with my heel then returned to Gus to take up my role as Mama. When the city was safe, and the fighting over, the Queen could take her rightful place leading the revolt against the gods.

And I'd go back for my son.

382

TWENTY FIVE
ALESSANDRA

A common danger unites even the bitterest enemies
– ARISTOTLE

T HE VOICES CAME FROM THE DARKNESS OF MY MIND. At first, I didn't know them, where they came from or why they spoke to me.

We are not your enemies. This one was female.

You have been misled. This one male.

Destroy us, and you destroy your world. Help us, and we will help you.

More voices, more messages like these continued to whisper into my thoughts. No one gave a name, but the theme was the same across the speakers.

Gradually, as the darkness lifted and my slumber slid away, I became aware of myself again. I was cold, lying on what felt like metal, and my head throbbed. The calming scents of amber, sulfur, and other spices soothed my initial fear of not knowing where I was or what had happened.

Those freaky memories surfaced when I was about to open my eyes.

"Can you hear them?" This voice was outside my head.

My eyelashes fluttered open. I was lying on my belly on the metal table where I'd been knocked out, staring at the floor through the cut out for my face. Groggy from drugs, intoxicated to the point of dizzy from the fumes, I wasn't able to react how I felt I probably should.

"Alessandra."

"Oh, gods … what now?" I lifted my head and gasped. The pain drove away the fog, and I stretched back with one wooden arm to touch the part of my head that hurt. They'd shaved a strip of hair away above the back of my head. I couldn't feel what they'd done but I felt the roughness of a bandage and smelled blood beneath pungent astringent.

"Don't bother it. The microchip is fused to your spine." Someone grasped my hand to keep me from picking at the bandage. "I only have a minute."

Blinking, I sat up and met Lantos' gaze. He steadied me, the sparkle gone from his eyes for the first time since we'd met. Before I could curse him back to the day he was born, he held up the teal gem, a reminder of how he'd threatened Adonis.

"I can't call him back. Not yet, but I will soon. In the meantime, you need to make the Magistrate believe you're on his side," he said. "I don't have time to explain what I've done and why."

384

"You're an asshole. You threatened your own friend."

"So you would cooperate. I'd never hurt him. Send him to the monster arena? In a heartbeat, but he likes it there." He gave a small smile. "My goal has always been the same. This was the only way to reach it," he said without apology. "But ... I am not an ally of the Magistrate's. He's a means to an end for me. I swore to Adonis I'd never let your fate come to you, and this was the only way to keep that promise."

No part of me believed him sincere or capable of regret or compassion. If I had any sort of strength, I'd punch him.

"Do you hear them?" he asked again.

The whispers had faded to the point I couldn't make out the words. "Who are they?"

"The Magistrate needs me because I'm an ambassador to the gods. They ... asked a favor of me. They asked for the ability to speak to you as they do me."

"So ... you put them in my head?" I was having a hard time following anything. I simultaneously wanted to dance and nap, and my headache was so intense behind one eye, I was pretty sure I'd vomit if I attempted either.

"You were born with the skill to speak to them. I simply lifted the last block in your mind we put to help control your magic. Your memories are fully returned. No trace of my father's magic remains. I did, however, block Adonis. Your connection runs quite deep. I can't have him returning before I'm done."

"Adonis will not forgive you so easily." His betrayal of Adonis felt personal, as if he were betraying me. In a way, I knew he was. Adonis swore to protect me and trusted Lantos.

"I am prepared to confess when the timing is right for him to return." Regret flickered in Lantos' eyes.

"Why are they talking to me? I want them gone from the Earth."

"You have much to learn about what's really going on." He stepped back from the table. "And I am out of time." He retreated to a shadowy corner and became one with it.

Even his lies have lies. I couldn't imagine how anything ever got done among the members of the Triumvirate – or how I was supposed to trust anything any of them told me. I squinted then grimaced at the pain. Seconds later, a doctor approached and checked my vitals. I struggled to hear the voices without success.

"Any pain?" the doctor asked.

"You just did brain surgery on me. What do you think?" I snapped moodily.

He withdrew a syringe from his pocket and injected its contents into me. "The Magistrate wants you awake, so no morphine. This will take the edge off," he said.

Its effects were immediate, and I released a sigh as the pain from my right eye receded. "Thanks."

Before *he* entered the room, I felt him. It was similar to the sense I had about Adonis yet different as well. This was superficial. Adonis was entwined with me on a primal level, an extension of me and me of him.

But the Magistrate … he was like a permanent burr in my sock. I didn't like how he felt inside my head. It was unnatural.

He didn't belong.

"I felt you awaken." The normally subdued man was borderline excited for once. Cunningness gleamed in his eyes, and his hands were clenching and releasing. "I have never experienced such a connection."

Ugh. Great.

He was studying me closely.

I pushed off the table, wobbled, and touched the back of my skull gingerly.

"You can see the rainbows?" he asked.

"Rainbows?"

He motioned to the area above my head.

Wow. So the chip and the magic of Dolos had plugged him straight into my brain. Unease trickled through me. Did that mean he could read my mind? Control my thoughts? Just how deep in my head was he?

"Yeah," I said. "Those are what the Oracle uses to create, destroy and whatever else she's supposed to do."

"How do I create?"

"I haven't figured that out yet. Seems kind of random or accidental."

"Then how do I destroy?"

I shifted weight between my feet, not wanting to answer. A streak of pain shot through me, originating in my brain and smashing through my body. I staggered.

"So it works," he said in satisfaction. "I had a control mechanism built into the chip. If you disobey, displease or otherwise refuse to do my bidding, I can punish you until you cooperate."

More pain. I dropped to my knees, gasping. White dots filled my gaze and my ears rang.

"Tell me how to destroy," he ordered quietly.

"Okay!" I gasped. "You just take ... the rainbows and crush them. Or ... push them into your body if you want them to disappear."

The pain stopped immediately. I struggled to regain myself. When I stood, he was frowning, trying to grip the ribbons above a table.

"Perhaps you alone retain this ability," he said and turned to me. "Try it."

Not yet ready for another round of pain, I obeyed and held out my hand. I took the ribbons above the table he wanted to destroy and crushed them.

It crumpled.

"Interesting. Although I can see what you do, and sense what you do, you alone control your magic," he observed.

Thank the gods for that tiny blessing.

"What else can you do?" he faced me again.

"That's it," I said. "Until my trials are over."

"This was not your third?"

I shook my head.

"The queen." Understanding crossed his features, followed by tension. "I'm afraid she's made her escape. She had the opportunity to task you. I saw to it at her tea party. She didn't give you your trial?"

"No," I lied and then waited to see if he could sense my

deception with the same ease Adonis did.

"There is a reason Lantos is here and she is not," he growled. "Come. Let's send Her Majesty and her divine patroness a message." He motioned to someone from the corner.

I almost sighed in relief. So he couldn't read my mind or feel it when I lied. This gave me some wiggle room. My only real challenge: keeping my powers from emerging completely by refusing to carry out the Silent Queen's trial. It should be easy, assuming Cecelia could hang on as long as I needed to figure out how to undo what the Magistrate had done to me.

Niko emerged from the shadows, and I almost screamed. I felt like crap – and he was not the person I wanted around.

Cleon went to the elevator. Niko gripped my arm and we trailed at my slow pace. My step was unsure; the world was moving a little too fast for me to keep up with. It wasn't until we reached the outside world that my sense began to clear. It was close to midnight and chilly. I shivered in my gown.

"Amazing," Cleon breathed.

I lifted my eyes and saw the world once more exploding with life and activity only we could see. The ribbons soothed me. Their movement was gentle and swaying to the point of mesmerizing. A car was waiting, but Cleon appeared lost as he gazed around.

It wasn't the ribbons that had my attention, though. It was the smoldering, bombed out remains of the Silent Queen's villa. The largest on the compound, its disappearance was impossible to miss and ran for half a block. Smoke trickled into the sky. If not for the reassurance she had escaped, I'd be panicking.

"Sir," Niko prodded.

Cleon blinked and strode to the car, a small smile on his face.

Dread and throbbing pain replaced the giddy euphoria of the caverns, and I slid into the backseat beside him. I ached too much from the abuse of the arena, Mama's people and impromptu brain surgery to want to speak or move, and I was at a loss of what to think about Adonis still or his boss, who was turning out to have more sides than a dice.

My villa was still standing, which meant Leandra and Mrs. Nettles were hopefully safe. I needed Leandra, to know how wide and capable her spy network really was. Could she get word to Theodocia? Could they get me away from Cleon and expel him from my mind?

If anything, I had the desire to sleep for about a week. Closing my eyes, I rested my head back against the seat then hissed as the tender base of my skull erupted into pain. Agitated, I shifted onto my side the best I could. My head pounded too hard for me to find a comfortable position.

"I have spent my lifetime studying the Oracle and her powers," Cleon said.

Even when I knew he was the super villain of my life, I was compelled to listen, unable to prevent the tension from sliding out of me. His presence was always so calming, his voice soothing.

"I am truly, *truly* pleased to know I do not have to hurt you as my predecessors did Cecelia in order to access your power."

He was so good at pretending to be sincere, I almost believed him. Straightening in my seat, I studied him in the dimness of what streetlights managed to penetrate the car.

"You want to open the portal again?" I asked.

"Not exactly. I want to do more than return the world to the way it's been for centuries."

"What more is there?"

"There are no limits to what I can do now that I can control you." He glanced at me, a trace of a smile on his face. It was cold, calculating, the first time I'd seen malice in his otherwise expressionless features.

"So … world domination?" I asked.

"Something like that. With your power at my disposal, I can crush the gods beneath my heel and anyone else who opposes me. They will do my will or suffer."

It sounded a little like what the Queen had wanted, except her goal was to make the world a better place after she exacted her revenge. I had a sense the Magistrate's ambition was more self-serving.

I said nothing. Whether it was from knowing the man beside me was a monster behind a kind face and warm personality or the drugs, I was nauseated.

The streets were clear, the military lining every intersection in riot gear and flanked by armored vehicles. I had never seen Niko's men inside the city before this, but they were everywhere.

"I declared martial law behind the wall," Cleon said. "I

heard rumors of the Silent Queen's plans. Her underground army."

I wanted to ask about SISA stepping aside so easily but didn't. Adonis was gone, and the Supreme Priest was playing a dangerous game to get what he wanted. I hoped ... *prayed* ... one of them knew what they were doing giving in to a man like Cleon and turning on the Queen. I stared out the window, heart quickening. I wasn't about to reveal anything of the Silent Queen's plans.

"I think I need a long nap," I said in the tense quiet. "I'm not feeling so well."

"You've had a trying few days," he agreed. "I promise you time to rest, after a simple demonstration of your power."

"Demonstration. You want me to destroy something."

"I do. No one has to know your powers are limited. This will convince them otherwise."

I tensed, unable to imagine what his target was. He admitted to wanting to rule the world. It wasn't like he'd hold back, now that he had the shot to do it.

We were silent the rest of the trip. He was taking us toward the wall, but to an area unreachable by Mama's people. We entered a secure military base and traveled through soldier-packed streets to the foot of the wall. Rather than carve out stairs inside the wall, as Theodocia's people had done, the military had created an elevator running to the top of the wall protected by no less than a dozen heavily armed soldiers.

We got out of the car. The guards gave away once they spotted Cleon and saluted Niko. Niko strode through them and the barriers between us and the wall. I trailed him, limping, eyeing the heavily armed men uneasily. There was pretty much no chance of me escaping the demonstration, unless I let Cleon kill me through the control mechanism he'd implanted in my brain.

I didn't see him letting me die when he wanted to control me.

Cleon and a man with stars on his collar spoke quietly and followed. They grew quiet as we all climbed into the elevator. The ride was too fast for me – my stomach turned, and I steadied myself against the cool metal wall.

The voices were louder, though still hard to understand. One voice, a male one, seemed to be the only one whose words I could make out.

You must stop him. Let us help you.

I didn't know how to respond or even if I should. The gods were supposed to be my enemies. The priests at my orphanage believed so. The Silent Queen swore as much, and even Leandra still believed the gods to be against everything the Old Ways stood for.

The more I learned and experienced of the outside world, the less I truly understood it. A man like Cleon had to be stopped. But so did Lantos, who was willing to sacrifice me and everyone else to exact the revenge of the Titans. And the Holy Wars, the condition the world outside this wall lived in …

Who exactly was an ally to me? Because I wasn't seeing how any of these people were remotely near my side of the fence.

This time, when my head ached, it wasn't from the surgery. It was because I was once more feeling like a victim of my circumstances rather than the powerful Oracle I was supposed to be.

We reached the top of the wall and stepped off the elevator. Soldiers lined the city and open sides as far as I could see in both directions. DC and the surrounding areas glowed to my right while the darkness, all I ever saw of the rest of the world, was to my left.

Niko led us to a point on the wall and waved away the soldiers standing guard. I joined him, admiring the lights of the city beneath Nyx's sky and how the ribbons seemed to dance among them. What we were doing here? Why did I have the feeling I never should've left my forest?

"Shut up and do what you're told, kid," Niko said quietly, for my ears only, before he stepped back for Cleon to replace his presence at my side.

"Beautiful, is it not?" Cleon asked, a smile on his features as he viewed the city and surrounding areas. "The most powerful city in the world, perhaps the most powerful the world has ever known, right at your feet."

The lump forming in my throat was too large for me to swallow.

"Reports indicate the Silent Queen has focused her underground army there." He pointed towards an area that included the central temple of Artemis.

I studied it. I had no idea if he were right or not. I had seen a small part of the underground city but didn't know DC enough to understand where it was in correlation to the above ground world. The area he indicated, though, was also residential. I counted at least four apartment buildings, a neighborhood of townhouses, police station and a park among several quiet streets lined with businesses surrounding the temple.

"That's where we'll start. Destroy it all."

My eyes flew up to him. "You can't be serious!"

Cleon met my gaze. I saw no emotion or compassion in his eyes and recoiled. How I was ever convinced he was kind or worthy or anything good was beyond me. None of these people could be trusted.

"Won't ... won't that anger Artemis?" I managed.

"Artemis favored the Queen and her High Priestess. Which is why this will be a demonstration to both sides." He motioned towards it, supreme satisfaction on his face. "Destroy everything for a five block radius from the central temple."

I couldn't believe I'd heard the words. This had to be a nightmare, another alternate reality like the one Mnemosyne created. For an agonizing moment, I stood shocked, too surprised and horrified to move.

"No," I said finally. "I'm not a monster like you. I won't let you turn me into one!"

Agony pierced my brain, and I staggered, dropping to my knees as the pain spread rapidly, crippling me. I could barely breathe and wasn't able to move or see, not with the paralyzing pain stabbing me in the brain.

"I gave you an order, Oracle," Cleon said softly.

"There … are … people!" I gasped out.

"If we are to be taken seriously, this needs to be done."

I barely registered the words.

The pain stopped as suddenly as it started. I shook from head to toe. "I don't care. I won't do it!"

"If you refuse me, I'll put you on the wall next to Cecelia."

Survive, Adonis had told me. But if faced with knowing it meant hundreds, if not thousands, of innocent people died, would he tell me to do whatever it took? Because I didn't think I could live with hurting someone innocent. He killed without restraint, but I wasn't him. I wasn't like any of these people!

"What's your answer?" Cleon demanded.

"Never," I whispered. I was better off diving off the wall to my death than doing what he said.

"Let me try," Niko's said.

Nothing the asshole could say was going to change my mind. With what strength I could muster, I managed to peel myself off the ground and sit. Even this movement left me dizzy.

Niko crouched beside me, close enough for his body heat to warm me and for our discussion to be private. Not that I was going to listen to a word the asshole said. He titled my chin up to meet his dark gaze. My original captor, my first betrayer, the man who showed me how different the real world was, appeared grim.

"My son's name is Tommy. He has a brilliant, strong, idealistic mother who will stop at nothing to serve the greater good. She's a true visionary, one who would sacrifice anything

– and anyone, including you, me and her own son – to see her goals realized," he began. "I'm a pragmatist. I don't care about the world she wants to create for our son tomorrow. I care about him surviving the one we live in today. It's why I serve the Magistrate. There's no second guessing who's had the upper hand here for quite some time. I'm always going to be on the winning team, because I'm not willing to sacrifice my son. I do whatever it takes to win, and he stays alive."

Startled by his honesty, I found myself listening mere minutes after swearing I wouldn't.

"She and I are alike in that way," he continued. "I will do anything, kill anyone, for my greater purpose, for my Tommy. What you need to figure out real quick: what's your greater calling, and what will you sacrifice to ensure you're able to see the day when it becomes reality? When what and who you love are no longer in danger?"

I knew the answer the moment he asked the question. It was instinctual, a whisper, perhaps from the depths of me that were tied to Adonis. Niko's damning pep talk left me quaking.

"But … those people are innocent," I whispered, tears pricking my eyes. "How do you live with knowing what you've done?"

"It's easy. I take one look at my son and realize there is no cost I'm not willing to pay to ensure he lives." He touched the exposed double omega birthmark visible on my arm. "I have a feeling this mark means you're not just another Oracle, and Cleon seems to think you're the strongest Oracle since the first who opened the portal between worlds. You aren't destined for the same fate as Cecilia. You're destined for the end of days, whatever form that takes, whoever's days those are."

Survive. My purpose, to restore the Old Ways, to end the tyranny of gods and men alike, made sense for the first time since leaving the forest. Without me, the world was stuck with Cleon. Without me, the people would continue to suffer through the Holy Wars. Without me, the future of everyone I loved was so very, very dark.

"I also know that today I'm on the winning team. But tomorrow, this might change. Nothing you do tonight will stop Theodocia or the Queen from whatever their plans are. By now they're safely out of the city or so deeply hidden, no one can touch them," he added. "No one you kill tonight will have a better life living under Cleon's rule than dying quietly in their sleep. If anything, you're doing them the same favor I did your priests."

I flinched at the reminder of him mercy-killing the people who helped raise me.

Niko's gaze was steady, and I began to understand who he was better than I did before. "So I ask again. What's your greater purpose, kid? What would you do to see it happen?"

Tears rolled down my face. A week ago, I'd been desperate to leave the forest and eager to do what I thought I was supposed to: help humanity return to a time where people were happy and free. I had no idea what price would be exacted to do what was right.

Several days later, I was contemplating the mass murder of thousands just so I'd one day have the chance to change the world for the better for anyone who survived the gods, Cleon and me.

Niko drew a breath. "I also know there's something going on between you and Adonis. I hate the man, but I know he'd tell you this, just as Dosy would. There is no tomorrow without you, kid. There's no future where gods and men are not at war, where the human race has a remote chance in Hades of surviving. If you care about anyone – Adonis or otherwise – you'll do whatever you have to today so you can save their lives tomorrow."

Wrong person. Right message. I wanted to weep. My resistance yielded the moment he put it into perspective. The thought of Adonis in danger was as crippling as the pain. The bond between us ran deeper than even I suspected. How had I missed what he was to me? How had I not seen it from the first meeting?

Your name is seared into my soul. His claim had stunned me, and it was only now sinking into me how deeply he felt. He would do anything for me without hesitation and had told me to do the same – survive. At all costs.

"I'll do you the favor of clearing out any other area Cleon wants destroyed, if you have time to give me a head's up. That's all I can offer," Niko said. "You need to decide if those you love are worth you choosing to be on the winning team."

If I followed in Cecelia's footsteps, I'd never be able to do what I had to. But choosing this path meant I, too, would bear the taint of this war. I, too, was destined to become a different kind of monster. The worst kind, if I had to guess, with the power of a god and controlled by a maniac with delusions of ruling over gods and men.

Niko rose. "You have two minutes before we drag you back down to the caverns to join Cecelia."

My gaze went to the city. I ached for Adonis to be here or for Herakles to guide me. I ached knowing I'd judged both of them for what they'd done to others when they didn't have the luxury of a choice.

Mostly, I hurt knowing Niko was right as had Adonis been when he claimed I'd have to risk unleashing the apocalypse in order to become who everyone thought I was.

I was made to believe an Oracle with incredible power could face a god, but only just learning that it took a monster to face another monster. I had to survive, because someone had to defend my world, no matter what that made me.

"Forgive me, Artemis," I murmured and climbed to my feet. With a deep breath, I looked back at Niko, whose expression was emotionless, then faced the city again.

I spread out both hands and gathered the ribbons, herding them together so I could grip them better.

Choking back a sob, with tears blurring my vision, I crushed them between my hands.

The ground beneath the wall shook, and the area I'd targeted began collapsing in upon itself. Artemis' pristine white temple went dark and then crumbled. It was followed by the apartment buildings full of people I'd never meet, the school and police station, the businesses and townhomes. Everything and everyone was turned to rubble instantly and toppled into the sinkhole forming beneath them.

"Incredible," the Magistrate whispered, awed by the sight of destruction.

You are forgiven, came the soft, sad whisper of Artemis from the depths of my mind.

I dropped my hands, not caring about the hot tears sliding down my cheeks or anything else in the world. The raw pain inside me was worse than anything Cleon could inflict upon me. It stemmed as much from what I'd just done as knowing this was just the beginning.

To survive, I had to become a monster like everyone else around me.

To save my world, I just might have to destroy it first.

OMEGA SERIES

OMEGA
THETA (2016)
ALPHA (2017)

LOVE ꙨMEGA?

Continue reading for an exclusive look at how Alessandra and Mismatch met twelve years before ꙨMEGA begins!

ALESSANDRA

OMEGA BEGINNINGS MINISERIES
Episode One

ONE

The gargoyle was crying.

Only I could see it.

Later on in life, I would learn that the ribbons I witnessed around everything were fields of energy, sparks of magic and the flow of life, each with its own unique color range. The world was filled with them. Inanimate objects had two ribbons. People had three.

At the age of five, all I really understood was that the stone creature being tormented by teen boys was alive – and hurting.

"Leave him alone!" I shouted and ran towards them.

The boys faced me briefly and dismissed me as quickly as most adults did. One of them wacked the gargoyle with his bag, and its ear chipped off.

Where a little girl wasn't listened to, a screaming kid generally was. "You're hurting him!" I shrieked.

"Hey! What're you boys doing to her?" one of the teachers called from the group of students touring the temple nearby.

One of the boys pushed me away. "You got us in trouble, you stupid kid," he snapped.

"You boys should be with your group!" Mrs. Thatcher approached and pointed to the other teens gathered around one of the priestesses giving the tour. "You leave kindergartners alone."

"We didn't do nothing, Mrs. Thatcher," one of them protested.

But they left, which was all I wanted. My attention was fixated on the stone monster whose ear was broken in half. The ribbons around him were agitated. Unlike most people, who had three ribbons, there were four around this beast: purple, faded teal, bright red and sunny yellow. The teal one sparkled in a way I had never seen before. I didn't know enough to understand what this meant – aside from the fact he wasn't like the other rocks and stones in the world.

I bent down and retrieved the cool limestone piece of his ear. On tiptoes, I reached up to replace it. His ugly face and large fangs were scary to me, but knowing he was in pain trumped my fear. I struggled to reach the broken stone.

"What're you doing, Alessandra?" Mrs. Thatcher asked, finished with the boys.

"He's hurt. I'm fixing him."

"You have such the imagination!"

I rolled my eyes and rested my cheek against that of the hideous statue. "Don't worry. I'll take care of you," I whispered to him.

"Oh, his ear is broken." Mrs. Thatcher took the piece from me and replaced it. "Do you know what this is, Alessandra?"

"A gargoyle."

"No, Alessandra. You should've been paying attention to the tour guide."

I watched anxiously as she balanced the part of the ear back where it belonged. It wasn't helping the creature's pain, and its suffering was moving into me. The ribbons of everyone around me always reached out to me, as if I was supposed to do something or know something about them. I could take those ribbons and manipulate them, bring the unliving to life and fix those that were hurt. I had even combined ribbons to create my own best friend: a monster-like creation consisting of my cat and my favorite stuffed animal. Its name was Mrs. Nettles. It purred and looked like a koala.

But I was too young to know why the ribbons existed, how I alone saw them or what I was supposed to do, if not bring my stuffies to life for tea parties.

"Gargoyles have water spouts," Mrs. Thatcher told me. "This is a grotesque. It's a statue monster. Can you say grotesque?"

I ignored her.

"They're here to protect the gods," she continued. "Do you see how large their eyes are?"

While each was unique, every beast had oversized wings, fangs and eyes. This one had eyes that were different sizes, the mane of a lion and face of a panther, a long tail, and wings like a dragon. He was larger, too, and facing the wrong direction.

Dozens of scary-faced stone monsters peered over the edges of the rooftop on the Temple of Artemis at the heart of Washington DC, glaring down at anyone who came to visit. Only my monster looked inward, guarding the rooftop. This was my first field trip to the Temple, and nothing had interested me about the place where the goddess visited aside from the stone creatures with their four ribbons. But this one had my absolute attention before the incident with the boys; he was special like me.

"It's said the gods can see through the eyes of the grotesques and make sure no one is here to hurt them," the teacher said. "But they can't hurt you. They're just stone."

"I don't care!" I snapped at her, my anxiety reaching a pitch. "You're not helping him right!"

"Alessandra, what have we discussed about these outbursts?"

"Leave me alone!"

"I'm getting your teacher."

I climbed onto the paws of the grotesque and grabbed the piece of stone from her. She walked away. I planted the ear where it belonged, albeit sloppily, and then I did *it*. I closed my eyes and imagined his ribbons smoothing out, twisted the two yellow ones beginning to separate and wrapped him with the ribbons only I possessed: the green ones.

I took his pain away and went one step further. I willed his ear healed. The stone shifted beneath my fingers and grew together. His ear was sideways, but it was back where it belonged.

"You'll be okay now," I told him softly. "I'm sorry they hurt you." I touched his scary features. "You need a name. How about ... Mismatch?" I touched his misshapen eye and uneven fangs. "I don't care what she says. You're a gargoyle. You're *my* gargoyle."

"Alessandra!" My teacher called.

I was always in trouble as a child, obsessed with the ribbons no one else could see. The grotesque didn't answer me or move the way my stuffies did when I wrapped them in green ribbons. I hopped off his paws and waited for the teacher to come lecture me, as usual.

"Honey," my teacher's voice was gentle but firm. "It's time to go sit in the bus."

"I know," I said and sighed. Uncertain how to address a stone creature, I curtseyed the way I'd seen the princesses in Disney movies do. "Goodbye, Mismatch."

TWO

"Mrs. Nettles! I'm home!" I shouted and shoved the front door open.

With my participation in the temple tour cut short after the gargoyle incident, I couldn't wait to get home. My parents worked until seven each night for the government; I didn't expect them to be there. I dropped my book bag on the floor by the door and flung off my shoes.

My purring, stuffed koala waddled down the stairs to the door.

"I had an awful day, Mrs. Nettles," I told her the way my father did my mother when he got home from work. "I made us a new friend! But then I forgot to tell him where I live." With a sigh, I began to think this was the worst day of my life so far.

Mrs. Nettles picked up my shoes – she loved shoes – and

waddled towards the stairs.

"Don't you want a snack?" I asked her.

She paused and then switched directions, clutching the shoes to her fuzzy chest. We went to the kitchen, and I told her all about my day – the stupid tour, the stupid boys, the ugly gargoyle and being sent to the bus to sit because of my temper.

"I don't *have* a temper, Mrs. Nettles!" I complained while heating us both cups of water for tea in the microwave and digging the chocolate pudding out of my mother's hiding spot in the pantry.

Lifting her off the counter to the floor, I precariously balanced a tray of tea and snacks and climbed the stairs to my room on the second floor. I turned on *Frozen,* my current favorite movie, which always cheered me up, and sat down on the floor with Mrs. Nettles.

She sat on my shoes and then pawed at the stuffed horse at our tea table.

"Okay. I guess he can come out. He almost got us in trouble last time," I reminded her.

Weaving the ribbons that floated around the stuffy quickly, I counted to three and smiled when Horsey came to life.

Clumsy and oddly proportioned, Horsey's first move was to knock over Mrs. Nettles' tea.

"Can this day get any worse?" I moaned.

It could and did.

My parents came home early, soon after I did. Irritated by my day, I went to the top of the stairs to greet them and fetch my book bag before my mother yelled at me.

They were speaking tersely in quiet voices. This, of course, warranted me sneaking down the stairs to hear their secrets. My sixth birthday was coming up. It was possible they were planning a party.

"… neighbors disappearing," my father said. Tall and handsome with brown hair, he stormed into the kitchen – the place they went to talk in private – and was followed by my pretty, tiny mother. "Seven, Kaitlin! They're closing in."

I crept down the stairs. It didn't sound like a discussion about my party, but I wanted to be sure.

"If we move now, they'll know," my mother was saying in her calm I-told-you-this-before voice. "We have to wait."

"For how long? For our entire neighborhood to end up at the House?" my father asked. "For us to be arrested and interrogated?"

"Relax, Howie. We've been careful. We always are."

"Not careful enough. They found her somehow. We've tried everything to make her normal, to make her fit in."

I was too young to understand they spoke about *me.* That knowledge didn't click until I was close to ten. I stood and listened, wondering whom they were talking about.

"Hey, Mrs. Nettles," my mother greeted my special pet. "No snacks before dinner."

Mrs. Nettles curled up at her feet.

"*This* is why," my father said and pointed at her. "We can't keep hiding these … things she makes."

Offended by how they treated my only real friend, I gasped.

"Lyssa, is that you?" my mother called.

413

I ducked behind the doorway.

"Come on out, baby," my father said.

"Who were you talking about?" I asked and entered the kitchen. I gave Mama a hug first and then Daddy before picking up Mrs. Nettles.

"No one, baby. Just a neighbor."

I was too young to know when my parents lied to me, too. "Oh. You aren't planning my birthday party?"

"Not yet." Mama smiled.

"Will people come this year?"

They exchanged a look. "Lyssa, we might have to keep it a family affair again this year," Daddy said gently. "You can bring all your toys to life at once. Won't that be fun?"

"It's the worst day of my life, daddy."

He laughed and picked me up, hugging me. "You want nuggets for dinner?"

"Yes."

My mother wrapped her arms around both of us. We rested our foreheads against one another's, the way we did every day before bed. The worry faded from both their faces.

"You are our world, Lyssa," Mama told me. "You know that, right?"

"I knoooooow." I said with another dramatic sigh. I took her face in my chubby hands, kissed her forehead and did the same to my father.

"I'll put Mrs. Nettles away so you can start dinner," I said with all the seriousness a child possesses.

My father set me down. I picked up Mrs. Nettles and hefted

her up the stairs to my room.

Dinner was quiet. I knew enough to sense something was wrong. Rather than watch a movie after eating like we usually did, my parents went to their room. I couldn't make out their muffled words and remained in my room, alone, as usual. Mrs. Nettles played with me, though Horsey was grounded after spilling her tea.

My parents didn't emerge at bedtime, so I changed into my pajamas and brushed my teeth then turned off the lights. I climbed into bed with Mrs. Nettles. Streetlight slipped past my curtains and made lines on my ceiling. I watched them. Mrs. Nettles burrowed into the covers beside me, and soon, her purring lulled me to sleep.

Until sometime very late, when a scratching at my window woke me. Mrs. Nettles was at the wall beneath the window, clawing at it. I sat up, shuffled to the window and peered out. Shadows and light played with my eyes. I wiped sleep from them. Something resembling a huge bird was hovering outside my window. I leaned through the curtains to see it more clearly. It was in the unlit backyard, and moonlight glinted off its wings as it settled next to my sandbox.

Unable to make out its form among the pool and landscaping of the yard, I focused on the ribbons to identify what it was.

There were five – and one was green.

With a gasp, I shoved my feet into my slippers and grabbed Mrs. Nettles. I raced out of my room, down the stairs and to the back door, all but slinging it open in my excitement to see my guest.

My step slowed when I reached the bottom of the stairs. I set down Mrs. Nettles. None of my stuffed animals or toys were nearly as big as the gargoyle before me.

Mismatch was huge, larger than he had seemed crouched on the rooftop of the temple. His wings were as wide as my yard, his eyes glowing dark teal, and his athletic body like something I had seen in cartoons about superheroes. His tail swished back and forth, tapping against the swing set, wagging the way my neighbor's dog's tail did when I fed it treats.

"You found me, Mismatch!" I exclaimed in a quiet squeal I hoped didn't awaken my parents. "I am so sorry! I forgot to give you my address!"

He was still ugly though less frightening than he had been crouched and scowling on the temple. I dashed to him and flung my arms around his thighs. He was warm like a human, not cold like a rock.

"Mrs. Nettles! Come meet Mismatch!" I cried in a muffled voice.

How did you awaken me, little one? His voice entered my head rather than my ears.

I looked up at him. His fangs were too large for his lips to cover, and his oddly shaped eyes and face were nowhere near normal. A small gem matching his teal eyes was at the base of his neck on a black choker. But I wasn't afraid; he was *mine.* Everything I awoke became part of my world.

"I gave you a new ribbon," I told him. "It woke you up. It

woke her up." I pointed to the purring koala bear that drew near. Mrs. Nettles was worried, pawing at one of her ears.

Ribbon? The gargoyle's voice was low and dark like the night. He knelt in front of me, his wings closing around us as if to keep my parents from hearing. *What is this ribbon? Magic?*

"Magic?" I echoed and scrunched my face. "I can't have magic, silly. Only the gods and Oracle have magic."

He touched my face with his cool fingers. His nails were long and pointed. They tickled, and I giggled. *You are but a child,* he said, sounding puzzled. *How can a child have this gift?*

"I don't know," I answered. "Do you want to meet the others?"

What others?

"My toys. I bring them all to life sometimes but they're sleeping now. You can stay with me, too."

I cannot stay, little one. He laughed quietly into my mind. *I am too large.*

"But how will I take care of you?"

You wish to take care of me? He tilted his head.

"Yes, of course. Mama says if I awaken something, it must stay with me, because it's my responsibility. No neighbors can know, and especially not the government or they'll take you away. So I bring everything to my room." I looked him over skeptically. "You might fit in my closet."

You gave me life, little one. I can take care of myself. I can take care of you.

"Me?" I giggled. "That's why I have Mrs. Nettles." I

417

stretched to grab my favorite pet and best friend.

This is your protector? Mismatch picked up Mrs. Nettles with one hand.

"Yes. She sleeps most of the time, except in the afternoon."

You need a protector while you sleep.

"Why? *Everyone* is asleep at night," I pointed out. "The only monsters are the ones I sometimes dream about. They come to life and sneak into the neighbor's house, but they never hurt me."

Mismatch was quiet. He swept hair from my face and gazed at me through his gemstone eyes. I shivered in the cool night air, and his wings closed around us. I snuggled into the plush wings.

"Oooohhhh!" I ran my fingers through the soft fleece covering the inside.

You will need a protector before this is done.

I smiled at him without understanding. "So you will stay in my closet?"

No, little one. But I will be here at night looking over you.

"We can have midnight tea."

If you wish it. He set Mrs. Nettles on the ground and reached for the gem at his neck. *If you should need me, I will come.* He handed it to me.

"This is beautiful," I murmured and accepted the gem. It appeared small on him but took up most of my palm. "I will take care of it."

I know you will. His wings swept away from me as he rose. *I must go, little one.*

418

"So soon?"

Yes. I have been asleep for a very long time and have forgotten this world. There are people and places I must visit. But I will return to you soon.

"My birthday is in two days. Will you be back in time?"

Yes.

"We'll have cake, and you can take me and Mrs. Nettles flying."

I do not feel Mrs. Nettles wishes to fly.

Mrs. Nettles hid behind my leg, her face pressed to my thigh. "Well, you can take *me* flying," I decided. "Mrs. Nettles will make us tea."

I agree, little one. I must go.

"Okay. Goodbye, Mismatch." I curtseyed to him once more.

Goodbye, little one. I will see you on your birthday. He bowed and then stepped back from me to unfurl his wings.

He leapt into the sky. I watched him, enthralled and delighted by the sight of my gargoyle flying in the night. He disappeared into the clouds rolling in for another spring storm. I stood in the backyard, gaze on the sky.

My gargoyle. He was beautiful. I closed my hand around the gem and swept up Mrs. Nettles into a hug before dashing back to my room.

THREE

I missed my bus the next morning, and it was raining. Not that I wanted to go to school anyway. I had an appointment with the principal to discuss my outburst at the temple.

I had thought Wednesday was my worst day ever, but Thursday was, too.

Watching my bus turn a corner, I debated going inside and telling my dad I needed a ride to school. Mama was always good about it, but she went to work early today, and Daddy would lecture me.

If I ended up late, I was going to be in even more trouble. Upset already, I turned around and trudged home. Wet and shivering in the spring weather, I started up the sidewalk to our house when I heard the sirens. I turned to see several police cars, trailed by a large black van, barreling down the street.

"Lyssa, what're you doing?" my father asked, emerging from the house.

"I missed the bus," I told him and pointed towards the vehicles. "Do you think someone is hurt?"

He approached and rested his hands on my shoulders. When he didn't answer, I peered up at him.

"Daddy, do you think someone is hurt?" I asked again, shouting to be heard over the sirens.

Daddy didn't seem to hear me. He was staring at the oncoming cars the way I did Halloween masks at the store. I *hated* Halloween. The more scared I got, the more monsters left my nightmares to roam around the neighborhood, and the longer I was grounded for not controlling them.

Daddy's fingers dug into my shoulders the nearer the vehicles came.

They whipped by our house and screeched to a halt three houses down, at the Adderleys, where my nightmare monsters went to hide last time.

"Daddy!" I complained and wriggled.

"Sorry, Lyssa." He released me and smiled without taking his eyes off the emergency vehicles. "Let's get you to school."

The day went as badly as I expected. Hours later, I made tea while filling in Mrs. Nettles about the principal, getting teased by a stupid boy, Shelby Lane stealing my crayons and having a runny nose after the rain that morning.

Listening, Mrs. Nettles sat on the counter while I

microwaved my tea. I helped her down and let her grab our pudding. Then we both climbed up the stairs to my room with snacks and tea. I turned on the television.

"Look, Mrs. Nettles! *American Oracle* is on!" A spinoff of the singing competition, *American Idol,* the talent show was about teenage girls who thought they could be the next Oracle of Delphi. I sat too close to the television, not caring if I was caught or not. Mama had refused to let me watch this when it came on Sunday night, and it was all the kids at school talked about. Even our teacher had seen it.

I punched buttons on the remote control until the DVR came on so I could record it.

"Who will be the next *American Oracle?*" the host asked, facing the screen. "Judges have selected the most promising young women to replace the dying Oracle of Delphi. Ten hopefuls are present for our debut season, but only one will be chosen by *you* to represent America to the gods in Greece! If she wins, she will become the voice of the gods, the opener of the gateway between heaven and earth ... and so much more! Are you ready to meet the candidates?"

"YES!" I screeched along with the crowd.

Ten teenaged women were led onto the stage, and each was told to give her name and what her magical power was.

I strained to see the ribbons around each girl. Some said they could read minds or move objects with their thoughts. Others claimed they could give inanimate objects life or absorb magic or other magical powers I didn't understand.

"No, no, no, no, no," I said, pointing out each girl. "No, no

"... maybe." I tilted my head. Only one girl had four ribbons. The girl labeled *Lilian* had a green ribbon so faint, I could barely make it out. "Mrs. Nettles, what do you think?" I twisted to see her lapping up the creamer at the center of our tray of tea. "Mrs. Nettles! Pay attention!"

I took the pot of creamer away.

She joined me.

"Her." I pointed once more.

Mrs. Nettles shook her head.

"Hmm. They all look normal," I said. "Maybe the Oracle has normal ribbons, too?"

Mrs. Nettles shook her head again. She climbed to her feet and waddled to the scrapbook collection I had hidden away about the Oracle of Delphi, the only human in the world with the power of a god. Once found and tested, she disappeared. Mama said she went to work with the gods doing good. Daddy said the Oracle should never be spoken of.

Which was why I hid the newspaper and magazine clippings Mama brought me, so he wouldn't find them. He always got upset when I mentioned the Oracle.

Mrs. Nettles brought me one of my scrapbooks and set it down. I picked it up and flipped through it to find pictures of the current Oracle of Delphi. She hadn't been seen in thirty years. The pictures of her were all older and her clothing was funny. Normally, I wasn't able to see ribbons on pictures, but I saw hers, because she was magical.

"Six," I said and counted. "I guess you're right. None of them have six." The Oracle had a green ribbon like mine. I put the book away. "But maybe they still can do wonderful things."

Mrs. Nettles brought me a toy dragon.

"You want to play?" I asked.

She set it down on the scrapbook.

"Okay, but don't bite his tail off this time. You really hurt him." I brought the dragon to life for her to play with and returned to watching the show. "I bet the Oracle never gets yelled at by the principal," I said grumpily.

I watched the two-hour *American Oracle* premiere over. And over. And over. Four times total, before Mrs. Nettles' snoring jarred me out of my utter fascination with the girls.

Pushing myself off my belly, I looked around my dark room briefly before crossing to turn on the lights. It was nine o'clock. My parents hadn't yelled up at me to say they were home. Mrs. Nettles was lying on her back, the toy dragon curled on her stomach. Both were asleep.

I left my room and stood at the top of the stairs. The house was completely dark. Flipping on the lights of the stairwell, I held the railing as I made my way to the bottom floor. This had happened once or twice before. My parents sometimes had to work late. They usually called and left me a message when they did.

Turning on lights as I went, I returned to the kitchen and climbed on top of a chair so I could reach the answering machine on the counter. The light was flickering. I pushed play.

"Baby …" Mama's voice was hushed. She almost sounded sad. "I need you to do two things for me. One, delete this voicemail when it's over. Press the button with the red x like I showed you that one time. Two, you remember the special hiding place we send you to when bad storms come? Grab your emergency bag out of the pantry. Take Mrs. Nettle and go hide in the storm center the moment you receive this message. Don't come out until Saturday morning. The storm will be over by then. Call your grandma from the cell phone in your emergency pack and tell her to come get you. Okay? Listen to this again until you're sure you know what to do and then delete it. We love you, Baby, so much."

At first I was worried about the storm, and then I recalled that tomorrow was my birthday. My parents were planning something huge for me – and it involved my grandma. Excited, I listened dutifully until certain I understood exactly what Mama wanted me to do before I deleted the recording.

Darting to the pantry, I found the emergency pack labeled with my name. It was a small backpack I was supposed to take with me if there was a bad storm, which happened often in spring. My parents took storms and tornadoes seriously. We practiced hiding in a safe place once a month.

We all had emergency packs, and theirs were present still. I didn't think twice about it. They had packs in their cars, if there really was a storm. And if not, if they were planning a surprise party for me, they wouldn't need them anyway. I put the backpack on eagerly.

Assuming their absence was tied to them waiting for me to hide so they could plan, I hurried up the stairs to my room fast enough that I tripped and banged my shin. Ignoring the pain, I made it to my room.

"Mrs. Nettles! We have to hide!" I exclaimed. I picked her up quickly and descended to the main floor before heading to the basement and the storm shelter. The hidden underground space was half the size of the ground floor of our house. It had a small kitchen, a big bed for my parents, a bunk bed for me, a bathroom, and even a television in the living area. The entrance was hidden under a tile in the floor.

I put Mrs. Nettles on the floor. Placing my hand on the secret panel to open the door, I was barely able to stand still. Mrs. Nettles pawed at me and pointed towards the upstairs.

"Oh! We left Thor out!" I said, recalling the dragon. "It's okay. Mama and Daddy can make sure he stays in my room. I'll turn him back on Saturday before my parteeeeeeee!" The last word ended in a squeal.

Mrs. Nettles lifted her arms so I could carry her down the ladder into the storm shelter. I reached the bottom and closed the door. The lights went on automatically, and I sighed, happy and exited about my party after my bad day.

FOUR

I went to bed soon after arriving in the shelter. Mrs. Nettles and I lay down in my parents' bed to be sure I woke up if they came down.

They didn't.

During our monthly drills, they sometimes told me I might be alone for a long time down here but that they'd always come find me. I was supposed to sit put and watch my favorite movies and drink tea until they returned.

It was Friday, my birthday. I was a little disappointed to wake up and find they weren't there, and Daddy hadn't made me my birthday waffles. The knowledge they were planning a surprise party soon swept away my concern.

I spent the morning watching movies, the *American Oracle*

premiere again and drinking tea. Mama had taught me how to microwave food and make sandwiches, so I did both for Mrs. Nettles and me while we waited for the day to pass.

I followed Mama's instructions and knew they were planning something for me, but I still felt lonely. I hadn't brought down any other stuffies aside from Mrs. Nettles. They were my favorite to play with, my only friends.

After an afternoon nap and two more Disney movies, I was bored. I dumped my emergency backpack onto the bed to see its contents. Sorting food from toys and the phone, I smiled as I saw the card my mama had included. She hadn't written anything except for a heart on the inside.

Pulling out my notebook and crayons, I practiced drawing hearts. I was learning to write but wasn't very good at it.

I wasn't very good at anything in school, even arts and crafts. My teacher said I'd grow out of my temper and impatience and not to worry, because one day, I'd catch up to the others. Until then, I was special in my own way.

"What do you think, Mrs. Nettles?" I asked and pointed to the heart that took me a long time to complete. "It almost looks like Mama's."

Mrs. Nettles shook her head.

"Okay. I'll keep trying." I scribbled over it.

Mrs. Nettles picked up a crayon and drew a diamond. She tapped it.

"What?" I asked, gazing at it.

She drew the moon, a bird, a house …

"Oh!" I sat up quickly. "Mismatch's gift!"

She nodded.

"But Mama said ..." I drifted off, beginning to panic about the gift I'd left upstairs. What if it was swept away in a storm? It was so beautiful, and it was from my gargoyle. "Mrs. Nettles! Mismatch is supposed to be here tonight! I can't tell him I lost it."

My mind decided, I put on my shoes and tied my hair into a sloppy ponytail. Mrs. Nettles appeared to be trying to tell me something, but I swept her up in my arms and dashed to the ladder. She squirmed.

"Stop, Mrs. Nettles. We have to be quiet, in case they're planning," I reminded her.

She went still. I climbed the ladder slowly and reached the top. Placing my hand against the pad in front of me, I waited while the door overhead opened.

There was no sound of rain or a storm, and I finished my climb in excitement, now firmly convinced my parents had asked me to hide so they could plan my party. It didn't matter that it was happening the day after my birthday. It was going to be my first birthday party ever that I could remember. We'd always had quiet, family gatherings. I didn't have any friends at school, but I had cousins who lived out of town who were my age. I went to *their* parties. Maybe they were finally coming to mine.

I closed the entrance to the shelter behind me the way I had been taught before setting down Mrs. Nettles. Blinking in the dark basement, I experienced a strange sense, one I had never felt before.

It was the fear from a nightmare, but I was awake. I would later learn to identify the uncomfortable instinct as one of danger. Soft ribbons outlined my surroundings. None of them were out of place, even if I couldn't see the objects they floated around in the darkness.

I went up the wooden stairs to the door leading into the house and pushed it open.

The ribbons in the kitchen were out of place. It was chaotic, as if there really had been a storm, and it blew over everything inside the kitchen. Pacing to the living room, I was upset to see it in the same condition. In fact, everything on the ground floor was in a similar state of disarray and none of the lights worked.

My hope about having a birthday party began to fade at the damage done to the first floor. I hurried upstairs, to my room, and was pleased to find all the ribbons where they were supposed to be. Except ...

"Thor?" I called quietly. "Are you here?"

Everything in my room gave off two ribbons – inanimate objects. I had left Thor out and alive. He should have stood out easily with his three ribbons. But he didn't.

"Mrs. Nettles, can you find him?" I called behind me. I went to the bottom drawer of the dresser where I had hidden the jewel Mismatch gave me and other treasures. Relieved to find it safe, I slid the glowing gem into my pocket. Mama and Daddy had made me stash flashlights all over the house in case of a storm like this, and I pulled out a small one and flipped it on. "Mrs. Nettles!"

Her purring came from under the bed. She poked her head out.

"He's not here?"

She shook her head.

"Weird. Where could he have gone?" I searched the room quickly but already knew from the ribbons he wasn't present. "The storm messed up the living room and kitchen. Maybe it swept him away?" I was grateful it had passed over my bedroom but also worried about Thor. Mama said I had to take care of my friends, and I had never lost one yet.

Picking up my pet, I walked to the hallway and my parent's room. I knocked as they had taught me before walking in. Their room, too, had been hit by the storm. Thor wasn't present either.

The instinct I didn't like was tickling the back of my neck like I had left the window open. Shivering, I scratched my neck, puzzled, and returned to the top of the stairs.

"Something isn't right," I whispered to Mrs. Nettles. I was starting to feel scared.

Hoping my parents left me a message, I returned to the messy kitchen, righted a chair and checked the answering machine. It was off, like the lights. Their emergency packs were in the pantry. They had left no notes on the fridge, and their cars weren't in the garage or in the driveway. A black van was parked out front. It was big like the one I saw go to the Adderleys the other day, but it meant nothing to me at that time.

Ribbons. They were everywhere, jumbled and out of place,

distressing me. My eyes settled on one in the living room that didn't fit in, and I went to the doorway to get a better look. Something was behind the overturned couch. Something with three ribbons, but it wasn't the right pattern and colors to be Thor or my parents. Shining the light on the couch, I wasn't able to see what was behind it.

There was another set of three ribbons in the formal dining room, behind the toppled table.

I turned off my flashlight and listened for anything indicating what – or who – was in my house.

I heard nothing, but the ribbons were never wrong. Stepping back into the hallway, I clutched Mrs. Nettles to me hard enough that she began to squirm.

I whirled to head back to the shelter and spotted another set of three ribbons. This one was now between the door to the basement and me. Panic set in, and I raced to the back door and burst outside.

My swing set and sand box, the ball I'd been kicking with Mrs. Nettles Tuesday, and other toys were scattered around the yard where I left them. The storm hadn't hit my backyard.

Or my room. The air didn't smell of rain, and the sky was clear.

"I don't think it was a storm, Mrs. Nettles," I said, wanting to cry.

I heard it then, someone moving around the bottom floor of my house.

Panicking, I darted to the tree in the corner of my yard and climbed the wood plank ladder to the tree house at the top. It was where I went when I was mad at my parents. There was no television or emergency supplies, but it was quiet and small, cozy with a mini-couch and rugs on the floor.

I set Mrs. Nettles down and crept to the window overlooking my yard and the back of my house. Someone emerged from the back door and stepped into the backyard. I didn't recognize his ribbons, or those of the three people who followed him.

Ducking back down, I stared at Mrs. Nettles in the dark, my heart pounding so hard, I could hear it in my ears. "Keep quiet, Mrs. Nettles."

Her purring grew softer, and she cuddled against me.

My focus turned to the dark night visible through the skylight. I slipped a hand into my pocket, and I gripped the jewel.

"Mismatch, come get us," I whispered. "I think we're in trouble."

The men in the backyard spoke quietly to one another. I couldn't make out their words, but they were getting closer.

My eyes stayed on the sky. I had full faith in the gargoyle I had just met. My friends always came when I called, no matter where I was in the house, and Mismatch had said if I needed him, he'd come.

I waited and waited, starting to cry when I heard the men approach the tree where I hid. Clinging to Mrs. Nettles, I squeezed the jewel even tighter. Her plush coat soaked up my tears.

"Please, Mismatch. I'm scared!"

Another long moment passed, and one of the men began to climb the makeshift ladder to the tree house.

I huddled with my favorite pet, pressing my face into her fur, and waited for them to find me.

Wind whipped the tree branches together, and they clattered. My eyes flew open, and I stared out the skylight at the wide wings beating the air above the tree.

"I knew you'd come," I said, smiling happily through my tears. My heart swelled with love for the creature I brought to life and came when I needed him.

You are in danger, little one. His words slid into my mind.

"I know."

Stay where you are until I tell you to come out. Do not look outside. Do you understand?

"Yes." I hunkered down and closed my eyes.

He said nothing else, and the clatter of branches stopped. Someone in the backyard shouted. I tensed, scared and worried about my gargoyle.

"We're going to be okay, Mrs. Nettles." I wiped my running nose on her head. She snuggled against me. "Don't you worry. Mismatch is here. He'll take care of us and tomorrow, we'll go to Grandma's and Mama and Daddy will be there waiting for us."

Little did I know at the innocent age of six, I'd never see my family again.

MISMATCH

EPISODE TWO

$\mathcal{O}$NE

Grotesque by night and human by day, I didn't know what I really was or how it came to be that I was stuck between forms and worlds. No temple guardian in history had ever been reanimated. I didn't seem to be a man or a beast but a combination of both with sentience and the senses of an animal.

"What *is* that?"

I froze in my position leaning over the rooftop of a hotel. As a statue, no one paid me any heed. But as a living creature, I had to remind myself constantly I could not simply dwell amongst the humans the way a statue did. I was a monster to them, as I discovered when I first awoke last night and terrified a janitor on the roof of the Temple of Artemis.

"Maybe it's a vampire," one of the teen girls below

437

whispered.

I am not a vampire.

They didn't hear me. Only one person had – the little girl who broke the curse. I visited her last night before flying here. As much as I wanted to stay and discover how she possessed the magic needed to awaken me, I had to take care of something very important first.

I was as still as possible, until those below lost interest. Then I crept over the edge of the roof and down the wall like a spider to peer into the hotel room I was stalking. I had hoped to talk to the Crown Princess of Greece during the daylight, when I was human, but her security was too tight.

One of her handmaidens was with her.

I alighted and landed lightly on the railing of the balcony of the royal suite of the Four Seasons in New York City. Sitting back on my haunches, I decided to wait, closed my eyes and … breathed.

I never knew how incredible it was to breathe.

My first inhale of night air after four thousand years as a statue was indescribable, and every one since was a blessing. I was never meant to awaken from the living death cursing every heir of my bloodline. I became stone at the age of seventeen.

The little girl – whose name was one of many things lost in the chaos of my mind – had awoken me yesterday afternoon, but I did not move until dark fell. There was a presence in my head that hadn't been there before her touch, a sense I innately knew was her. I could *feel* her and where she was. She was a beacon, which I took to be the result of whatever magic she used. It tied us to one another. Only the gods could give life to stone. Her magic was such that the priesthood was going to find her, if the gods didn't first. She didn't know her danger when she woke me.

There could be no competition or threat to either priests or gods. She hadn't been found yet, but she would be, and I intended to be there when it happened, even if my plan of what to do hadn't formed.

A day after she reanimated me, I could fly clumsily and barely stand. I was in no shape to defend her from a god. My body had not yet adjusted to being alive after so long in stone. My mind, however, had exploded with activity.

Everything I had witnessed over the millennia was jumbled and churning through my thoughts all at once. I had trouble processing the wind sweeping beneath my wings or the way moonlight outlined everything below me. I couldn't grapple with the idea of the continent I was on hadn't been discovered when I became stone or that Greece was not the center of the world anymore – even if the Olympic deities were.

There was too much information for my man or beast brain to process.

I still hear them. The connection I shared with the other grotesques remained but only when I was a beast. We were able to talk to one another from our perches atop the temples. It was necessary, for each of us had a very slim lane of sight, and we had to warn one another about any danger.

Their voices added to the chaos of my mind. Some of them were begging me to free them, while others wanted to know what the world smelled like or to find their favorite food and remind them how it tasted. The most devout and oldest of the Bloodline chastised me for accepting the gift of life and abandoning my sacred duty as a temple guardian.

I was too overwhelmed to decipher what was honorable and what wasn't. I didn't know *why* Little One had brought me to life and no other. What I did know: I had no intention of returning to the living death and would save my descendants from the same destiny, no matter how long it took or what I had to do.

This resolution started here, tonight.

Opening my eyes, I peered into the princess's room once more. She was climbing into bed. A security guard did one final sweep, and her matronly handmaiden tucked her in.

The lights went out. I dropped to my feet on the balcony, righted my balance and tucked my wings so I didn't appear quite so scary.

My nails were two inches long. I used them to scratch at the glass pane of her door.

The Crown Princess, a blonde girl with a permanent look of graveness on her features, sat up and stared in my direction.

I scratched again. Standing was taxing and walking cumbersome. I had spent too long hunched over on all fours and knelt, unable to remain upright for long.

She approached, stopped when she saw me, and then opened the door.

Children did not fear the unusual the way adults did. For the second time in as many days, I was grateful for their innocent faith that the monster I was bid them no harm.

"Are you lotht?" she asked, peering at me. Around six, she bore the chiseled cheekbones and jawline of our Bloodline. One of her ears stuck out too far, and she'd recently lost her two front teeth. Her lisp was much more pronounced than it should be with her missing teeth. She had a speech impediment.

Her hair was white-blonde, and her eyes bright blue. She was as Greek looking as I was at the moment. Hunched over, my head was at the level of hers. There was sadness in her gaze. Unlike Little One, who was sheltered from what she was, this child appeared much wiser than her years, as if she knew already how ugly the world outside her palace was.

I am not lost. I came to see you. I told her and waited to see if she could understand.

"Oh. What are you?" she asked.

I am … was a statue.

She touched my cheek with cool fingertips. "You aren't thtone," she observed wisely.

Not anymore. I do not know what I am. I am called … Mismatch. The name wasn't right, but my confused brain wasn't either. I couldn't recall who exactly I had been long ago.

"I'm Phoibe."

Like the Titan.

"Yeth."

Why are you not in Greece where you belong?

"I have to be here. The motht powerful priethteth liveth here, and I do now, too, now that Mama ith dead. Why are you here?"

441

I came to find you. The others like me – we're called grotesques – can communicate through our minds to one another. Those in the temple nearby told me where you were.

"Why?"

Phoibe, I was the Crown Prince of Greece once, a very long time ago. You are a descendant of mine, and you are in trouble.

She tilted her head to the side, listening without interrupting, but confused as well. She glanced down at her wrist, and I knew she sought the mark we all shared.

I presented my inner wrist to her, so she could see the distinctive birthmark identifying us as touched by the gods. The omega letter was prominent on my skin.

She held out her wrist beside mine. "But you're a living gargoyle," she said, puzzled. "I'm not a gargoyle."

Our family bears a curse, one that turns you into what I am. I came to warn you about it.

"Everyone dithappearth, like Mama," she whispered. "Ith it the curthe, too?"

Yes, Phoibe. We are turned to stone and placed atop the temples of the gods and goddesses to protect them. Your mother is on a temple somewhere, too. As soon as an heir is born and deemed healthy enough to survive childhood, the curse claims the parent. I was seventeen when my son was born, and I became stone.

"But the priesteth thaid she wath dead."

It is a living death. Her mind and eyes are awake. But she cannot move. She is a statue, a temple guardian.

"How awful." Phoibe's eyes watered. "Will I be a thtatue?"

442

I hesitated. A girl this age couldn't fully understand the importance of what I told her. I didn't know if she was capable of withstanding the pressures that would come, if she followed the instructions I came here to give her.

As an adult, I understood how every generation of heir to the throne was led willingly to his or her fate. We were rendered vulnerable by the sudden loss of our parents and tricked into saying the spell that would turn us to stone. Often times, the priests and priestesses we became dependent upon in place of our parents had us speak the spell before we were ten. When the subsequent heir was born, the curse automatically imprisoned us.

We were innocent children when we sealed our own fates, led into the trap by the people we trusted. There was a chance I was too late already.

But I had to make her understand in case I had arrived in time to save her.

"Forgive me, Mithmatch," she said and regained her composure. She squared her shoulders and lifted her chin, every bit the tiny, regal princess trained from an early age to hide her emotions. "That wath very inappropriate of me. I am prepared for what you have to thay and will not cry."

For the first time in four thousand years, I felt an emotion. It was sadness, and it twisted my heart to think of how many little girls had succumbed to the curse ahead of this one. I couldn't help them.

I could only help her – maybe. Vulnerable and sad, Phoibe's steady gaze stirred emotions I couldn't yet name or process in the mess of my mind.

The curse is brought on by a spell your priests will have you speak aloud, I told her.

"Then I will not thpeak it," she reasoned with the simple logic of a child.

They will trick you. They can make you say one word every few months until the spell is complete.

"Oh." She gazed at our wrists. "Can I come with you?"

Taken aback, I wasn't certain how to respond. I had thought only to warn her; it never occurred to me to take her away.

The request also made sense. How else could I protect her from her fate? She was far too young and trusting to fend off the cunning people who would surely do whatever it took to force her into her destiny as a temple guardian.

She gazed at me hopefully, waiting.

Yes. There was no other answer to give. *But since I have just awoken, I have nowhere for us to live, no food or paper money like they use here. Let me secure these things first, and then I will come for you.*

"Tomorrow?"

In two or three days.

"Okay." There was a light in her gaze.

You cannot tell anyone about me, not your priestess or even your friends.

"I don't have any friendth, Mithmatch," she said softly. "I only talk to my shadow."

I resisted the urge to sweep her up into my arms and take

444

her away now. I had forgotten how lonely a life it was to be the heir to the Greek throne and therefore, the heir to the Bloodline favored by the gods. Children were groomed to rule from the time they walked. They were fastidiously protected from anyone who might take advantage of them or seek to gain favor with the gods through the innocent trust of the sacred heir of the Bloodline.

I, too, had been raised alone and isolated until the age of fourteen, when an heir was considered old enough to rule without a regent and navigate his path through the politics of the world.

I understood our duty was to the greater good. I had never questioned my upbringing, even on the day I was turned to stone.

But I did now. It had taken millennia to turn me from an arrogant prince into a wise beast who finally saw my privileged childhood for what it really was: a prison tended by manipulative men and women whose sole goal was to preserve the Bloodline.

It was wrong. The wide-eyed, lonely Phoibe deserved better, and I was in a position to help her.

I will come for you in three days, I said resolutely and stood. *In the meantime, do not speak to anyone. At all. Not until I return for you. Do you understand?*

She nodded.

Take care, Phoibe.

She opened her mouth to speak then slapped a hand over it. With her other hand, she waved.

I stepped through the balcony doors and leapt into the air, determined to make it back to Little One's city by the time dawn came. It was an eight hour flight. With any luck, I'd reach the city just before the sun rose and turned me human.

I had a birthday to attend, and I wasn't about to miss the special day of the Little One who reanimated me after so long.

***

If you enjoyed reading the first of the "*OMEGA BEGINNINGS*" miniseries short stories, check out the rest, available in ebook format from Amazon, Barnes and Noble, iBooks, Kobo, Smashwords, etc.; and meet the main characters from Omega twelve years before they collide!

You can also order the paperback from your local bookstore!

Coming soon:
"*THETA BEGINNINGS*"
featuring novelettes about the Silent Queen, Mercenary, Shadow Titan and Mercenary!

JOIN THE FANDOM!

For giveaways, sneak peeks, scoops on the upcoming "Theta Beginnings Miniseries," future book releases and more!

OmegaFandom.com

About The Author

Lizzy Ford is the author of over fifty titles written for young adult, new adult and adult romance readers, to include the internationally bestselling "Rhyn Trilogy," "Witchling Series," "Zoey Rogue" and the "War of Gods" series. Lizzy's books span multiple subgenres of romance, to include contemporary, paranormal and dystopian, among others.

Lizzy has focused on keeping her readers happy by producing brilliant, gritty romances that remind people why true love is a trial worth enduring. Her books have been featured in Publishers Weekly, Glamour UK, Romantic Times, USA Today, Huffington Post, Kirkus Reviews, and many other places. She lives in southern Arizona with her husband, sister, three dogs and a cat.

Lizzy's books can be found on every major ereader library, to include: Amazon, Barnes and Noble, iBooks, Kobo, Sony and Smashwords.

Connect With Lizzy

Website: LizzyFord.com
Facebook: Facebook.com/LizzyFordBooks
Twitter: @lizzyford2010
Instagram: @LizzyFordAuthor

Also by Lizzy Ford ...

Omega Series
Omega
Theta
Alpha

Omega Beginnings Miniseries
Alessandra
Mismatch
Phoibe
Lantos
Theodocia
Niko
Cleon
Herakles

Theta Beginnings Miniseries
Silent Queen
Mercenary
Shadow Titan
People's Champion

History Interrupted
West
East
North
South

Non-Series (2014-2015)
Black Moon Draw
Highlander Enchanted
The Door

Sons of War (Standalones)
Semper Mine

Soldier Mine
SEAL Mine

UNNATURAL SERIES
Unnatural
Unmade

STARWALKERS SERIALS (with Julia Crane)
Severed
Trapped
Exiled
Revealed
Escaped

HEART OF FIRE
Charred Heart
Charred Tears
Charred Hope

RHYN TRILOGY
Katie's Hellion
Katie's Hope
Rhyn's Redemption

RHYN ETERNAL
Gabriel's Hope
Deidre's Death
Darkyn's Mate
The Underworld
Twisted Fate

WAR OF GODS
Damian's Oracle
Damian's Assassin
Damian's Immortal
The Grey God

DAMIAN ETERNAL
Xander's Chance
The Black God

ANSHAN SAGA
Kiera's Moon
Kiera's Home (novelette)
Kiera's Sun

SHORT STORIES
A Night Worth Dying For
Santa's Ninja Elves: Natasha
Santa's Ninja Elves: Hunter
Mind Café
Snow Whisperers
The Phoenix and the Darkness

NON-SERIES TITLES (2011-2014)
Star Kissed
A Demon's Desire
The Warlord's Secret
Maddy's Oasis
Rebel Heart

By Lizzy Ford and Published by Evatopia Press

WITCHLING
Dark Summer
Autumn Storm
Winter Fire
Spring Rain

INCUBATTI
Zoey Rogue
Zoey Avenger

BROKEN BEAUTY NOVELLAS

Broken Beauty
Broken World

Voodoo Nights
Cursed
Chosen

... AND MORE COMING SOON!

WITH SO MANY BOOKS, IT'S HARD TO KNOW WHERE TO START! HERE'S A QUICK LIST OF SUGGESTIONS!

FAN FAVORITES (paranormal): "Katie's Hellion," "Dark Summer," "Damian's Oracle"

ABOUT A READER WHO GETS SUCKED INTO A BOOK: "Black Moon Draw"

CONTEMPORARY ROMANCE: "Semper Mine"

SPICY URBAN FANTASY/PARANORMALS: "Zoey Rogue","Charred Heart"

SWEET (FADE TO BLACK SEX SCENES) PARANORMAL ROMANCE: "Damian's Oracle," "Katie's Hellion," "Xander's Chance"

NOVELLAS: (paranormal) "A Demon's Desire," (contemporary romance) "Maddy's Oasis"

TEEN PARANORMALS: "Dark Summer," "Omega," "Cursed"

TEEN LITERARY FICTION: "Broken Beauty"

LIZZY'S FIRST BOOK EVER: "Damian's Oracle"

TIME TRAVEL: "West"

SCI-FI ROMANCE: (dystopian) "Rebel Heart," (alien) "Kiera's Moon," (futuristic) "Star Kissed"

FIRST BOOKS IN EACH SERIES
"Damian's Oracle" (War of Gods)
"Katie's Hellion" (Rhyn Trilogy)
"Gabriel's Hope" (Rhyn Eternal)
"Charred Heart" (Heart of Fire)

"Dark Summer" (Witchlings)
"Zoey Rogue" (Incubatti)
"Hear No" (Hidden Evil)
"West" (History Interrupted)
"Omega" (Omega Series)